Unto Caesar

Baroness Emmuska Orczy

ISBN: 978-1-64799-139-5

TABLE OF CONTENTS

CHAPTER I

"Beautiful for situation, the joy of the whole earth, is Mount Zion...."—Psalm xlviii. 2.

And it came to pass in Rome after the kalends of September, and when Caius Julius Cæsar Caligula ruled over Imperial Rome.

Arminius Quirinius, the censor, was dead. He had died by his own hand, and thus was a life of extortion and of fraud brought to an ignominious end through the force of public opinion, and by the decree of that same Cæsar who himself had largely benefited by the malpractices of his minion.

Arminius Quirinius had committed every crime, sunk to every kind of degradation which an inordinate love of luxury and the insatiable desires of jaded senses had suggested as a means to satisfaction, until the treachery of his own accomplices had thrown the glaring light of publicity on a career of turpitude such as even these decadent times had seldom witnessed ere this.

Enough that the end had come at last. A denunciation from the rostrum, a discontented accomplice thirsting for revenge, an angry crowd eager to listen, and within an hour the mighty, much-feared censor was forced to flee from Rome to escape the fury of a populace which would have torn him to pieces, and was ready even to massacre his family and his womenfolk, his clients and his slaves.

He escaped to his villa at Ostia. But the Emperor Caligula, having duly enjoyed the profits derived from his favourite's extortions, hurled anathema and the full weight of his displeasure on the man who had been not only fool enough to be found out, but who had compromised the popularity of the Cæsar in the eyes of the people and of the army. Twenty-four hours later the imperial decree went forth that the disgraced censor must end his days in any manner which he thought best—seeing that a patrician and member of the Senate could not be handed over to common justice—and also that the goods of Arminius Quirinius should be publicly sold for the benefit of the State and the profit of those whom the extortioner had wronged.

The latter phrase, though somewhat vague, pleased the people and soothed public irritation, and the ephemeral popularity of a half-crazy tyrant was momentarily restored. Be it said however, that less than a month later the Cæsar decided that he himself had been the person most wronged by Arminius, and that the bulk of the profits derived from the sale of the late censor's goods must therefore find its way into the imperial coffers.

The furniture of Arminius' house within the city and that of his villa at Ostia had fetched vast sums at a public auction which had lasted three days. Everything had been sold, from the bed with the gilt legs on

1

which the body of the censor had been laid after his death, to the last vase of murra that adorned his walls and the cups of crystal from which his guests had drunk. His pet monkeys were sold and his tame magpies, the pots of flowers out of the hothouses and the bunches of melons and winter grapes ripening under glass.

After that it was the turn of the slaves. There were, so I understand, over seven thousand of these: scribes and carpenters, litter-bearers and sculptors, cooks and musicians; there were a quantity of young children, and some half-witted dolts and misshapen dwarfs, kept for the amusement of guests during the intervals of supper.

The bulk of them had been sent to the markets of Delos and Phaselis, but the imperator had had the most valuable items amongst the human goods set aside for himself, and not a few choice pieces had found their way into the households of the aediles in charge of the sales: the State too had appropriated some hundreds of useful scribes, sculptors and mechanics, but there were still a thousand or so who—in compliance with the original imperial edict—would have to be sold by public auction in Rome for the benefit of the late censor's defrauded victims.

And thus, on this ninth day of September, a human load panting under the heat of this late summer's sun, huddled one against the other, pushed and jostled by the crowd, was exposed to the public gaze in the Forum over against the rostrum Augustini, so that all who had a mind, and a purse withal, might suit their fancy and buy.

A bundle of humanity—not over-wretched, for the condition of the slaves in the household of Arminius Quirinius had not been an unhappy one—they all seemed astonished, some even highly pleased, at thus finding themselves the centre of attraction in the Forum, they who had spent their lives in getting humbly out of other people's way.

Fair and dark, ivory skin and ebony, male and female, or almost sexless in the excess of deformity, there were some to suit all tastes. Each wore a tablet hung round the neck by a green cord: on this were writ the chief merits of the wearer, and also a list of his or her defects, so that intending purchasers might know what to expect.

There were the Phrygians with fair curly hair and delicate hands skilled in the limner's art; the Numidians with skins of ebony and keen black eyes that shone like dusky rubies; they were agile at the chase, could capture a lion or trap the wild beasts that are so useful in gladiatorial games. There were Greeks here, pale of face and gentle of manner who could strike the chords of a lyre and sing to its accompaniment, and there were swarthy Spaniards who fashioned breast-plates of steel and fine chain mail to resist the assassin's dagger: there were Gauls with long lithe limbs and brown hair tied in a knot high above the forehead, and Allemanni from the Rhine with two-coloured hair heavy and crisp like a lion's mane. There was a musician from Memphis whose touch upon the sistrum would call a dying spirit back to the land of the living, and a cook from Judæa who could stew a peacock's tongue so that it melted like nectar in the mouth: there was a white-skinned Iceni from Britain, versed in the art of healing, and a negress from Numidia who had killed a raging lion by one hit on the jaw from her powerful fist.

Then there were those freshly brought to Rome from overseas, whose merits or demerits had not yet been appraised—they wore no tablet round the neck, but their feet were whitened all over with chalk; and there were those whose heads were surmounted by an ugly felt hat in token that the State treasury tendered no guarantee for them. Their period of servitude had been so short that nothing was known about them, about their health, their skill, or their condition.

Above them towered the gigantic rostrum with tier upon tier of massive blocks of marble, and in the centre, up aloft, the bronze figure of the wolf—the foster-mother of the great city—with metal jaws distended and polished teeth that gleamed like emeralds in the sun.

And all around the stately temples of the Forum, with their rich carvings and colonnades and walls in tones of delicate creamy white, scarce less brilliant than the clouds which a gentle morning breeze was chasing westwards to the sea. And under the arcades of the temples cool shadows, dense and blue, trenchant against the white marble like an irregular mosaic of lapis lazuli, with figures gliding along between the tall columns, priests in white robes, furtive of gait, slaves of the pontificate, shoeless and silent and as if detached from the noise and bustle of the Forum, like ghosts that haunt the precincts of graves.

Throughout all this the gorgeous colouring that a summer's mid-morning throws over imperial Rome. Above, that canopy of translucent blue, iridescent and scintillating with a thousand colours, flicks of emerald and crimson, of rose and of mauve that merge and dance together, divide and reunite before the retina, until the gaze loses consciousness of all colour save one all-pervading sense of gold.

In the distance the Capitol, temple-crowned, rearing its deified summit upwards to the dome of heaven above, holding on its triple shoulders a throng of metal gods, with Jupiter Victor right in the centre, a thunderbolt in his hand which throws back ten thousand reflections of dazzling light—another sun engendered by the sun. And to the west the Aventine wrapped in its mantle of dull brown, its smooth incline barren and scorched, and with tiny mud-huts dotted about like sleepy eyes that close beneath the glare.

And far away beyond the Aventine, beyond the temples and palaces, the blue ribbon of the Tiber flowing lazily to the sea: there where a rose-coloured haze hung in mid-air, hiding with filmy, transparent veil the vast Campania beyond, its fever-haunted marshes and its reed-covered fastnesses.

The whole, a magnificent medley of cream and gold and azure, and deep impenetrable shadows trenchant as a thunder cloud upon an horizon of gold, and the moving crowd below, ivory and bronze and black, with here and there the brilliant note of a snow-white robe or of crimson head-band gleaming through dark locks.

Up and around the rostrum, noise that was almost deafening had prevailed from an early hour. On one of the gradients some ten or a dozen scribes were squatting on mats of twisted straw, making notes of the sales and entries of the proceeds on rolls of parchment which they had for the purpose, whilst a swarthy slave, belonging to the treasury, acted as auctioneer under direct orders from the praefect of Rome. He was perched high up aloft, immediately beneath the shadow of the yawning bronze wolf; he stood bare-headed under the glare of the sun, but a linen tunic covered his shoulders, and his black hair was held close to his head by a vivid crimson band.

He shouted almost incessantly in fluent Latin, but with the lisp peculiar to the African races.

A sun-tanned giant whose massive frame and fair hair, that gleamed ruddy in the sun, proclaimed some foreign ancestry was the praefectus in command of this tangled bundle of humanity.

He had arrived quite early in the day and his litter stood not far from the rostrum; its curtains of crimson silk, like vivid stains of blood upon the walls of cream and gold, fluttered restlessly in the breeze. Around the litter a crowd of his own slaves and attendants remained congregated, but he himself stood isolated on the lowest gradient of the central rostrum, leaning his powerful frame against the marble, with arms folded across his mighty chest; his deep-set eyes were overshadowed by heavy brows and his square forehead cut across by the furrow of a perpetual frown which gave the whole face a strange expression of untamed will and of savage pride, in no way softened by the firm lines of the tightly closed lips or the contour of the massive jaws.

His lictors, at some little distance from him, kept his person well guarded, but it was he who, with word or nod, directed the progress of the sale, giving occasional directions to the lictors who—wielding heavy flails—had much ado to keep the herd of human cattle within the bounds of its pens. His voice was harsh and peremptory and he pronounced the Latin words with but the faintest semblance of foreign intonation.

Now and then at a word from a likely purchaser he would with a sign order a lictor to pick out one of his wares, to drag him forward out of a compact group and set him up on the catasta. A small crowd would then collect round the slave thus exposed, the tablet on his neck would be carefully perused and the chattel made to turn round and round, to walk backwards and forwards, to show his teeth and his muscle, whilst the African up on the rostrum would with loud voice and profuse gesture point out every line of beauty on a lithe body and expatiate on the full play of every powerful muscle.

4

The slave thus singled out for show seemed neither resentful nor distressed, ready enough most times to exhibit his merits, anxious only for the chance of a good master and the momentary avoidance of the lictor's flail. At the praefect's bidding he cracked his knuckles or showed his teeth, strained the muscles of his arm to make them stand up like cords, turned a somersault, jumped, danced or stood on his head if ordered so to do.

The women were more timid and very frightened of blows, especially the older ones; the younger shoulders escaped a chastisement which would have marred their beauty, and the pretty maids from Corinth or Carthage, conscious of their own charms, displayed them with good-natured naïveté, deeming obedience the surest way to comfort.

Nor did the praefect perform his duty with any show of inhumanity or conscious cruelty. Himself a wealthy member of the patriciate, second only to the Cæsar, with a seat in the Senate and a household full of slaves, he had neither horror nor contempt for the state of slavery—a necessary one in the administration of the mightiest Empire in the world.

Many there were who averred that the praefect of Rome was himself the descendant of a freedman—a prisoner of war brought over by Cæsar from the North—who had amassed wealth and purchased his own freedom. Indeed his name proclaimed his foreign origin, for he was called Taurus Antinor Anglicanus, and surnamed Niger because of his dark eyes and sun-tanned skin. Certain it is that when the sale of Arminius' goods was ordered by imperial edict for the benefit of the State, no one complained that the praefect decided to preside over the sale himself.

He had discharged such duties before and none had occasion to complain of the manner in which he did it. In these days of unbridled excesses and merciless outbursts of rage, he remained throughout—on these occasions—temperate and even impassive.

He only ordered his lictor to use the flail when necessary, when the bundle of human goods was so huddled up that it ceased to look attractive, and likely purchasers seemed to fall away. Then, at his command, the heavy thongs would descend indiscriminately on the bronze shoulder of an Ethiopian or the fair skin of a barbarian from the North; but he gave the order without any show of cruelty or passion, just as he heard the responsive cry of pain without any outward sign of pity.

CHAPTER II

"To be laid in the balance, they are altogether lighter than vanity."—Psalm lxii. 9.

As the day wore on, trade became more brisk and the work of the lictors more arduous, for the crowd was dense and the bargain-hunters eager to push to the front.

Now a bronze-skinned artisan with slender limbs and narrow tapering hands was attracting attention. He was standing on the platform, passive and indifferent, apparently unconscious alike of the scorching sun which bit into his bare flesh, as of the murmurs of the dealers round him and the eloquence of the African up on the rostrum, who was shouting himself hoarse in praise of his wares.

"A leather worker from Hispania," he thundered with persuasive rhetoric, "his age but two dozen years, his skill unequalled on either bank of the Tiber ... A tunic worked by him is softer than the fleeciest wool, and the sheath of a dagger becomes in his hands as hard as steel.... Good health and strength, two thousand sesterces were a poor price to pay for the use of these skilled hands.... Two thousand sesterces.... His lordship's grace, the censor Arminius Quirinius paid four thousand for him...."

He paused a moment whilst a couple of Jews from Galilee, in long dark robes and black caps covering their shaggy hair, turned critically round this paragon from Hispania, lifted his hands and gazed on each finger-tip as if trying to find traces on these of that much-vaunted skill.

"Two thousand sesterces, kind sirs, and you will have at your disposal the talent of a master in the noble art of leather working; pouches and coverings for your chairs, caskets and sword-hilts, nothing comes amiss to him.... Come! shall we say two thousand sesterces?"

The Jews were hesitating. With a rapid glance of their keen, deep-set eyes they consulted one with the other, whilst their long bony fingers wandered hesitatingly to the wallets at their belts.

"Two thousand sesterces!" urged the auctioneer, as he looked with marked severity on the waverers.

He himself received a percentage on the proceeds of the sale, a few sesterces mayhap that would go to swell the little hoard which ultimately would purchase freedom. The scribes stilet in hand waited in patient silence. The praefect, indifferent to the whole transaction, was staring straight in front of him, like one whose thoughts are strangers to his will.

"One thousand we'll give," said one of the Jews timidly.

"Nay! an you'll not give more, kind sirs," quoth the auctioneer airily, "this paragon among leather workers will bring fortune to your rival dealers...."

"One thousand," repeated one of the intending purchasers, "and no more."

The African tried persuasion, contempt, even lofty scorn; he threatened to withdraw the paragon from the sale altogether, for he knew of a dealer in leather goods over in Corinth who would give two fingers of his own hand for the exclusive use of those belonging to this Hispanian treasure.

But the Jews were obstinate. With the timid obstinacy peculiar to their race, they stuck to their point and refused to be enticed into purposeless extravagance.

In the end the wonderful worker in leather was sold to the Jew traders from Galilee for the sum of one thousand sesterces; his dark face had expressed nothing but stolid indifference whilst the colloquy between the purchasers and the auctioneer had been going on.

The next piece of goods however was in more pressing demand; a solid German, with massive thorax half-hidden beneath a shaggy goatskin held in at the waist by a belt; his hairy arms bare to the shoulder, his gigantic fists clenched as if ready to fell an ox.

A useful man with plough or harrow, he was said to be skilled in smith's work too. After a preliminary and minute examination of the man's muscles, of his teeth, of the calves of his legs, bidding became very brisk between an agriculturist from Sicilia and a freedman from the Campania, until the praefect himself intervened, desiring the slave for his own use on a farm which he had near Ostia.

Some waiting-maids from Judæa fetched goodly money; an innkeeper of Etruria bought them, for they were well-looking and knew how to handle and carry wine jars without shaking up the costly liquor; and the negroes were sought after by the lanistae for training to gladiatorial combats.

Scribes were also in great demand for copying purposes. The disseminators of the news of the day were willing to pay high prices for quick shorthand writers who had learned their business in the house of Arminius the censor.

In the meanwhile the throng in the Forum had become more and more dense. Already one or two gorgeously draped litters had been seen winding their way in from the Sacra Via or the precincts of the temples, their silken draperies making positive notes of brilliant colour against the iridescent whiteness of Phrygian marble walls.

The lictors now had at times to use their flails against the crowd. Room had to be made for the masters of Rome, the wealthy and the idle, who threw sesterces about for the gratification of their smallest whim, as a common man would shake the dust from his shoes.

Young Hortensius Martius, the rich patrician owner of five thousand slaves, had stepped out of his litter, and a way being made for

7

him in the crowd by his men, he had strolled up to the rostrum, and mounting its first gradient he leaned with studied grace against the block of white marble, giving to the common herd below the pleasing spectacle of a young exquisite, rich and well-favoured—his handsome person carefully perfumed and bedecked after the morning bath, his crisp fair hair daintily curled, his body clad in a tunic of soft white wool splendidly worked in purple stripes, the insignia of his high patrician state.

He passed a languid eye over the bundle of humanity spread out for sale at his feet and gave courteous greeting to the praefect.

"Thou art early abroad, Hortensius Martius," quoth Taurus Antinor in response; "'tis not often thou dost grace the Forum with thy presence at this hour."

"They told me it would be amusing," replied young Hortensius lazily, "but methinks that they lied."

He yawned, and with a tiny golden tool he began picking his teeth.

"What did they tell thee?" queried the other, "and who were they that told?"

"There was Caius Nepos and young Escanes, and several others at the bath. They were all talking about the sale."

"Are they coming hither?"

"They will be here anon; but some declared that much rubbish would have to be sold ere the choice bargains be put up. Escanes wants a cook who can fry a capon in a special way they wot of in Gaul. Stuffed with ortolans and covered with the juice of three melons—Escanes says it is mightily pleasing to the palate."

"There is no cook from Gaul on the list," interposed the praefect curtly.

"And Caius Nepos wants some well-favoured girls to wait on his guests at supper to-morrow. He gives a banquet, as thou knowest. Wilt be there, Taurus Antinor?"

He had spoken these last words in a curious manner which suggested that some significance other than mere conviviality would be attached to the banquet given by Caius Nepos on the morrow. And now he drew nearer to the praefect and cast a quick glance around him as if to assure himself that the business of the sale was engrossing everyone's attention.

"Caius Nepos," he said, trying to speak with outward indifference, "asked me to tell thee that if thou wilt come to his banquet to-morrow thou wilt find it to thine advantage. Many of us are of one mind with regard to certain matters and could talk these over undisturbed. Wilt join us, Taurus Antinor?" he added eagerly.

"Join you," retorted the other with a grim smile, "join you in what? in this senseless folly of talking in whispers in public places? The Forum this day is swarming with spies, Hortensius Martius. Hast a wish to make a spectacle for the plebs on the morrow by being thrown to a pack of tigers for their midday meal?"

And with a nod of his head he pointed up to the rostrum where the dusky auctioneer had momentarily left off shouting and had thrown himself flat down upon the matting, ostensibly in order to speak with one of the scribes on the tier below, but who was in reality casting furtive glances in the direction where Hortensius Martius stood talking with the praefectus.

"These slaves," said Taurus Antinor curtly, "all belong to the imperial treasury; their peculium is entirely made up of money gained through giving information—both false and true. Have a care, O Hortensius Martius!"

But the other shrugged his shoulders with well-studied indifference. It was not the mode at this epoch to seem anything but bored at all the circumstances of public and private life in Rome, at the simple occurrences of daily routine or at the dangers which threatened every man through the crazy whims of a demented despot.

It had even become the fashion to accept outwardly and without the slightest show of interest the wild extravagances and insane debaucheries of the ferocious tyrant who for the nonce wielded the sceptre of the Cæsars. The young patricians of the day looked on with apparent detachment at his excesses and the savage displays of unbridled power of which he was so inordinately fond, and they affected a lofty disregard for the horrible acts of injustice and of cruelty which this half-crazy Emperor had rendered familiar to the citizens of Rome.

Nothing in the daily routine of life amused these votaries of fashion—nothing roused them from their attitude of somnolent placidity, except perhaps some peculiarly bloody combat in the arena—one of those unfettered orgies of lust of blood which they loved to witness and which have for ever disgraced the glorious pages of Roman history.

Then horror would rouse them for a brief moment from their apathy, for they were not cruel, only satiated with every sight, every excitement and luxury which their voluptuous city and the insane caprice of the imperator perpetually offered them; and they thirsted for horrors as a sane man thirsts for beauty, that it might cause a diversion in the even tenor of their lives, and mayhap raise a thrill in their dormant brains.

Therefore even now, when apparently he was toying with his life, Hortensius Martius did not depart outwardly from the attitude of supercilious indifference which fashion demanded. They were all actors, these men, always before an audience, and even among themselves they never really left off acting the part which they had made so completely their own.

But that the indifference was only on the surface was evidenced

9

in this instance by the young exquisite's scarce perceptible change of position. He drew away slightly from the praefect and anon said in a loud tone of voice so that all around him might hear:

"Aye! as thou sayest, Taurus Antinor, I might find a dwarf or some kind of fool to suit me. Mine are getting old and dull. Ye gods, how they bore me at times!"

And it was in a whisper that he added:

"Caius Nepos specially desired thy presence at supper to-morrow, O Taurus Antinor! He feared that he might not get speech with thee anon, so hath asked me to make sure of thy presence. Thou'lt not fail us? There are over forty of us now, all prepared to give our lives for the good of the Empire."

The praefect made no reply this time; his attention was evidently engrossed by some close bidding over a useful slave, but as Hortensius now finally turned away from him, his dark eyes under the shadow of that perpetual frown swept over the figure of the young exquisite, from the crown of the curled and perfumed head to the soles of the daintily shod feet, and a smile of contempt not altogether unkind played round the corners of his firm lips.

"For the good of the Empire?" he murmured under his breath as he shrugged his broad shoulders and once more turned his attention to his duties.

Hortensius in the meanwhile had spied some of his friends. Gorgeously embroidered tunics could now be seen all the time pushing their way through the more common crowd, and soon a compact group of rich patricians had congregated around the rostra.

They had come one by one—from the baths mostly—refreshed and perfumed, ready to gaze with fashionable lack of interest on the spectacle of this public auction. They had exchanged greetings with the praefect and with Hortensius Martius. They all knew one another, were all members of the same caste, the ruling caste of Rome. Young Escanes was now there, he who wanted a cook, and Caius Nepos—the praetorian praefect who was in search of pretty waiting-maids.

"Hast had speech with Anglicanus?" asked the latter in a whisper to Hortensius.

"Aye! a few words," replied the other, "but he warned me of spies."

"Will he join us, thinkest thou?"

"I think that he will sup with thee, O Caius Nepos, but as to joining us in——"

"Hush!" admonished the praetorian praefect, "Taurus Antinor is right. There are spies all around here to-day. But if he comes to supper we'll persuade him, never fear."

And with a final significant nod the two men parted and once more mixed with the crowd.

More than one high-born lady now had ordered her bearers to

set her litter down close to the rostrum whence she could watch the sale, and mayhap make a bid for a purchase on her own account; the rich Roman matrons with large private fortunes and households of their own, imperious and independent, were the object of grave deference and of obsequious courtesy—not altogether unmixed with irony, on the part of the young men around them.

They did not mix with the crowd but remained in their litters, reclining on silken cushions, their dark tunics and richly coloured stoles standing out in sombre notes against the more gaily-decked-out gilded youth of Rome, whilst their serious and oft-times stern manner, their measured and sober speech, seemed almost set in studied opposition to the idle chattering, the flippant tone, the bored affectation of the outwardly more robust sex.

And among them all Taurus Antinor, praefect of Rome, with his ruddy hair and bronzed skin, his massive frame clad in gorgeously embroidered tunic, his whole appearance heavy and almost rough, in strange contrast alike to the young decadents of the day as to the rigid primness of the patrician matrons, just as his harsh, even voice seemed to dominate the lazy and mellow trebles of the votaries of fashion.

The auctioneer had in the meanwhile cast a quick comprehensive glance over his wares, throwing an admonition here, a command there.

"That yellow hair—let it hang, woman! do not touch it I say.... Slip that goatskin off thy loins, man ... By Jupiter 'tis the best of thee thou hidest.... Hold thy chin up girl, we'll have no doleful faces to-day."

Sometimes his admonition required more vigorous argument. The praefect was appealed to against the recalcitrant. Then the harsh unimpassioned voice with its curious intonation in the pronouncing of the Latin words, would give a brief order and the lictor's flail would whizz in the air and descend with a short sharp whistling sound on obstinately bowed shoulder or unwilling hand, and the auctioneer would continue his perorations.

"What will it please my lord's grace to buy this day? A skilled horseman from Dacia?... I have one.... A pearl.... He can mount an untamed steed and drive a chariot in treble harness through the narrowest streets of Rome.... He can ... What—no?—not a horseman to-day?... then mayhap a hunchback acrobat from Pannonia, bronzed as the tanned hide of an ox, with arms so long that his finger-nails will scrape the ground as he runs; he can turn a back somersault, walk the tight-rope, or ... Here, Pipus the hunchback, show thine ugly face to my lord's grace, maybe thou'lt help to dissipate the frown between my Lord's eyes, maybe my lord's grace will e'en smile at thine antics.... Turn then, show thy hump, 'tis worth five hundred sesterces, my lord ... turn again ... see my lord, is he not like an ape?"

My lord was smiling, so the auctioneer prattled on, and the deformed creature upon the catasta wound his ill-shapen body into every kind of contortion, grinning from ear to ear, displaying the

11

malformation of his spine, and the hideousness of his long hairy arms, whilst he uttered weird cries that were supposed to imitate those of wild animals in the forest.

These antics caused my lord to smile outright. He was willing to expend two thousand sesterces in order to have such a creature about his house, to have him ready to call when his guests seemed dull between the courses of a sumptuous meal. The deal was soon concluded and the hunchback transferred from the platform to the keeping of my lord's slaves, and thence to my lord's household.

CHAPTER III

"Fairer than the children of men."—Psalm xlv. 2.

"Hun Rhavas, dost mind thy promise made to Menecreta?" whispered a timid voice in the African's ear.

"Aye, aye!" he replied curtly, "I had not forgotten."

There was a lull in the trade whilst the scribes were making entries on their tablets.

The auctioneer had descended from the rostrum. Panting after his exertions, perspiring profusely under the heat of the noonday sun, he was wiping the moisture from his dripping forehead and incidentally refreshing his parched throat with copious drafts from out a leather bottle.

His swarthy skin streaming with perspiration shone in the glare of the noonday sun like the bronze statue of mother-wolf up aloft.

An elderly woman in rough linen tunic, her hair hidden beneath a simple cloth, had succeeded in engaging his attention.

"It had been better to put the child up for sale an hour ago, whilst these rich folk were still at the bath," she said with a tone of reproach in her gentle voice.

"It was not my fault," rejoined the African curtly, "she comes one of the last on the list. The praefect made out the lists. Thou shouldst have spoken to him."

"Oh I should never dare," she replied, her voice trembling at the mere suggestion of such boldness, "but I did promise thee five aurei if I succeeded in purchasing the child."

"I know that," quoth the African with a nod of satisfaction.

"My own child, Hun Rhavas," continued the pleading voice; "think on it, for thou too hast children of thine own."

"I purchased my son's freedom only last year," acquiesced the slave with a touch of pride. "Next year, an the gods will, it shall be my daughter's and after that mine own. In three years from now we shall all be free."

"Thou art a man; 'tis more easy for thee to make money. It took me six years to save up twenty-five aurei which should purchase my child: twenty for her price, five for thy reward, for thou alone canst help me, an thou wilt."

"Well, I've done all I could for thee, Menecreta," retorted Hun Rhavas somewhat impatiently. "I've taken the titulus from off her neck and set the hat over her head, and that was difficult enough for the praefect's eyes are very sharp. Ten aurei should be the highest bid for a maid without guarantees as to skill, health or condition. And as she is not over well-favoured——"

But this the mother would not admit. In weary and querulous tones she began expatiating on the merits of her daughter: her fair hair, her graceful neck—until the African, bored and impatient, turned on her roughly.

"Nay! an thy daughter hath so many perfections, thou'lt not purchase her for twenty aurei. Fifty and sixty will be bid for her, and what can I do then to help thee?"

"Hun Rhavas," said Menecreta in a sudden spirit of conciliation, "thou must not heed a mother's fancies. To me the child is beautiful beyond compare. Are not thine own in thy sight beautiful as a midsummer's day?" she added with subtle hypocrisy, thinking of the ugly little Africans of whom Hun Rhavas was so proud.

Her motherly heart was prepared for every sacrifice, every humiliation, so long as she obtained what she wanted—possession of her child. Arminius Quirinius had given her her freedom some three years ago, but this seeming act of grace had been a cruel one since it had parted the mother from her child. The late censor had deemed Menecreta old, feeble, and therefore useless: she was but a worthless mouth to feed; but he kept the girl not because she was well-favoured or very useful in his house, but because he knew that Menecreta would work her fingers to the bone until she saved enough money to purchase her daughter's freedom.

Arminius Quirinius, ever grasping for money, ever ready for any act of cupidity or oppression, knew that from the mother he could extract a far higher sum than the girl could possibly fetch in the open market. He had fixed her price as fifty aurei, and Menecreta had saved just one half that amount when fate and the vengeance of the populace overtook the extortioner. All his slaves—save the most valuable—were thrown on the market, and the patient, hard-working mother saw the fulfilment of her hopes well within sight.

It was but a question of gaining Hun Rhavas' ear and of tempting his greed. The girl, publicly offered under unfavourable conditions, and

13

unbacked by the auctioneer's laudatory harangues, could easily be knocked down for twenty aurei or even less.

But Menecreta's heart was torn with anxiety the while she watched the progress of the sale. Every one of these indifferent spectators might become an enemy through taking a passing fancy to her child. These young patricians, these stern matrons, they had neither remorse nor pity where the gratification of a whim was at stake.

And was not the timid, fair-haired girl more beautiful in the mother's eyes than any other woman put up on the platform for the purpose of rousing a momentary caprice.

She gazed with jealous eyes on the young idlers and the high-born ladies, the possible foes who yet might part her from the child. And there was the praefect too, all-powerful in the matter.

If he saw through the machinations of Hun Rhavas nothing would save the girl from being put up like all the others as the law directed, with the proper tablet attached to her neck, describing her many charms. Taurus Antinor was not cruel but he was pitiless. The slaves of his household knew that, as did the criminals brought to his tribunal. He never inflicted unnecessary punishment but when it was deserved he was relentless in its execution.

What hope could a poor mother have against the weight of his authority.

Fortunately the morning was rapidly wearing on. The hour for the midday rest was close at hand. Menecreta could watch, with a glad thrill in her heart, one likely purchaser after another being borne in gorgeously draped litter away from this scene of a mother's cruel anxiety. Already the ladies had withdrawn. Now there was only a group of men left around the rostrum; Hortensius Martius still lounging aimlessly, young Escanes who had not yet found the paragon amongst cooks, and a few others who eyed the final proceedings with the fashionable expression of boredom.

"I wonder we have not seen Dea Flavia this day," remarked Escanes to the praefect. "Dost think she'll come, Taurus Antinor?"

"Nay, I know not," he replied; "truly she cannot be in need of slaves. She has more than she can know what to do with."

"Oh!" rejoined the other, "of a truth she has slaves enough. But 'tis this new craze of hers! She seems to be in need of innumerable models for the works of art she hath on hand."

"Nay, 'tis no new craze," interposed Hortensius Martius, whose fresh young face had flushed very suddenly as if in anger. "Dea Flavia, as thou knowest full well, Escanes, hath fashioned exquisite figures both in marble and in clay even whilst thou didst waste thy boyhood in drunken revelries. She——"

"A truce on thine ill-temper," broke in Escanes with a good-humoured laugh. "I had no thought of disparagement for Dea Flavia's genius. The gods forbid!" he added with mock fervour.

"Then dost deserve that I force thee down to thy knees," retorted Hortensius, not yet mollified, "to make public acknowledgment of Dea Flavia's beauty, her talents and her virtues, and public confession of thine own unworthiness in allowing her hallowed name to pass thy wine-sodden lips."

Escanes uttered a cry of rage; in a moment these two—friends and boon companions—appeared as bitter enemies. Hortensius Martius, the perfumed exquisite, was now like an angry cockbird on the defence, whilst Escanes, taller and stronger than he, was clenching his fists, trying to keep up that outward semblance of patrician decorum which the dignity of his caste demanded in the presence of the plebs.

Who knows how long this same semblance would have been kept up on this occasion? for Hortensius Martius, obviously a slave to Dea Flavia's beauty, was ready to do battle for the glorification of his idol, whilst Escanes, smarting under the clumsy insult, had much ado to keep his rage within bounds.

"If you cut one another's throats now," interposed the praefect curtly, "'twill be in the presence of Dea Flavia herself."

Even whilst he spoke a litter gorgeously carved and gilded, draped in rose pink and gold, was seen slowly winding its way from the rear of the basilica and along the Vicus Tuscus, towards the Forum. In a moment all eyes were turned in its direction; the two young men either forgot their quarrel or were ashamed to prolong it in the presence of its cause.

Now the litter turned into the open. It was borne by eight gigantic Ethiopians whose mighty shoulders were bare to the sun, and all round and behind it a crowd of slaves, of clients, of sycophants followed in its trail, men running beside the litter, women shouting, children waving sprays of flowers and fans of feathers and palm leaves, whilst the air was filled with cries from innumerable throats:

"Augusta! Augusta! Room for Dea Flavia Augusta."

The retinue of Dea Flavia of the imperial house of the Cæsars was the most numerous in Rome.

At word of command no doubt the bearers put the litter down quite close to the rostrum even whilst four young girls stepped forward and drew the silken curtains aside.

Dea Flavia was resting against the cushions; her tiny feet in shoes of gilded leather were stretched out on a coverlet of purple silk richly wrought with gold and silver threads. Her elbow was buried in the fleecy down of the cushions; her head rested against her hand.

Dea Flavia, imperial daughter of Rome, what tongue of poet could describe thy beauty? what hand of artist paint its elusiveness?

Have not the writers of the time told us all there was to tell? and exhausted language in their panegyrics: the fair hair like rippling gold, the eyes now blue, now green, always grey and mysterious, the delicate hands, the voluptuous throat, those tiny ears ever filled with flattery?

15

But methinks that the carping critic was right when he deemed that the beauty of her face was marred by the scornful glance of the eyes and the ever rigid lines of the mouth. There was those who had dared aver that Dea Flavia's snow-white neck had been more beautiful if it had known how to bend, and that the glory of her eyes would be enhanced a thousandfold when once they learned how to weep.

This, however, was only the opinion of very few, of those in fact who never had received the slightest favour from Dea Flavia; those on whom she smiled—with that proud, cold smile of hers—fell an over-ready victim to her charm. And she had smiled more than once on Hortensius Martius, and he, poor fool! had quickly lost his head.

Now that she was present he soon forgot his quarrel; neither Escanes nor the rest of the world existed since Dea Flavia was nigh. He pushed his way through her crowd of courtiers and was the first to reach her litter even as she put her dainty feet to the ground.

Escanes too and Caius Nepos, and Philippus Decius and the other young men there, forgot the excitement of the aborted quarrel and pressed forward to pay their respects to Dea Flavia.

The aspect of her court was changed in a moment. Her lictors chased the importunate crowd away, making room for the masters of Rome who desired speech with their mistress. The rough and sombre garments of the slaves showed in the background now, and all round the litter tunics and mantles of fleecy wool gorgeously embroidered in crimson and gold, or stripes of purple, crowded in eager medley.

All at once too the immediate neighbourhood of the rostrum was deserted, the human chattels forgotten in the anxious desire to catch sight of the great lady whom the Cæsar himself had styled Augusta—thus exalting her above all women in Rome. Her boundless wealth and lavish expenditure, as well as her beauty and acknowledged virtue, had been the talk of the city ever since the death of her father, Octavius Claudius of the House of Augusta Cæsar, had placed her under the immediate tutelage of the Cæsar and left her—young and beautiful as she was—in possession of one of the largest fortunes in the Empire. No wonder then that whenever her rose-draped litter was perceived in the streets of Rome a crowd of idlers and of sycophants pressed around it, curious to see the queen of society and anxious to catch her ear.

This same instant of momentary excitement became that of renewed hope for an anxious mother's heart. Menecreta, with the keenness of her ardent desire, had at once grasped her opportunity. Hun Rhavas fortunately glanced down in her direction. He too no doubt saw the possibilities of this moment of general confusion. The five aurei promised him by Menecreta sharpened his resourceful wits. He signalled to one of the lictors below—an accomplice too, I imagine, in this transaction—and whilst a chorus of obsequious greetings round Dea Flavia's litter filled the noonday air like the hum of bees, a pale-faced, delicate-looking girl was quickly pushed up on to the platform.

16

Hun Rhavas very perfunctorily declaimed her age and status.

"Of no known skill," he said, mumbling his words and talking very rapidly, "since my lord's grace the late censor had made no use of her. Shall we say ten aurei for the girl? she might be made to learn a trade."

As the auctioneer started on his peroration those among the crowd who were here for business, and not for idle gaping, turned back towards the catasta. But the little maid who stood there so still, her hair entirely hidden by the ungainly hat, her head bent and her eyes downcast, did not seem very attractive; the lack of guarantee as to her skill and merits represented by the hat and the absence of the tablet round her neck caused the buyers to stand aloof.

As if conscious of this, a deep blush suffused the girl's cheeks. Not that she was ashamed of her position or of her exposure before the public gaze, for to this ordeal her whole upbringing had tended. Born in slavery, she had always envisaged this possibility, and her present position caused her in itself neither pain nor humiliation.

She knew that her mother was there in the crowd, ready for this opportunity; that the present state of discomfort, the past life of wretchedness would now inevitably be followed by a brighter future: reunion with her mother, a life of freedom, mayhap of happiness, marriage right out of the state of bondage, children born free!

No! it was not the gaping crowd that mattered, the exposure on the public platform, the many pairs of indifferent eyes fixed none too kindly upon her: it was that hat upon her head which brought forth in her such a sense of shame that the hot blood rushed to her cheeks; that, and the absence of the tablet round her neck, and Hun Rhavas' disparaging words about her person.

Others there had been earlier in the day—her former companions in Arminius' household—on whom the auctioneer had lavished torrents of eloquent praise, whom for the first bidding he had appraised at forty or even fifty aurei, the public being over willing to pay higher sums than those.

Whilst here she stood shamed before them all, with no guarantee as to her skill and talents, though she knew something about the art of healing by rubbing unguents into the skin, could ply her needle and dress a lady's hair. Nor was a word said about her beauty, though her eyes were blue and her neck slender and white; and her hair, which was of a pretty shade of gold, could not even be seen under that hideous, unbecoming hat.

"Ten aurei shall we say?" said Hun Rhavas with remarkable want of enthusiasm; "kind sirs, is there no one ready to say fifteen? The girl might be taught to sew or to trim a lady's nails. She may be unskilled now but she might learn—providing that her health be good," he added with studied indifference.

The latter phrase proved a cunning one. The few likely buyers

17

who had been attracted to the catasta by the youthful appearance of the girl—hoping to find willingness, even if skill were wanting—now quickly drew away.

Of a truth there was no guarantee as to her health and a sick slave was a burden and a nuisance.

"Ten aurei then," said Hun Rhavas raising the hammer, whilst with hungry eyes the mother watched his every movement.

A few more seconds of this agonising suspense! Oh! ye gods, how this waiting hurts! She pressed her hands against her side where a terrible pain turned her nearly giddy.

Only a second or two whilst the hammer was poised in mid air and Hun Rhavas' furtive glance darted on the praefect to see if he were still indifferent! Menecreta prayed with all her humble might to the proud gods enthroned upon the hill! she prayed that this cycle of agony might end at last for she could not endure it longer. She prayed that that cruel hammer might descend and her child be delivered over to her at last.

CHAPTER IV

"Hope deferred maketh the heart sick."—Proverbs xiii. 12.

Alas, the Roman gods are the gods of the patricians! They take so little heed of the sorrows and the trials of poor freedmen and slaves!

"Who ordered the hat to be put on this girl's head?" suddenly interposed the harsh voice of the praefect.

He had not moved away from the rostrum all the while that the throng of obsequious sycophants and idle lovesick youths had crowded round Dea Flavia. Now he spoke over his shoulder at Hun Rhavas, who had no thought, whilst his comfortable little plot was succeeding so well, that the praefect was paying heed.

"She hath no guarantee, as my lord's grace himself hath knowledge," said the African with anxious humility.

"Nay! thou liest as to my knowledge of it," said Taurus Antinor. "Where is the list of goods compiled by the censor?"

Three pairs of willing hands were ready with the parchment rolls which the praefect had commanded; one was lucky enough to place them in his hands.

"What is the girl's name?" he asked as his deep-set eyes, under their perpetual frown, ran down the minute writing on the parchment roll.

18

"Nola, the daughter of Menecreta, my lord," said one of the scribes.

"I do not see the name of Nola, daughter of Menecreta, amongst those whom the State doth not guarantee for skill, health or condition," rejoined the praefect quietly, and his rough voice, scarcely raised above its ordinary pitch, seemed to ring a death-knell in poor Menecreta's heart.

"Nola, the daughter of Menecreta," he continued, once more referring to the parchment in his hand, "is here described as sixteen years of age, of sound health and robust constitution, despite the spareness of her body. The censor who compiled this list states that she has a fair knowledge of the use of unguents and of herbs, that she can use a needle and plait a lady's hair. Thou didst know all this, Hun Rhavas, for the duplicate list is before thee even now."

"My lord's grace," murmured Hun Rhavas, his voice quivering now, his limbs shaking with the fear in him, "I did not know—I——"

"Thou didst endeavour to defraud the State for purposes of thine own," interposed the praefect calmly. "Here! thou!" he added, beckoning to one of his lictors, "take this man to the Regia and hand him over to the chief warder."

"My lord's grace——" cried Hun Rhavas.

"Silence! To-morrow thou'lt appear before me in the basilica. Bring thy witnesses then if thou hast any to speak in thy defence. To-morrow thou canst plead before me any circumstance which might mitigate thy fault and stay my lips from condemning thee to that severe chastisement which crimes against the State deserve. In the meanwhile hold thy peace. I'll not hear another word."

But it was not in the negro's blood to submit to immediate punishment now and certain chastisement in the future without vigorous protestations and the generous use of his powerful lungs. The praefect's sentences in the tribunal where he administered justice were not characterised by leniency; the galleys, the stone-quarries, aye! even the cross were all within the bounds of possibility, whilst the scourge was an absolute certainty.

Hun Rhavas set up a succession of howls which echoed from temple to temple, from one end of the Forum to the other.

The frown on the praefect's forehead became even more marked than before. He had seen the young idlers—who, but a moment ago, were fawning round Dea Flavia's litter—turning eagerly back towards the rostrum, where Hun Rhavas' cries and moans had suggested the likelihood of one of those spectacles of wanton and purposeless cruelty in which their perverted senses found such constant delight.

But this spectacle Taurus Antinor was not like to give them. All he wanted was the quick restoration of peace and order. The fraudulent auctioneer was naught in his sight but a breaker of the law. As such he was deserving of such punishment as the law decreed and no more. But his howls just now were the means of rousing in the hearts of the crowd that most despicable of all passions to which the Roman—the master of civilisation—was a prey—the love of seeing some creature, man or beast, in pain, a passion which brought the Roman citizen down to the level of the brute: therefore Taurus Antinor wished above all to silence Hun Rhavas.

"One more sound from thy throat and I'll have thee scourged now and branded ere thy trial," he said.

The threat was sufficient. The negro, feeling that in submission lay his chief hope of mercy on the morrow, allowed himself to be led away quietly whilst the young patricians—cheated of an anticipated pleasure—protested audibly.

"And thou, Cheiron," continued the praefect, addressing a fair-skinned slave up on the rostrum who had been assistant hitherto in the auction, "do thou take the place vacated by Hun Rhavas."

He gave a few quick words of command to the lictors.

"Take the hat from off that girl's head," he said, "and put the inscribed tablet round her neck. Then she can be set up for sale as the State hath decreed."

As if moved by clockwork one of the lictors approached the girl and removed the unbecoming hat from her head, releasing a living stream of gold which, as it rippled over the girl's shoulders, roused a quick cry of admiration in the crowd.

In a moment Menecreta realised that her last hope must yield to the inevitable now. Even whilst her accomplice, Hun Rhavas, received the full brunt of the praefect's wrath she had scarcely dared to breathe, scarcely felt that she lived in this agony of fear. Her child still stood there on the platform, disfigured by the ugly headgear, obviously most unattractive to the crowd; nor did the awful possibility at first present itself to her mind that all her schemes for obtaining possession of her daughter could come to naught. It was so awful, so impossible of conception that the child should here, to-day, pass out of the mother's life for ever and without hope of redemption; that she should become the property of a total stranger who might for ever refuse to part from her again—an agriculturist, mayhap, who lived far off in Ethuria or Macedon—and that she, the mother, could never, never, hope to see her daughter again—that was a thought which was so horrible that its very horror seemed to render its realisation impossible.

But now the praefect, with that harsh, pitiless voice of his, was actually ordering the girl to be sold in the usual way, with all her merits exhibited to the likely purchaser: her golden hair—a perfect glory—to tempt the artistic eye, her skill recounted in fulsomeness, her cleverness with the needle, her knowledge of healing herbs.

The mother suddenly felt that every one in that cruel gaping crowd must be pining to possess such a treasure, that the combined wealth of every citizen of Rome would be lavished in this endeavour to obtain the great prize. The praefect himself, mayhap, would bid for her, or the imperator's agents!—alas! everything seemed possible to the anxious, the ridiculous, the sublime heart of the doting mother, and when that living mass of golden ripples glimmered in the noonday sun, Menecreta—forgetting her timidity, her fears, her weakness—pushed her way through the crowd with all the strength of her despair, and with a cry of agonised entreaty, threw herself at the feet of the praefect of Rome.

"My lord's grace, have mercy! have pity! I entreat thee! In the name of the gods, of thy mother, of thy child if thou hast one, have pity on me! have pity! have pity!"

The lictors had sprung forward in a moment and tried to seize the woman who had dared to push her way to the praefect's closely guarded presence, and was crouching there, her arms encircling his thighs, her face pressed close against his knees. One of the men raised his flail and brought it down with cruel strength on her thinly covered shoulders, but she did not heed the blow, mayhap she never felt it.

"Who ordered thee to strike?" said Taurus Antinor sternly to the lictor who already had the flail raised for the second time.

"The woman doth molest my lord's grace," protested the man.

"Have I said so?"

"No, my lord—but I thought to do my duty——"

"That thought will cost thee ten such lashes with the rods as thou didst deal this woman. By Jupiter!" he added roughly, whilst for the first time a look of ferocity as that of an angry beast lit up the impassiveness of his deep-set eyes, "if this turmoil continues I'll have every slave here flogged till he bleed. Is the business of the State to be hindered by the howlings of this miserable rabble? Get thee gone, woman," he cried finally, looking down on prostrate Menecreta, "get thee gone ere my lictors do thee further harm."

But she, with the obstinacy of a great sorrow, clung to his knees and would not move.

"My lord's grace, have pity—'tis my child; an thou takest her from me thou'lt part those whom the gods themselves have united—'tis my child, my lord! hast no children of thine own?"

"What dost prate about?" he asked, still speaking roughly for he was wroth with her and hated to see the gaping crowd of young, empty-headed fools congregating round him and this persistent suppliant hanging round his shins. "Thy child? who's thy child? And what hath thy child to do with me?"

"She is but a babe, my lord," said Menecreta with timid, tender voice; "her age only sixteen. A hand-maiden she was to Arminius Quirinius, who gave the miserable mother her freedom but kept the daughter so that he might win good money by and by through the selling of the child. My lord's grace, I have toiled for six years that in the end I might buy my daughter's freedom. Fifty aurei did Arminius

Quirinius demand as her price and I worked my fingers to the bone so that in time I might save that money. But Arminius Quirinius is dead and I have only twenty aurei. With the hat of disgrace on her head the child could have been knocked down to me—but now! now! look at her, my lord, how beautiful she is! and I have only twenty aurei!"

Taurus Antinor had listened quite patiently to Menecreta's tale. His sun-tanned face clearly showed how hard he was trying to gather up the tangled threads of her scrappy narrative. Nor did the lictors this time try to interfere with the woman. The praefect apparently was in no easy temper to-day, and when ill-humour seized him rods and flails were kept busy.

"And why didst not petition me before?" he asked, after a while, when Menecreta paused in order to draw breath.

And his face looked so fierce, his voice sounded so rough, no wonder the poor woman trembled as she whispered through her tears:

"I did not dare, my lord—I did not dare."

"Yet thou didst dare openly to outrage the law!"

"I wanted my child."

"And how many aurei didst promise to Hun Rhavas for helping thee to defraud the State?"

"Only five, my lord," she murmured.

"Then," he said sternly, "not only didst thou conspire to cheat the State for whose benefit the sale of the late censor's goods was ordered by imperial decree, but thou didst bribe another—a slave of the treasury—to aid and abet thee in this fraud."

Menecreta's grasp round the praefect's knees did not relax and he made no movement to free himself, but her head fell sideways against her shoulder whilst her lips murmured in tones of utter despair:

"I wanted my child."

"For thy delinquencies," resumed the praefect, seemingly not heeding the pathetic appeal, "thou shalt appear before my tribunal on the morrow like unto Hun Rhavas thine accomplice, and thou shalt then be punished no less than thou deservest. But this is no place for the delivery of my judgment upon thee, and the sale must proceed as the law directs; thy daughter must stand upon the catasta, thou canst renew thy bid of twenty aurei for her, and," he added with unmistakable significance, as throwing his head back his imperious glance swept over the assembled crowd, "as there will be no higher bid for Nola, daughter of Menecreta, she will become thy property as by law decreed."

The true meaning of this last sentence was quite unmistakable. The crowd who had gathered round the rostrum to watch, gaping, the moving incident, looked on the praefect and understood no one was to bid for Nola, the daughter of Menecreta. Taurus Antinor, surnamed Anglicanus, had spoken and it would not be to anyone's advantage to quarrel with his arbitrary pronouncement for the sake of any slave girl, however desirable she might be. It was not pleasant to encounter the wrath of the praefect of Rome nor safe to rouse his enmity.

So the crowd acquiesced silently, not only because it feared the praefect, but also because Menecreta's sorrow, the call of the despairing mother, the sad tragedy of this little domestic episode had not left untouched the hearts of these Roman citizens. In matters of sentiment they were not cruel and they held family ties in great esteem; both these factors went far towards causing any would-be purchaser to obey Taurus Antinor's commands and to retire at once from the bidding.

As for Menecreta, it seemed to her as if the heavens had opened before her delighted gaze. From the depths of despair she had suddenly been dragged forth into the blinding daylight of hope. She could scarcely believe that her ears had heard rightly the words of the praefect.

Still clinging to his knees she raised her head to him; her eyes still dimmed with tears looked strangely wondering up at his face whilst her lips murmured faintly:

"Art thou a god, that thou shouldst act like this?"

But obviously the small stock of patience possessed by the praefect was now exhausted, for he pushed the woman roughly away from him.

"A truce on thy ravings now, woman. The midday hour is almost on us. I have no further time to waste on thine affairs. Put the girl up on the catasta," he added, speaking in his usual harsh, curt way, "and take this woman's arms from round my shins."

And it was characteristic of him that this time he did not interfere with his lictors when they handled the woman with their accustomed roughness.

CHAPTER V

"Cast thy bread upon the waters: for thou shalt find it after many days."—Ecclesiastes xi. 1.

The fair-skinned Cheiron up on the rostrum now took over the duties of the disgraced Hun Rhavas.

The interlude had caused the crowd to linger on despite the approach of noonday, an hour always devoted, almost sacred, to rest. But now that decorum was once more restored and the work of the sale could be proceeded with in the methodical manner approved by the praefect, interest began to flag.

The crowd seemed inclined to wait just a brief while longer in order to see Nola put up on the catasta and to hear the bid of twenty aurei made for her by her mother—a bid which, at the praefect's commands, was to be final and undisputed. Just to see the hammer come clashing down as an epilogue to the palpitating drama was perhaps worth waiting for. The human goods still left for sale after that would have to be held over for a more favourable opportunity.

The praefect was preparing to leave.

Up on the platform Nola, the daughter of Menecreta, smiled at the world through a few lingering tears. She was very happy now that her golden hair was allowed to stream down her shoulders, and that it was only because the praefect had so ordered it that the low price of twenty aurei would be accepted for her.

"Nola, daughter of Menecreta," shouted Cheiron, the new auctioneer, "aged sixteen years, skilled in the art of healing, and the knowledge of unguents and herbs. Her health is good, her teeth perfect, and her eyes keen for threading the finest needle. Shall we say fifteen aurei for the girl?"

He recited his peroration quickly and perfunctorily, like one repeating a lesson, learned from the praefect.

"I'll give twenty," rang out Menecreta's voice, clearly and loudly. She, too, had learned her lesson, and learned it well, whilst gratitude and an infinity of joy gave her strength to overcome her natural timidity.

"Twenty aurei! twenty aurei! will no one bid more for Nola, the daughter of Menecreta," shouted the auctioneer, hammer in hand, ready to bring it down since no more bidding would be allowed for this piece of goods. "Twenty aurei! no one bids more—no one—no——"

"I'll give thirty aurei!"

It was a pure, young voice that spoke, the voice of a young girl, mellow and soft-toned as those of a pigeon when it cooes to its mate; but firm withal, direct and clear, the voice of one accustomed to command and even more accustomed to be obeyed.

The sound rang from temple to temple right across the Forum, and was followed by silence—the dead silence which falls upon a multitude when every heart stops beating and every breath is indrawn.

Cheiron paused, hammer in hand, his lips parted for the very words which he was about to utter, his round open eyes wandering irresolutely from the praefect's face to that of the speaker with the melodious voice.

And on the hot noonday air there trembled a long sigh of pain, like the breaking of a human heart.

But the same voice, soft and low, was heard again:

24

"The girl pleases me! What say you, my lord Escanes, is not that hair worthy to be immortalised by a painter's hand?"

And preceded by her lictors, who made a way for her through the crowd, Dea Flavia advanced even to the foot of the catasta. And as she advanced, those who were near retreated to a respectful distance, making a circle round her and leaving her isolated, with her tall Ethiopian slaves behind her holding broad leaves of palm above her head to shield her from the sun. Thus was the gold of her hair left in shadow, and the white skin of her face appeared soft and cool, but the sun played with the shimmering folds of her white silk tunic and glinted against the gems on her fingers.

Tall, imperious and majestic, Dea Flavia—unconscious alike of the deference of the crowd and the timorous astonishment of the slaves—looked up at Cheiron, the auctioneer, and resumed with a touch of impatience in her rich young voice:

"I said that I would bid thirty aurei for this girl!"

Less than a minute had elapsed since Dea Flavia's sudden appearance on the scene. Taurus Antinor had as yet made no movement or given any sign to Cheiron as to what he should do; but those who watched him with anxious interest could see the dark frown on his brow grow darker still and darker, until his whole face seemed almost distorted with an expression of passionate wrath.

Menecreta, paralysed by this sudden and final shattering of her every hope, uttered moan after moan of pain, and as the pitiful sounds reached the praefect's ears, a smothered oath escaped his tightly clenched teeth. Like some gigantic beast roused from noonday sleep, he straightened his massive frame and seemed suddenly to shake himself free from that state of torpor into which Dea Flavia's unexpected appearance had at first thrown him. He too, advanced to the foot of the catasta and there faced the imperious beauty, whom the whole city had, for the past two years, tacitly agreed to obey in all things.

"The State," he said, speaking at least as haughtily as Dea Flavia herself, "hath agreed to accept the sum of twenty aurei for this slave. 'Tis too late now to make further bids for her."

But a pair of large blue eyes, cold as the waters of the Tiber and like unto them mysterious and elusive, were turned fully on the speaker.

"Too late didst thou say, oh Taurus Antinor?" said Dea Flavia raising her pencilled eyebrows with a slight expression of scorn, "nay! I had not seen the hammer descend! The girl until then is not sold, and open to the highest bidder. Or am I wrong, O praefect, in thus interpreting the laws of Rome?"

"This is an exceptional case, Augusta," he retorted curtly.

"Then wilt thou expound to me that law which deals with such exceptional cases?" she rejoined with the same ill-concealed tone of gentle irony. "I had never heard of it; so I pray thee enlighten mine

25

ignorance. Of a truth thou must know the law, since thou didst swear before the altar of the gods to uphold it with all thy might."

"'Tis not a case of law, Augusta, but one of pity."

The praefect, feeling no doubt the weakness of any argument which aimed at coercing this daughter of the Cæsars, prompted too by his innate respect of the law which he administered, thought it best to retreat from his position of haughty arrogance and to make an appeal, since obviously he could not command. Dea Flavia was quick to note this change of attitude, and her delicate lips parted in a contemptuous smile.

"Dost administer pity as well as law, O Taurus Antinor?" she asked coldly.

Then, as if further argument from him were of no interest to her, she once more turned to the auctioneer, and said with marked impatience:

"I have bid thirty aurei for this girl; art set there slave, to gape at the praefect, or to do thy duty to the State that employs thee? Is there a higher bid for the maid? She pleaseth me, and I'll give sixty or an hundred for her. This is a public auction as by law directed. I appeal to thee, oh Taurus Antinor, to give orders to thy slaves, ere I appeal to my kinsman, the Emperor, for the restoration of a due administration of the law."

Those who had cause to know and to fear the praefect's varying moods, were ready to shrink away now from the threatening darkness of his glance. He seemed indeed like some tawny wild beast, chained and scorned, whom a child was teasing from a point of vantage just beyond the reach of his powerful jaws.

She was so well within her rights and he so absolutely in the wrong as far as the law was concerned, that he knew at once that he must inevitably give way. If Dea Flavia chose to desire a slave she could satisfy the caprice, since no man's fortune could hold out against her own. This too did the praefect know. He himself was passing rich and would gladly have paid a large sum now, that he might prove the victor in this unequal contest but Dea Flavia had the law and boundless wealth on her side. Taurus Antinor had only his personal authority which had coerced the crowd, but was of no avail against this beautiful woman who defied him openly before the plebs and before his slaves.

"Have no fear, O Dea Flavia," he said, trying to speak calmly, but his voice trembling with the mighty effort at control, "justice hath never yet suffered at my hands. I told thee that 'tis not a case of law here but one of mercy. This girl's mother has toiled for years to save enough money with which to buy the freedom of her child. She hath twenty aurei to command, and the girl is not worth much more than that. The State would have been satisfied, for my own purse would have made up the deficiency. I had bought the girl myself and given her to the mother, but the poor wretch was so proud and happy to buy her child's freedom herself, that I allowed her to make the bid. That is this slave-girl's story, Augusta! Thou seest that the law will not suffer, neither shall the State be defrauded. What thou art prepared to give for the girl that will I make good in the coffers of the State. Art satisfied, I hope! Thou art a woman, and canst mayhap better understand than I did at first when Menecreta threw herself at my knees."

His rugged voice softened considerably whilst he spoke, and those who were watching him so anxiously saw the ugly dark frown gradually lighten on his brow. No wonder! since he was just a man face to face with an exceptionally beautiful woman, to whose pity he was endeavouring to make appeal. At all times an easy and a pleasant task, it must have been doubly so now when the object of mercy was so deserving. Taurus Antinor looked straight into the lovely face before him, marvelling when those exquisite blue eyes would soften with their first look of pity. But they remained serene and mysterious, neither avoiding his gaze nor responding to its appeal. The delicately chiselled lips retained their slight curve of scorn.

He gave a sign to Menecreta, and she approached, tottering like one who is drunken with wine, or who has received a heavy blow on the head. She stood before Dea Flavia, with head trembling like poplar leaves and great hollow eyes fixed in meaningless vacancy upon the great patrician lady.

"This is Menecreta, O Dea Flavia," concluded the praefect; "wilt allow her to plead her own cause?"

Without replying directly to him, Dea Flavia turned for the first time to the slave-girl on the platform.

"Is this thy mother?" she asked.

"Yes!" murmured the girl.

"Hast a wish that she should buy thy freedom?"

"Yes."

"That thou shouldst go with her to the hovel which is her home, the only home that thou wouldst ever know? Hast a wish to become the slave of that old woman, whose mind hath already gone wandering among the shadows, and whose body will very shortly go in search of her mind? Hast a wish to spend the rest of thy days scrubbing floors and stewing onions in an iron pot? Or is thy wish to dwell in the marble halls of Dea Flavia's house, where the air is filled with the perfume of roses and violets and tame songbirds make their nests in the oleander bushes? Wouldst like to recline on soft downy cushions, allowing thy golden hair to fall over thy shoulders the while I, mallet or chisel in hand, would make thy face immortal by carving it in marble? The praefect saith thine is a case for pity, then do I have pity upon thee, and give thee the choice of what thy life shall be. Squalor and misery as thy mother's slave, or joy, music, and flowers as mine."

Her voice, ever low and musical, had taken on notes of tenderness and of languor. The tears of pity which the praefect had vainly tried to conjure up gathered now in her eyes as her whole mood seemed to melt in the fire of her own eloquence.

Nola hung her head, overwhelmed with shame. She was very young and the great lady very kind and gentle. Her own simple heart, still filled with the selfish desires of extreme youth, cried out for that same life of ease and luxury which the beautiful lady depicted in such tempting colours before her, whilst it shrank instinctively from the poverty, the hard floors, the stewing-pots which awaited her in that squalid hut on the Aventine where her mother dwelt.

She hung her head and made no reply, whilst from the group of the young and idle sycophants who had hung on Dea Flavia's honeyed words just as they had done round her litter a while ago, came murmurs of extravagant adulation and well-chosen words in praise of her exquisite diction, her marvellous pity, her every talent and virtue thus freely displayed.

Even the crowd stared open-mouthed and agape at this wonderful spectacle of so great a lady stooping to parley with a slave.

The praefect alone remained seemingly unmoved; but the expression of hidden wrath had once more crept into his eyes, making them look dark and fierce and glowing with savage impotence; and his gaze had remained fixed on the radiantly beautiful woman who stood there before him in all the glory of her high descent, her patrician bearing, the exquisite charm of her personality, seductive in its haughty aloofness, voluptuous even in its disdainful calm.

Neither did Menecreta fall a victim to Dea Flavia's melodious voice. She had listened from a respectful distance, and with the humble deference born of years of bondage, to the honeyed words with which the great lady deigned to cajole a girl-slave: but when Dea Flavia had finished speaking and the chorus of admiration had died down around her, the freedwoman, with steps which she vainly tried to render firm, approached to the foot of the catasta and stood between the great lady and her own child.

She placed one trembling, toil-worn hand on Nola's shoulder and said gently:

"Nola, thou hast heard what my lady's grace hath deigned to speak. A humble life but yet a free one awaits thee in thy mother's home on the Aventine; a life of luxurious slavery doth my lady's grace offer thee. She deigns to say that thou alone shalt choose thy way in life. Thou wast born a slave, Nola, and shouldst know how to obey. Obey my lady then. Choose thy future, Nola. The humble and free one which I, thy mother, have earned for thee, or the golden cage in which this proud lady would deign to keep her latest whim in bondage!"

Her voice, which at first had been almost steady, died down at the end in a pitiful quiver. It was the last agony of her hopes, the real parting from her child, for even whilst Menecreta's throat was choked with sobs, Nola hung her head and great heavy tears dropped from her

28

eyes upon her clasped hands. The child was crying and the mother understood.

She no longer moaned with pain now. The pain was gone; only dull despair remained. Her heart had hungered for the one glad cry of joy: "Mother, I'll come to thee!" It was left starving even through her daughter's tears.

But those who watched this unwonted scene could not guess what Dea Flavia felt, for her eyes were veiled by her long lashes, and the mouth expressed neither triumph nor pity. Menecreta now once more tried to steady her quivering voice; she straightened her weary back and said quite calmly:

"My lady's grace has spoken, and the great lords here assembled have uttered words of praise for an exquisite act of pity. My lady's grace hath spoken and hath told the poor slave, Nola, to choose her own life. But I, the humble freedwoman, will speak in my turn to thee, O Dea Flavia of the imperial house of immortal Cæsar, and looking into thine eyes I tell thee that thy pity is but falsehood and thine eloquence naught but cruelty. By thy words thou didst take my child from me as effectually as if thou already hadst bought and paid for her. Look at the child now! She hangs her head and dares not look on me, her mother. Oh! thou didst well choose thy words, oh daughter of imperial Cæsar, for thy honeyed words were like the nectar which hid the poison that hath filtrated into my daughter's heart. Thou hast said it right—her life with me had been one of toil and mayhap of misery, but she would have been content, for she had never dreamed of another life. But now she has heard thee speak of marble halls, of music and of flowers, of a life of ease and of vanity, and never again would that child be happy in her mother's arms. Be content, O Augusta! the girl is thine since thy caprice hath willed it so. Even though she chose her mother now, I would not have her, for I know that she would be unhappy in that lonely hut on the Aventine; and though I have seen much sorrow and endured much misery, there is none greater to bear than the sight of a child's sorrow. Take her, Dea Flavia! thine eloquence has triumphed over a mother's broken heart."

Strangely enough, and to the astonishment of all those present, Dea Flavia had listened patiently and silently whilst the woman spoke, and now she said quite gently:

"Nay! thou dost wrong thine own child, Menecreta; see how lovingly she turns to thee!"

"Only because in her shallow little heart there has come the first twinge of remorse," replied the woman sadly. "Soon, in the lap of that luxury which thou dost offer her, she will have forgotten the mother's arms in which she weeps to-day."

"That's enough," suddenly interposed the praefect harshly. "Menecreta, take thy child; take her, I say. Dea Flavia hath relinquished her to thee. Be not a fool and take the child away!"

29

But with a gesture of savage pride the freedwoman tore herself away from Nola.

"No!" she said firmly, "I'll not take her. That proud lady here hath stolen the soul of my child; her body, inert and sad, I'll not have the while her heart longs to be away from me. I'll not have her, I say! let the daughter of Cæsar account to the gods above for her tempting words, her honeyed speech and her lies."

"Silence, woman!" ordered Dea Flavia sternly.

"Lies, I tell thee, lies," continued the woman who had lost all sense of fear in the depth of her misery; "the life of luxury thou dost promise this child—how long will it last? thy caprice for her—when will it tire? Silence? nay! I'll not be silent," she continued wildly in defiant answer to angry murmurs from the crowd. "Thou daughter of a house of tyrants, tyrant thyself! a slave to thy paltry whims, crushing beneath thy sandalled feet the hearts of the poor and the cries of the oppressed! Shame on thee! shame on thee, I say!"

"By the great Mother," said Dea Flavia coldly, "will no one here rid me of this screaming vixen?"

But even before she had spoken, the angry murmurs around had swollen to loud protestations. Before the praefect's lictors could intervene the crowd had pushed forward; the men rushed and surrounded the impious creature who had dared to raise her voice against one of the divinities of Rome: Augusta the goddess.

One of Dea Flavia's gigantic Ethiopians had seized Menecreta by the shoulder, another pulled her head back by the hair and struck her roughly on the mouth, but she, with the strength of the vanquished, brought down to her knees, frenzied with despair, continued her agonised cry:

"A curse upon thee, Dea Flavia, a curse spoken by the dying lips of the mother whom thou hast scorned!"

How she contrived momentarily to free herself from the angry crowd of lictors and of slaves it were impossible to say; perhaps at this moment something in Menecreta's wild ravings had awed their spirit and paralysed their hands. Certain it is that for one moment the freedwoman managed to struggle to her feet and to drag herself along on her knees until her hands clutched convulsively the embroidered tunic of Dea Flavia.

"And this is the curse which I pronounce on thee," she murmured in a hoarse whisper, which, rising and rising to higher tones, finally ended in shrieks which reached to the outermost precincts of the Forum. "Dea Flavia, daughter of Octavius Claudius thou art accursed. May thine every deed of mercy be turned to sorrow and to humiliation, thine every act of pity prove a curse to him who receives it, until thou on thy knees, art left to sue for pity to a heart that knoweth it not and findest a deaf ear turned to thy cry. Hear me, ye gods—hear me!... Magna Mater, hear me!... Mother of the stars—hear me!"

Superstition, deeply rooted in every Roman heart, held the crowd enthralled even whilst Menecreta's trembling voice echoed against the marble walls of the temples of the gods whom she invoked. No one attempted to stop her. Dea Flavia's slaves dared not lay a hand on her. It seemed as if Magna Mater herself, the great Mother, had thrown an invisible mantle over the humble freedwoman, shielding her with god-like power.

"Menecreta, raise thyself and come away," said a harsh voice in tones of command. The praefect had at last with the vigorous help of his lictors managed to push his way through the crowd. It was he now who attempted to raise the woman from her knees. He sharply bade his own men to silence the woman and to take her away.

Dea Flavia had remained silent and still. She had not attempted to interrupt the frenzied woman who called this awful curse upon her; only once, when Menecreta invoked the gods, did a shudder pass through the delicate body, and her heavy lids fell over her blue eyes, as if they were trying to shut out some awful vision which the woman's ravings had conjured up.

Then in a sudden her mood seemed to change, her serenity returned, and when the praefect interposed she put out a restraining hand, warning the lictors not to approach.

She bent to Menecreta and called her by name, her mellow voice vibrating with tender tones like the chords of the harp that are touched by a master hand, and her blue eyes, veiled with tears, looked down with infinite tenderness on the prostrate figure at her feet.

"Menecreta," she said gently, "thy sorrow hath made thee harsh. The gods, believe me, still hold much happiness in store for thee and for thy daughter. See how they refuse to register thy curse which had been impious were it not the dictate of thy poor frenzied mind. See, Menecreta, how thou didst misjudge me; what I did, I did because I wished to test thy love for thy child. I wished to test its true selflessness. But now I am satisfied and Nola need no longer choose, for she shall have the luxury for which her young heart doth pine, but she shall never by me be deprived of her mother's love."

Even while she spoke, Menecreta struggled to her knees. Her wide-open eyes, over which a mysterious veil seemed to be slowly descending, were fixed on the radiant vision above her. But comprehension had not yet reached her mind. Her spirit had not yet been dragged from the hell of despair to this glorious sight of heaven.

"Menecreta," continued the gentle voice, "thou shalt come to my house. A free woman, thou shalt be my friend and thy daughter shall be thy happy bondswoman. I'll give thee a little home in which thou shalt dwell with her and draw thy last breath in her arms; there shall be a garden there which she will plant with roses. Thy days and hers will be

31

one continuous joy. Come to me now, Menecreta! Take thy daughter by the hand and come and dwell with her in the little house which my slaves shall prepare for thee."

Her face now was almost on a level with that of Menecreta, whose hollow eyes gazed upwards with a look of ecstatic wonder.

"Who art thou?" murmured the freedwoman; "there is a film over my eyes—I cannot see—art thou a goddess?"

"Nay!" replied Dea Flavia gently, "only a lonely maiden who has no friends e'en in the midst of all her riches. A lonely maid whom thou didst try to curse, asking the gods that her every act of mercy be turned to bitter sorrow. See, she takes thee to her heart and gives thee back thy daughter, a home and happiness."

"My daughter?" murmured Menecreta.

"She shall dwell with thee in the house which shall be thine."

"A home?" and the trembling voice grew weaker, the hollow eyes more dim.

"Aye! in the midst of a garden, with roses and violets all around."

"And happiness?" sighed Menecreta.

And her head fell back against Dea Flavia's arm; her eyes, now veiled by the film of death gazed, sightless, up at the dome of blue.

"Menecreta!" cried Dea Flavia, horror-stricken as she felt the feeble body stiffening against her with the approaching rigidity of death.

"Mother!" echoed Nola, striving to smother her terror as she threw herself on her knees.

"The woman is dead," said the praefect quietly.

CHAPTER VI

"I am Alpha and Omega, the beginning and the end, the first and the last."—Revelations xxii. 13.

And after that silence and peace.

Silence save for the moanings of the child Nola, who in a passionate outburst of grief had thrown herself on the body of her mother.

Dea Flavia stood there still and calm, her young face scarce less white than the clinging folds of her tunic, her unfathomable eyes fixed upon the pathetic group at her feet: the weeping girl and the dead woman.

She seemed almost dazed—like one who does not understand and a quaint puzzled frown appeared upon the whiteness of her brow.

Once she raised her eyes to the praefect and encountered his gaze—strangely contemptuous and wrathful—fixed upon her own, and anon she shuddered when a pitiable moan from Nola echoed from end to end along the marble walls around.

And the crowd of idlers began slowly to disperse. In groups of twos and threes they went, their sandalled feet making a soft rustling noise against the flagstones of the Forum, and their cloaks of thin woollen stuff floating out behind them as they walked.

The young patricians were the first to go. The scene had ceased to be amusing and Dea Flavia was not like to bestow another smile. They thought it best to retire to their luxurious homes, for they vaguely resented the majesty of death which clung round the dead freedwoman and the young living slave. They hoped to forget in the course of the noonday sleep, and the subsequent delights of the table, the painful events which had so unpleasantly stirred their shallow hearts.

Dea Flavia paid no heed to them as they murmured words of leave-taking in her ear. 'Tis doubtful if she saw one of them or cared if they went or stayed.

At an order from the praefect the auction sale was abruptly suspended. The lictors drove the herds of human cattle together preparatory to taking them to their quarters on the slopes of the Aventine where they would remain until the morrow; whilst the scribes and auctioneers made haste to scramble down from the heights of the rostrum, the heat of the day having rendered that elevated position well-nigh unbearable. Only Dea Flavia's retinue lingered in the Forum. Standing at a respectful distance they surrounded the gorgeously draped litter, waiting, silently and timorous, the further pleasure of their mistress; and behind Dea Flavia her two Ethiopian slaves, stolidly holding the palm leaves to shield her head against the blazing sun which so mercilessly seared their own naked shoulders.

"Grant me leave to escort thee to thy litter, Augusta!" murmured a timid voice.

It was young Hortensius Martius who spoke. He had approached the catasta and now stood timid, and a suppliant, beside Dea Flavia, with his curly head bare to the scorching sun and his back bent in slave-like deference. But the young girl seemed not to hear him and even after he had twice repeated his request she turned to him with uncomprehending eyes.

"I would not leave thee, Dea," he said, "until I saw thee safely among thy slaves and thy clients."

Then at last did she speak. But her voice sounded toneless and dull, as of one who speaks in a dream.

"I thank thee, good Hortensius," she said, "but my slaves are close at hand and I would prefer to be left alone."

To insist further would have been churlish. Hortensius Martius, well versed in every phase of decorum, bowed his head in obedience and retired to his litter. But he told his slaves not to bear him away from the Forum altogether but to place the litter down under the arcades of the tabernae, and then to stand round it so that it could not be seen, whilst he himself could still keep watch over the movements of Dea Flavia.

But she in the meanwhile remained in the same inert position, standing listlessly beside the body of Menecreta, her face expressing puzzlement rather than horror, as if within her soul she was trying to reconcile the events of the last few moments with her previous conceptions of what the tenor of her life should be.

The curse of Menecreta had found sudden and awful fulfilment, and Dea Flavia remained vaguely wondering whether the gods had been asleep on this hot late summer's day and forgotten to shield their favoured daughter against the buffetings of fate. A freedwoman had roused superstitious fear in the heart of a daughter of the Cæsars! Surely there must be something very wrong in the administration of the affairs of this world. Nay, more! for the freedwoman, unconscious of her own impiety, had triumphed in the end; her death—majestic and sublime in its suddenness—had set the seal upon her malediction.

And Dea Flavia marvelled that the dead woman remained so calm, her eyes so still, when—if indeed Jupiter had been aroused by the monstrous sacrilege—she must now be facing the terrors of his judgments.

And Taurus Antinor watched her in silence whilst she stood thus, unconscious of his gaze, a perfect picture of exquisite womanhood set in a frame of marble temples and colonnades, a dome of turquoise above her head, the palm leaves above her throwing a dense blue shadow on her golden hair and the white tunic on her shoulders.

He had heard much of Dea Flavia—the daughter of Claudius Octavius and now the ward of the Emperor Caligula—since his return from Syria a year ago, and he had oft seen her gilded and rose-draped litter gliding along the Sacra Via or the Via Appia, surrounded with its numberless retinue: but he had never seen her so close as this, nor had he heard her speak.

She was a mere child and still under the tutelage of her despotic father when he—Taurus Antinor—tired of the enervating influences of decadent Rome, had obtained leave from the Emperor Tiberius to go to Syria as its governor. The imperator was glad enough to let him go. Taurus Antinor, named Anglicanus, was more popular with the army and the plebs than any autocratic ruler could wish.

He went to Syria and remained there half a dozen years. The jealousy of one emperor had sent him thither and 'twas the jealousy of another that called him back to Rome. Syria had liked its governor over well, and Caius Julius Cæsar Caligula would not brook rivalry in the allegiance owed to himself alone by his subjects—even by those who dwelt in the remotest provinces of the Empire.

But on his return to Rome the powerful personality of Taurus Antinor soon imposed itself upon the fierce and maniacal despot. Caligula—though he must in reality have hated the Anglicanus as much and more than he hated all men—gave grudging admiration to his independence of spirit and to his fearless tongue. In the midst of an entourage composed of lying sycophants and of treacherous minions, the Cæsar seemed to feel in the presence of the stranger a sense of security and of trust. Some writers have averred that Caligula looked on Taurus Antinor as a kind of personal fetish who kept the wrath of the gods averted from his imperial head. Be that as it may, there is no doubt that tyrant exerted his utmost power to keep Taurus near his person, showering upon him those honours and titles of which he would have been equally ready to deprive him had the stranger at any time run counter to his will. Anon, when the Cæsar thought it incumbent upon his dignity to start on a military expedition, he forced Antinor to accept the praefecture of the city in order to keep him permanently settled in Rome.

The Anglicanus accepted the power—which was almost supreme in the absence of the Cæsar. He even gave the oath demanded of him by the Emperor that he would remain at his post until the termination of the proposed military expedition, but it was easy to see that the dignities for which others would have fought and striven to their uttermost were not really to the liking of Taurus Antinor.

Avowedly wilful of temper, he had since his return from Syria become even more silent, more self-centred than before. Many called him morose and voted him either treacherous or secretly ambitious; others averred that he was either very arrogant or frankly dull. Certain it is that he held himself very much aloof from the society of his kind and persistently refused to mix with the young elegants of the day either in their circles or their baths, their private parties or public entertainments.

Thus it was that the praefect found himself to-day for the first time in the near presence of Dea Flavia, the acknowledged queen of that same society which he declined to frequent, and as he grudgingly admitted to himself that she was beautiful beyond what men had said of her, he remembered all the tales which he had heard of her callous pride, her cold dignity, and of that cruel disdain with which she rejected all homage and broke the hearts of those whom her beauty had brought to her feet.

For the moment, however, she struck him as more pathetic than fearsome; she looked lonely just now like a stately lily blooming alone in a deserted garden. He was wroth with her for what she had done to Menecreta and for her childish caprice and opposition to his will, but at the same time he who so seldom felt pity for those whom a just punishment had overtaken, was sorry for this young girl, for in her case retribution had been severe and out of all proportion to her fault.

Therefore he approached her almost with deference and forced his rough voice to gentleness, as he said to her:

"The hour is late, O Dea Flavia. I myself must leave the Forum now. I would wish to see thee safe amongst thy women."

She turned her blue eyes upon him. His voice had roused her from her meditations and recalled her to that sense of proud dignity with which she loved to surround herself as with invisible walls. She must have seen the pity in his eyes for he did not try to hide it, but it seemed to anger her as coming from this man who—to her mind—was the primary cause of her present trouble. She looked for a moment or two on him as if trying to recollect his very existence, and no importunate slave could ever encounter such complete disdain as fell on the praefect at this moment from Dea Flavia's glance.

"I will return to my palace at the hour which pleaseth me most, O praefectus," she said coldly, "and when the child Nola, being more composed, is ready to accompany me."

"Nay!" he rejoined in his accustomed rough way, "the slave Nola is naught to thee now. She will be looked after as the State directs."

"The slave is mine," she retorted curtly. "She shall come with me."

And even as she spoke she drew herself up to her full height, more like, he thought, than ever to a stately lily now. The crown of gold upon her head caught a glint from the noonday sun, and the folds of her white tunic fell straight and rigid from her shoulders down to her feet.

It seemed strange to him that one so young, so exquisitely pure, should thus be left all alone to face the hard moments of life; her very disdain for him, her wilfulness, seemed to him pathetic, for they showed her simple ignorance of the many cruelties which life must of necessity have in store for her.

As for yielding to her present mood, he had no thought of it. It was caprice originally which had caused her to defy his will and to break old Menecreta's heart. She had invoked strict adherence to the law for the sole purpose of indulging this caprice. Now he was tempted also to stand upon the law and to defy her tyrannical will, even at the cost of his own inclinations in the matter.

He would not trust her with the child Nola now. He had other plans for the orphan girl, rendered lonely and desolate through a great lady's whim, and he would have felt degradation in the thought that Dea Flavia should impose her will on him in this.

He knew her power of course. She was a near kinswoman of the Emperor, and the child of his adoption; she was all-powerful with the Cæsar as with all men through the might of his personality as much as through that of her wealth.

36

But he had no thought of yielding nor any thought of fear. It seemed as if in the heat-laden atmosphere two mighty wills had suddenly clashed one against the other, brandishing ghostly steels. His will against hers! The might of manhood and of strength against the word of a beautiful woman. Nor was the contest unequal. If he could crush her with a touch of his hand, she could destroy him with one word in the Cæsar's ear. She had as her ally the full unbridled might of the House of Cæsar, while against her there was only this stranger, a descendant of a freedwoman from a strange land. For the nonce his influence was great over the mind of the quasi-madman who sat on the Empire's throne, but any moment, any event, the whisper of an enemy, the word of a woman, might put an end to his power.

All this Dea Flavia knew, and knowing it found pleasure in toying with his wrath. Armed with the triple weapon of her beauty, her purity and her power, she taunted him with his impotence and smiled with scornful pity upon the weakness of his manhood.

Even now she turned to Nola and said with gentle firmness:

"Get up, girl, and come with me."

But at her words the last vestige of deference fled from the praefect's manner; pity now would have been weak folly. Had he yielded he would have despised himself even as this proud girl now affected to scorn him.

He interposed his massive figure between Dea Flavia and the slave and said loudly:

"By thy leave, Nola, the daughter of Menecreta, is the property of the State and 'tis I will decide whither she goeth now."

"Until to-morrow only, Taurus Antinor," she rejoined coldly, "for to-morrow she must be in the slave market again, when my agents will bid for and buy her according to my will."

"Nay! she shall not be put up for sale to-morrow."

"By whose authority, O praefectus?"

"By mine. The State hath given me leave to purchase privately a number of slaves from the late censor's household. 'Tis my intention to purchase Nola thus."

"Thou hast no right," she said, still speaking with outward calm, though her whole soul rebelled against the arrogance of this man who dared to thwart her will, to gainsay her word, and set up his dictates against hers, "thou hast no right thus to take the law in thine own hands."

"Nay! as to that," he replied with equal calm, "I'll answer for mine own actions. But the slave Nola shall not pass into thy hands, Augusta! Thou hast wrought quite enough mischief as it is; be content and go thy way. Leave the child in peace."

In these days of unbridled passions and unfettered tyranny, a man who spoke thus to a daughter of the Cæsars spoke at peril of his life. Both Dea Flavia and Taurus Antinor knew this when they faced one another eye to eye, their very souls in rebellion one against the other—his own turbulent and fierce, with the hot blood from a remote land coursing in his veins, blinding him to his own advantage, to his own future, to everything save to his feeling of independence at all cost from the oppression of this family of tyrants; her own almost serene in its consciousness of limitless power.

For the moment her sense of dignity prevailed. Whatever she might do in the future, she was comparatively helpless now. The praefect in the discharge of his functions—second only to the Cæsar—was all-powerful where he stood.

Taurus Antinor was still the praefect of Rome, still a member of the Senate and favourite of Caligula. He had her at a disadvantage now, just as she had held him a while ago when she forced on the public sale of the girl Nola. Therefore, though with a look she would have crushed the insolent, and her delicate hands were clenched into fists that would have chastised him then and there if they had the strength, she returned his look of fierce defiance with her usual one of calm.

"Thou hast spoken, Taurus Antinor," she said coldly, "and in deference to the law which thou dost represent I bow to thy commands. Art thou content?" she added, seeing that he made no reply.

"Content?" he asked, puzzled at her meaning.

"Aye!" she said; "I asked thee if thou wert content. Thou hast humiliated a daughter of Cæsar, a humiliation which she is not like to forget."

"I crave thy pardon if I have transgressed beyond the limits of my duty."

"Thy duty? Nay, Taurus Antinor, a man's duties are as varied as a woman's moods, and he is wisest who knows how to adapt the one to the other. 'Tis not good, remember, to run counter to Dea Flavia's will. 'Tis much that thou must have forgotten, O praefect, ere thou didst set thy so-called duty above the fulfilment of my wish."

"Nay, gracious lady," he said simply, "I had forgotten nothing. Not even that Archelaus Menas, the sculptor, died for having angered thee; nor that Julius Campanius perished in exile and young Decretas in fetters, because of thine enmity. Thou seest that—though somewhat of a stranger in Rome—I know much of its secret history, and though mine eyes had until now never beheld thy loveliness, yet had mine ears heard much of thy power."

"Yet at its first encounter thou didst defy it."

"I have no mother to mourn o'er my death like young Decretas," he said curtly, "nor yet a wife to make into a sorrowing widow like the sculptor Menas."

If it was his desire to break through the barrier of well-nigh insolent calm which she seemed to have set round her dainty person, then he succeeded over well, for she winced at his words like one who has received a blow and her eyes, dark with anger, narrowed until they became mere slits fringed by her golden lashes.

"But thou hast a life, Taurus Antinor," she said, "and life is a precious possession."

He shrugged his massive shoulders, and a curious smile played round his lips.

"And thou canst order that precious possession to be taken from me," he said lightly. "Is that what thou wouldst say?"

"That and more, for thou hast other precious treasures more precious, mayhap, than life; so guard them well, O Taurus Antinor!"

"Nay, gracious lady," he rejoined, still smiling, "I have but one soul as I have one life, and that too is in the hands of God."

"Of which god?" she asked quaintly.

He did not reply but pointed upwards at the vivid dome of blue against which the white of Phrygian marbles glittered in the sun.

"Of Him Whose Empire is mightier than that of Rome."

She looked on him in astonishment. Apparently she did not understand him, nor did he try to explain, but it seemed to her as if his whole appearance had changed suddenly, and her thoughts flew back to that which she had witnessed a year ago when she was in Ostia and she had seen a raging tempest become suddenly stilled. "There is no mightier empire than that of Rome," she said proudly, "and methinks thou art a traitor, oh Taurus Antinor, else thou wouldst not speak of any emperor save of Cæsar, my kinsman."

"I spoke not of an emperor, gracious lady," he said simply.

"But thy thoughts were of one whose empire was mightier than that of Rome."

"My thoughts," he said, "were of a Man Whom I saw whilst travelling through Judæa a few years ago. He was poor and dwelt among the fishermen of Galilee. They stood around Him and listened whilst He talked; when He walked they followed Him, for a halo of glory was upon Him and the words which He spoke were such that once heard they could never be forgotten."

"Didst thou too hear those marvellous words, O Taurus Antinor?" she asked.

"Only twice," he replied, "did I hear the words which He spoke. I mingled with the crowd, and once when His eyes fell upon me, it seemed to me as if all the secrets of life and death were suddenly revealed to me. His eyes fell upon me.... I was one of a multitude ... but from that moment I knew that life on this earth would never be precious to me again—since the most precious gift man hath is his immortality."

"Thou speakest of strange matters, O praefect," she rejoined, "and meseems there's treason in what thou sayest. Who is this man, whose very look hath made a slave of thee?"

"A slave to His will thou sayest truly, O daughter of Cæsar! Could

I hear His command I would follow Him through life and to death. At times even now meseems that I can hear His voice and see His eyes ... thou hast never seen such eyes, Augusta—fixed upon my very soul. I saw them just now, right across the Forum, when the wretched freedwoman clung shrieking round my shins. They looked at me and asked me to be merciful; they did not command, they begged ... asking for the pity that lay dormant in my soul. And now I know that if those same eyes looked at me again and asked for every drop of my blood, if they asked me to bear death, torture, or even shame, I would become as thou truly sayest—a slave."

Once or twice whilst he spoke she had tried to interrupt him, but every time the words she would have spoken had died upon her lips. He looked so strange—this praefect of Rome—whose judgments everyone feared, whose strict adherence to duty the young elegants of the day were ever fond of deriding. He looked very strange now and spoke such strange words—words that she resented bitterly, for they sounded like treason to the House of Cæsar of which she was so coldly proud.

To her Cæsar was as a god, and she as his kinswoman had been brought up to worship in him not the man—that might be vile—but the supreme power in the Empire which he represented. She did not pause to think if he were base, tyrannical, a half-crazy despot without mind or heart or sensibilities. She knew what was said about him, she had even seen at times things from which she recoiled in unspeakable horror; but her soul, still pure and still proud, was able to dissociate the abstract idea of the holy and mighty Cæsar from its present hideous embodiment. And this same holy reverence for Cæsar she looked for in all those who she deemed were worthy to stand—not as his equals, for only the gods were that—but nigh to his holy person—his own kinsmen first, then his Senate, his magistrates, and his patricians, and above all this man—almost a stranger—whom the Cæsar had deigned to honour with his confidence.

And yet this same stranger spoke calmly of another, of a man whom he would obey as a slave in all things, whom he would follow even to death; a man whose might he proclaimed above that of Cæsar himself.

"But who is this man?" she exclaimed at last, almost involuntarily.

"A poor Man from Galilee," he replied.

"What is he called?"

"Out there they called Him Jesus of Nazareth."

"And where is he now?"

"He died upon the cross, in Jerusalem, seven years ago."

"Upon the cross?" she exclaimed; "what had he done?"

"He had dwelt among the poor and brought them contentment and peace; He had lived amongst men and taught them love and charity. So the Roman proconsul ordered Him to be crucified, and those whom He had rendered happy rejoiced over His death."

"Methinks that I did hear something of this. I was a child then but already I took much interest in the affairs of State, and my father spoke oft freely in my presence. I remember his talking of a demagogue over in Judæa who claimed to be the King of the Jews and who was punished for treason and sedition. But I also heard that he did but little mischief, since only a troop of ignorant fisher-folk followed and listened to him."

"Ignorant fisher-folk thou saidst it truly, O Dea Flavia, yet I have it in my mind that anon the knee of every patrician—aye! of every Cæsar—shall bend before the mighty throne of that Man from Galilee."

"And thus didst learn thy lesson of treason, O praefect," she retorted; "demagogues and traitors from Judæa have sown the seeds of treachery in thy mind, and whilst thou dost receive with both hands the gifts of the Cæsar my kinsman, thou dost set up another above him and dost homage to him in thy heart."

"Aye! in my heart, gracious lady; for I am even more ignorant than those fishermen from Galilee who heard every word spoken by Jesus of Nazareth. I heard Him but twice in my life and once only did His eyes rest upon me, and they enchained my heart to His service, though I know but little yet of what He would have me do."

"No doubt he would have thee turn traitor to thine Emperor and to acclaim him—the demagogue—as imperator before the Senate and the army. He——"

"I told thee that He was dead," he interposed simply.

"And that his words had made thee rebellious to Cæsar and insolent to me."

"Thine humble servant, O Augusta," he rejoined, smiling in spite of himself, for now she was just like an angry child. "Wilt but command and see how I will obey."

"The girl Nola!" she said haughtily.

"In that alone I must deny thee."

"Then tie my shoe, it hath come undone."

The tone with which she said this was so arrogant and so harsh that even her slaves behind her turned frightened eyes on the praefect who was known to be so proud, and on whom the curt command must have had the effect of a sudden whip-lash on the face.

She had spoken as if to the humblest of her menials, finding pleasure in putting this insult on the man who had dared to thwart and irritate her; but she had not spoken deliberately; it had been an impulse, an irresistible desire to see him down on his knees, in a position only fit for slaves.

Directly the words had left her mouth, she already regretted them, for his refusal now would have been doubly humiliating for herself, and her good sense had told her already that no patrician—

41

least of all Taurus Antinor—would submit quietly to public insult and ridicule even from her.

The quick, more gentle word was already on her lips, the look of mute apology was struggling to her eyes, when to her astonishment the praefect, without a word, was down on his knees before her.

"Nay!" she said, "I did but jest."

"The honour," he said quietly, "is too great, O daughter of Cæsar, that I should forego it now."

His powerful shoulders were bent almost to the level of the ground, and she looked down on him, more puzzled than ever at this stranger whose every action seemed different from those of his fellow-men. She put her little foot slightly forward, and as he tied the string of her shoe she saw how slender was his hand, firm yet tapering down to the elegant finger-tips; the hand of a patrician even though he hailed from the barbaric North.

Suddenly she smiled. But this he did not see for he was still intent upon the shoe, but she felt that those slender hands of his were singularly clumsy. And she smiled because she had recollected how like his fellowmen he really was, how he evidently forgot his wrath and sank his pride for the pleasure of kneeling at her feet.

To this homage she was well accustomed. Many there were in Rome who at this moment would gladly have changed places with the praefect. More than one great patrician had craved the honour of tying her shoe, more than one patrician hand had trembled whilst performing this service.

And Dea Flavia smiled because already she guessed—or thought that she guessed—what would follow the tying of her shoe—a humble kiss upon her foot, the natural homage of a man to her beauty and to her power.

The daughter of Cæsar smiled because the spirit of child-like waywardness was in her, and she thought that she would like the slave-like homage from this man whom her wrath and threats had left impassive but whom her beauty had at last brought down to his knees; and thus smiling she waited patiently, content that he should be clumsy, glad that in the distance, under the arcade of the tabernae, she had spied Hortensius Martius watching with wrathful eyes every movement of the praefect. She wondered if the young exquisite had heard the wordy warfare between herself and the proud man who now knelt quite awkwardly at her feet, and she guessed that what Hortensius had seen and heard, that he would retail at full length to his friends in the course of the banquet given by Caius Nepos to-morrow night.

For the moment she felt almost sorry for the giant brought down to his knees; the kiss which she so confidently anticipated would of a truth complete his surrender, since she had resolved to make him kiss the dust by suddenly withdrawing her foot from under his lips, and

42

then to laugh at him, and to allow her slaves to laugh and jeer at him as he lay sprawling in the dust, his huge arms lying crosswise on the flagstones before her.

The spirit of mischief was in her, the love to tease a helpless giant; so for the nonce anger almost died out within her and her eyes looked clear and blue as triumph and joy danced within their depths.

But now Taurus Antinor had finished tying her shoe. He did not stoop further nor did he embrace the dust; but he straightened his broad shoulders and raised himself from his knees without rendering that homage which was expected of him.

"Hast further commands for thy servant, O daughter of Cæsar?" he asked calmly.

"None," she replied curtly.

And calling her slaves to her she entered her litter, and drew its curtains closely round her so that she should no longer be offended by his sight.

CHAPTER VII

"The fool hath said in his heart, There is no God."—Psalm xiv. 1.

And late that day when Dea Flavia was preparing for rest she dismissed her tire-women, keeping only her young slaves around her, and then ordered Licinia to attend on her this night.

Licinia was highly privileged in the house of Dea Flavia. She had nursed the daughter of proud Claudius Octavius at her breast, and between the wizened old woman and the fresh young girl there existed perfect friendship and the confidence born of years. Dea's first tooth was in Licinia's keeping and so was the first lock of hair cut from Dea's head. Licinia had been the confidante of Dea's first childish sorrow and was the first to hear the tales of the young girl's social triumphs.

No one but Licinia was allowed to handle Dea's hair. It was her shrivelled fingers that plaited every night the living stream of gold into innumerable little plaits, so that the ripple in it might continue to live again on the morrow. It was Licinia who rubbed Dea's exquisite limbs with unguents after the bath, and she who trimmed the rose-tinted nails into their perfect, pointed shape.

To-night Dea Flavia was lying on a couch covered with crimson silk. Her elbows were buried in a cushion stuffed with eiderdown, her chin rested in her two hands and her eyes were fixed on a mirror of polished bronze held up by one of her younger slaves.

43

Licinia, stooping over the reclining body of her mistress, was gently rubbing the white shoulders and spine with sweet-scented oil.

"And didst see it all, Licinia?" asked Dea Flavia, as with a lazy stretch of her graceful arms she suddenly swung herself round on to her back and looked straight up at the wrinkled old face bending tenderly over her.

"Aye, my precious," replied Licinia eagerly, "everything did I see; for thou didst draw the curtains of thy litter together so quickly, I had no time to take my place by thy side. I meant to follow immediately, and was only waiting there for a moment or two until the crowd of thy retinue had dispersed along the various streets. Then it was that I spied my lord Hortensius, and something in the expression of his face made me pause then and there to see if there was aught amiss."

"And was aught amiss with my lord Hortensius?" asked Dea Flavia with studied indifference.

"He looked wrathful as a tiger in the arena when the guards come and snatch his prey from him. There was a frown on his face darker than that which usually sits on Taurus Antinor's brow."

"He was angered?"

"Aye! at the praefect," rejoined Licinia. "He strode forward from under the arcades directly after the crowd of thy slaves had disappeared, and the Forum was all deserted save for Taurus Antinor standing there as if he had been carved in marble and in bronze and rooted there to the spot. My lord Hortensius came close up to the praefect and greeted him curtly. I dared no longer move away lest I should be seen, so I hid in the deep shadow behind the rostrum, and I heard Taurus Antinor's response to my lord Hortensius."

"Yes! yes!" said Dea Flavia impatiently, "of course they greeted one another ere they came to blows. But 'tis of the blows I would like to hear, and what my lord Hortensius said to the praefect."

"He spoke to him of thee, my child, and taunted him with having angered thee," said Licinia. "The praefect is so proud and so impatient, I marvelled then he did not hit my lord Hortensius in the face at once. He looked so huge, I bethought me of a giant, and his head looked dark like the bronze head of Jupiter, for his face had flushed a deep and angry crimson, whilst his mighty fists were clenched as if ready to strike."

"What caused him to strike, then?"

"My lord Hortensius called him a stranger, and this the praefect did not seem to resent. 'There are other lands than Rome,' he said, 'and one of these gave my ancestors birth. Proud am I of my distant land, and proud now to be a patrician of Rome.' Then did my lord Hortensius break into loud laughter, which to mine ears sounded mirthless and forced. He raised his hand and pointed a finger at the praefect and shouted, still laughing: 'Thou a patrician of Rome? thou a tyrant's minion! slave and son of slave! Nay! if the patriciate of Rome had its

44

will with thee, it would have thee publicly whipped and branded like the arrogant menial that thou art!' This and more did my lord Hortensius say," continued Licinia, whose voice now had sunk to an awed whisper at the recollection of the sacrilege; "I hardly dared to breathe for I could see the praefect's face, and could think of naught save the wrath of Jupiter, when on a sultry evening the thunder clouds are gathering in the wake of the setting sun."

But Dea Flavia's interest in the narrative seemed suddenly to have flagged. She stretched her arms, yawned ostentatiously, and with the movement of a fretful child she threw herself once more flat upon the couch, with her elbows in the cushions and her face buried in her hands.

With some impatience she snatched the mirror from the young slave's hand, and then she put it on the pillow and looked straight down into it, whilst her hair fell like golden curtains down each side of her face.

"Go on, Licinia," she said with curt indifference.

"There is but little more to tell," said the old woman, who with stolid placidness had resumed her former occupation, and once more rubbed the white shoulders with the sweet-smelling unguent; "nor could I tell thee how it all happened. A sort of tempestuous whirlwind seemed to sweep before my eyes, and the next thing that I saw clearly was an enormous figure clad in a gorgeous tunic, and standing high, high above me on the very top of the marble rostrum beside the bronze figure of the god. It was the praefect. From where I stood, palsied with fear, I could see his face, dark now as the very thunders of Jupiter, his hair around his head gleamed like copper in the sun; but what caused my very blood to freeze and the marrow to stiffen in my bones, was to see his two mighty arms high above his head holding the body of my lord Hortensius. He looked up there like some god-like giant about to hurl an enemy down from the mountains of Olympus. The rostrum stands a terrific height above the pavement of the Forum; the marble balustrades, the outstanding gradients, the carvings along its sides, all stood between that inert body held up aloft by those gigantic arms and the flagstones below where Death, hideous and yawning, seemed to be waiting for its prey. And still the praefect did not move, and I could see the muscles of his arms swollen like cords and the sinews of his hands almost cracking beneath the weight of my lord Hortensius' body."

Licinia paused and passed a wrinkled hand over her moist forehead. She was trembling even now at the recollection of what she had seen. The beautiful figure lying stretched out upon the couch had not moved in a single one of its graceful lines. The tiny head beneath its crown of gold was bent down upon the mirror.

"Couldst see my lord Hortensius' face?" came in the same cold tones of indifference from behind the veil of wavy hair.

"No!" said Licinia. "I thank the gods that I could not. One cry for

45

mercy did he utter, one cry of horror when first he felt himself uplifted and looked down into the awful face of Death which awaited him below. Then mayhap he lost consciousness for I heard not a sound, and the whole city lay still in the hush of the noonday sleep. Less than one minute had intervened since first I saw that avenging figure outlined against the blue curtain of the sky: less than one minute even whilst my heart had ceased to beat. And then did a cry of horror escape my lips, and the praefect looked down into my face. Nor did he move as yet, but slowly meseemed as if the ruddy glow died from out his cheeks and brow, and after a while the tension on the mighty arms relaxed, and slowly were they lowered from above his head. He no longer was looking at me now, for his eyes were fixed upon the distant sky, as if they saw there something that called with irresistible power. And upon the heat-laden air there trembled a long sigh as of infinite longing. Then the praefect gathered my lord Hortensius' inanimate body in his arms as a mother would her own child, and with slow and steady steps he descended the gradients of the rostrum. At its foot he caught sight of me, and called me to him: 'My lord hath only fainted,' he said to me; 'do thou chafe his hands and soothe his forehead, whilst I send his slaves to him.' He laid the precious burden down in the cool shadow, taking off his own cloak and making of it a pillow for my lord Hortensius' head. Then he went from me, and as he went I could hear him murmur: 'In Thy service, oh Man of Galilee.'"

Even as these last words still trembled on Licinia's lips there came a sharp cry of rage, followed by one of terror, as with quick and almost savage movement Dea Flavia picked up the heavy mirror of bronze and hurled it across the chamber. It fell with a loud crash against the delicate mosaic of the floor, but as it swung through the air its sharp metal edge hit a young slave girl on the shoulder; a few drops of blood trickled down her breast and she began to whimper in her fright.

It had all happened so suddenly that no one—least of all Licinia— could guess what it was that had so angered my lady. Dea Flavia had raised herself to a sitting posture, and thrown her hair back, away from her face which looked flushed and wrathful, whilst two sharp furrows appeared between her brows.

The women were silent, feeling awed and not a little frightened; the girl, whose shoulder was now bleeding profusely, continued her whimpering.

"Get up, girl," said Licinia roughly, "and staunch thy scratch elsewhere, away from my lady's sight. Hark at the baggage! One would think she is really hurt. Get thee gone, I say, ere I give thee better cause for whining."

But in a moment Dea Flavia was on her feet. With a quick cry of pity she ran to her slave, kneeled beside her and with a fine white cloth herself tried to staunch the wound.

"Art hurt?" she said gently, "art hurt, child? I did not wish to hurt thee. Stop thy weeping—and I'll give thee that amber locket which thou dost covet so. Stop thy weeping, I say! Is it my white rabbit thou dost hanker after—thou shalt have it for thine own—or—or—the woollen tunic with the embroidered bands—or—or—Stop whining, girl," she added impatiently, seeing that the girl, more frightened than hurt, was sobbing louder than before. "Licinia, make her stop—she angers me with all this whining—stop, I tell thee. Oh, Licinia, where is thy whip? I vow I'll have the girl whipped if she do not stop."

But Licinia, accustomed to her mistress's quick changing moods, had in her turn knelt beside the girl and was busy now with deft hands in staunching the blood and tying up the wound. This done she dragged the child up roughly, though not unkindly, from the ground.

"Get thee gone and lie down on thy bed," she said; "shame on thee for making such a to-do. My lady had no wish to hurt thee, and thou hast upset her with all this senseless weeping. Get thee gone now ere I do give thee that whipping which thou dost well deserve."

She contrived to push the girl out of the chamber and ordered two others to follow and look after her; then once more she turned to her mistress, ready to tender fond apologies since what she had said had so angered her beloved.

Dea Flavia had thrown herself on the couch on her back; her arms were folded behind her head, her fair hair lay in heavy masses on the embroidered coverlet. She was staring straight up at the ceiling, her blue eyes wide open, and a puzzled frown across her brow.

"My precious one," murmured Licinia.

But Dea Flavia apparently did not hear. It seemed as if she were grappling in her mind with some worrying puzzle, the solution of which lay hidden up there behind that brilliant bit of blue sky which glimmered through the square opening in the roof.

"My precious one," reiterated the old woman appealingly, "tell me, Dea—was it aught that I said which angered thee?"

Dea Flavia turned large wondering eyes to her old nurse.

"Licinia," she said slowly.

"Yes, my goddess."

"If a man saith that there is one greater, mightier than Cæsar ... he is a traitor, is he not?"

"A black and villainous traitor, Augusta," said Licinia, whose voice at the mere suggestion had become hoarse with awe.

"And what in Rome is the punishment for such traitors, Licinia?" asked the young girl, still speaking slowly and measuredly.

"Death, my child," replied the old woman.

"Only death?" insisted Dea, whilst the puzzled look in her eyes became more marked, and the frown between her brows more deep.

"I do not understand thee, my precious one," said Licinia whose turn it was now to be deeply puzzled; "what greater punishment could there be for a traitor than that of death?"

"They torture slaves for lesser offences than that."

"Aye! and for sedition there is always the cross."

"The cross!" she murmured.

"Yes! Dost remember seven years ago in Judæa? There was a man who raised sedition among the Jews, and called himself their king—setting himself above Cæsar and above the might of Cæsar.... They crucified him. Dost remember?"

"I have heard of him," she said curtly. "What was his name?"

"Nay! I have forgot. Methinks that he came from Galilee. They did crucify him because of sedition, and because he set himself to be above Cæsar."

"And above the House of Cæsar?"

"Aye! above the House of Cæsar too."

"And they crucified him?"

"Aye! like a common thief. 'Twas right and just since he rebelled against Cæsar."

"And yet, Licinia, there are those in Rome who do him service even now."

"The gods forbid!" exclaimed Licinia in horror. "And how could that be?" she added with a shrug of the shoulders, "seeing that he died such a shameful death."

"I marvel on that also," said the young girl, whose wide-open blue eyes once more assumed their strangely puzzled expression.

"Nay! I'll not believe it," rejoined the old woman hotly. "Do that man service? A common traitor who died upon the cross. Who did stuff thine ears, my goddess, with such foolish tales?"

"No one told me foolish tales, Licinia. But this I do know, that there are some in Rome who set that Galilean above the majesty of Cæsar, and in his name do defy Cæsar's might."

"They are madmen then," said the slave curtly.

"Or traitors," added Dea Flavia.

"Thou sayest it; they are traitors and rebels, and never fear, they'll be punished ... sooner or later, they will be punished.... Defy the might of Cæsar?... Great gods above! the impious wretches! thou wert right, my princess! Death alone were too merciful for them.... The scourge first ... and then the cross ... that will teach them the might of thy house, oh daughter of Cæsar.... I would have no mercy with them.... Throw them to the beasts, say I!... brand them ... scourge them ... wring their heart's blood until they cry for death...!"

The old pagan looked evil and cruel in her fury of loyalty to that house which begat her beloved Dea. Her eyes glistened as those of a cat waiting to fall upon its prey; her wrinkled hands looked like claws that were ready to tear the very flesh and sinew from the traitor's breast. Her voice, always hoarse and trembling, had risen to a savage shriek

48

which died away as in a passionate outburst of love she threw herself down on the floor beside the couch, and taking Dea's tiny feet between her hands, she covered them with kisses and with tears.

But Dea Flavia once more lay back on the coverlet of crimson silk and her blue eyes once more were fixed upwards to the sky. Above her the glint of blue was now suffused with tones of pink merging into mauve; somewhere out west the sun was slowly sinking into rest. Tiny golden clouds flitted swiftly across that patch of sky on which Dea Flavia gazed so intently.

"Come kiss me, Licinia," she said slowly after a while. "I'll to rest now. To-morrow I shall see my kinsman the Cæsar again, after a year's absence from him. I desire to be very beautiful to-morrow, Licinia, for mayhap I'll to the games with him. That new tunic worked with purple and gold. I'll wear that and my new shoes of antelope skin. In my hair the circlet of turquoise and pearls ... dost think it'll become me, Licinia?"

"Thou wilt be more beautiful, my precious one, than man's eyes can conveniently endure," said Licinia, whose whole face became radiant with the joy of her perfect love for the girl.

"Ah! thou hast soothed my heart and mind, Licinia. I feel that I shall sleep well to-night."

She allowed the old woman to lead her gently to her bedchamber, where within the narrow alcove she lay all that night tossing upon the silken mattress that was stuffed with eiderdown. Sleep would not come to her, and hour after hour she lay there, her eyes fixed into the darkness on which, at times, her fevered fancy traced a glowing cross.

CHAPTER VIII

"The lot is cast into the lap, but the whole disposing thereof is of the Lord."—Proverbs xvi. 33.

And even thus did the mighty Empire hurry headlong to its fall; with shouts of joy and cries of exultation, with triumphal processions, with music, with games and with flowers.

The Cæsar had returned from Germany and Gaul having played his part of mountebank upon the arena of the world. Eaten up with senseless and cynical vanity, Caius Julius Cæsar Caligula desired to be the Cæsar of his army as he was princeps and imperator, high pontiff and supreme dictator of the Empire. But as there was no war to

49

conduct, no rebellion to subdue, he had invented a war and harassed some barbarians who had no thought save that of peace.

He stage-managed conspiracies and midnight attacks, drilling his own soldiers into acting the parts of malcontents, of escaped prisoners, of bloodthirsty barbarians, the while he himself—as chief actor in the play—vanquished the mock foes and took from them mock spoils of war.

Then he upbraided Rome for her inertia whilst he, the Emperor, confronted dangers and endured hardships for her sake. His letters, full of glowing accounts of his supposed prowess, of the ferocity of the enemy, of the fruits of victory snatched at the cost of innumerable sacrifices were solemnly read to the assembled senators in the temple of Mars, and to a vast concourse of people gathered in the Forum.

They listened to these letters with awe and reverence proud of the valour of their Cæsar, rejoicing in the continued glory of the mightiest Empire of the world—their own Empire which they, the masters of the earth and of the sea, had made under the guidance of rulers such as he who even now was returning laurel-laden and victory-crowned from Germany.

And the triumphal procession was begun. First came the galley in which Caligula was said to have crossed the ocean for the purpose of subduing some rebel British princes, but in which he in verity had spent some pleasant days fishing in the bay. It was brought back to Rome in solemn state by land, right across the country of the Allemanni and carried the whole of the way by sixteen stalwart barbarians—supposed prisoners of war.

The galley was received with imperial honours as if it had been a human creature—the very person of the Cæsar. In the presence of a huge and enthusiastic crowd it was taken to the temple of Mars, where the pontiffs, attired in their festal robes, dedicated it with solemn ritual to the god of war and finally deposited it in a specially constructed cradle fashioned of citrus wood with elaborate carvings and touches of gilding thereon; the whole resting upon a pedestal of African marble.

Upon the next day a procession of Gauls entered the city carrying helmets which were filled with sea-shells. The men wore their hair long and unkempt, they were naked save for a goatskin tied across the torso with a hempen rope and their shins were encircled with leather bands. The helmets were said to have belonged to those of Cæsar's soldiers who had lost their lives in the expedition against the Germans, and the sea-shells were a special tribute from the ocean to the gods of the Capitol. By the Cæsar's orders the helmets were to be the objects of semi-divine honours in memory of the illustrious dead.

Thus the tragi-comedy went on day after day. The plebs enjoying the pageants because they did not know that they were being fooled, and the patricians looking on because they did not care.

And now the imperial mountebank was coming home himself,

having ordered his triumph as he had stage-managed his deeds of valour. Triumphal arches and street decorations, flowers and processions, he had ordained everything just as he wished it to be. From the statue of every god in the temples of the Capitol and of the Forum the bronze head had been knocked off by his orders, and a likeness of his own head placed in substitution. His intention was to receive divine homage, and this the plebs—who had been promised a succession of holidays, with races, games, and combats—was over-ready to grant him.

The vestibule connecting his palace with the temple of Castor had been completed in his absence, and he wished to pass surreptitiously from his own apartments to the very niche of the idol which was in full view of the Forum and there to show himself to the people, even whilst a sacrifice was offered to him as to a god.

To all this senseless display of egregious vanity the obsequiousness of the senators and the careless frivolity of the plebs easily lent itself; nor did anyone demur at the decree which came from the absent hero, that he should in future be styled: "The Father of the Armies! the Greatest and best of Cæsars."

All thought of dignity was dead in these descendants of the great people who had made the Empire; they had long ago sold their birthright of valour and of honour for the pottage of luxury and the favours of a tyrannical madman. What cared they if after they had feasted and shouted themselves hoarse in praise of a deified brute, the ruins of Rome came crashing down over their graves? What cared they if in far-off barbaric lands the Goths and Huns were already whetting their steel.

Only a few among the more dignified senators, a few among the more sober praetorian tribunes, revolted in their heart at this insane exhibition of egoism, these perpetual outrages on common sense and dignity; but they were few and their influence small, and they were really too indolent, too comfortable in their luxurious homes to do aught but accept what they deemed inevitable.

The only men in Rome who cared were the ambitious and the self-seekers, and they cared not because of Rome, not because of the glory of the Empire, or the welfare of the land, but because they saw in the very excess of the tyrant's misrule the best chance for their own supremacy and power.

Foremost amongst these was Caius Nepos, the praetorian praefect, all-powerful in the absence of the Cæsar, well liked by the army, so 'twas said. Some influential friends clung around him and also some malcontents, those who are ever on the spot when destruction is to be accomplished, ever ready to overthrow any government which does not happen to further their ambitions.

Most of these men were assembled this night beneath the gilded roof of Caius Nepos' house. He had gathered all his friends round him, had feasted them with good viands and costly wines, with roasted peacocks from Gaul and mullets come straight from the sea; he had amused them with oriental danœrs and Egyptian acrobats, and when they had eaten and drunk their fill he bade them good night and sent them home, laden with gifts. But his intimates remained behind; pretending to leave with the others, they lingered on in the atrium, chatting of indifferent topics amongst themselves, until all had gone whose presence would not be wanted in the conclave that was to take place.

There were now some forty of them in number, rich patricians all of them, their ages ranging from that of young Escanes who was just twenty years old to that of Marcus Ancyrus, the elder, who had turned sixty. Their combined wealth mayhap would have purchased every inhabited house in the entire civilised world or every slave who was ever put up in the market. Marcus Ancyrus, they say, could have pulled down every temple in the Forum and rebuilt it at his own cost, and Philippus Decius who was there had recently spent the sum of fifty million sesterces upon the building and equipment of his new villa at Herculaneum.

Young Hortensius Martius was there, too, he who was said to own more slaves than anyone else in Rome, and Augustus Philario of the household of Cæsar, who had once declared that he would give one hundred thousand aurei for a secret poison that would defy detection.

"Why is not Taurus Antinor here this evening?" asked Marcus Ancyrus when this little group of privileged guests once more turned back toward the triclinium.

"I think that he will be here anon," replied the host. "I have sent him word that I desired speech with him on business of the State and that I craved the honour of his company."

They all assembled at the head of the now deserted tables. The few slaves who had remained at the bidding of their master had re-draped the couches and re-set the crystal goblets of wine and the gold dishes with fresh fruit. The long narrow hall looked strangely mournful now that the noisy guests had departed, and the sweet-scented oil in the lamps had begun to burn low.

The table, laden with empty jars, with broken goblets, and remnants of fruits and cakes, looked uninviting and even weird in its aspect of departed cheer. The couches beneath their tumbled draperies of richly dyed silk looked bedraggled and forlorn, whilst the stains of wine upon the fine white cloths looked like widening streams of blood. Under the shadows of elaborate carvings in the marble of the walls ghost-like shadows flickered and danced as the smoke from the oil lamp wound its spiral curves upwards to the gilded ceiling above. And in the great vases of priceless murra roses and lilies and white tuberoses, the spoils of costly glasshouses, were slowly drooping in the heavy atmosphere. The whole room, despite its rich hangings and gilded pillars, wore a curious air of desolation and of gloom; mayhap Caius Nepos himself was conscious of this, for as he followed his guests from out the atrium he gave three loud claps with his hands, and a troupe of young girls came in carrying bunches of fresh flowers and some newly filled lamps.

These they placed at the head of the table, there, where the couches surrounding it were draped with crimson silk, and soft downy cushions, well shaken up, once more called to rest and good cheer.

"I pray you all take your places," said the host pleasantly, "and let us resume our supper."

He gave a sign to a swarthy-looking slave, who, clad all in white, was presiding at a gorgeous buffet carved of solid citrus-wood which—despite the fact that supper had just been served to two hundred guests—was once more groaning under the weight of mammoth dishes filled with the most complicated products of culinary art.

The slave, at his master's sign, touched a silver gong, and half a dozen henchmen in linen tunics brought in the steaming dishes fresh from the kitchens. The carver set to and attacked with long sharp knife the gigantic capons which one of the bearers had placed before him. He carved with quickness and dexterity, placing well-chosen morsels on the plates of massive gold which young waiting-maids then carried to the guests.

"Wilt dismiss thy slaves before we talk?" asked Marcus Ancyrus, the veteran in this small crowd. He himself had been silent for the past ten minutes, doing full justice to this second relay of Caius Nepos' hospitality.

The waiting-maids were going the round now with gilt basins and cloths of fine white linen for the cleansing and drying of fingers between the courses; others, in the meanwhile, filled the crystal goblets with red or white wine as the guests desired.

"We can talk now," said the host; "these slaves will not heed us. They," he added, nodding in the direction of the carver and his half-dozen henchmen, "are all deaf as well as mute, so we need have no fear of them."

"What treasures," ejaculated young Escanes with wondering eyes fixed upon his lucky host; "where didst get them, Caius Nepos? By the gods, I would I could get an army of deaf-mute slaves."

"They are not easy to get," rejoined the other, "but I was mightily lucky in my find. I was at Cirta in Numidia at a time when the dusky chief there—one named Hazim Rhan—had made a haul of six malcontents who I understood had conspired against his authority. It seems that these rebels had a leader who had succeeded in escaping to his desert fastness, and whom Hazim Rhan greatly desired to capture. To gain this object he commanded the six prisoners to betray their leader; this they refused to do, whereupon the dusky prince ordered their ears to be cut off and threatened them that unless they spoke on

53

the morrow, their tongues would be cut off the next day. And if after that they still remained obdurate, their heads would go the way of their tongues and ears."

Exclamations of horror greeted this gruesome tale, the relevancy of which no one had as yet perceived. But Caius Nepos, having pledged his friends in a draught of Sicilian wine, resumed:

"I, as an idle traveller from Rome had been received by the dusky chieftain with marked deference, and I was greatly interested in the fate of the six men who proved so loyal to their leader. So I waited three days, and when their tongues and ears had been cut off and their heads were finally threatened, I offered to buy them for a sum sufficiently large to tempt the cupidity of Hazim Rhan. And thus I had in my possession six men whose sense of loyalty had been splendidly proved and whose discretion henceforth would necessarily be absolute."

This time a chorus of praise greeted the conclusion of the tale. The cynical calm with which it had been told and the ferocious selfishness which it revealed seemed in no way repellent to Caius Nepos' guests. A few pairs of indifferent eyes were levelled at the slaves and that was all. And then Philippus Decius remarked coolly:

"So much for thy carvers and henchmen, O Caius Nepos, but thy waiting-maids?—are they deaf and dumb too?"

"No," replied the host, "but they come from foreign lands and do not understand our tongue."

"Then you all think that the next few days will be propitious for our schemes?" here broke in young Escanes who seemed the most eager amongst them all.

"Aye!" said Caius Nepos, "with a little good luck even to-morrow might prove the best day. The Cæsar is half frenzied now, gorged with his triumph, the mockery of which he does not seem to understand. He is more like a raving madman than ever, much more feeble in mind and body than before this insensate expedition to Germany."

"I suppose that there is no doubt as to the truth of the tales which are current about the expedition," quoth Marcus Ancyrus, whose years rendered him more cautious than the others.

"No doubt whatever," rejoined the host, "and some of the tales fall far short of the truth. There never was a real blow struck during the whole time that madman was away. He travelled from place to place in his litter borne by eight men, and sent his soldiers ahead of him with sprays and buckets of water that they should lay the dust along the road on which he would travel. At Trevirorum on the banks of the Rhine, he caused two hundred of his picked guard to dress up as barbarians and to make feint to attack the camp at midnight. This they did with necessary shoutings and clashings of steel against steel. Then did the greatest and best of Cæsars sally forth in full battle array followed by a few of his most trusted men, and in the darkness there was heard more shouting and more clashings of steel until Caligula returned in triumph at sunrise to his camp. He had passed hempen ropes round the necks of the mock barbarians, and ever after had them dragged in the wake of his litter, even as if they were prisoners of war. No doubt he had paid them well for acting such a farce."

"But was the army blind to all this folly?"

"The Cæsar only kept some five hundred picked men round him in his camp. These he bribed into acquiescence of all his mad pranks. The rest of the legions were some distance away all the time. They believed all that they were told; mayhap they thought it wisest to believe."

"I know that in Belgica, on the shores of the ocean——" began Augustus Philario after a while.

But he was not allowed to proceed. Shouts of derision broke in upon the tale, followed by expressions of rage.

"What is the good of retailing further follies," said Caius Nepos at last; "we all know that a madman, a vain, besotted fool wields now the sceptre of Julius Cæsar and of great Augustus. The numbers of his misdeeds are like the grains of sand on the seashore, his orgies have shamed our generation, his debauches are a disgrace upon the fame of Rome. Patricians awake! The day hath come, the hour is close at hand. To-morrow, mayhap, at the public games ... a tumult amongst the people ... it should be easy to rouse that ... then a well-edged dagger ... and the Empire is rid of the most hideous and loathsome tyrant that ever brutalised a nation and shamed an empire."

Even as he spoke, and despite the deaf-mute slaves and the foreign girls, he lowered his voice until it sank to the merest whisper. Reclining upon the couches with elbows buried in silken cushions the others all stretched forward now, until two score of heads met in one continued circle, forehead to forehead and ear to ear, whilst in the midst of them an oil lamp flickered low and lit up at fitful intervals the sober, callous faces with the hard mouths and cruel, steely eyes.

The slaves—those who had lost ears and tongue and those who spoke no language save their own foreign one—had retreated to the far corners of the room, up against the columns of Phrygian marble or the hangings of Tyrian tapestries; their great uncomprehending eyes were fixed on that compact group at the head of the table, where round the bowls of roses and of lilies and the goblets of wine, the future of the Empire of Rome was even now being discussed.

"The tumult can be easily provoked," said one of the guests presently—a young man whose black hair and dark eyes bespoke his Oriental blood. "The Cæsar is certain to provoke it himself by some insane act of tyrannical folly. Ye must all remember how, two years ago, during the Megalesian games he ordered the women of his retinue to descend into the arena and to engage the gladiators in combat. At this outrage the discontent among the people nearly broke out into open revolt. It was thou, Caius Nepos, who checked the tumult then."

"The hour was not ripe," said the latter, "and we were not allied. It will be different to-morrow."

"How will it be to-morrow?"

"When the tumult is at its highest, he who has the surest hand shall strike the Cæsar down. I, in the meanwhile——"

"Then thou, Caius Nepos, art not certain of the sureness of thy hand?" interposed Hortensius Martius who hitherto had taken no active part in the discussion.

He lay on a couch at some distance from his host and had declined every morsel offered to him by the waiting-maids; but he had drunk over freely, and his good-looking young face looked flushed and dark beneath its wealth of curls. Unlike his usual self he was ill-humoured and almost morose to-night, and there was a dark, glowering look in his eyes as from time to time he cast furtive glances towards the door.

"Nay, good Hortensius," said the host loftily, "mine will be the greater part. The praetorian guard know and trust me. It will be my duty when the Cæsar is attacked to keep them from rushing to his aid. The army is apt to forget a tyrant's crime, and to think of him only as a leader to be obeyed. But when the guard hear my voice, they will understand and will be true to me."

"'Tis I will strike," now broke in young Escanes, with all the enthusiasm of his years. The ardour of leadership glowed upon his face, and he seemed to challenge this small assembly to dispute his right to the foremost place in the great event of the morrow.

But his challenge was not taken up; no one else seemed eager to dispute his wish. Somewhat sobered, he resumed more calmly:

"The Cæsar hath much affection for me. I oft sat beside him in the Circus or at the games last year. The Augustas too like to have me beside them, to talk pleasing gossip in their ears. 'Twill be easiest for me, at a signal given, to strike with my dagger in the Cæsar's throat."

"Thine shall be that glory, O Escanes, since thou dost will it so," said Caius Nepos, not without a touch of irony. "Directly the deed is done, the praetorian guard shall raise the cry: 'The Cæsar is dead!'"

"And it should at once be followed by another," said Marcus Ancyrus, the elder, "by 'Hail to thee, O mighty Cæsar!'"

"'Tis thou shouldst raise that cry, O Caius Nepos," said Hortensius with a sarcastic curl of his lip.

"Oh! as to that——" began the other with some hesitation.

"Aye! as to that," said Escanes hotly, "if I slay the tyrant to-morrow with mine own hand, then must I know at least for whom I do the deed."

There was silence after that. Everyone seemed absorbed in his own thoughts. Dreamy eyes gazed abstractedly in crystal goblets, as if vainly trying to trace in its crimson depths the outline of an imperial sceptre. At last Caius Nepos spoke:

"Let us be rid of the tyrant first. The army then will soon elect its new chief."

"And is it on the support of the army, O praefect! that thou dost base thine own hopes of supreme power?" asked Hortensius, whose ill-humour seemed to grow on him more and more.

"Nay!" retorted Caius Nepos, "I did not know that by so doing I was dashing thine!"

"Silence," admonished Marcus Ancyrus, the elder. "Are we children or slaves that we should wrangle thus? Have we met here in order to rid the Empire of an abominable and bloodthirsty tyrant, or are we mere vulgar conspirators pursuing our own ends? There was no thought in our host's mind of supreme power, O Hortensius! nor in thine, I'll vow. As for me, I care nought for the imperium," he added naïvely, "it is difficult to content everyone, and a permanent consulship under our chosen Cæsar were more to my liking. Bring forth thy tablets, O Caius Nepos, and we'll put the matter to the vote. There are not many of the House of Cæsar fit to succeed the present madman, and our choice there will be limited."

"There is but Claudius, the brother of Germanicus," interposed the host curtly.

"Germanicus' brother to succeed Germanicus' son," said another with a contemptuous shrug of the shoulders.

"And he is as crazy as his nephew," added Caius Nepos.

He had not assembled his friends here to-night, he had not feasted them and loaded them with gifts with a view to passing the imperium merely from one head to another. He was fairly sure of the support of the praetorian guard, whose praefect he was, and had counted on the adherence of these malcontents, who he hoped would look to him for future favours whilst raising him to supreme dignity.

He liked not this talk of the family of Cæsar which took the attention of his closest adherents away from his own claim.

"The entire House of Cæsar," he said, "is rotten to the core. There is not one member of it fit to rule."

"But of a truth," said prudent Ancyrus, "they have the foremost claim."

"Then if that be the case," broke in young Hortensius Martius suddenly, "let us turn to the one member of the House of Cæsar who is noble and pure, exalted above all."

"There is none such," said Caius Nepos hotly.

"Aye! there is one," retorted the younger man.

"His name?" came loudly from every side.

"I spoke of a woman."

"A woman!"

And shouts of derisive laughter broke from every lip. Only Marcus Ancyrus remained grave and thoughtful, and now he said:

"Dost perchance speak of Dea Flavia Augusta?"

"Even of her," replied Hortensius.

Involuntarily at the name, the voice of the older man had assumed a respectful tone, and all around the vulgar sneers and bitter mockery had died away as if by magic contact with something hallowed and pure.

Even Caius Nepos thought it wise to subdue his tone of contempt, and merely said curtly:

"A goddess of a truth, but a woman cannot lead an army or rule an empire."

"No," rejoined Hortensius Martius, "but a wise and virtuous woman can rule wisely and virtuously over the man whom she will choose for mate."

There was silence for a moment or two, whilst young Hortensius' glowing eyes swept questioningly over the assembly. Everyone there knew of his passion for the Augusta, a passion, in truth, shared by many of those who had the privilege of knowing her intimately, and strangely enough though the proposal had so much daring in it, it met with but little opposition.

"Wouldst thou then suggest, O Hortensius Martius," quoth Marcus Ancyrus, the elder, after a slight pause, "that the Augusta's husband be made Emperor of Rome?"

"Why not?" retorted the other simply.

"It is not a bad notion," mused young Escanes, who thought himself high in the favour of Dea Flavia.

"An admirable one," assented Ancyrus, "for we must remember that Dea Flavia Augusta is of the true blood of the Cæsars—the blood of the great Augustus—and there is none better. Since she, as a woman, cannot rule men or lead an army, what more fitting than that her lord, whoever he might be, should receive the imperium through her hands?"

"He might prove to be a more miserable creature than the Caligula himself," suggested Philario, who was too ill-favoured to have hopes of winning the proud and imperious beauty for himself.

"Nay! that were impossible," asserted Hortensius hotly; "the man whom Dea Flavia will favour will be a brave man else he would not dare to woo her; he will be honourable and noble else he could never win her."

"Methinks that thou art right, O Hortensius," added Ancyrus, who had taken upon himself the rôle of a wise and prudent counsellor, "and moreover he will be rich by virtue of the wealth which the Augusta will have as her marriage portion; her money, merged with the State funds, would be of vast benefit to the land."

"And on his death his son and hers—a direct descendant of great Augustus—would be the only fitting heir," concluded another.

"Meseems," now said Ancyrus decisively, "that we would solve a grave difficulty by accepting the suggestion made by Hortensius

Martius. The imperium—as is only just—would remain in the family of the great Augustus. We should have a brave, noble and rich Cæsar whose virtuous and beautiful wife would wield beneficial influence over him, and for the present we should all be working for unselfish ends; not one of us here present can say for a certainty whom the Augusta will choose for mate. Directly the tyrant is swept out of the way, we, who have brought about the great end, will ask her to make her choice. Thus our aims will have been pure and selfless; each one of us here will have risked all for the sake of an unknown. What say you friends? Shall we pledge our loyalty to the man whom not one of us here can name this day—a man mayhap still unknown to us: the future lord of Dea Flavia Augusta of the House of Cæsar?"

The peroration seemed greatly to the liking of the assembled company: the thought that they would all be working with pure and selfless motives flattered these men's egregious vanity; vaguely every one of them hoped that all the others would believe in his unselfish aims, even whilst everyone meant to work solely for his own ends. Hortensius Martius' proposal pleased because it opened out such magnificent possibilities: the imperium itself, which had seemed infinitely remote from so many, now appeared within reach of all.

Anyone who was young, well-favoured, and of patrician birth might aspire to the hand of the Augusta, and not one of those who possessed at least two of those qualifications doubted his own ability to win.

Raising himself to a more upright position, Marcus Ancyrus the elder, goblet in hand, looked round for approval on all the guests.

The murmur of acquiescence was well-nigh general, and many there were who held their goblets to the waiting-maids in order to have them filled and then drained them to the last dregs. But there were a few dissentient voices, chiefly among the less-favoured who, like Philario, could hardly dare approach a beautiful woman with thoughts of wooing her.

Caius Nepos had not taken up the pledge, nor had he taken any part in the discussion since Dea Flavia's name first passed the lips of young Hortensius. Indeed, as the latter seemed to lose his ill-humour and become flushed and excited with the approval of his friends, so did the host gradually become more and more morose and silent.

Clearly the proposal to leave the matter of the choice of a Cæsar in the hands of a woman was not to his liking. Though good-looking and still in the prime of life he had never found favour with women, and Dea Flavia had often shown open contempt for him, and for the selfish ambition which moved his every action, and which he was at no pains to conceal.

It was easy to see, by the glowering look on his face, that the meeting this night had not turned out as he had wished.

"We cannot decide this matter otherwise than by vote," said one of the guests when the murmurs of approval and those of dissent had equally died down.

"Thou art right, O friend," assented Ancyrus, "and I pray thee, Caius Nepos, order thy slaves to bring us the tablets, and let each man record his vote according to his will."

Caius Nepos could find no objection to this, even though the question of voting was in no way to his liking. He had a vague hope, mayhap, that by gaining time he might succeed in sowing seeds of discord amongst those who had been so ready to accede to the new proposal; any moment even now—a chance word spoken, a trifling incident, an incipient quarrel might sway these men and bring them back to their allegiance to himself. He had been so sure of their support; the banquet this night had been destined to set the seal to their fealty and to cement their friendship: it was more than exasperating that the suggestion of a young fool should have caused them to swerve from their promised adherence.

For the moment however, he could not help but acquiesce outwardly in the wish of the majority. After an imperceptible moment of hesitation, he called to one of his deaf-mute slaves and made him understand by signs that he wanted forty wax tablets prepared and brought hither with forty stylets wherewith to write. Then he cheerily bade his guests once more to eat and drink and to make merry.

And it was characteristic of these strange products of a decadent age, that in the midst of grave discussions wherein their own lives and their future aggrandisement were at stake, these men were quite ready to respond to their host's invitation and momentarily to forget their own ambitious schemes in the enjoyment of epicurean delights.

Wine and fruit were once more handed round; both were excellent, and during a brief interval mighty issues were set aside and conversation became more general and more free. The pageant of games and combats which was to last for over thirty days in honour of the deification of Caligula and his safe return from Germany became the subject of eager talk. There had been rumours of a remarkable load of African lions arrived in the Tiber a day or two ago, which were to make a gorgeous spectacle in the arena pitted against some tigers from Numidia. There was also talk of a novelty in the shape of crocodiles who were said to fight with great cunning and power against a pack of hyenas from the desert.

Then there would be the chariot races and gladiatorial combats; heavy betting on these events had been in progress for some time all over the city among the wealthy patricians as well as among the impoverished plebs; the respective merits of the blues, the greens, the reds, and the yellows were the subject of heated discussions, and Caius Nepos was glad to note that more than a suspicion of antagonism was aroused between his guests in the defence of their respective choice.

He only took a very cursory part in the discussion, putting in a word here and there where contradiction or approval might further inflame overheated tempers.

And he ordered his slaves to pour the wine with a free hand, and himself was ready to pledge every one of his guests over and over again for as long as they were ready to drink.

Inside the room the heat had become excessive, the evening air only entered through narrow windows, and the gentle breeze did no more than fan the flames of the oil lamps or make the petals of dying roses tremble and fall. The noise grew louder and louder as the fumes of heady wines obscured the brains of these makers of future empires. Slaves were called for loudly to undo the tunics and to help cast off all but the necessary garments.

Every face round the table now was flushed and moist; every forehead streaming with perspiration. Escanes, goblet in hand, was singing a ribald song, the chorus of which was taken up by the group of young men nearest to him. The older ones were making insane bets and driving preposterous bargains over horses and slaves.

By the time that the slaves had returned with the tablets the praetorian praefect had cause to be satisfied with the temper of his guests. Coarse jests and drunken oaths were heard more often than whispered serious talk, the names of popular gladiators seemed of more account than those of future Cæsars. Arguments were loud and violent; every mouth slobbered, every lip trembled and every eye glowed with unnatural brightness: curls were dishevelled and laurel crowns awry; the silken draperies on the couches had become tattered rags and the cushions were scattered all about the floor; debris of crystal vases littered the table and bunches of dying flowers were tossed about by unsteady hands.

Given a little more time, a few more draughts of Sicilian wine, and all thoughts of voting for a future Cæsar would be beyond the mental power of these degenerates, and drunken quarrels would turn to violent enmity. This Caius Nepos had in mind when he took the tablets from the slaves, and threw them down with affected carelessness on the table before him.

"We cannot vote," he said loudly, "whilst Taurus Antinor is not here."

His words were even more potent than he had hoped; all that he had wanted was further delay, and most of his guests nodded approval with drunken solemnity and then called for more wine. But Hortensius Martius who, though he had drunk as heavily as the others, had not joined in the ribald songs or the senseless orgy of shouts and of laughter, now jumped up with a violent oath.

"What hath Taurus Antinor to do with us?" he shouted at the top of his voice, "or we with Taurus Antinor? Ye do not intend, I trust, to raise a freedman to the imperium and place the sceptre of Cæsar in the hands of a descendant of slaves!"

He was trembling with such unbridled fury, his eyes glowed with the lust of such deadly hate that instinctively the ribald songs and immoderate laughter were hushed, and eyes, veiled with the film of intoxication were turned wonderingly upon him.

But Caius Nepos was smiling blandly: the ire of Hortensius pleased him even though he did not understand its cause.

"Nay, as to that," he said, "are we not all descended from slaves? Taurus Antinor hath the ear of the plebs. Doth suggest, O Hortensius, that he also hath the ear of Dea Flavia Augusta?"

He had shot this arrow into the air, little guessing how hard and truly it would hit.

Hortensius was making vigorous efforts to curb his temper, biting his lips until tiny drops of blood slowly trickled down his chin. But he felt that the mocking eyes of his host were upon him, and had just a sufficiency of reason left in him to see through the machinations of Caius Nepos. He would not hold himself up to ridicule now before those who should prove his strong supporters in the future; his proposal had not yet been put to the vote, and he did not mean to alienate his adherents by an insane show of maniacal rage.

"Of that," he said in response to his host's taunt, and in a voice quivering with the mighty effort of control, "of that there is but little fear. The Augusta is too proud to look with favour on a stranger; as for me, I would sooner ask Escanes to plunge his dagger in my throat than I would serve the Empire under the Cæsarship of Taurus Antinor."

"Thou canst record thy vote as thou thinkest best," said Caius Nepos with calm urbanity. And those who were sufficiently sober nodded approval with solemn gravity.

"Nay," here interposed Marcus Ancyrus with stern reproof, "before we begin to vote let us be agreed on one point: let us be prepared to swear by the gods that we will adhere truly and loyally to the choice of the majority—and if, as meseems is likely, we agree that the unknown future husband of Dea Flavia Augusta become the ruler of us all, then must we swear to proclaim him the Cæsar with one accord, else doth our voting become a mere farce. Friends, before ye vote, are you ready to take this oath?"

"Aye! aye!" came from almost every mouth round the table. But they nodded like automatons, with heavy heads that rolled on bowed shoulders and blurred eyes half-hidden behind closing lids.

"I'll not swear allegiance to Taurus Antinor," persisted Hortensius obstinately.

"Dost think it likely that the Augusta favours him?" asked the host ironically.

"No—but——"

"Then what hast thou to fear?"

"As for me," interposed young Escanes in a thick voice broken by hiccoughs, "I am ready to swear as Marcus Ancyrus directs. If we are not satisfied with the new Cæsar, whoever he may be, my dagger will not rust in the meanwhile; I can easily whet it again."

Even as these last cynical words left the young man's lips there came from outside the noise of much shouting and shuffling of naked feet, and anon the sound of a voice, loud and harsh, asking for leave to speak with the praetorian praefect. Caius Nepos paused, tablets in hand. Strangely enough the voice, though well-known, seemed to have a sobering effect on all these ebullient tempers. Marcus Ancyrus, who was the most calm among them all, threw a quick glance of inquiry on his host, one or two furtive glances were exchanged, a look that was half-ashamed crept into some of the faces, and there were hurried, whispered calls to the slaves to bring the bags of ice.

Quickly the tunics were re-adjusted and an attempt made at re-establishing some semblance of decorum round the table. Caius Nepos was giving hastily whispered directions to the waiting-maids.

"Pull that coverlet straight, quick!" he ordered, "and those cushions, pick them off the ground ... that broken vase, set it aside.... There! try and hide that wine stain with a fresh cloth."

And all the while rapid, eager questions flew from mouth to mouth.

"Wilt tell him at once, O Caius Nepos?"

"Or wilt ply him with wine first?"

"'Twere safer."

"Nay! nay!" said Escanes, whose wrists and ankles were being bathed, "that would take too long. Taurus Antinor hath a strong head, and I, for one, could not keep sober another half-hour."

"Dost know if he is at one with us?" was the query that came from every side.

Hortensius Martius alone had remained silent. He did not call either for water or for ice. It was his hatred that had sobered him, making the lines of his face set and hard, causing the flush to die from his cheeks and leaving them ashy pale.

"Dost know if he is at one with us?" reiterated Augustus Philario impatiently.

He had ordered a slave to hold lumps of ice to his forehead, whilst Philippus Decius—lying next to him—was having perfume rubbed into the back of his neck.

"We must look stern and deliberate," said Ancyrus. "Dost know, O Caius Nepos, if he is at one with us?"

"We must enlist him," rejoined the latter hurriedly; "he holds the plebs, and without his help our position might become difficult. A word from him to the crowd and the new Cæsar is assured of peace within the city."

"Then do thou tell him what has been decided," said one of the others who was busy smoothing his tangled hair.

"No, no!" whispered cautious Ancyrus, the elder, "have a care ... thou, Caius Nepos, must probe him ere thou speakest."

"Tell him naught of Escanes' dagger," added another hurriedly.

"Speak of abdication," said the older man, "of anything that comes in thy mind. Some men there are who——"

But he had no time to explain his meaning further, for the next moment Taurus Antinor stepped into the room.

CHAPTER IX

"There is a lion in the way; a lion is in the streets."—Proverbs xxvi. 13.

He had exchanged his embroidered tunic for a gorgeous synthesis of crimson embroidered with gold, which set off to perfection the somewhat barbaric splendour of his personality, and as he stood there massive and erect, beneath the gilded beams of Caius Nepos' dining-hall, with the slaves at his feet undoing the strings of his shoes, he looked every inch the ruler for whom all these men here were blindly and senselessly seeking.

His deep-set eyes beneath that stern frown had swept quickly over the assembly as he entered, and though now comparative order had been restored and a semblance of calm reigned around the table, Taurus Antinor did not fail to note the flushed faces and glowing eyes, the broken goblets, and stained and tattered cloths which gave ugly evidence of the riotous orgy that had gone before.

But though forty pairs of eyes were fixed upon his face, none could boast that they had perceived any change in its somewhat severe impassiveness as he now advanced towards his host.

"Greeting to thee, O Caius Nepos!" he said. "I crave thy pardon for my late coming, but I had other duties to which to attend."

"Duties?" said Caius Nepos lightly; "nay, Taurus Antinor, there are just now duties so high and sacred that others must of necessity stand aside for these! But of this more anon. Wilt rest now and partake of wine?"

"I thank thee, good Caius," replied the praefect, "but I have supped, and only came at thy bidding, because thou didst say that affairs of State would claim our attention this night."

To all those present he gave courteous if not very hearty greeting. Then did his glance encounter that of Hortensius Martius who alone had said no word or made a movement to welcome him.

There was a vacant place beside young Hortensius, and Taurus Antinor took it, but he did not lie along the cushions as the others did but half sat, half leaned on the couch, and turning to the young man said simply:

"I give thee greeting, O Hortensius! I had no thought of meeting thee here."

"I told thee yesterday that I would be present," said the other curtly.

"I remember now and am proud and honoured to sit by thy side; wilt pledge me in a goblet of wine?"

He had forced his rough voice to tones of gentleness. Hortensius Martius raised his glowering eyes with some curiosity on his face.

But a day and a night had elapsed since his life had lain wholly at the mercy of this powerful giant whom he had insulted, and who had been on the point of punishing that insult with death.

Young Hortensius, held aloft in the mighty grip of the praefect twenty feet above the flagstones of the Forum, seeing a hideous death waiting for him below, did not even now realise how it came to pass that—when he recovered from the swoon into which horror and fear had thrown him—he found himself being tended by an old woman, and anon delivered safe and sound into the keeping of his slaves; he had entered his litter and been borne to his home still marvelling, but of the praefect of Rome he had not since then seen a trace.

He had questioned his slaves who swore that from the arcades of the tabernae, where they had been waiting, they had seen nothing of what went on around the rostra. Hortensius knew that they lied, they must have seen something of the quarrel; they must have seen him being carried like a recalcitrant child up to the top of the highest rostrum, and threatened with awful punishment by the very man whom he had affected to despise. They must also have seen the praefect relenting, carrying him down again, content apparently with the fright which he had given him.

His slaves must have been witnesses to his humiliation, and now were afraid to tell him what they had seen; and for the first time in his life Hortensius Martius felt a wave of cruelty pass over him, in an insensate desire to make the slaves speak under pressure of torture.

At the time he was ashamed to seem too eager and had forborne to question further. But he allowed his humiliation to breed the quick-growing weed of hate. When first the name of Taurus Antinor was mentioned he realised how that weed had grown apace, and now that he sat beside him, and felt the inquisitive eyes of his host fixed with ill-concealed mockery upon him, he knew in his innermost heart that after this day there would no longer be room in the city of Rome for himself as well as for this man who had vanquished and humiliated him.

For the moment, however, he did not care to proclaim before all these men the hatred which he felt for Taurus Antinor. Thoughts of

65

supreme grandeur were coursing through his brain. He knew that no one stood so high in Dea Flavia's graces as he himself had done this year past, and that no one was so like to win her for wife, since she had in her own proud and aloof way already accepted his respectful wooing.

Therefore, putting a rein upon his jealousy and upon his unruly tongue, he took up a goblet and responded to the pledge of the man whom he hated. But whilst Antinor drained the crystal cup to the dregs young Hortensius scarcely wetted his lips, and pretending to drink deeply, he kept his eyes fixed upon the praefect of Rome.

It seemed to him as if he had never really seen him before, so sharp are the eyes of hate that they see much that is usually hidden to those of indifference. Young Hortensius, over the edge of his goblet, embraced with a steady glance the whole person of his enemy—the massive frame, the strong limbs, the hands and feet slender and strong. He looked straight into those deep-set eyes over which a perpetual frown always cast a shadow, and saw that they were of an intense shade of blue and with a strange look in them of kindliness and of peace, which belied the stern fierceness of the face and the wilful obstinacy of the massive jaw.

But now Caius Nepos began to speak. Taking the advice of Marcus Ancyrus the elder, he spoke vaguely, trying to probe the thoughts that lay hidden behind the Anglicanus' furrowed brow. He had received advice, he said that the Cæsar was tired of government and wished to spend some quiet days in the Palace of Tiberius, on the island of Capraea; all this cleverly interwoven with sighs of hope as to what a happier future might bring if the Empire were rid—quite peaceably, of course—of the tyranny of a semi-brutish despot.

Then, as Taurus Antinor made no comment on his peroration, he recalled in impassioned language all that Rome had witnessed in the past three years of depravity, of turpitude, of senseless and maniacal orgies and of bestial cruelty, all perpetrated by the one man to whom blind Fate had given supreme power.

"And to whom, alas!" said Taurus Antinor in calm response to the glowing speech, "we have all of us here sworn loyalty and obedience."

There was silence after this. Despite the lingering fumes of wine that obscured the brain, everyone felt that with these few words the praefect of Rome had already given an answer, and that nothing that could be said after this would have the power of making him alter his decision. But Marcus Ancyrus, conscious of his own powers of diplomacy, took up the thread of his host's peroration.

"Aye! but we should be obeying him," he said simply, "if we accept his abdication."

"There is no disloyalty," asserted Escanes, "in rejoicing at such an issue, if the Cæsar himself doth will it so."

"None," admitted the praefect; "but there would be grave difficulty in choosing a successor."

"To this," said the host, "we have given grave consideration."

"Indeed!"

"And have come to a decision which we all think would best serve the welfare of the State."

"May I hear this decision?"

"It means just this, O praefect! that since the sceptre of Cæsar must, if possible, remain in the House of Cæsar, and since no man of that House is worthy to wield it, we would ask the Augusta Dea Flavia to take to herself a lord and husband, on whom, by virtue of his marriage, the imperium would rest for his life, and after his death fall on the direct descendant of great Augustus himself."

Taurus Antinor had not made a sign whilst Caius Nepos thus briefly put before him the main outline of the daring project, and Hortensius Martius, who was watching him closely, could not detect the slightest change in the earnest face even when Dea Flavia's name was spoken. Now, when Nepos paused as if waiting for comment, Antinor said gravely:

"Ye must pardon me, but I am a stranger to the social life in Rome. Will you tell me who this man is whom the Augusta will so highly favour?"

"Nay, as to that," said Caius Nepos, "we none of us know it as yet! Dea Flavia has smiled on many, but up to now hath made no choice."

"Then 'tis to an unknown man ye would all pledge your loyalty?"

"Unknown, yet vaguely guessed at, O praefect," here broke in Escanes, with his usual breezy cheerfulness; "we all feel that Dea Flavia's choice can but fall on an honourable man."

"Thou speakest truly," rejoined Taurus Antinor earnestly; "but I fear me that for the present your schemes are too vague. The Augusta hath made no choice of a husband as yet, and the Cæsar is still your chosen lord."

"A brutish madman, who——"

"You chose him——"

"Since then he hath become a besotted despot."

"Still your Emperor—to whom you owe your dignities, your power, your rank——"

"Thou dost defend him warmly, O praefect of Rome," suddenly interposed Hortensius Martius who had followed every phase of the discussion with heated brow and eyes alert and glowing. "Thou art ready to continue this life of submission to a maniacal tyrant, to a semi-bestial mountebank——"

"The life which I lead is of mine own making," rejoined Taurus Antinor proudly; "the life ye lead is the one ye have chosen."

And with significant glance his dark eyes took in every detail of the disordered room—the littered table, the luxurious couches, the

67

numberless empty dishes and broken goblets as well as the flushed faces and the trembling hands, and involuntarily, perhaps, a look of harsh contempt spread over his face.

Hortensius caught the look and winced under it; the words that had accompanied it had struck him as with a lash, and further whipped up his already violent rage.

"And," he retorted with an evil sneer, "to the Cæsar thou wilt render homage even in his most degraded orgies, and wilt lick the dust from off his shoes when he hath kicked thee in the mouth."

Slowly Taurus Antinor turned to him, and Hortensius Martius appeared just then so like a naughty child, that the look of harshness died out of the praefect's eyes, and a smile almost of amusement, certainly of indulgence, lit up for a moment the habitual sternness of his face.

"Loyalty to Cæsar," he said simply, "doth not mean obsequiousness, as all Roman patricians should know, oh Hortensius!"

"Aye! but meseems," rejoined the young man, whose voice had become harsher and more loud as that of Taurus Antinor became more subdued and low, "meseems that at the cost of thy manhood thou at least art prepared to render unto Cæsar——"

But even as these words escaped his lips the praefect, with a quick peremptory gesture, placed one slim, strong hand on Hortensius' wrist.

It seemed as if in a moment—and because of those words—a strange power had gone forth from the soul within right down to the tips of the slender fingers that closed on those of the younger man with a grip of steel.

He had raised himself wholly upright on the couch, his massive figure, in the gorgeous crimson tunic, standing out clear and trenchant against the shadowy whiteness of the marble walls behind him. His head, with the ruddy mass of hair on which the flickering lamps threw brilliant, golden lights, was thrown back, and the eyes, deep, intent, and glowing with unrevealed ardour, looked straight out before him into the shadows.

"Render unto Cæsar," he said slowly, "the things which are Cæsar's, and unto God the things that are God's."

His voice was low and unmodulated, as of one who repeats something that he has heard before, whilst the eyes suddenly shone as if with a fleeting memory of an exquisite vision.

The action, the words, were but momentary, but for that brief moment the angry retort was checked on Hortensius' lips, even as were the sneers and the bibulous scowls on the faces of those around. Taurus Antinor, towering above them all, and imbued with a strange dignity, seemed to be gazing into a space beyond the walls of the gorgeous dining-hall; into a space hidden from their understanding but peopled with the sweet memory of a sacred past. And even as he gazed a strange

68

spell fell over these voluptuaries; a spell which they were unable to withstand. Whilst it lasted every ribald word was stilled and every drunken oath lulled to silence. The very air seemed hushed and only from a bunch of dying roses the withered petals were heard to fall one by one.

Then the grasp on Hortensius' wrist relaxed, the dark head was lowered, the falling lids once more hid the mysterious radiance of the eyes. The spell was broken as Taurus Antinor resumed quietly:

"The Cæsar," he said, "hath not yet abdicated; he is still our chosen ruler and Emperor. To speak of his successor now savours of treachery and——"

"And what thou sayest stinks of treachery," broke in Hortensius Martius with redoubled wrath, and shaking himself free from the brief spell of superstitious awe which Antinor's words and Antinor's grip on his arm had momentarily cast over him. "Hast come here, O praefect, but to spy on us, to probe our souls and use them for thine own selfish ends?"

"Silence, Hortensius!" admonished Ancyrus, the elder.

"Nay, I'll not be silent!" retorted the young man, who seemed at last to have lost all control over his jealous passion. His eyes, in which gleamed the fire of intense hate, swept from the face of his enemy to that of his friends whom they challenged. His voice had become raucous and hoarse and his tongue refused him service, making his words sound inarticulate.

"Do ye not see," he shouted, turning his flushed face toward the others, "do you not see how you are being fooled? The praefect stands high in the Cæsar's favour, he has the Cæsar's ear——"

"Silence!" broke in in peremptory accents the voice of Caius Nepos, the host.

"Silence!" cried some of the younger men.

"No! No! I'll shout! I'll shout!" persisted Hortensius with the crazy obstinacy of one whose mind is obscured with liquor and with passion, "I'll shout until you understand. Fools, I tell ye! Fools are ye all! You tell this man of your schemes, of your plans! He listens blandly to you!... You fools! you fools! Not to have suspected ere this that his so-called loyalty to Cæsar masks his treachery to us!"

He was kneeling now upon his couch, and with clenched hands was pounding against the cushions like an angry child. The tumult became general; everyone was shouting. Those who were nearest to this raving young maniac were trying to seize him, but he waved his arms about like the wings of a night bird, and anon he seized a goblet of heavy solid metal and struck out with it to the right and left of him, so that none dared come nigh.

But the praefect stood quietly beside him, with arms held very tightly across his mighty chest, his dark eyes fixed upon the raving figure on the couch. No one had ventured to approach him, for the

69

feeling of superstitious awe which he had aroused in them a while ago had not wholly died down, and now there was such a look of contempt and of wrath in his face that instinctively the most sober drew away from him, and those whose minds were obscured with wine looked upon him in ever growing terror.

Suddenly Hortensius, brandishing the heavy goblet, raised it high above his head, and with a drunken and desperate gesture he flung it in the direction of the praefect, but his hand had trembled and his arm was unsteady. The goblet missed the head of Taurus Antinor and fell crashing along the marble-topped table, bringing a quantity of crystal down with it in its fall.

A few drops of the wine from the goblet had fallen on Taurus Antinor's tunic, and from the parched throat of young Hortensius there rose a hoarse and immoderate laugh and a string of violent oaths. But even before these had fully escaped his lips he saw the praefect's dark face quite close to his own, and felt a grip as of a double vice of steel fastening on both his shoulders.

He knew the grip and had felt it before; no claw of desert beast was firmer or more unrelenting. Young Hortensius felt his whole body give way, his very bones crack beneath that mighty grip. His head, overheated with wine, fell back against the cushions of his couch, and he felt as if the last breath in him was leaving his enfeebled body.

"Thou art a fool indeed, Hortensius," murmured a harsh voice close to his ear; "a fool to provoke a man beyond the power of his control."

Then as at a word from the host, the other men—those who were steady on their feet—tried to interpose, Taurus Antinor turned his face to them.

"Have no fear," he said quite calmly, "for this man. He shall come to no harm. Twice hath he insulted me and twice have I held his life in my hands."

Then, as Hortensius uttered an involuntary cry of rage or of pain, Taurus Antinor spoke once more to him:

"Thy life is in my hands yet will I not kill thee, even though I could do it with just the tightening of my fingers round thy throat. But provoke me not a third time, O Hortensius, for I have in my possession a heavy-thonged whip, and this would I use on thee even as I order it to be used on the miscreant thieves that are brought to my tribunal. So cross not my path again, dost understand? I am but a man and have not an inexhaustible stock of patience."

Whilst he spoke he still held young Hortensius down pinioned amongst the cushions. No one interfered, for it had dawned on every blurred mind there that here lay a deeper cause for quarrel than mere political conflict. Hortensius, though vanquished now, had been like a madman; his unprovoked insults had come from a heart overburdened with jealousy and with hate. Now when the praefect relaxed his grip

70

upon him, he lay for a while quite still, and anon Caius Nepos beckoned to his slaves, and they it was who ministered to him, bathing his forehead with water and holding lumps of ice to the palms of his hands.

Taurus Antinor had straightened out his tall figure. For a moment he looked down with bitter scorn on the prostrate figure of his vanquished foe. The awed silence which his strange words of a while ago had imposed upon the others, still hung upon them all. They stood about in groups, whispering below their breath, and the slaves were huddled up one against the other in the distant corners of the room. An air of mystery still hung over the magnificent triclinium, its convivial board, its abandoned couches, over the vases of murra and crystal and the fast dying roses. It seemed as if some personality—great, majestic, divine—had passed through the marble hall and that the sound of sacred feet still echoed softly along its walls.

It almost seemed as if there clung a radiance in that shadowy corner where the eyes of an enthusiast had sought and found the memory of the Divine Teacher; and that in the fume-laden air there lingered the odour of the sacrifice offered by a rough, untutored heart to the Man Who had spoken unforgettable words seven years ago in Galilee.

CHAPTER X

"That the world through Him might be saved."—St. John iii. 17.

Taurus Antinor had bidden farewell to his host, and to the other guests and then departed.

Not another word had been spoken on the subject of the Cæsar or of his probable successor. The conspirators, somewhat sobered, had allowed the praefect to go without attempting further effort to gain him to their cause. They had had their answer. Though many of them did not quite understand the full depth of its meaning, yet were they satisfied that it was final. They bade him farewell quietly and without enmity; somehow the thought of their murderous plan had momentarily fled from their mind, and the quarrel between Hortensius Martius and the praefect of Rome seemed to have been the most important event of the day.

Taurus Antinor emerged alone from the peristyle of Caius Nepos' house. An army of slaves belonging to the various guests were hanging about the vestibule, talking and laughing amongst themselves and feasting on the debris from the patricians' table, brought out to them by servitors from within; some forty litters encumbered the floor, but Antinor, paying no heed to these, passed through the crowd of jabbering men and women and made his way across to the steps which led upwards to the street.

The day was done, had been done long ago; already the canopy of the stars was stretched over the sleeping city, and far away to the east, beyond the gilded roof of Augustus' palace, the waning moon, radiant and serene, outlined the carvings on every temple with a thin band of gold and put patches of luminous sapphires and emeralds on the bronze figures that crowned the Capitol.

Taurus Antinor paused awhile, enjoying the restfulness of the night; from his broad chest came a long-drawn breath of voluptuous delight at the exquisite sweetness of the air. How far away now seemed that long, luxurious room, with its stained cloths and crumpled cushions, with the low tables groaning under the debris of past repasts and the rows of couches luring to sensuous repose. For the moment even the wranglings of Caius Nepos' guests seemed remote, their selfish aims and their lying tongues. Here, beneath the stars, there was stillness and peace.

A gentle breeze from over the distant hills blew on the dreamer's forehead and eased the wild throbbings of his temples; from somewhere near tiny petals of heliotrope, chased by the breeze, brought sweet-scented powder to his nostrils.

He looked around him, gazing with wondering eyes on the mighty city sleeping upon her seven hills, on the gorgeous palaces of Tiberius and Caligula and the squalid huts far away on the Aventine Hill, on the mighty temples with their roofs of gold and the yawning arena down below, desolate and silent now, but where on the morrow men and beasts would tear one another to pieces to make holiday for the masters of the world.

And even as his restless eyes swept over the surrounding landscape, they turned to where, in the shadow of the stately palaces of Tiberius and of Augustus, lay the house of Dea Flavia. Its gilded portals threw back with brilliant intensity the weird and elusive light of the waning moon, and high above, upon the balustrade of the roof, gigantic bronze groups of quaint and misshapen beasts looked ghoul-like against the canopy of the sky.

All within the massive walls was dark and still; near to the vestibule a couple of ancient cypresses made a natural arch overhead, and in the tender branches of a group of acacias close by, the evening breeze sighed with gentle, melancholy murmurings amongst the leaves.

Instinctively Taurus Antinor turned to walk a few steps toward the house, and soon reached a spot from whence his gaze could command the colonnaded vestibule, with its mosaic pavement sunk a few steps below the level of the street. Somewhere near him, though he could not see it, a bosquet of heliotrope and white lilies sent an intoxicating fragrance into the air.

From far away—where the marshes stretched their limitless expanse toward the sea—came the melancholy cry of a bittern, calling to his absent mate.

A vague longing surged in the strong man's heart; he stretched out his arms up to the dark, starlit canopy above, and a sigh, half impatient, wholly melancholy, escaped his half-closed lips.

His eyes tried to pierce the marble walls behind which there bloomed—stately and proud—a beautiful white lily.

Wholly against his will, the man's thoughts flew back to that midday hour in the Forum, when Dea Flavia had stood before him in all the exquisite glory of her youth and her loveliness, with that wilful curl round her chiselled lips and the delicate brows drawn together in a frown of child-like obstinacy. How beautiful she was and how strangely pathetic had been her isolation in the midst of so much grandeur.

Even now he thought of her—asleep possibly somewhere in this gorgeous palace—all alone, despite the thousands of slaves around her; friendless, despite the might of the House of Cæsar of which she was so proud.

Through one of the tiny windows there peeped a flickering light. Taurus Antinor marvelled if that were her sleeping-room and, closing his eyes, pictured her there, resting on embroidered coverlets and cushions, her fair hair falling in waves around her face at rest; and he wondered whether in sleep a dewy tear had perchance put a priceless diamond on her golden lashes.

Bitter thoughts of the men whom he had just quitted surged back in his heart; they wished to make of this young girl a tool for the fashioning of their own ambitious schemes.

"The Augusta shall choose one of us for mate, and him we shall ask to hold the sceptre of Cæsar."

One of them for mate! One of those sensuous self-seekers who would use her as a stepping-stone, and, having obtained supreme power through her dainty hands, would cast her aside as a useless tool and break her heart ere she realised even that she had one.

And from the thoughts of the beautiful girl his mind flew back as if instinctively to that strange phase of his life—those unforgettable days in Judæa which had seemed like unto the turning point of his whole existence. He recalled every moment of that memorable day when he had stood among a multitude on the barren wastes of Galilee and, wrapped in a dark cloak, had listened in solitary silence to words and teachings such as he had never dreamed of before.

"If only I could have understood Thee better then," he murmured; "if more of Thy precious words had fallen on mine ear.... I might have told her then something of what Thou didst say ... I could have found the words to make her understand.... But now I am

73

ignorant and forlorn.... Oh, Man of Galilee! Thou didst die so soon ... and left so many of us groping in the darkness.... Thou Son of God, come back to me, if only in a dream ... show me the way, the truth, the light; show me the star which they say guided the shepherds to Thy cradle ... give me Thy cross, and let me walk once more on Golgotha to Thee."

And even as these words of passionate longing escaped half audibly from his lips his eyes wandered round the seven hills of Rome, and suddenly the highest peak beyond the Forum appeared to him transfigured in the night. Memory with a swift hand drew aside the veil of the present and in a vision showed him a picture of the past. The marble temples of pagan gods disappeared, the hill became bleak and precipitous and dark; great stillness reigned around, save where from afar there came at times the distant roll of thunder. The sky was overcast, great banks of cloud, the colour of lead, with blood-red lights within their massive bosoms, swept storm-tossed across the firmament.

Then from the valley below there came, vaguely remote at first, then rising louder and louder, a sound as when a mighty torrent rushes onwards in its course; and as Taurus Antinor gazed now on that dream-hill, memory showed him, surging like a tempestuous sea, thousands upon thousands of human heads, all tending upwards to the summit of the hill.

They came—the great multitude—they came, and still they came; and like gigantic breakers on a smooth shore, waves of human beings scattered themselves and dispersed upon that hill.

And amongst them all, isolated, walking with bent back and thorn-crowned head well-nigh bowed to the dust, came a Man bearing a Cross.

Taurus Antinor saw Him even now as he had seen Him then, with blood and sweat dripping from His brow, the pale, patient face serene and set, the eyes half closed in agony still glowing with unutterable love and with the perfect peace of complete sacrifice.

And among the sea of faces that gazed on that solitary figure Taurus Antinor had recognised himself.

He saw himself as he was then, a rough voluptuary, a thoughtless, sentient beast who up to that time had lived a life of emptiness and of mockery, eating and drinking and sleeping and waking again day after day, year after year. And he saw himself as he was on that day, he one of thousands and thousands of lookers-on gazing on the three hours' agony of a just Man upon the Cross.

He remembered every minute of those three hours, which the hill of imperial Rome now pictured back to him as in a dream. He had stood there a mere unit amongst the crowd, wrapped in a dark cloak, unrecognised and unknown, but with every nerve strained to catch the words that fell from those dying lips. He had heard the cry of bitterness: "Lord! Lord! why hast Thou forsaken Me?" and that of infinite love and of supreme pardon: "Oh God, forgive them, for they know not what they do."

And above and around the sky grew darker and the air more still, and round that dying figure alone there shone a radiance unseen by most; for had they seen it as Taurus Antinor saw it then, then surely would they have known, would they have understood.

And at the foot of that Cross women and men stood weeping, and thoughtless soldiers hurled insults on their dying Lord. The lips that had only uttered words of perfect charity thirsted for a drop of water, and a sponge filled with gall was pressed mockingly to them.

But the arms were still extended wider and wider, so it seemed, as if in their almighty love they would embrace all that surging humanity; all those that suffered, those that hoped as well as those that doubted, those who mocked Him and those who adored.

Taurus Antinor's very manhood had cried out to him then to fight the multitude single-handed, to shake the power of Rome and defy the will of the people, and to rush up to that one Cross, towering above the others, to pick out with firm fingers every cruel nail, to wrap the sacred body in soft, soothing cloths, and to kiss every wound until it closed in health.

Even now, after all these years, the rough soldier's cheeks were burning with the shame of impotence.

To look on that sacrifice and be unable to stop it. To look on such a death and to continue to live on, still blind, still ununderstanding, even though the Teacher Who had come to explain had sighed ere he died: "It is finished!" And yet Taurus Antinor, now looking back upon his own past self, knew that at the time, despite the horror, the pity and the sorrow, there was also in his heart a sense of happiness and even a vague feeling of triumph.

What he saw there—with eyes that comprehended not—that he knew was because it must be; because it had been preordained and done by One Whose will was mightier than death. Though with aching heart and seared eyes he had watched every minute of the supreme agony, yet something within him, even then, had told him that every minute of that agony was a sacrifice that would not be in vain. And whilst in weakness he groaned with the pathos of it all, yet did his heart thrill with strange exultation, and from that Cross—even when all was silent—there rang in his ear the last words of perfect fulfilment of a perfect sacrifice:

"It is finished!"

And even as the words rang once again in Taurus Antinor's ears, the awful darkness of that momentous hour fell upon the dream-hill far away. Golgotha, with its three towering crosses vanished from before the visionary's gaze. Once more there rose before him the marble temples of pagan Rome that crowned the Capitol—the gorgeous idols

75

covered in gold, these gods of mockery before whom the mightiest Empire in the world was satisfied to bow the knee.

And that same sweet, sad longing rose in the dreamer's heart.

"Could I but have heard Thee speak more often!... Could I but have touched Thy hands, methinks that I would have understood.... But now ... now all is still dark before me ... and the way is so difficult."

And even as the sigh died upon his lips there came from behind him the sound of prolonged and hoarse laughter, followed by snatches of a drinking song and loud calls for slaves and litters.

Caius Nepos' guests were leaving the hospitable house at last. Drunk with wine, smothered in flowers, replete with every epicurean delight they were going home now, having, mayhap, forgotten that they had plotted to murder Cæsar and to raise themselves to power at all costs, even if that cost was to be a sea of blood or the ruins of Rome.

The song and laughter soon died away in the distance. Taurus Antinor had distinguished the voice of Hortensius Martius and that of Ancyrus, the elder. The sigh of sadness turned to one of bitterness, his arms dropped by his side, and a cry of harsh contempt escaped his parched? throat.

"Oh, Man of Galilee," he murmured, "didst die for such as these?"

CHAPTER XI

"Come unto Me, all ye that labour and are heavy laden, and I will give you rest."—St. Matthew xi. 28.

A timid voice roused Taurus Antinor from his dream:

"My gracious lord, thy litter is here!"

He started as a man suddenly wakened from sleep, and once or twice his eyes closed and opened again ere they rested finally on the broad back bent in a curve before him.

"Methought my gracious· lord was waiting," continued the speaker in the same timid voice, "and mayhap did not see the litter among the shadows."

"I fear me I was dreaming, my good Folces," said the praefect with a sigh, "for truly I did know that thou wast here. Is the girl Nola with thee?"

"Aye, gracious lord. She waits on thy pleasure, and thy bearers—"

"Nay, did I not tell thee that I would have no bearers?"

"The way is long, gracious lord——"

"I told thee that I would walk."

"But my lord——"

"Silence now," he said with some of his habitual impatience; "send my litter and bearers home; bring me the mantle I required, and do thou and Nola follow me."

Reluctantly the old man obeyed.

"My gracious lord will be footsore—the way is long and ill-paved——" he muttered, half audibly, even as he made his way to the rear of the bosquet of lilies where a group of slaves stood waiting desultorily.

Anon he returned carrying a mantle of dark woollen stuff, and Taurus Antinor, having wrapped himself in this, slowly turned to walk down the hill.

Leaving the imperial palaces behind him, he went rapidly along the silent and deserted street. It wound its tortuous way at first on the crest of the hill, skirting the majestic temple of Magna Mater with its elevated portico and noble steps that lost themselves in the shadows of labyrinthine colonnades.

The street itself—narrow and unpaved—was in places rendered almost impassable by the piles of constructor's materials and rubbish that encumbered it at every step—debris or future requisites of the gigantic and numberless building operations which the mad Emperor pursued with that feverish energy and maniacal restlessness that characterised his every action. Palaces here and temples there, a bridge over the Forum, a new circus, new baths, the constant pulling down of one edifice to make room for the construction of another: all this work—commenced and still unfinished—had changed the whole aspect of the great city, turning it into a wilderness of enormous beams and huge blocks of uncut marble and stone that littered its every way.

But Taurus Antinor paid no heed to the roughness and inaccessibility of the road. Unlike the rich patricians of the time he hated the drowsy indolence of progress in a litter, and after the fatigues of a nerve-racking day, the difficulties of ill-paved roads were in harmony with his present mood.

Assuring himself that old Folces and the girl Nola were close at his heels, he stepped briskly along the now precipitous incline of the hill. The rapid movement did him good. The air came to him from across the gardens of the palaces, sweetly scented by late lilies and clumps of dying roses.

Soon he had left the great circus behind him too, and now he started climbing again, for his way led him upwards on the slope of the Aventine Hill. The silence here seemed more absolute than among the dwellings of the rich, for there, at times, a night watchman would emerge from a cross-road and give challenge to the belated passer-by, whilst a certain bustle of suspended animation always reigned around the palace of the Emperor even during the hours of sleep; some of his slaves and guard were always kept awake, ready to minister to any fancy or caprice that might seize the mad Cæsar in the middle of the night.

But here where there were no palaces to guard, no insane ruler to protect, no one came to question the purpose of the benighted wanderers, nor did sudden outbursts of laughter or good cheer pierce the mud walls of the humble abodes that lay scattered on the slope of the hill.

The waning moon had hidden her light behind a heavy bank of clouds, a dull greyness pervaded the whole landscape, causing it to look weird and forlorn in the gloom. The few trees dotted about here and there looked starved and gaunt on the barren hill-side, with great skeleton-like arms that waved mournfully in the breeze; the ground uneven and parched—after the summer's drought—rose and sank in fantastic mounds and shapes like tiny fortresses of ghosts or ghouls; the street itself soon became merged in the general surroundings, only a tiny footway, scarcely discernible in the gathering darkness, wound upwards to the summit of the hill.

From time to time a solid block of what appeared only as impenetrable blackness loomed up from out the shadows, with all the grandeur of exaggerated size which the darkness of the night so generously lends. Soon it would reveal itself as a small mud-covered box, with four bare walls and a narrow doorway facing toward the south. Herein lived and suffered a family of human beings—freedmen and women without the stigma of slavery, but with all the misery of destitution and often of complete starvation.

Here and there the little house would be surrounded by a vestibule—a mere projection from the roof supported on a few rough beams—but never a garden, scarcely a tree to cast a cooling shade on hot summer afternoons, or clump of lilies or mimosa to sweeten the air that came dank and fetid from over the marshes beyond the hill.

Not a sound now disturbed the stillness of the night save when a bat fluttered overhead, or when furtive footsteps—on unavowable errand bent—glided softly off the beaten track and quickly died away among the shadows.

The praefect walked on, heedless of his surroundings. The mood that had been on him ever since he left Caius Nepos' house still caused his mind to wander restlessly in the illimitable regions of perplexity and doubt. He scarcely looked where he was going, for he kept his eyes fixed upon the starlit canopy above him and upon the crest of the hill which lost itself in the darkness overhead.

Suddenly, out of the gloom, two pairs of hands emerged, and without warning fastened themselves on the praefect's throat: thin, claw-like hands they were, and above them gaunt arms, mere bones covered with wrinkled flesh that proclaimed starvation and misery.

The old slave from the rear uttered a cry of terror; Nola clung to

78

him paralysed with fear. The slopes of the Aventine were noted for the gangs of malefactors that infested them, and defying the power of the aediles, rendered them unsafe for wayfarers even in the light of day.

Taurus Antinor, instantly brought back from the land of dreams, had no great difficulty in freeing himself from the claw-like grasp. With a quick gesture of his own powerful hands, he had in a moment succeeded in dragging the gaunt fingers from off his throat, and, holding the thin wrists with a firm grip, he gave them a sudden sharp twist, which elicited two cries of pain and brought two pairs of knees in hard contact with the ground.

It had all occurred in the space of a few seconds, and now a bundle of soiled rags seemed to be lying huddled up under the praefect's foot, and he looked like some powerful desert beast that has placed a massive paw on a pair of puny rats.

The thin arms wriggled like worms in his mighty grasp.

"Pity, my lord! Pity!" came in hoarse murmurs from the bundle of rags under his foot.

"Pity? Of that have I in plenty," he replied gruffly. "But methinks 'twas not pity ye sought by trying to strangle me."

"Pity, my lord, my children are starving...."

"Pity, my lord, I have not tasted food to-day——"

"Pity, my lord!" retorted the praefect with a grim laugh, and mimicking the wretched man's words, "I would have murdered you had I had the power."

Then he relaxed his grip, and with his foot pushed the bundle of dirt further away from him. He groped in his wallet and drew out some silver coins. These he threw, one by one, into the midst of the shapeless rags, and he stooped forward, striving in the darkness to see something of the faces that were wilfully hidden from him, something of the mouths that had uttered the pitiable groans.

Vaguely he discerned the outline of cadaverous cheeks, of sunken temples, of furtive eyes veiled by thin lids; he saw the glances half of fear, wholly of doubt, that were thrown on the silver coins, heard the muttered oaths, the incipient quarrel over the distribution of the unexpected hoard.

Then did the strange perplexities which had assailed him throughout this night find expression in bitter words. He threw down a few more coins and said slowly:

"These are for pity's sake, and in the name of One Whom mayhap ye will know one day. He died that ye should live! Bear that in mind and ponder on it. Mayhap ye will find the solution to that riddle. That such as you should live in eternity, therefore did He die.... When ye have understood this and can explain the value of your lives as compared with His, come and tell it to the praefect of Rome and he will shower on you wealth beyond your dreams."

Then, without waiting to hear protestations, or heeding the

ironical laughter that came from the bewildered night-prowlers, he turned on his heels and resumed his interrupted walk along the slope of the hill.

The footpath—scarce more than a beaten track—soon disappeared altogether. Presently Taurus Antinor paused and called to Folces to come up to him.

"Methinks we must be near the house," he said.

"Aye, gracious lord," replied the man, "just on thy right, some two hundred steps from here. The way is very dark, wilt permit me to walk by thy side?"

"Walk by my side an thou wilt. Thou canst direct me more easily; but as to the darkness I can see through it well."

"But my gracious lord did not see those evil malefactors that set upon him."

"No, Folces, I was dreaming as I walked. They came upon me unawares."

"And my gracious lord allowed them to go. They were notorious miscreants."

"They were the embodiment of a strange riddle, good Folces. They helped to puzzle me—and Heaven knows that I was puzzled enough ere I saw those miserable wretches. Mayhap some day I'll understand the riddle which their abject persons did represent. But now tell me, is this the house?"

The wanderers had struck to their right and walked on some two hundred paces. Now they paused beside one of those square mud-walled boxes, of which they could only discern the narrow door made of unplaned wood, and through the chinks of which a faint light glimmered weirdly. Two or three steps fashioned in the earth itself led down toward the threshold. Taurus Antinor descended these and knocked boldly on the door.

It was opened from within, and under the rough lintel there appeared the figure of a man of short stature, clad in a long grey tunic. His head, which he held forward in an attempt to peer through the darkness, looked almost unnaturally large, owing to the mass of loose greyish hair that fell away from his forehead like a mane, and the long beard that straggled down upon his breast.

"May we enter, friend?" asked Taurus Antinor.

At the sound of the voice the man drew aside, and through the narrow doorway was now revealed the interior of the house—a straight, square room, with a few wooden seats disposed about, and at the top end an oblong table covered with a snow-white cloth. An aperture in the wall appeared to lead to an inner chamber, which must indeed have been of diminutive size, for the central room seemed to occupy almost the whole of the interior of the house. Suspended by an iron chain from the ceiling above there hung a small lamp in which flickered a tiny flame fed by some sweet-smelling oil. It threw but little light around and left deep and curious shadows in the angles of the room.

From out these, as the praefect entered, there emerged the figure of an old woman, with smooth grey hair half-hidden beneath a kerchief of strange oriental design, and straight dark robe, foreign in cut and appearance to those usually seen in the streets of Rome.

The massive figure of Taurus Antinor seemed almost to fill the entire room, but he stood to one side now disclosing the old slave and the girl Nola.

"This," he said, addressing the woman, "is the child of whom I spoke to thee. She is friendless and motherless, but she is free, and I have brought her so that thou mayest teach her all thou knowest."

In the meanwhile the man with the leonine head had closed the door on the little party. He came forward eagerly, and raising himself on the tips of his toes, he put his hands on Antinor's shoulder, and with gentle pressure forced him to stoop. Then he kissed him on either cheek.

"Greeting to thee, dear friend," he said cheerily. "Thou hast done well to bring the girl. My mother and I will take great care of her."

"And ye will teach her your religion," said Taurus Antinor earnestly; "because of that did I bring her. She is young and will be teachable. She'll understand as a child will, that which hardened hearts are unable to grasp."

"Nay, friend," said the man simply, "there is not a great deal to teach, nor a great deal to understand. Love and faith, that is sufficient ... and, as our dear Lord did tell us, love is the greatest of all."

For the moment the praefect made no reply. The man had helped him to cast off his heavy mantle, and he stood now in all the splendour of barbaric pomp, a strangely incongruous figure in this tiny bare room, both to his surroundings and to his gentle host and hostess with their humble garb and simple, timid ways.

She—the woman—had drawn Nola with kindly gesture to her. The child was crying softly, for she was half-frightened at the strangeness of the place, and also she was tired after her long walk up and down the rough road. The woman, with subtle feminine comprehension, soon realised this, and also understood that the girl, reared in slavery, felt awed in the presence of so great a lord. So, putting a kindly arm round the slender form of the child, she led her gently out of the main room to the tiny cubicle beyond, where she could rest.

The three men were now left alone. Folces, squatting in a dark corner, kept his eyes fixed upon his master. He took no interest in what went on around him; he cared nothing about the strangeness of the surroundings, his master was lord and praefect of Rome, and could visit those whom he list. But Folces, like a true watch-dog, remained on the alert, silent and ever suspicious, keeping an eye on his master, remaining obedient and silent until told to speak.

The man, in the meanwhile, had asked the praefect to sit.

"Wilt rest a while, O friend," he said, "whilst I make ready for supper."

But Antinor would not sit down. In his habitual way he leaned against the wall, watching with those earnest eyes of his every movement of his host, as the latter first passed a loving hand over the white cloth on the table and then smoothed out every crease on its satiny surface. Anon he disappeared for a moment in the dark angle of the room, where a rough wooden chest stood propped against the wall. From this he now took out a loaf of fine wheaten bread, also a jar containing wine and some plain earthenware goblets. These things he set upon the table, his big leonine head bent to his simple task, his small grey eyes wandering across from time to time in kindliness on his friend.

Intuition—born of intense sympathy—had already told him that something was amiss with the praefect. He knew every line of the rugged face which many deemed so fierce and callous, but in which he had so often seen the light of an all-embracing charity.

When Taurus Antinor used to visit his friend in the olden days he was wont to shed from him that mantle of rebellious pride with which, during the exercise of his duties in Rome, he always hid his real personality. People said of the praefect that he was sullen and morose, merciless in his judgments in the tribunal where he presided. They said that he was ambitious and intriguing, and that he had gained and held the Cæsar's ear for purposes of his own advancement. But the man and woman who had come recently on the Aventine and who called the praefect of Rome their friend, knew that his rough exterior hid a heart brimming over with pity, and that his aloofness came from a mind absorbed in thoughts of God.

But to-day the praefect seemed different. The look of joy with which he had greeted his friends had quickly faded away, leaving the face darkened with some hidden care; and as the man watched him across the narrow room, he seemed to see in the strong face something that almost looked like remorse.

Therefore, whilst accomplishing the task which he loved so well, he quietly watched his friend and resolved that he should not recross the threshold of this house without having unburdened his soul.

"Friend," he now said abruptly, "I have a curious whim to-night. Wilt indulge it?"

"If it be in my power," responded the praefect, rousing himself from his reverie.

A look of deep affection softened for the moment the hard look on his face, as his deep-set eyes rested on the quaint figure of the man with the leonine head.

82

"What is thy whim?" he asked.

"Over in Judæa we were so little alone," rejoined the latter, "and then we had such earnest things to talk about, that I have never heard from thy lips how it came to pass that thou didst hear our dear Lord preach in Galilee."

"Yet I did tell thee," said the praefect, "when first thou didst ask my confidence."

"Then 'tis my whim to hear thee tell me again," rejoined the man simply. "All that pertains to our dear Lord doth lie so close to my heart, and 'tis long now since I have spoken of Him to one who hath seen and heard Him. 'Tis great joy to me to hear of every impression which He made on the heart of those whose life was gladdened by a sight of His face."

"Whose life was gladdened by a sight of His face!" repeated Taurus Antinor gently. "Aye! there dost speak the truth, O friend! for my life too was gladdened by a sight of His face. I was travelling through Judæa, on my way to Syria, and the Cæsar had desired me to visit the proconsul. Thus did I halt in Jerusalem one day. Having done the Emperor's bidding, I had time to kill ere I started further on my journey. So I bethought me that I would like to see something of the Man from Nazareth of Whom I had heard speak."

"And God prompted thee, friend, to go and hear Him."

"God, sayest thou?" rejoined the praefect slowly. "Aye! mayhap thou'rt right. 'Twas God then that sent me. Disguised in humble raiment I went forth one day and made my way to the desert lands of Galilee."

"And didst see Him there?"

"I saw Him sitting on a low mound of earth with the canopy of blue above His head, and all around Him a multitude that hung entranced upon His lips. He spoke to them of the Kingdom of Heaven— a Kingdom of whose existence, alas! I had never dreamed. But His words did wring my heart, and the majesty of His presence has ever since been before mine eyes. To-day it all came back to me, the gentle face, the perfect mouth framing exquisite words. Above Him a curtain of azure, and far away, the illimitable stretch of horizon merging into the water beyond. The very air was still and listening to His words; from under jagged boulders tiny lizards peeped out, and on the branches of starved, gaunt trees the birds had stopped to rest. Then it was that panther-like, sleek sleuth-hounds hovered round Him, trying to entangle Him in His talk. They made their way close to Him, and with honeyed words and deft insinuations, spoke of allegiance and of the tribute due to Cæsar. I stood not far off and could hear what they said. My very heart seemed to still its beating, for did not their questions embrace the whole riddle of mine own life. God and Cæsar! I, the servant of Cæsar—the recipient of rich gifts from his hands—should I forswear the Cæsar and follow Jesus of Nazareth?"

"And didst hear what He answered, friend?"

"Aye! I heard it. And to-day when traitors spoke, it seemed as if the Divine Presence stood close to me amongst the shadows. Once more I saw the bleak and arid land, the skeleton arms of the trees, the blue firmament above my head, I saw the multitude of simple folk around Him and the leer in the eyes of the tempters. And above the din of drunken revelries to-night I heard again the voice that bade me then to render unto Cæsar the things which are Cæsar's, and unto God the things that are God's."

The other sighed, a sigh of glad content.

"I thank thee, friend, for telling me this. 'Tis a joy to hear thee speak of Him. It is so long since we talked of this matter. And—tell me yet again—thou wast in Jerusalem when He died?"

"I stood on Golgotha," said the praefect slowly, "on that day before the Jewish Passover, seven years ago. Once again wrapped in a dark cloak, one among a multitude, I gazed with eyes that I felt could never look on anything else again. I saw the patient face smeared with blood, the God-like head crowned with thorns, the eyes—still brimming over with love—slowly closing in agony. Overhead the heavens murmured, vivid flashes of lightning rent the canopy of the sky, and men around me mocked and jeered, whilst the Divine Soul fled upwards back to God. At that moment, O friend! I seemed to lose mine own identity. I—even I alone—became the whole multitude. I was no longer just mine own self, but I was all of us who looked, who heard and saw and did not yet understand.... A multitude was looking through my eyes ... a multitude heard through mine ears ... I was the crowd of poor, of helpless slaves, and I was the whole of the patriciate of Rome. I was barbarian and Italian, I was British and Roman, all in one ... and my voice was the voice of the entire world, as suddenly I cried out to Him: 'Do not die now and leave us desolate!'"

His harsh voice broke down in a great sob that came from out the depths of an overburdened heart. He took a few steps forward and slowly dropped on his knees right against the table, his clasped hands resting on the cloth, his forehead buried in his hands.

The man had listened to him silently and patiently with, in his heart, that subtle understanding for another's sorrow, which his own mission had instilled into him. And thus understanding he went up to that end of the table where knelt the rich and mighty praefect of Rome, the friend of Cæsar, all-powerful in the land, with burning head buried in his hands, and eyes from which despite his will hot tears gushed up that would not be suppressed.

He placed a kindly hand on the bowed shoulder of his friend.

"Wilt tell me what troubles thee?" he said gently.

Taurus Antinor passed his hand across his forehead as if to chase away the brain-searing thoughts. He raised himself from his knees and gratefully pressed the hand that had recalled him to himself.

"Nay, friend," he said, "I'll not do that. Thy friendship is too precious a guerdon that I should jeopardise it by showing thee the blackness of my soul."

"Dost talk at random," said the other firmly; "my friendship doth not come and go like fleeting sunshine on a winter's day. I gave it thee on that self-same unforgettable day when I saw thee standing alone upon the hill after the crowd had departed and we who loved Him were lifting Him down from His Cross."

"Thou didst take pity then on my loneliness."

"I saw in thee one who had faith," said the man simply. "I grasped thy hand in friendship then, not knowing who thou wast. When I knew, then did I follow thee to Rome, for I needed thy help. My Master sent me here. I do His work that He did enjoin on all His disciples. Thy protection and friendship, O mighty praefect of Rome, hath been an infinite help to me. Thy kindness and charity hath saved from want the many humble followers of Christ who have been forced to give up all for His sake. Therefore whatever doth burden thy soul now, I pray thee share it with me, so that I might bear it with thee and mayhap ease thy load."

"May God bless thee for these words."

"And thy burden, friend?"

"Ask not to share it—'tis one of treachery."

"Of treachery?... Whose treachery?..."

"Mine."

"Thine?... I'll not believe it.... Thou a traitor ... against Cæsar?"

"No."

"Against whom, then?"

"Against Him Whose death I witnessed seven years ago."

"Then I'll not believe it. And 'tis sacrilege thus to jest."

"Jest?" said Taurus Antinor, with a laugh that rang unnatural and hoarse. "Jest! when for a day and a night my soul hath been on the rack and mocking demons have jeered at my torments? Jest! When—?"

He broke off abruptly and looked down with an earnest gaze on the upturned face of his friend.

"If thou wouldst tell me more it would ease thy heart," said the man simply.

For a moment or two the praefect was silent. His hand rested on his friend's shoulder, and his eyes, with their deep furrow between the brows, were fixed on the kind face that invited confidence.

"For seven years," he said abruptly, but speaking very slowly, "whilst I served the Cæsar, every one of my waking thoughts and many of my dreams tended to that day in Jerusalem and the three hours' agony which I had witnessed on Golgotha. Yesterday did a woman cross my path—and now I have thoughts only of her."

"Who is this woman?" asked the other.

"She is of the House of Cæsar, pure and chaste as the lilies in my

85

garden at Ostia, proud and unapproachable as the stars ... her heart is a closed book wherein man hath never read ... but since her eyes have mocked me with their smile, my heart is enchained to her service and I see naught but her loveliness."

"Look upwards, man; a glowing Cross will blind thine eyes to all save to itself."

"Have I not looked," said the praefect, with a sharp, quick sigh, "until mine eyes have ached with trying to see that which once was so clear. But now, between me and that sacred memory that methought had been branded into my very soul, there always rises the vision of a girl, tall and slender as the lilies, clad all in white as they. She stands between me and memory, and mine eyes grow weary and dim trying to see beyond that vision, recalling to my mind the picture of that Cross, the thorn-crowned head, the pierced hands and feet. She stands between me and memory, and with laughing eyes defies me not to see her, and I look and look, and the vision of the Cross grows more faint, and she stands there serene and white and silent, with blue eyes smiling on my treachery and scornful voice upraised, denying God and Christ. She is of the House of Cæsar and she is ignorant, and she laughs at my belief and scorns all thought of God, and I do find it in my treacherous heart to pity her and pitying her to kneel at her feet. And all the while a thousand demons shout mockingly unto mine ear: 'Thou art a traitor—a traitor to thy God—for were she to beckon, 'tis to her that thou wouldst go, forgetting all—thine immortal soul, thy crucified God...?' And thus do devils mock me, and my soul grows darker and darker and greater and greater grows the mystery, for my heart, broken, miserably doubting and weak, cries out not with resignation, not in patience, but in a spirit of angry rebellion: 'God, my God! why hast thou forsaken me?'"

He raised his arms up to heaven as if in a last desperate appeal; but now he did not kneel—he stood beside his friend shamed and yet proud, and the look in his eyes was that of one who sees a vision that is exquisitely beautiful and dear. The other saw the look, and with the kind indulgence taught by a sublime teacher, he found it in his heart to pity and to love. Once more he placed his thin, wrinkled hand on the praefect's shoulder, and his small eyes beamed with perfect faith and trust as he said gently:

"Do not try and probe any mystery just now, O friend, the day has been long and thou art weary and sad. Come and sit beside me here at table; my mother will join us and the girl Nola too, and the man who is thy slave, if thou wilt so allow it. Together we'll think of that day in Judæa seven years ago, and we'll break bread and drink wine, and—without trying to understand anything—we'll do it all together in memory of Him!"

For a moment Taurus Antinor was silent. In the strong face every line told of the great storm within the innermost heart.

And slowly the man beside him repeated the most exquisite words that have ever been spoken to a troubled soul.

"Come unto Me all ye that travail and are heavy laden and I will refresh you."

Taurus Antinor's head fell upon his breast. He closed his eyes, for not even his friend should see that they were wet with tears. But even whilst the heartstrings were torn by the ruthless hand of passion, it seemed as if—when the man had finished speaking—the magic words had already left upon the soul their impress of infinite peace.

And without another word, he went slowly forward and took his place at the table.

At a call from the man, the old woman entered softly, her woollen shoes making no sound upon the wooden floor. She had Nola by the hand who seemed comforted and rested. The praefect beckoned to Folces, who silently obeyed and came forward to the table.

Then the five of them sat down and quietly partook of supper, sitting side by side, the disciple from Judæa and his mother, the two slaves and the praefect of Rome. The Christians sat beside the pagans, the mighty lord beside his slave, and they broke bread and drank wine, all in memory of Him.

CHAPTER XII

"Hell from beneath is moved for thee to meet thee at thy coming."—Isaiah xiv. 9.

I pray you follow me now to an inner chamber in the palace of the mighty Cæsar. A square room with walls of marble inlaid with precious stones, and with hangings of crimson silk to exclude the searching light of day. The air heavy with the fumes of burning incense that wound in spiral curves upwards to the domed roof, and escaped— ethereal and elusive—through the tiny openings practised therein, the seats of gilded wood with downy cushions that seemed to melt at a touch, and in a recess a monumental bed of solid and priceless citrus, carved by the hand of a Greek sculptor, with curtains of purple silk wrought all over with stars.

In vases of delicate murra huge bunches of blood-red roses hung their drooping heads, and beneath the feet carpets of heavy silk hid the exquisite beauty of mosaics of lapis-lazuli and chrysoprase.

And in the midst of all this stately gorgeousness a creature— hardly human—raging round like a thwarted beast.

Caius Julius Cæsar Caligula was in one of his maddest moods; his hollow eyes glowed with unnatural fire, his scanty, light-coloured hair stood up around his head like the bristly mane of a hyena. Up and down the room he stamped with heavy feet; his robe, weighted with precious stones, striking out around him as he trod the smooth surface of silken carpets or the slippery mosaic of the floor. His thin arms and ankles were covered with numerous bracelets and on his feet were shoes studded with diamonds.

At first sight it would indeed have been difficult to say if it was a man or a woman who was thus pacing this magnificent cage, with wild gestures of the arms and hoarse cries that seemed to proceed from no human throat. The face, white and puffy, might have been of either sex, and the flowing garment and wealth of jewellery suggested a woman rather than a man.

The Cæsar was crazy with rage, and all round the room slaves and attendants cowered, terrified. In his hand he had a short whip with five thongs of solid, knotted leather, at the end of each of which was an iron hook. From these five hooks a few drops of blood were trickling down his white silk tunic. At intervals, at the slightest noise or sound from the cowering slaves, he struck out savagely with the whip, and the thongs with their sharp hooks would descend whizzing on some naked shoulder and tear out a piece of flesh and start the flow of a fresh stream of blood.

Then the madman would break out into a diabolical fit of laughter, and strike out with his whip again and again all around him, wildly and indiscriminately, until his garments and his face were spattered all over with blood, and to right and left of him shrieking figures fell fainting to the ground.

The Cæsar was crazy with rage, and he who had thus angered him reclined on a couch, out of the reach of the shrieking demon, and his thin lips were curled in a smile of satisfaction. It was Caius Nepos who was here that he might betray those of his accomplices who had swerved from their allegiance to himself, and behind him—well hidden by the draperies of the couch—cowered Hun Rhavas, the dusky slave of the treasury, he who yesterday had appeared before the tribunal of the praefect of Rome for conspiracy to defraud the State in connection with the sale of the slave-girl Nola.

The law in such matters was severe. It demanded that a delinquent against the State—if he be a slave—shall lose his right hand, or his tongue, or his ears; that he should moreover forfeit his entire hard-saved belongings to the treasury and lose all chance of ever obtaining his freedom. But the praefect had been lenient, and though he could not dismiss the offender, he mitigated his punishment.

Hun Rhavas was publicly scourged and branded, but he lost neither ears, tongue, nor hand, nor was he deprived of the peculium with which ultimately he hoped to purchase his own freedom and that of his children. Yet such was the African's nature, such the result of the training which slavery in the imperial entourage had drilled into him, that Hun Rhavas forgot the clemency and only remembered the punishment.

With bleeding back and mind saturated with hate, he sought audience of the Emperor, and obtained it half an hour after Caius Nepos, the praetorian praefect, had himself been introduced in the presence of Caligula. The story which Hun Rhavas—the paid spy—brought to the ear of Cæsar, was but a confirmation of what Caius Nepos had to tell.

A conspiracy was on foot to murder the father of the armies, the greatest and best of Cæsars. The flower of the Roman patriciate was wallowing in this monstrous treachery. Hortensius Martius was in it up to the neck, so was Marcus Ancyrus, the elder, and Philippus Decius and Philario, of the imperial household.

Hun Rhavas had seen them consorting together and whispering among themselves the day of the sale of the late censor's slaves. He was able to state positively that the praefect of Rome was at one with the band of traitors.

This last fact had brought the frenzied Cæsar to the verge of death. He nearly choked with the violence of his rage. He had believed in the honesty of Taurus Antinor: had even looked on him as a lucky fetish. This man's treachery was more infuriating than that of a thousand others. In the madness of his wrath he would have killed Hun Rhavas with his own hands had not the latter succeeded in hiding himself out of the raving maniac's reach.

Had he dared, Caligula would have tortured Caius Nepos until he too gave him evidence against Taurus Antinor; but on this point the praetorian praefect was guarded. He had not yet made up his mind whether friendship or enmity with the praefect of Rome would be to his own advantage. All that he wanted at this moment was to be rid of those who had opposed him last night for the sake of their own schemes. Therefore in measured words he only spoke of the whisperings which he had overheard in the vestibule of his own house, between a certain band headed by Hortensius Martius and Marcus Ancyrus, the elder.

"During the Circensian games, O Cæsar," he explained, "they hope to raise a tumult amongst the people ... and whilst the attention of thy faithful guard is drawn away from thy sacred person, one of the miscreants is to plunge a dagger in thy throat——"

Here he was forced to silence by a cry like that of a slaughtered ox, which shook the marble pillars of the hall. Caligula had thrown himself upon the bed and was writhing there like a mad beast, biting the coverlets, beating with clenched fists against the woodwork, while foam dripped from the corners of his mouth.

"Tell me more—tell me——" he bellowed at last, during an interval between two of these maniacal spasms.

The slaves all round the room were trembling with fear; Hun Rhavas, huddled under the couch, was shaking like a leaf.

But Caius Nepos, calm and dignified, waited in silence until the paroxysm had abated, then he quietly went on with his tale.

"There is but little else to tell, O Cæsar. I came to warn thee ... for 'tis easy for thee to wear a shirt of mail to cover thy throat and breast against the dagger of assassins. But the conspirators hushed their talk in my presence. I tried to hear more and played the spy in thy service, but my heart was burdened with loyalty for thee, so I came thus early to put thee on thy guard."

The Cæsar had once more resumed his restless walk up and down the room. He was biting his fists, trying to restrain himself from striking the noble informer as brutally as he did his slaves, for he loathed the bearer of evil tidings almost as much as the secret traitors. He suffered from an overwhelming fury of hatred and from an unquenchable thirst for blood.

But three years ago the people and patricians had acclaimed him with shouts and rejoicings; they had feasted in his honour, proclaimed his godhead and his power, and now they were plotting to murder him! The madman threw out his arms in a passionate longing for revenge.

"They would kill me," he cried hoarsely, "kill me!" ... And a demoniacal laugh broke from his swollen throat. He tore the garments from off his chest and buried his nails in his own flesh, whilst roar upon roar of his mad laughter woke the echoes of his stately palace.

Then suddenly the paroxysm died completely down. An unnatural calm succeeded the violent outbursts of rage. Caligula, with a corner of his silken robe, wiped the perspiration from his streaming face. He threw himself on a seat, and resting both elbows on his knees and his chin in his hands, he stared contemplatively before him.

Of a truth this calm seemed even more awe-inspiring than the snarls and cries of a while ago. Caius Nepos' sallow cheeks became still more ashen in colour as he cast a quick glance round the room, feeling perhaps for the first time to-day how completely he was at the mercy of a raving lunatic if the latter should turn against him. But the Cæsar sat there for some time, ruminating, with great hollow eyes fixed on one spot on the ground and gusts of stertorous breathing escaped from his chest.

After a while he spoke:

"Thou didst not tell me yet, O kind friend!" he said dully, "what the traitors mean to do once they have murdered their Cæsar. Whom would they set up as his successor? They cannot all be emperors of Rome. For whose sake then do they intend to commit this damnable treachery?"

"Nay, great Cæsar!" replied Caius Nepos drily, "methinks they all have a desire to become Emperor of Rome, and this being impossible, there was a vast deal of wrangling in my vestibule last night. I caught the purport of several words, and——"

"And of several names?" asked Caligula in the same even voice.

"I heard one name spoken in particular, O Cæsar."

"Tell me."

"That of the Augusta, thy kinswoman," said Caius Nepos, after a slight moment of hesitation.

"Of Dea Flavia?"

"Even hers."

"But she is a woman, and cannot lead an army," said the Emperor, whose voice sounded hollow and distant, as if it came from out the depths of a grave.

"Nor was that suggested, O Cæsar."

"What then?"

"The conspirators, methinks, have agreed amongst themselves that the future husband of Dea Flavia Augusta—whoever he might be—should be the successor of the murdered Cæsar."

"Whoever he might be," repeated the Emperor, mechanically echoing the other's words.

"Aye! The Augusta, I understand, favours no one as yet."

"She hath made no choice ... to thy knowledge?"

"No, no ... her choice was to be made after ... afterwards."

"Her choice to be made by her—or by them?"

"That I know not, great Cæsar. The Augusta, I feel sure, was not a consenting party to the treachery. The traitors would use her for their own ends."

After this there was silence for a while. Caligula still sat staring with wide-open eyes before him, whilst the slaves held their breath, staring fascinated on that terrible whip, lying momentarily forgotten.

Caius Nepos, pale as a withered maple leaf, was from time to time moistening his dry lips with his tongue.

The minutes sped on. Who shall say what fiendish thoughts were coursing through the mad tyrant's brain?

At last he rose, and resumed his walk up and down the room. But no longer did he rave now, no longer did he strike about him like one bereft of reason. His face, though flushed and streaming with perspiration, was set and calm; his footsteps across the carpets were measured and firm. He had cast his whip aside and his hands were clenched behind his back, and on his brow there had appeared a deep furrow, the sign of concentrated thought.

Then at last he paused in his walk and stood in the centre of the room facing the informer.

"I thank thee, good Caius Nepos," he said, "for thy loyalty to me. To-morrow, mayhap, I shall think of a reward in accordance with thy service, but for the nonce I would wish to be alone. I have much to

91

think of. The present crisis demands of me those qualities of courage and of statesmanship for which the citizens of Rome already know me. To-morrow I go to the opening of the games in the Circus. Mayhap there will be a tumult amongst the people, and mayhap a damnable traitor will make an attempt against the sacred life of one who is god and Cæsar and emperor all in one. If all this occurs, and I find that thou didst not lie, then will I give thee such reward as even thou dost not at present dream of. But if between now and to-morrow I find that thou didst lie, that thou didst try to gain my favour and didst rouse my wrath only for the gaining of thine own ends, that thou didst slander Roman patricians with a view to removing thine own personal enemies, then will I devise for thee such punishment that on thy knees wilt beg of death to release thee from torment. And thou didst know, O Caius Nepos, that in the inventing of torture thy Cæsar has the genius of a god."

His voice had become perfectly steady and natural in its tones; all his restless, jerky movements had ceased. Outwardly he seemed to be completely master of himself. But of a truth the aspect of the madman now was more terrible than before. His sallow cheeks were the colour of lead, his pale eyes had narrowed down till they were mere slits through which gleams of deadly hate shot mercilessly on the informer.

Caius Nepos had great difficulty in keeping up an appearance of dignity. It was obviously in his interest to show neither confusion nor fear just now. Nothing but calm demeanour and a proud show of loyalty would ensure his personal safety at this moment. The praetorian praefect knew enough of the imperial despot to appreciate the danger of this outwardly quiet mood, which hid the utter callousness of demoniacal cruelty.

Therefore, in response to the horrible threat, Caius Nepos merely bent his head as if in humble submission to the will of one who was as a god. He felt his teeth chattering against one another, his limbs trembling, his blood frozen within him, and with it all he had the additional horror of knowing that the brutish tyrant was looking him through and through, that he saw the fear in him and was gloating on it with delight.

It was with a feeling of inexpressible relief that he at last understood that he was being dismissed. Steadying his limbs as best he could, he rose from his couch and made obeisance before the Cæsar. Then almost mechanically and like one in a dream, but holding himself erect and composed, he walked backwards out of the room.

The silken curtains weighted with gold fell together with a swishing sound behind him. And even as they did so a loud and prolonged roar of laughter, like that of a hundred demons let loose, echoed throughout the length and breadth of marble halls. Caius Nepos took to his heels and fled like one possessed, with hands pressed to his ears, trying to shut out the awful sounds that pursued him all down the corridors: the shrieks of pain, the whizzing of whipcord through the air, and, rising above all these, that awful laugh which must have found its origin in hell.

CHAPTER XIII

"Can there any good thing come out of Nazareth?"—St. John i. 46.

Dea Flavia was standing beside a tall stool, on the top of which—on a level with her hands—was a shapeless mass of clay. Her fingers buried themselves in the soft substance or ran along the surface, as the exigencies of her task demanded.

Now and then she paused in her work, drew back a step or two from the stool, and with head bent on one side surveyed her work with an anxious frown.

Some few paces from her, at the further end of the room, a young girl sat on an elevated platform, with shoulders bare and head straight and rigid, the model for the proposed statue. Dea Flavia, in a simple garment of soft white stuff falling straight from her shoulders, looked peculiarly young and girlish at this moment, when she was free from all the pomp and paraphernalia of attendants that usually surrounded her wherever she went.

The room in which she indulged her artistic fancy was large and bare, with stuccoed walls on which she herself had thrown quaint and fantastic pictures of goddesses and of beasts, and groups of charioteers and gladiators, drawn with a skilful hand. The room derived its light solely from above, where, through a wide opening in the ceiling, came a peep of cloud-covered sky. There was little or no furniture about, and the floor of iridescent mosaic was innocent of carpet. Only in the corners against the wall stood tall pots of earthenware filled with flowers, with a profusion of late summer lilies and roses and with great branches of leaves on which the coming autumn had already planted its first kiss that turns green to gold.

"Hold thy head up, girl, a little higher," said Dea Flavia impatiently; "thou sittest there like a hideous misshapen bunch of nothing-at-all. Dost think I've paid a high price for thee that thou shouldst go to sleep all day upon that trestle?"

And the girl, roused from semi-somnolence, would pull herself together with a little jerk, would straighten her shoulders and lift her chin, whilst a quickly smothered sigh of weariness would escape her lips.

The air was heavy both within and without, with the presage of a coming storm. It had been terribly hot the last few days. The weather-wise—for there were many such at this time in Rome—had prophesied that Jupiter would send his thunders roaring before very long, and the feeling of thunder in the air caused the model to feel very sleepy, and on the forehead of Dea Flavia beads of perspiration would appear at the roots of tiny fair curls.

She was working with a will but with strange, fretful movements, like one whose mind seems absent from the present task. Short sighs of impatience escaped her parted lips at intervals and a frown appeared and disappeared fitfully between her brows.

"Chin up, girl ... shoulders straight!" came in curt admonitions once or twice to the drowsy model.

Whereupon from the furthest corner of the room Licinia would emerge, rod in hand, to emphasise the necessity of keeping awake when a beloved mistress so desired it.

"Let her be, Licinia," said Dea Flavia with angry impatience when for the fifth time now the model fell in a huddled heap, with nose almost touching her knees, and heavy lids falling over sleepy eyes. "It's no use ... there is something in the air to-day. I cannot work.... Phew!... methinks I feel the approach of thunder."

She threw down her modelling tools with a fretful gesture and then nervily began to destroy her morning's work, patting the clay aimlessly here and there until once more it became a shapeless mass.

"That lazy baggage hath spoilt thy pleasure," said Licinia gruffly; "but I'll teach her——"

"No, no, good Licinia!" interposed the young girl with a weary smile. "Teach her nothing to-day.... The air is too heavy for serious lessons. Send her away and bring me water for my hands."

Then as Licinia—muttering various dark threats—drove the frightened girl before her, Dea Flavia breathed a sigh of relief. Her hands were covered with clay, so she stood quite still waiting for the reappearance of Licinia with the water; and all the while the frown on her face grew darker and the look of trouble in her eyes more pronounced.

Soon the old woman returned with a basin full of water in her hands and a white cloth over her arm. With her wonted loving care she washed Dea's hands between her own and dried them on the towel. Dea allowed her to perform this kindly office for her, standing quite still and gazing absently out into vacancy.

"What can I do now for thee, my precious?" asked Licinia anxiously.

"Nothing, Licinia, nothing," replied Dea with a sigh. "Just leave me in peace.... I have a desire for solitude and silence."

It was the old woman's turn to sigh now, for she did not like this unwonted mood of her beloved. Dea Flavia, when in the privacy of her own house, was always gay and cheerful as a bird, prattling of all sorts of things, telling amusing anecdotes to her old nurse and playing light-heartedly with her young slaves, whenever she was not occupied with her artistic work. This frown upon the smooth, white brow was very unusual, and the fretful, impatient gestures were as unwonted as was that dreamy, absent gaze which spoke of anxious, troubled thoughts.

Dea Flavia herself could not understand her own mood. She could not have confided in the faithful old woman, even had she been so minded, for truly she would not have known what to confide.

Her thoughts worried her. They were so insistent, dwelling obstinately on one moment which had flitted by yesterday—the moment when she stood facing the praefect of Rome, and looking into his deep, dark eyes, which then and there had reminded her of a stormy sea suddenly lulled to rest. It seemed as if nothing now or ever hereafter would chase from her mind the memory of his look and of his rugged voice, softened to infinite gentleness as he said: "I told thee that He died upon the Cross."

She could hear that voice now, even as at this moment from afar a muffled sound of thunder went echoing over the hills, and, strive as she might, wherever she looked her eyes were haunted by the vision which he had conjured up of a man with arms outstretched upon a cross, whose might was yet greater than that of Rome.

At the time she had been greatly angered. The praefect had spoken traitorous words, and she had hated him—she hated him still—for that allegiance which he seemed to have given to another. Then, with a quick, elusive trick, memory showed her the massive shoulders bent humbly at her feet, tying the strings of her shoe—a simple homage due to the daughter of Cæsar—and the sharp pang of wrath once more shot through her heart with the remembrance that he had not deigned to press his lips against her foot.

The man's face and figure haunted her for it was the face and the figure of one whom she had learnt to hate. Yes! She hated him for his treason to Cæsar, for his allegiance to that rebel from Galilee; she hated every word which he had spoken in that arrogant, masterful way of his, when he smiled upon her threats and calmly spoke of immortality. She hated the voice which perpetually rang in her ear, the voice with which he spoke of his own soul being in the keeping of God—of One Whose Empire is mightier than that of Rome.

Yet vaguely still—for she was but a girl—the woman in her was stirred; the power and desire which exists in every woman's soul to conquer that which seems furthest from her reach. She hated the man, and yet within her inmost heart there had sprung the desire to curb and possess his; to disturb the perfect serenity that dwelt in his deep-set eyes, to kindle in them a passion which would make of that proud spirit a mere slave to her will.

There was in her just now nothing but the pagan desire to rule, and to break a heart if need be, if she could not otherwise subdue it.

Memory had fanned her wrath. She saw him now as she had seen him yesterday, arrogantly thwarting her will, his bitter tongue lashing her with irony; and now, as yesterday, the blush of humiliation burned her cheeks, and her pride and dignity rose up in passionate revolt against the one man who had ever defied her and who had proudly proclaimed his allegiance to a man who was not the Cæsar.

That allegiance belonged to Cæsar and to his might alone; beyond that there was the House of Cæsar, and failing that, nothing but rebellious treachery. And the troubled look grew deeper in Dea Flavia's face, and now she buried her hot cheeks in her hands, for the humiliation which she had endured yesterday from one man seemed to shame her even now.

"I'll break thy will," she murmured, whilst angry tears rose, burning, to her eyes. "I'll shame thy manhood and never rest until I see thee crawling—an abject slave—at the feet of Cæsar, who shall kick thee in the face. Cæsar and the House of Cæsar brook no rivalry in the heart of a Roman patrician."

Her hands dropped from before her face. She threw back her head, and looked straight before her into the darkest corner of the room.

"Jesus of Nazareth, he called thee!" she said slowly and as if speaking to an invisible presence. "And he said at thy call he would give up the world, and suffer death and torture and shame for thee!... Then so be it! And I do defy thee, O man of Galilee! even I, Dea Flavia Augusta, of the imperial House of Cæsar! For that man whom I hate and despise, for that man who has defied and shamed me, for that man whose heart and allegiance thou hast filched from Cæsar, for him will I do thee battle ... and that heart will I conquer; and it shall be Cæsar's and mine—mine—for I will break it and crush it first and then wrest it from thee!"

And even as she spoke, from far away over the hills and beyond the Campania the thunder rolled dully in response.

CHAPTER XIV

"Hast thou an arm like God? or canst thou thunder with a voice like him."—Job xl. 9.

A few moments later Licinia came running back into the room.

"Augusta!" she exclaimed excitedly even before she had crossed the threshold. "Augusta! quick! the Cæsar!"

Dea Flavia started, for she had indeed been suddenly awakened from a dream. Slowly, and with eyes still vague and thoughtful, she turned to her slave.

"The Cæsar?" she repeated, whilst a puzzled frown appeared between her brows and the young blood faded from her cheeks. "The Cæsar?"

"Aye," said the old woman hurriedly. "He is in the atrium even now, having just arrived, and his slaves fill the vestibule. He desires speech with thee."

"He does not often come at this hour," said Dea Flavia, whose face had become very white and set at mention of a name which indeed had the power of rousing terror in every heart just now. "Doth he seem angered?" she asked under her breath.

"No, no," said Licinia reassuringly, "how could he be angered against thee, my pet lamb? But come quickly, dear, to thy robing room; what dress wilt put on to greet the Cæsar in?"

"Nay, nay," she said with a tremulous little laugh, "we'll not keep my kinsman waiting. That indeed might anger him. He has been in this room before and hath liked to watch me at my work. Let him come now, an he wills."

Licinia would have protested for she loved to deck her darling out in all the finery that, to her mind, rendered the Augusta more beautiful than a goddess, but there was no time to say anything for even now the Cæsar's voice was heard at the further end of the atrium.

"Do not disturb your mistress. I'll to her myself. Nay! I'll not be announced. 'Tis an informal cousinly visit I am paying her this morning."

"He seemeth in good humour," whispered Dea Flavia, whose little hands were trembling as they made pretence once more of taking up the modelling tools. Licinia hurriedly tried to smooth down the golden hair which had become unruly during the course of the morning, but in her haste only succeeded in completely disarranging it and it fell in wavy masses down the young girl's shoulders, all but one plait which remained fixed over her brow like a wide band of gold.

Dea uttered an exclamation of horror and made a quick gesture, trying to capture the recalcitrant curls, even at the very moment that the Emperor Caligula entered the room.

97

He paused on the threshold and her arms dropped down to her side. Her golden hair fell all round her as she bent her knees making obeisance to the Cæsar. There was nothing regal about her now, nothing imperious or proud; she looked just like a child caught unawares at play.

Blushing with confusion she advanced toward her kinsman, and with head bent received his kiss upon her pure forehead. Nor did she shrink at this loathsome contact which would have filled almost any other woman's heart with horror. To her this man was not really human—he was the Cæsar—a supernatural being blessed by the gods, and endowed by them with supreme majesty and power.

"Dismiss thy slaves," he said curtly, "I would have speech with thee."

He had well schooled his turbulent temper to calmness. After Caius Nepos' departure and a final outburst of unbridled violence, he had plunged into a cold bath and given himself over for half an hour to the ministrations of his slaves. Then, cool and refreshed—at any rate outwardly—he had dressed himself in simple robes, and passing right through the halls of the Palace of Tiberius which adjoined his own, he had reached the precincts of Dea Flavia's house, which in its turn abutted on that built by Germanicus.

At any other time but the present one—when his frenzied mind was wholly given over to thoughts of the terrible treachery against his own person—he would have been conscious of Dea Flavia's exquisite beauty, as she stood before him, humble with the proud humility of one who has everything to give and nothing to receive; chaste with that pure ignorance which refuses to know what it cannot condone, and withal a perfect woman, imbued with a fascination which no man had ever been able to resist, for it was the fascination of youthful loveliness combined with the stately aloofness of conscious power.

At any other time but this, the unscrupulous voluptuary would have gazed on his beautiful kinswoman with eyes that would have shamed her with their undisguised admiration, and mayhap his look and actions would have placed a severe test on her loyalty and on her respect for him.

But to-day Caligula only saw in her the tool whom conspirators meant to use for their treacherous ends, her loveliness paled in his eyes before the awful suspicion which he had of her guilt, and whilst she stood quietly awaiting his pleasure, he marvelled how much she knew of the traitors' plans and whether her white fingers would effectually thrust the dagger into an assassin's hand.

She had dismissed her slaves at his bidding—all unconscious as she was of any danger that might threaten her through him. He waited for a while in silence, then he said abruptly:

"Dea Flavia, what is thine age?"

She looked up at him, smiling and puzzled.

"Some twenty years, great Cæsar," she replied, "but of a truth I had not kept count."

"Twenty years?" he retorted, "then 'tis high time that I chose a husband for thee."

This time she looked up at him boldly, and although in her glance there was all the respect due to the immortal Cæsar, yet was there no show of humility in her attitude as she threw back the heavy masses of her hair and drew up her slender figure to its full stately height.

"Was it to tell me this," she asked simply, "that the greatest of Cæsars sought his servant's house to-day?"

"In part," he rejoined curtly, "and I would hear thine answer."

"My lord has not deigned to ask a question?"

"Art prepared to accept the husband whom I, thine Emperor will choose for thee?"

"In all things do I give thee honour and reverence, O Cæsar," she replied, "but——"

"But what?"

"But I had no thought of marriage."

"No thought of marriage!" he retorted roughly as, unable to sit still, harassed by rage and doubt, he once more started on that restless walk of his up and down the room.

She watched him with great wondering eyes. That something serious lay behind his questionings was of course obvious. He had not paid her this matutinal visit for the sole purpose of passing the time of day; and she did not like this strange mood of his nor his reference to a topic over which he had not worried her hitherto.

In truth the thought of marriage had never entered her head, even though Licinia—with constant garrulousness—had oft made covert allusions to that coming time. She knew—for it had been instilled into her from every side ever since her father had left her under the tutelage of the Cæsar—that she must eventually obey him, if one day he desired that she should marry.

A young patrician girl would never dream of rebellion against the power of a father or a guardian, and when that guardian was the Cæsar himself and the girl was of the imperial house, the very thought of disobedience savoured of sacrilege.

But hitherto that question had loomed ahead in Dea Flavia's dreams of the future only as very shadowy and vague. She had never given a single thought to any of the young men who paid her homage, and their efforts at winning her favours had only caused her to smile.

She had felt herself to be unconquerable, even unattainable, and Caligula, before this mad frenzy had fully seized hold of him, had—in his own brutish way—indulged her in this, allowing her to lead her own life and secretly laughing at the machinations that went on around him to obtain the most coveted matrimonial prize in Rome.

Now suddenly this happy state of things was to come to an end; her freedom, on which she looked as her most precious possession, was to be taken roughly from her. One of the men whom she had despised, one of that set of libertines, of idle voluptuaries who had dangled round her skirts whilst casting covetous eyes upon her fortune, was to become her master, her supreme lord, and she—a slave to his desires and to his passions.

Strangely enough the thought of it just now was peculiarly horrible to her—the thought of what the Cæsar's wish might mean—the inevitableness of it all nauseated her until she felt sick and faint, and the walls of the room began to swing round her so that she had to steady herself on her feet with a mighty effort of will, lest she should fall.

She knew the Cæsar well enough to realise that if he had absolutely set his mind on her marriage nothing would make him swerve from the thought. If he once desired a thing he would never rest night or day until his wish had been fulfilled.

Men and women of Rome knew that. Patricians and plebs, senators and slaves, had died horrible deaths because the Cæsar had demanded and they had merely thought to disobey.

Therefore it was with wide-open, terror-filled eyes that she watched that tyrannical master in his restless walk up and down the room.

Outside greater darkness had gathered, heavy clouds obscured the light, and the gorgeous figure of the Cæsar now and then vanished into the dark angles of the room, reappearing a moment later like some threatening ghoul that comes and goes, blown by the wind which foretells the coming storm.

After a while Caligula paused in his walk and stood close beside her, looking as straight as he could into her pale face.

"No thought of marriage?" he repeated, with one of his mirthless laughs, "no thought, mayhap, of the husband whom I would choose for thee? No doubt there is even now lurking somewhere in this palace a young gallant who alone has the right to aspire to Dea Flavia's grace."

"My lord is pleased to jest," she said coolly, "and knows as well as I do that no patrician can boast of a single favour obtained from me."

"Then 'tis on a slave thou hast chosen to smile," he said roughly.

Then as she did not deign to make reply to this insult, he continued:

"Come! Art mute that thou dost not speak when Cæsar commands?"

"What does my lord wish me to say?"

"Hast a lover, girl?"

"No, my lord."

"Thou liest."

100

"Did I deceive my lord in this, then had I not the courage to look boldly in the Cæsar's face."

"Bah!" he said with a snarl, "I mistrust that maidenly reserve which men call pride, and I, clever coquetry. The women of Rome have realised, fortunately by now, that they are the slaves of their masters, to be bought and sold as he directs. The wife must learn that she is the slave of her husband, the daughter that she belongs to the father; the women of the House of Cæsar that they belong to me."

"It is a hard lesson my lord would teach to one half of his subjects."

"It is," he said with brutal cynicism, "but I like teaching it. I hope to live long enough—nay! I mean to live long enough—to establish a marriage market in Rome, where the lords of the earth can buy what women they want openly, for so many sesterces, as they can their cattle and their pigs."

She recoiled from the man a little at these words and a blush of shame slowly rose to her cheek. But she retorted calmly:

"The gods do speak through Cæsar's mouth and he frames the laws even as they wish."

Her words flattered his egregious vanity which had even as great, if not a greater, hold upon him than his tyrannical temper. He knew that to this proud girl he was as a god, and that her respect for his Cæsarship made her blind to every one of his faults, but this additional simple testimony from her pure lips caused him to relent towards her, and quite instinctively made him curb the violent grossness of his tongue.

"Thou speakest truly, O Dea Flavia," he said complacently. "The gods will, when the time comes, speak through my mouth and make known their will through my dictates even as they have done hitherto— even as they do at this moment when I tell thee that I desire to see thee married."

"My lord hath spoken," she said calmly.

"Do not think, O Dea Flavia," he continued, carried away by his own eloquence, "that I desire aught but thy happiness. If I decide to give thee for wife to a man, it shall only be to one who is worthy of thee in every respect. Thou shalt help me to choose him ... for I have not yet made my choice ... he shall testify before thee as to his nobility and his bravery.... An thou dost assure me that thou hast not yet bestowed thy regard on any man——"

He paused midway in his phrase with indrawn breath, waiting for her reply. She gave it firmly and without hesitation.

"I have cast my eyes on no man, my lord, and have no desire to marry."

"Wouldst consecrate thy virginity to Vesta then?" he asked with a sneer.

"Rather that," she replied, "if my lord would so deign to command."

"Tush!" he broke in impatiently. "Herein thou dost offend the gods and me! 'Tis impious to waste thy beauty in barren singleness; the gods hate the solitary maid unless she be ill-favoured and unpleasing to every man. Thou of the House of Cæsar hast a mission to fulfil and canst not fulfil it thus in isolation, fashioning clay figures that have no life which they can consecrate to Cæsar. But have no fear, for I, thy lord, do watch over thy future—the man whom I will choose for thee will be worthy of thy smiles."

He drew up his misshapen figure to its full height and beamed at the young girl with an expression of paternal benignness. He was delighted with himself, delighted with his own oratory. He was such a born mountebank that he could even act the part of kindness and benevolence, and he acted it at this moment so realistically that the ignorant, confiding girl was taken in by his tricks.

She saw the gracious smile and was too inexperienced, too devoted, to see the hideous leer that he was at pains to conceal.

"The choice will be difficult, gracious lord," she said, feeling somewhat reassured, "and will take some time to make."

"Therefore will I trust to inspiration," he rejoined blandly.

"The gods no doubt will speak when the time comes."

"Aye! They will thunder forth their decree at midday to-morrow," said Caligula, with well-assumed majesty.

"To-morrow, O my lord?"

"Thou hast said it. I have a fancy to make known my decree in this matter during the games at the Circus to-morrow. So put on thy richest gown, O Dea Flavia Augusta," he added with a sneer, "so as to appear pleasing in thy future husband's sight."

"My gracious lord is pleased to jest," she said, all her fears returning to her in a moment with an overwhelming rush that made her sick with horror.

"Jest!" he retorted with a snarl, showing his yellow teeth like a hyena on the prowl, "nay! I never was so earnest in my life. Is not the future of my beloved ward of supreme importance to me?"

"Nay, then, good my lord," she pleaded earnestly, her young voice trembling, her blue eyes fixed appealingly on the callous wretch, "I do beg of thy mightiness to give me time ... to think ... to ..."

"I have done all the thinking," he broke in roughly, "thou hast but to obey."

"Indeed, indeed," she entreated, "I have no wish to disobey ... but my gracious lord ... do I pray thee deign to consider ..."

"Silence, wench!" he shouted, with a violent oath, for what he deemed her resistance was exasperating his fury and reawakened all his former suspicions of her guilt. "Cease thy senseless whining.... I, thine Emperor, have spoken. Let that suffice. Who art thou that I should parley with thee? To-morrow thou'lt go to the Circus. Dost hear? And until then remain on thy knees praying to the gods to pardon thy rebellion against Cæsar."

And with an air which he strove to render majestic he turned on his heel and prepared to go. But in a moment she was down on her knees, her hands clutching his robe. She would not let him go, not now, not yet, whilst she had not exhausted every prayer, every argument, that would soften his heart towards her.

"My gracious lord," she pleaded, whilst her trembling voice was almost choked with sobs, "for pity's sake do hear me! I am not rebellious, nor disobedient to thy will! I am only a humble maid who holds all her happiness from thee! My gracious lord thou art great, and thou art mighty, thou art kind and just. Have mercy on me, for my whole heart is brimming over with loyalty for thee! I am free, and am happy in my freedom; the men who fawn round me, coveting my fortune, fill me with disgust. I could not honour one of them, my lord! I could not give one of them my love. Thou who art so great, must know how I feel. I implore thee leave me my freedom, the most precious boon which I possess, and my lips will sing a pæan of praise to thee for as long as I live."

But Caligula was not the man whom a woman's entreaties would turn from his purpose, more especially when that purpose was his own self-interest. This wretch had no heart within him, no sensibility, not one single feeling of pity or of loyalty.

His instinct must have told him that Dea Flavia was loyal to the core, loyal to the Cæsar and to his House, but so blinded was he by rage and humiliation and by the terror of assassination, that he saw in the earnest, simple pleadings of a young girl and devoted partisan nothing but the obstinate resistance of a would-be traitor.

The more did Dea plead, the more did he become convinced that already her choice of a husband was made, and that that husband was destined to wrench the sceptre of Cæsar from him and to mount Cæsar's throne over his murdered body. With a brutal gesture he pushed the young girl from him.

"Silence!" he shouted, as soon as choking rage enabled him to speak. "Silence, I say! ere I strike thee into eternal dumbness. What I have said, I've said. Dost hear me? To-morrow, at the Circus, I will name thy husband, and then and there thou shalt accept him, whoever he may be. I have a reason for wishing this—a reason of State far beyond the comprehension of a mere fool. To-morrow thou shalt accept the man of my choice as thy future lord. That is my will. Look to it, O daughter of Cæsar, that thou dost obey. Cæsar hath spoken."

"Cæsar hath spoken," she pleaded, "but my gracious lord will relent."

"Dost know me, girl?" he retorted, as, bending down to her, he seized her wrists in his and brought his flushed face all distorted by fury, close to her own. "Dost know me? For if so hast ever seen me relent once I have set my will? Look into my eyes now! Look, I say!" he shouted hoarsely, giving her wrists and arms a brutal wrench. "Do they look as if they meant to relent? Is there anything in my face to lead thee to hope that thou wouldst have thy treacherous way with me?"

He held her wrists so cruelly that she could have screamed with the pain, but she bit her lip to still the cry.

Daylight now was yielding to the oncoming storm. Dense shadows hung all round the room, making the objects in it seem weird and ghost-like in the gloom. Sudden gusts of wind swept angrily round, causing the withered leaves and dying flowers in the vases to murmur with unearthly sounds, as of the sighing of disembodied souls. Only through the aperture above a streak of greyish light struck full upon the Cæsar, as, with glowing eyes and cruel grasp, he compelled her to look on him.

For a moment she closed her eyes after she had looked, for never before had she seen anything so hideous and so evil. His misshapen head looked unnaturally large as it seemed to loom out at her from out the gathering darkness, his hair stood up sparse and harsh all round his forehead. His eyes were protruding and shot through with blood; his lips were dry and cracked, his cheeks of a dull crimson and heavy sweat was pouring down his face.

When she turned away from him in horror, he broke into that wild laugh of his which had in it the very sounds of hell.

"Well!" he said with a leer, "hast seen my face? Art still prepared to disobey?"

"No, my lord," she said slowly, and fixing her eyes fully upon his now, "but I am prepared to die."

"To die? What senseless talk is this?"

"Not senseless, my good lord. Even the gods do allow us poor mortals to find refuge from sorrow in death."

"So!" he said slowly, still gripping her wrists and peering into her face till his scorching breath made her feel sick and faint. "That is the way thou wouldst defy the will of Cæsar? Death, sayest thou?... Death and disobedience—rather than submission to the wish of him who has god-like power on earth. Death!" and he laughed loudly even whilst from afar there came, faint and threatening, the nearer presage of the coming storm. "What death? A pleasing, dreamless sleep brought on by drugs? A soothing draught that lulls even as it kills—or hadst perchance thought of the arena?... of the tiger that roars?... or the lictor's flail that drives?... hadst thought ... hadst thought ..."

He was foaming at the mouth, his rage was choking him; he had only just enough strength left in him to tear at the neck of his tunic, for the next moment he would have fallen, felled like an ox by the power of his own fury. But as soon as he had released Dea Flavia's wrists and she felt herself free to move, she rose from her knees, and with quick, almost mechanical gesture, she rearranged her disordered robe and shook back the heavy masses of her hair. Then she stood quite still, with arms hanging by her side, her head quite erect and her eyes fixed upon that raving monster. When she saw that he had at last regained some semblance of reason she said quite calmly:

"My gracious lord will work his way with his slave, and deal her what death he desires."

"What!" he murmured incoherently, "what didst thou say?"

"'Tis death I choose, my lord," she said simply, "rather than a husband who was not of mine own seeking."

For a moment then she did look death straight and calmly in the face, for it was death that looked on her through those blood-shot eyes. He had thrust his lower jaw forward, his teeth, large and yellow, looked like the fangs of a wolf; stertorous breathing escaped his nostrils, and his distorted fingers were working convulsively, like the claws of a beast when it sees its prey.

Caligula would have strangled her then and there without compunction and without remorse. She had defied him and thwarted him even more completely than she knew herself; and there was no death so cruel that he would not gladly have inflicted upon her then.

"Dost dare to defy me...!" he murmured hoarsely, "hast heard what I threatened ..."

She put out her hand, quietly interrupting him.

"I heard the threat, my lord ... and have no fear," she said.

"No fear of death?"

"None, gracious lord. There is no yoke so heavy as a bond unhallowed. No death so cruel as the breaking of a heart."

There was dead silence in the room now; only from a far distant rolls of ceaseless thunder sent their angry echo through the oppressive air. Caligula was staring at the girl as he would on some unearthly shape. Gasping he had fallen back a few steps, the convulsive twitching of his fingers ceased, his mouth closed with a snap, and great yellow patches appeared upon his purple cheeks.

Then he slowly passed his hand across his streaming forehead, his breathing became slower and more quiet, the heavy lids fell over the protruding eyes.

Caius Julius Cæsar Caligula was no fool. His perceptions, in fact, became remarkably acute where his own interests were at stake, and he had the power of curbing that demoniacal temper of his, even in its maddest moment, if self-advantage suddenly demanded it.

He had formed a plan in his head for the trapping of the unknown man who was to mount the throne of Cæsar over the murdered body of his Emperor. Before dealing with the whole band of traitors he wished to know who it was that meant to reap the greatest benefit by the dastardly conspiracy. There was one man alive in Rome at the present moment who thought to become the successor of

Caligula; that one man would be bold enough to woo and win Dea Flavia for wife.

Caligula's one coherent thought ever since Caius Nepos had betrayed the conspiracy to him, was the desire to know who that man was likely to be. That was the man he most hated—the unknown man. Him he desired to punish in a manner that would make all the others endure agonies of horror ere they in turn met their doom. But his identity was still a mystery. To discover it, the Cæsar had need of the help of this girl who stood there so calmly before him, defying his power and his threats. He looked on her and understanding slowly came to him ... understanding of the woman with whom he had to deal. It dawned upon him in the midst of his tumultuous frenzy that here he had encountered a will that he could never bend to his own—an irresistible force had come in contact with an unbending one. One of the two must yield, and Caligula, staring at the young girl who seemed so fragile that a touch of the hand must break her, knew that it was not she who would ever give in.

His well-matured plan he would not give up. He had thought it all out whilst he refreshed himself in his bath after Caius Nepos' visit, and it was not likely that any woman could, by her obstinate action, move Caligula from his resolve. But obviously he must alter his tactics if he desired Dea Flavia's help. He could gain nothing by her death save momentary satisfaction, and the matter was too important to allow momentary satisfaction to interfere with the delights of future complete revenge.

Therefore he forced himself to some semblance of calm. He was a perfect mountebank, a consummate actor, and now he called to his aid his full powers of deception. Cunning should win the day since rage and coercion had failed.

Slowly his face lost every vestige of anger and sorrowful serenity crept into his eyes. Tottering like one who feels unmanned, he sought the support of a chair and fell sitting into it, with his elbows on his knees and his head buried in his hands.

"Woe is me!" he moaned, "woe to the House of Cæsar when its fairest daughter turns traitor against her kin!"

"I! a traitor, good my lord!" she rejoined quietly. "There is no treachery in my desire to serve Cæsar in single maidenhood, or to offer thee my life rather than my freedom."

"There is black treachery," he said with tremulous voice like one in deep sorrow, "in refusing to obey the Cæsar."

"In this alone——"

But it was his turn now to interrupt her with a quick raising of the hand.

"Aye! That is what the waverer says: 'Good my lord, I'll obey in all save in what doth not please me!' Dea Flavia Augusta, I had thought thee above such monstrous selfishness."

"Selfishness, my lord?"

"Aye! Art thou not of the House of Cæsar? Art thou not my kinswoman? Dost thou not receive at my hands honour, position, everything that places thee above the common herd of humanity? Were I not the Cæsar, where wouldst thou be? Not in this palace surely, not the virtual queen of Rome, but, mayhap, a handmaid to another Cæsar's wife, an attendant on his daughter.... Thou dost seem to have forgot all this, Augusta."

"Nay, gracious lord, I have forgot nothing! Your goodness to me——"

"And yet wouldst deliver me over into the hands of mine enemies," he said with increased dolefulness, "and not raise a finger to save me."

"I would give my life for the Cæsar," she interposed firmly, "and this the Cæsar knows."

"Wouldst not even take a husband, when by so doing thou wouldst save the Cæsar from death."

"My gracious lord speaks in riddles ... I do not understand."

"Didst not understand, girl, that I but wished to test thy loyalty to me? Thou—like so many alas!—dost so oft prate of unbounded attachment to Cæsar. To-day, for the first time, did I put that attachment to the test, and lo! it hath failed me."

"Try me, my lord," she said, "and I'll not fail thee. But give me thy trust as well as thy commands."

She advanced close to where he sat, apparently a broken-down, sorrowful man, stricken with grief. The mighty Cæsar now was far more powerful than he had been a while ago when he raged and stormed and threatened, for he had appealed to the strongest feeling within her—he had appealed to her loyalty.

Slowly she sank once more on her knees, not in entreaty now, not with thoughts of self, but in the humble subjection of herself to the needs of him whom the gods had anointed. She sank upon her knees, and with that simple action she offered her happiness on the altar of her loyalty to him and to her house.

Gone was the look of defiance from her eyes, the pride had vanished and all the joy of life; no thought was left in the young mind now save an overwhelming sense of loyalty, no feeling lingered in the heart save the desire for self-sacrifice.

The Cæsar had commanded and since she could not disobey she was ready to die; memory had in a swift flash called up before her the vision of a man who, rather than yield to her caprice, had smiled at the thought of death. And she, too, had almost smiled, for suddenly she had understood how small a thing was life when slavery became its price.

But now all that had changed. The Cæsar pleaded and made appeal to her loyalty. Her refusal to obey him was no longer pride, it was disloyalty—almost sacrilege. The Cæsar called to her! It was as if the gods had spoken, and she fell on her knees, ready to obey.

The consummate actor was clever enough to hide the triumph that lit up his eyes when he saw her thus kneeling, and understood that she was prepared to yield.

He stretched out a paternal hand, and with weary sadness stroked her golden hair.

"Trust me, gracious lord," she reiterated, "my life is thine, do with it what thou wilt."

"Traitors are at work, Dea Flavia, to murder the Cæsar," he said gently.

"Ye gods!" she murmured, horrified.

"Aye! wouldst think mayhap that the gods will interfere? They will? I tell thee that they will! but they have need of thee, Augusta! I, thy Cæsar, thy god do have need of thee!"

With both hands now he took her own in his, not roughly, but with infinite tenderness, and cunningly contrived that two hot tears should fall upon her fingers.

"My gracious lord!" she whispered, "my life is at thy service."

"Accept the husband whom I propose for thee ... and my life will be safe.... Refuse to obey me in this and to-morrow the blood of Cæsar will be upon thy head...."

"My lord...."

"Wilt obey me, Augusta?"

"My gracious lord ... I do not understand," she pleaded; "have pity on my ignorance ... trust me but a little further...."

"I cannot tell thee more," he said with a sigh of patient weariness, "but this I do tell thee, that my life and with it the future of our House— of the Empire—now lie in thy hands. The abominable traitors would make a tool even of thee. 'The husband of Dea Flavia Augusta,' they say, 'shall succeed the murdered Cæsar!'"

She uttered a cry of horror.

"Their names," she murmured, "tell me their names."

"I know but a few."

"Which are they?"

"They speak of Hortensius Martius."

"Oh!"

"And of young Escanes ... also of Philario, my servant."

"Ye gods," she exclaimed, "let your judgments fall upon them."

"And of Taurus Antinor—the praefect of Rome," added the Cæsar, and a savage snarl escaped his lips even when he spoke the name.

"Taurus Antinor!" she exclaimed.

Then half-audibly she murmured to herself, repeating the Cæsar's words:

"They would make a tool of thee!"

She had fallen back, squatting on her heels, her hands clasped before her and her head sunk upon her bosom, bowed with shame and with horror. Her name had been bandied about by traitors, her person been bought and sold as the price of the blackest sacrilege that had ever disgraced the patriciate of Rome.

"And thou, Taurus Antinor," she whispered inaudibly, "art the blackest traitor amongst them all."

There was no need now for the Cæsar to make further appeal to her loyalty. She was loyal to him—body and soul—loyal to him and to her House, ready to sacrifice her pride, her freedom if need be at a word from the Cæsar, since he had said that by her action on the morrow she could help him fight the treacherous infamy.

Caligula could well be satisfied with his success; nor did he try to press his advantage further. All that he had wanted was the assurance that she would not thwart him when he put into execution the plan which he had conceived. The man-trap which he had set would not now fail through Dea's obstinacy.

He thought that the time had come for ending the interview. He desired that her receptive mind should retain a solemn impression of his majesty and of his power. A charlatan to the last, he now rose to his feet and with outstretched arm pointed upwards to the small glimpse of leaden-covered sky.

"Jove's thunders still speak from afar," he said with slow emphasis, "but to-morrow they will crash over Rome and over the traitors within her walls. The air will be filled with moanings and with gnashing of teeth; the Tiber will run red with blood, for the murdered Cæsar will mayhap be crying vengeance upon the assassins. Wilt save the Cæsar, O Dea Flavia? Wilt save Rome and the Empire from a deadly crime and the devastating vengeance of the outraged gods?"

He towered above her like some inspired prophet, with arms stretched out towards the fast approaching storm, and eyes uplifted to the thunderbolts of Jove.

"I await thine answer," he said, "O daughter of the Cæsars."

"My answer has been given, gracious lord," she murmured, "have I not said that my life was at thy service?"

"Thou'lt obey?"

"Command, O Cæsar!"

"To-morrow at the Circus ... dost understand?... I have a plan ... and thou must obey ... blindly ... dost understand?" he reiterated hoarsely.

"I understand, my lord."

"I'll name thy future husband to the public ... to the plebs ... to all ... and thou'lt accept him—before them all—without demur...."

"As my lord commands."

"This thou dost swear?"

"This do I swear."

"Then," said the mountebank with mock reverence as he placed his hand—blood-stained with the blood of countless innocent victims of his tyranny—upon the bowed head of the loyal girl, "receive the blessing of Jupiter the victorious, of Juno the holy goddess, and of Magna Mater the great Mother, for thou art worthy to be of the House of Cæsar."

But even as the last of these impious words had left his lips, the long awaited storm broke out in sudden fury; a vivid flash of lightning rent the sky from end to end and lit up momentarily every corner of the room, the kneeling figure of Dea Flavia, the misshapen figure of the imperial monster, the fading flowers in the vases. Then a mighty clap of thunder shook the very foundations of Dea Flavia's palace.

Caligula uttered a wild shriek of terror, and, calling loudly for his slaves, he fled incontinently from the room.

CHAPTER XV

"As he that bindeth a stone in a sling, so is he that giveth honour to a fool."—Proverbs xxvi. 8.

From the hour of midnight the streets and ways leading to the great Amphitheatre were alive with people, all tending toward the same goal: men and women in holiday clothes and little children running beside them. The men were heavily loaded with baskets of rush or bags of rough linen containing provisions, for many hours would be spent up there waiting for amusement, whilst the body would grow faint if food were not forthcoming.

So the men carried the provisions which the women had prepared the day before—eggs and cooked fish and such fruit as was cheap this season. And everybody was running, for though the Amphitheatre was vast and could hold—so 'twas said—over two hundred thousand people, yet considerably more than two hundred thousand people desired to be present at the opening of the games.

They were to last thirty-one days and spectacles would be varied and exciting. But the great day would be the opening day, the one on which everybody desired to be inside the Amphitheatre if possible and not outside.

Therefore an early start had to be made. But this nobody minded, as what is the want of a little sleep compared with the likelihood of missing the finest sight that had been witnessed in the city for years?

110

The Cæsar, of course, would be present. He would solemnly declare the games to be open. There were free gifts from him to the people: a thank-offering to the gods for his safe return from that arduous expedition in Germany; and he would show himself to his people, receive their acclamations and give them as much show and gaiety, music and combats, as they cared to see.

So they went in their thousands and their tens of thousands, starting in the middle of the night so as to be there when the great gates were opened, and they would be allowed to pour into the vast enclosure, and find as good seats for themselves and their families as they could.

And when at dawn, the great copper gates did slowly swing open, creaking upon their massive hinges, it was as if the flood-gates of a mighty sea had been suddenly let loose. In they poured, thousands upon thousands of them, scrambling, pushing and jumping, scurrying and hurrying, falling and tumbling, as they pressed onwards through the wide doors and then dispersed in the vastness of the gigantic arena, like ants that scamper away to their heaps.

Like so many pygmies they looked now, fussy and excited, perspiring profusely despite the cool breeze of this early dawn.

Give them half an hour and they'll all settle down, sitting row upon row, tier upon tier of panting, expectant humanity. After much bousculading the strong ones have got to the front rows, the weaker ones up aloft in the rear. But all can see well into the arena, and there are those who think that you get a better view if you sit more aloft; certain it is that you get purer air and something of the shadow of the encircling walls.

There is no sign of cloud or storm to-day. Jove's thunders spent themselves during the morning hours of yesterday when clap upon clap, awe-inspiring and deafening, made every superstitious heart quake with terror at this possible augury of some coming disaster. To-day the sky is clear and—soon after dawn—of that iridescent crystalline blue that lures the eye into myriads and myriads of atoms, the creations of the heat-laden ether that stretches away—far away to the infinite distance beyond.

The beauty of the late summer's day was accepted as a matter of course: as part and parcel of the holidays and festivals ordered by the Cæsar. These too were the people's just dues: emperors had to justify their existence by entertaining their people. Grumblings at their luxury and extravagances were only withheld because of other luxuries and extravagances perpetrated for the amusement of the people.

And from early dawn there was plenty to see. Even though you did not watch the citron-coloured sky overhead as it slowly changed its diaphanous draperies for others that were rose, then crimson, and then gold, finally casting off these two, and showing its blue magnificence unadorned. There were the soldiers on guard at the doors, their yellow

111

helmets shining in the sun, their naked legs bronzed below their tunics. There were the late-comers to watch, those who had not cared for a midnight vigil and were arriving late, like lazy ants creeping to their heaps, finding all places occupied, running hither and thither in search of an empty place.

Then, on the north side there were the tribunals of the senators, the patricians, and the knights, with—in the centre—gorgeous with purple draperies and standards—that which the Cæsar would occupy. Rich stuffs covered with gold embroideries fell over the edge of these tribunes and fluttered lazily in the morning breeze; chairs and cushions were disposed there, and it was interesting to make vague guesses as to who would occupy them.

The Emperor's tribune was decorated with flowers: huge bunches of lilies in pots of earthenware and crimson roses trailed in festoons overhead. There was no doubt that the Augusta Dea Flavia would be present then, lilies were her favourite flowers, they were always to be seen wherever she appeared.

The tribunes of the rich were so disposed that the sun would never shed an unpleasant glare into them, and over that part of the Amphitheatre an awning of white and purple striped stuff threw a pleasing and restful shadow.

Soon after the second hour the spectacle began. Processions of men and beasts who would take part in the combats and the shows. The Numidian lions—in heavy iron cages, drawn by eight pack horses— were snarling as they were dragged along, lean and hungry-looking, with bloodshot eyes that threatened, and dribbling jaws waiting to devour. The pack of hyenas from the desert, a novelty not yet witnessed at the games, the crocodiles from the Nile and the wolves from the Thracian forests.

It was amusing to hear the snarl of the lions and to think of them as they would appear anon pitted one against the other, or engaged in deadly combat against the crocodiles. But still more exciting would it be when the prisoners of war, lately captured in Germany, would have to try their heavy fists against the masters of the desert.

The procession of the beasts had lasted close upon an hour. The public waxed impatient. Beasts were well enough, but their prey was what the people desired to see. Women clamoured as loudly as the men. Children stood up upon the benches to catch sight of the prisoners, the malefactors, the rebellious slaves who would furnish the sport later on.

Presently they began to arrive and were greeted with loud acclamations—trembling, miserable bundles of humanity with hideous death staring at them all round, the pungent odour of wild beasts stinking of death, the glowering eyes of an excited populace testifying that no mercy would be shown.

The slaves mostly looked the prey of abject terror, backboneless, and with the cold sweat already pouring from their huddled-up bodies; they were men caught in the act of murder or of theft, confirmed malefactors most of them, now condemned to the arena to expiate their crimes and afford a holiday for the people.

Some of the most hardened criminals had been dressed up to look like the German rebels whom the Emperor was supposed lately to have vanquished, with tow-coloured wigs and coverings of goatskin around their torso: they were marched round the gigantic arena, with clanging chains on their wrists and ankles.

The public was delighted at their appearance. It confirmed the prowess of the Cæsar, for the men had been selected for this special exhibition because of their height or the breadth of their shoulders. Everyone was curious to see them, and howls of execration greeted them as they passed. It was felt that they deserved far more severe punishment than was meted to ordinary criminals. They had rebelled against the might of Cæsar, and in a manner had made attempt against his sacred life.

But the most interesting part of this early morning show was undoubtedly the black panther whom the native prince of Numidia had sent as a tribute to the imperator. Wild rumours as to its cunning and its ferocity had been in circulation for some time, but no one had ever seen it; it had been kept closely guarded and heavily chained in the gardens of the Cæsar's palace, and since its arrival from the desert was said to have grown to fabulous size and strength.

Its inclusion in the spectacle of to-day had come as an exciting surprise, for it was known that the Cæsar thought a great deal of the beast, going out daily to watch it through its iron bars, and delighting in its ferocity and cruel rapaciousness. He had caused a special house to be built for it in a secluded portion of his garden, with a swimming-bath carved out of a solid block of African marble. Its feeding trough was made of gold, and capons and pea-hens were specially fattened for its delectation.

Many were the tales current about the Cæsar's fondness for the creature and his pleasure in seeing it fed with live animals, which he would himself throw into the cage. It was even said he had fed the brute with human flesh, the flesh of slaves who had disobeyed or merely offended him: one of his chief amusements being to force one of these unfortunate wretches to thrust an arm into the cage, and then to watch the panther as it scrunched the human bones, and licked the human blood whilst cries of unspeakable horror and agony rent the air with their hideous sounds.

And now—in order to delight his people—the greatest and best of Cæsars would grant them the spectacle of his most precious pet. Loud clapping of hands and thunderous shouts of applause greeted the entrance of the magnificent cage which was drawn out into the arena by sixteen negro slaves. The bars of the cage were gilded, and it was

113

surmounted by the imperial standard and the insignia of imperial rank. Its pedestal was of carved wood and mounted on massive wheels of steel. In the front were four heavy chains of steel, and to these the sixteen negroes were harnessed. They were naked save for a loin-cloth of scarlet cloth, and on their heads were fillets of shining metal, each adorned with five long ostrich feathers which had been dipped in brilliant scarlet dye.

The weight of the cage, with its solid pedestal and heavy iron bars, must have been terrific, for the sixteen powerful Africans strained on the chains as they walked, burying their feet in the sand of the arena, their backs bent, the muscles of their shoulders and arms standing out like living cords. In a corner of the cage cowered the powerful creature, its broad, snake-like head thrust forward, its tiny golden eyes fixed before it, a curious snarl—like a grin—now and then contorted the immobility of its powerful jaws. The sinewy tail beat a restless tattoo on the floor of the cage.

Now and then when a jerk on the uneven ground disturbed it from its ominous quietude, the brute would jump up suddenly—quick as the lightning flash—and bound right across the cage, striking out with its huge black paw to where one of the rearmost negro's back appeared temptingly near.

The cunning precision with which that paw hit out exactly between two iron bars highly pleased the public, and once when the mighty claws did reach a back and tore it open from the shoulder to the waist, a wild shout of delight, echoed and re-echoed by thousands upon thousands of throats, shook the very walls of the gigantic Amphitheatre. Children screamed with pleasure, the women applauded rapturously, the men shouted "Habet! habet!" He has it! The unfortunate slave, who, giddy with the loss of blood, rolled inanimate beneath the wheels of the cage.

It was at this moment, when the excited populace went nearly wild with delight, that a loud fanfare of brass trumpets announced the approach of the Cæsar.

He entered his tribune preceded by an escort of his praetorian guard with flying standards. At sight of him the huge audience rose to its feet like one man and cheered him to the echoes, cheered him with just the same shouts as those with which, a few moments ago, it had acclaimed the ferocious prowess of the panther, cheered him with the same shouts with which it would have hailed his death, his assassination, the proclamation of his successor.

He was clad in a tunic of purple silk, wrought with the sun, moon and stars in threads of gold and silver, and on his chest was the breastplate of Augustus, which he had had dug up out of the vault where the great Emperor lay buried. On his head was a diadem of jewels in shape like the rays of the sun standing out all round his misshapen head, and in his hands he carried a gold thunderbolt, emblem of Jove, and a trident emblem of Neptune.

He was surrounded by his own guard, by a company of knights and a group of senators and patricians, and immediately behind him walked his wife, Cæsonia, and his uncle, Claudius, the brother of Germanicus.

He came to the front of the tribune, allowing the populace a full view of his grotesque person, and listening with obvious satisfaction to the applause and the cheers that still rose in ceaseless echoes upwards to the sky.

He did not hear the ironical laughter, nor yet the mocking comments on his appearance, which was more that of a caricature than of a sentient man. He was satisfied that all eyes were turned on himself and on the majestic pomp which surrounded him. The standard-bearers were ordered to wave the flags so that a cloud of purple and gold seemed to be wafted all round his head, and he ordered the Augustas to group themselves around him.

The people watched this pageant as they had done the earlier spectacles. It was all a part of the show stage-managed for their amusement. They were interested to see the Augustas, and those who knew mentioned the various names to their less fortunate neighbours.

"Cæsonia standeth next her lord. She gave him a love potion once, so 'tis said, because his passion for her was quickly on the wane. And 'tis that love potion which hath made him crazy."

"And there are the Cæsar's sisters, Drusilla and Livilla. Drusilla is very beautiful."

"And there is Julia, the daughter of Drusus. She had been willing to step into Cæsonia's shoes."

"But Dea Flavia, daughter of Claudius Octavius, is the most beautiful amongst them all!"

"Hail to Dea Flavia Augusta!" came from more than one enthusiastic throat.

She was clad all in white, with strings of pearls round her neck and a fillet of diamonds in her golden hair. Her face was very pale and her lips never smiled. In her hands she held three tall sprays of lilies scarce whiter than the smooth surface of her brow.

Everyone noticed that the Cæsar specially commanded her to sit on his left, Cæsonia being on his right, and that the Augustas all frowned with dissatisfaction at this signal honour paid to Dea Flavia.

Anon Caius Nepos, the praetorian praefect, came to the front of the tribune, and in stentorian voice commanded everyone to kneel. All those in the tribune did kneel immediately, the guard holding the standards, the senators and the knights. The Augustas all knelt too, and the patricians in the tribunes to right and left. Some of the people knelt, but not by any means all, and Caius Nepos had to repeat his command three or four times, and to threaten the immediate dispersal of the audience and the clearing of the Amphitheatre before everyone at last obeyed.

Caligula alone remained standing, and not far from him the praefect of Rome leaning against the partition wall.

The Cæsar then blessed his people, and at the word of Caius Nepos—the praetorian praefect—cries of "Hail Cæsar! Hail, O God! Hail the Father of the Armies! the greatest and best of Cæsars!" broke out on every side.

CHAPTER XVI

"Who knoweth the spirit of man that goeth upward, and the spirit of the beast that goeth downward to the earth."—Ecclesiastes iii. 21.

Caius Julius Cæsar Caligula was in excellent spirits, smiling and nodding to those around him and to his people all the time. His face certainly looked sallow and his eyes were bloodshot, but this may have been due to ill-health, for without doubt his temper was of the best. Only once had he frowned, when, looking behind him, he saw that the praefect of Rome had remained standing when everyone knelt to acclaim the Cæsar.

But even then the frown was quickly dissipated and he spoke quite pleasantly to the praefect later on. The Augustas grouped around him were continually laughing as he turned to them from time to time with a witty sally, or probably with what was more in keeping with his character—a coarse jest. And he watched the spectacle attentively from end to end. Firstly the play in verse on the subject of the judgment of Paris, a perversion of the legend favoured by the Greeks—a travesty wherein Paris—renamed Parisia—was a woman, and three gods were in rivalry for the golden apple, the emblem of her favours. Then the naval spectacle over the flooded arena, with ships and galleys executing complex manœuvres on waters rendered turbulent by cleverly contrived artificial means; then the wrestling and scenes of hunting with wolves and boars specially brought from the Thracian forests for the occasion.

He watched the Numidian lions tearing one another to pieces, he exulted with the audience over the fight between a pack of hyenas and some crocodiles from the Nile. He encouraged the gladiators in their fights, and joined in the excitement that grew and grew with every item of a programme which had been skilfully arranged so that it began with

116

simple and peaceful shows, and gradually became more bloodthirsty and more fierce.

It seemed as if a cunning mind, alert to the temper of the people, had contrived the entertainment so that with every stage of the proceedings something of the lustful love of cruelty, inherent in every Roman citizen, would be gradually aroused. The hunting scenes were a prelude to the combat between the lions, and these again were the forerunners of a more bloody bout between the hyenas and the crocodiles.

At last blood had begun to flow. The audience sniffed its sickening odour with a thrill of nostril and brain, and tongues and lips became parched with the fever of desire for more.

The other items—the play, the naval pageant, the scenes of hunting and combat of beasts amongst themselves—these were only the prologue. The real spectacle was at last to commence. For this the Romans thirsted—patricians and plebs alike, rich and poor, man, woman and child. These shows were their very life; they constituted the essence of their entire being; for these they rose at midnight and stood waiting, hour upon hour, that they might be near enough to smell the blood when it reddened the sand of the arena, and to see the last throe of agony on the face of those who fell in combat.

"Habet! Habet! Habet!"

The cry became more insistent and more hoarse. See the men and women leaning over the edge of the tribunes, their eyes wide open, their hands outstretched with thumb pointing relentlessly the way of death.

"Habet! Habet!" shrieked the women when a prostrate figure lay writhing on the ground, and the victor with head erect demanded the final verdict.

And up in the imperial tribune the Cæsar jested and laughed, the standards waved above his head, the striped awning threw a cool blue shadow over his gorgeous robes and the jewel-crowned heads of the Augustas.

The rest of the gigantic arena was a blaze of riotous colour now, with the mid-morning's sun darting its rays almost perpendicularly on the south side of the huge oval place. A sea of heads gold and brown, ruddy and black oscillating in unison to right or left like waters driven by the tide, as the combatants down below shifted their ground across the floor of the arena—fans of coloured feathers swinging, mantles caught by a passing breeze, every grain of sand on the floor of the arena a minute mirror radiating the light, everything glowed with an intensity of colour rendered all the more vivid by contrast with the dense shadows thrown against the marble walls.

On the south side every shade of russet and brown and green showed in the mantles and the tunics of the plebs, and seemed flecked with vivid gold under the light of the sun, whilst in the tribunes of the rich on the opposite side cool tones of amethyst and chrysoprase were veiled in tender azure by the shadow from the awning above. And at either end, to east and west the massive copper portals, like gigantic ruddy mirrors threw back these tones of gold and blue as if through a veil of sunset-kissed clouds.

Above, the sky of a vivid blue, translucent and iridescent with a myriad flecks of turquoise and rose and emerald that found their reflections in the marble walls of the arena or the shining helmets of the legionaries guarding the imperial tribune; and over the whole scene an impalpable veil of gold, made of tiny, unseen atoms that danced in the heat, and merged into an exquisite glowing harmony the russets and the purples, the emeralds and rubies and the trenchant notes of sardonyx and indigo that cut across the orgy of colour like a deep, gaping wound.

And through it all that sense of thrilling expectancy, so keen that it almost seemed palpable.

It vibrated in the air making every cheek glow with a crimson fire and kindling a light in every eye. It seemed to set every golden atom dancing, it was felt through every breath drawn by two hundred thousand throats.

Over the Emperor's head the striped awning flapped weirdly in the breeze, with strange insistent sound like the knocking of a ghostly hand upon the doors of hell.

Not a few miserable wretches whom the summary justice of the Cæsar's own tribunal had condemned to death were exposed to a band of swordsmen—executioners really, since the fight was quite unequal. Huge African giants with short naked swords pursuing a few emaciated wretches who ran howling round the arena, jumping improvised hurdles, rounding obstacles or crawling under cover, running, running with that unreasoning instinct of self-preservation which drives even before the certainty of death.

A hunting scene this, of novel diversion.

No one cared whether the victims were really guilty of crime, no one cared if they had been equitably tried and been justly condemned, all that the public cared about was that the spectacle was new and amusing. The African giants were well-trained for their part, playing with the miserable victims like 'a feline doth with its prey, allowing them to escape, now and then, to see safety close at hand, to make a wild dash for what looked like freedom, and then suddenly bounding on them with that short wide sword that cried death as it descended.

Rapturous applause greeted this show, and loud immoderate laughter hailed the fruitless efforts of the hunted, their falls over the obstacles, their look of horror, and the contortions of their meagre bodies when they were caught at last.

"Habet! Habet! Habet!" everyone shouted when one of the unfortunate wretches brought to bay tried to turn on his pursuer, and to pit two feeble arms against the relentless grip of well-trained giants, and against the death-dealing sword.

"Habet! Habet! Habet!"

"He has it!" they screamed. He has the hideous death, the gaping wound in the still panting chest. He has the final agony which helps to make a holiday for the great citizens of the world.

Now at last the sand of the arena has turned red with blood, the sickly odour mounts to every nostril; shrieks become more wild, like those of thousands of demons let loose. Anticipation and desire has been brought to its wildest pitch, and Caligula has every cause to be satisfied.

Cries of "The lions! the lions! Slaves to the lions!" resounded from every side. Thousands of feet beat a tattoo on the floor, and from behind the great copper gates a mighty roar filled the heat-laden air with its awesome echo.

In his gilded cage supported by carved pillars and drawn by eight Ethiopian slaves, the favourite of Caligula was slowly wheeled into the arena.

A huge sigh rose from every breast. The tumult was hushed; dead silence fell upon the vast concourse of people suddenly turned to stone, alive only by two hundred thousand pairs of eyes fixed upon the cage and its occupant.

The black panther—with its sleek black coat on which the midday sun threw tiny blotches of tawny lights—was cowering in a corner of its cage; its snake-like head, with the broad flat brow and wide curved jaws, was drawn back between its shoulders, its small golden eyes, gleaming like yellow topaz, were half closed in wary somnolence.

Slowly the cage was wheeled round by the panting negro slaves, and then it was brought to a standstill against the copper gates at the eastern end of the arena.

CHAPTER XVII

"Be thou faithful unto death."—Revelations ii. 10.

Up in the gorgeously draped tribune, beneath the striped awning, the Emperor Caligula watched the arrival of his pet panther with a grin of delight upon his face. He rubbed his hands together in obvious glee, and anon pointed out the beauty of the ferocious creature to the Augusta Dea Flavia, who coldly nodded in response.

She had sat beside the Cæsar all through the long, weary

119

morning, giving but few signs of life. Many there were who thought that, overcome with drowsiness owing to the heat, she had fallen asleep with her head buried in the fragrant depths of the lilies which she held.

Certain it is that throughout the spectacle she had kept her eyes closed, and when death-cries filled the air with their terrible echo, she had once or twice put her small hands to her ears.

Whenever she had done that the Cæsar had laughed, and apparently made jest of her with the other Augustas who, in their turn, appeared greatly amused.

The spectacle indeed had been somewhat tame, and but for the human chase of a while ago, would have been intolerably dull. There was surely nothing in the death of a few miserable slaves to upset the nerves of a Roman princess. As for the gladiators! well! they were trained and well paid to die.

Not far from the Cæsar's person, and leaning against the wall of the tribune in his wonted attitude, the praefect of Rome had also stood silently by. The Emperor had ordered his presence, nor could the praefect of the city be absent when the sacred person of the Cæsar was abroad amongst his people.

But no one could say whether the Anglicanus had seen or heard anything of what went on around him. His eyes of a truth were wide open, but they did not gaze down upon the arena; they were hidden by that dark frown upon his brow, and no one could guess whereon was his ardent gaze so resolutely fixed, no one could guess that from where he stood Taurus Antinor could perceive the outline of a delicate profile, with the softly rounded cheek, and a tiny shell-like ear half hidden by the filmy veil of curls.

He could see the lids with their fringe of golden lashes fall wearily over the eyes, he could trace the shudder of horror which shook the slender figure from time to time.

Once the lilies dropped from Dea Flavia's hand, and the soft swishing sound which they made in falling caused her to wake as from a reverie. She looked all round her with wide-open eyes, and her glance suddenly encountered those of the praefect of Rome. It seemed to him that her very soul was in her eyes then, a soul which at that moment appeared full of horror at all that she had seen.

But as quickly as she had thus involuntarily revealed her soul, so did she conceal it again beneath her favoured veil of unbendable pride. She frowned on him as if angered that he should have surprised a secret, and almost it seemed then that she flashed on him a look of hatred and contempt.

After that she turned away, and with her foot kicked away the fallen lilies. She sat now leaning forward, motionless and still, with her elbows buried in an embroidered cushion before her and her chin resting on her hands.

Oh! if he only could, how gladly would he have seized her even now and carried her away from this nauseating scene of bloodshed and cruelty. He crossed his arms over his powerful chest till every muscle seemed to crack with the effort of self-control. His very soul longed to take her away, his sinews ached with the desire to seize her and to bear her in his arms away, away beyond the cruel encircling walls of Rome, away from her marble palaces and temple-crowned hills, away over the marshes of the Campania and the belt of the blue sea beyond to that far-off land of Galilee where he himself had found happiness and peace.

The Cæsar had commanded his presence here to-day, and he had come because the Cæsar had commanded. To the last he would render unto Cæsar that which was Cæsar's. But he had stood by with eyes that only saw a golden head crowned with diamonds, a delicate oval cheek coloured like a peach and tiny fleecy curls that fluttered softly in the breeze.

There was no longer any sorrow in his heart, no longer any remorse or thought of treachery. The man in the little hut on the Aventine had shown him the way how to lay down his burden of weakness and of sin.

He knew that he loved Dea Flavia with all the ardour of an untamed heart that has never before tasted the sweetness of love. He knew that he loved her with all the passion of a soul that at last hath found a mate. But now he knew also that in this love there was no thought of treachery to Him in Whose service he was prepared to lay down his life. He knew that never again would the exquisite vision of this fair young pagan stand between him and the Cross, but rather that she would point to him—ignorantly and unconsciously—the way up to Golgotha.

For renunciation awaited him—that also did he know. A few more days in the service of the Cæsar, and his promise to remain in Rome would no longer bind him, since Caligula had returned from abroad.

The rest of his life was at the bidding of Him Who mutely from the Cross had demanded his allegiance: a lonely hut somewhere on the Campania, or further if God demanded it, a life of strenuous effort to win souls for Christ, and the renunciation of all that had made life easy and pleasant hitherto. God alone knew how easy that would have been to him forty-eight hours ago. Taurus Antinor hated and despised the life of Rome, the tyranny of a demented Cæsar, the indolence of the daily routine, the ever-recurrent spectacles of hideous, inhuman cruelty. Until that midday hour in the Forum four days ago, he had viewed his new prospective life with a sense of infinite relief.

But now renunciation meant something more. Detachment from Rome and all its pomps, its glories, and its cruelties meant also detachment from the presence of Dea Flavia. It meant the tearing out of his very heartstrings which had found root at a woman's feet. It meant the drawing of an impenetrable veil between life itself and all that henceforth could alone make life dear.

He had dreamed a dream, the exquisite beauty of which had wrought havoc in his innermost soul, but the awakening had come before the glorious dream had found its complete birth. Jesus of Nazareth had called to him from the Cross, but even as He called, the pierced, sacred hand had pointed to the broad path strewn with gold and roses, filled with the fragrance of lilies and thrilled with the song of mating birds: and the dying voice had gently murmured: "Choose!"

The soldier had chosen and was ready to go. But renunciation was not to be the easy turning away from a road that was none too dear—it was to be a sacrifice!—the taking up of the cross and the slow, weary mounting up, up to Calvary, with aching back and sweating brow and the dreary tragedy of utter loneliness.

It meant the giving up of every delight of manhood, of happiness in a woman's smile, of rapture in a woman's kiss. It meant the giving up of every joy in seeing her pass before him, of hearing the swish of her skirts on the pavement of the city; it meant the giving up of all hope ever to win her, of all thought of a future home, the patter of children's feet, the rocking of a tiny cradle. It meant the sacrifice of every thought of happiness and of every desire of body and of soul.

It meant the nailing of a heart to the foot of a cross.

CHAPTER XVIII

"So I gave them up unto their own heart's lust: and they walked in their own counsels."—Psalms lxxxi. 12.

In the meanwhile the stage-hands, the smiths and carpenters had been busily at work, setting the scene for the coming drama.

Huge gnarled tree-trunks were dragged into the arena, and so disposed as to afford shelter either for man or beast. By a mechanical device a stream of water some six foot wide was made to wind its course along the sands, and groups of tall reeds and other aquatic plants were skilfully arranged beside the banks of this improvised stream.

Soon the whole aspect of the arena was thus transformed into an open piece of country with trees here and there, and tufts of grass, mounds and monticules, with a stream and a reed-covered shore. The whole beautifully arranged and with due regard for realism.

The people watched, highly pleased; now that the Emperor's pet panther had appeared they were satisfied that a spectacle such as they loved was about to be unfolded before them.

But soon the workmen were engaged on other work, the purport of which could not at first be guessed. To understand it at all a vivid picture of the huge arena must appear before the mind.

Down below there was the artificial landscape, the trees, the stream, the sand and grass, and all around the massive marble walls rose to a height of some twelve feet to the lowest tier of the tribunes, beyond which sat row upon row in precipitous gradients two hundred thousand spectators.

At about four feet from the ground a narrow ledge—formed by the elaborate carving in the solid marble—ran right along the walls, and between this ledge and the top of the wall there was a low colonnaded arcade with deep niches set between the fluted columns.

From these niches the workmen now suspended short ladders of twisted crimson silk, of sufficient strength to bear the weight of a man. They affixed these to heavy steel rings imbedded in the bases of the columns, and when the ladders were in position, they hung down low enough, that a man—standing on the ledge below—could just contrive to seize the ends and to swing himself aloft, up into the niche.

The public watched these preparations with breathless interest, for soon their objects became evident. It was clear that those who were to be exposed to an encounter with the panther would be given a fair chance of escape. It was to be an even fight between man and beast.

A man hotly pursued by the brute could—if he were sufficiently agile—leap upon the narrow ledge, seize the rope-ladder and climb up it until he reached the safe haven of the niche, and could draw the ladder in after him. And fear of death doth lend a man wondrous agility.

It looked in fact as if the coming struggle were all to be in favour of the man and not of the beast, for the smooth surface of the walls and the narrow ledge above the carvings could not afford foothold to an enraged four-footed creature with sharp claws that would glance off the polished marble.

The public—realising this—waxed impatient. The novel spectacle did not, after all, promise to be to its liking. The panther would make but a sorry show if it was not given a helpless victim or two to devour.

Murmurs of dissatisfaction rose from every side as the work proceeded, and anon when all round the walls of the arena, the twelve ladders of safety were firmly fixed, seeming mutely to deride the excitement of the people, the murmur broke into angry cries.

But Caligula did not seem to heed either the murmur or those loud expressions of discontent which, at other times, would probably have maddened him with rage. He had watched the preparations with eager interest and had himself once or twice shouted directions to the workmen.

Now, when everything appeared complete, he turned to the tribune which was next to his own, and his small bloodshot eyes wandered over the assembly of patricians, of knights and of senators who were seated there.

He called my lord Hortensius Martius to him and appeared to be pointing out to him the advantages of the rope-ladders with obvious pride in the ingenuity of the device. Young Escanes too was bidden to admire the contrivance, which—it soon became evident—was the invention of the Cæsar himself.

The public—still feeling dissatisfied—watched desultorily for a while the doings in the imperial tribune. Then general interest was once more aroused, when the workmen—slaves and legionaries—having finished their preparations, hurried helter-skelter out of the arena.

The sliding doors of the panther's cage were being slowly drawn away.

For a few seconds the powerful brute remained wary, silent and cowering, then with one mighty, savage snarl it bounded into the arena.

Supple, graceful and splendid it walked round in solemn majesty, its flat head kept low to the ground, its sinuous body curving and winding as it walked, like that of a snake.

The public watched it, fascinated by the perfect grace of its movements and by the cruel ferocity of its tiny eyes.

Now at the eastern end of the Amphitheatre a small iron gate slowly swung upon its hinges, and in the dark recess beyond it a couple of men appeared. For a moment they stood there immovable, a closely huddled mass, shoulder to shoulder, with round open eyes dilated with fear and a cry of nameless terror still hovering unuttered on their lips.

They were hugely built men, with massive torso and legs bare, and tow-coloured hair brought straight up to the crown of the head and knotted there with a black band.

There was much shouting from the recess whence they had emerged, and anon some vigorous prodding and pushing from behind. But they dug their bare feet into the sand, refusing to move; arm against arm they made of themselves a wall which fear of death kept rigid and horror made unbreakable.

The public greeted them with mock applause. In them they had quickly recognised the German barbarians whom the Cæsar had brought back from his last expedition as prisoners of war; in truth they were hardened malefactors who had been offered a chance of life in exchange for the pitiable masquerade. But this the public did not know. To the two hundred thousand holiday-makers, craning their necks to see the miserable wretches, they were but the living proofs of the Cæsar's prowess in the field. With ironical cheers they were bidden to advance, even whilst at no great distance from them the black panther

124

sitting on its haunches was surveying them with lazy curiosity, licking its mighty jaws.

Then the public grew impatient, and from the recess behind the two men persuasion became more vigorous. Through the darkness behind the gates there appeared the red glow of a brazier, there was a quick hissing sound, an awful double howl of pain and the smell of burnt flesh filled the air. The next moment the two men fell scrambling forward into the arena, and the iron gate closed behind them with a thud.

CHAPTER XIX

*"Thou art become guilty in the blood that thou hast shed."—
Ezekiel xxii. 4.*

The hunter and the hunted! the lithe supple sinewy creature crawling with belly almost touching the ground and stealthy steps that made no sound on the sand of the arena.

Wary and silent the black beast crawled, now hiding amidst the scrubby grass, now bounding over trees and stream as if playing with herself, with her own desire for a taste of human blood.

At first terror had kept the two men rooted to the spot, paralysed, and with feet deeply imbedded in the sand. Only their eyes seemed alive, roaming along the wall, all round to where on either side the silken ladders made vivid crimson streaks on the white smoothness of the marble.

The panther waiting, watched them till they moved. The public, entranced, scarcely dared to draw breath.

Then came a sudden cry from thousands of throats; the two men, as if driven by a sudden sense of approaching death, had made a quick desperate rush, one to the right the other to the left, towards the crimson silk which meant safety to them.

But the panther was on guard and quicker twice than they. It seemed as if the brute had divined exactly where lay escape for its prey. It was guarding both sides of the arena at once, bounding from left to right, and back from right to left with giant leaps, soundless and swift.

The men paused again, because it seemed that when they were still, the panther too lay still and watched.

There was another lull, and from the imperial tribune above Dea Flavia watched the horrible spectacle, and Taurus Antinor drank into

125

his soul the beauty of her eyes as they watched—fascinated—every movement of the sleek black panther, and of those fair-skinned giants trying to escape from death; she watched the stealthy approach of the beast toward its prey; she watched, motionless and still, the while great beads of perspiration matted the fair curls on her brow.

And to the man who loved her, and who saw her thus watching the horrible spectacle which must have made her feel sick and faint, to him it seemed as if in her mind the hideous sight meant something more than just the brutal display of cruelty which was a familiar one enough in Rome.

It seemed as if to her some hidden meaning lay in this teasing of a ferocious brute, and in this apparent clemency in allowing the victims a chance of escape, for every now and then she turned as if involuntarily toward the Cæsar, and a quick glance of understanding seemed to pass between her and that inhuman monster.

Taurus Antinor, with his gaze fixed upon her every movement, wondered what all that could mean.

After a quarter of an hour of tense excitement, of alternate cries of horror and screams of delight, the two men had, by dint of cunning and agility, succeeded in evading the panther. They were safe within the protecting niches; the panther down below was roaring with baffled rage, and the public clapped and cheered vociferously.

Two more men were thrust into the arena, dressed in the same way as the others, pushed forward like the others to the accompaniment of a brazier's glow and the smell of burnt flesh.

The panther, more wary this time, did not allow both men to escape. Yet they had made a clever dash for safety; one of them was already swinging himself aloft, but the other had missed his footing once, when he jumped upon the ledge; he regained it and seized the swinging end of the ladder, but the panther, with a bound, had reached him and caught his foot in its jaws.

That hideous noise—the scrunching of a human bone—was drowned in tumultuous applause as the miserable wretch with the maimed and bleeding leg, but with that almighty instinct for life at any cost, toiled mangled and bleeding up that ladder less crimson than the trail which he left in his wake.

Dea Flavia's head fell forward on the cushion. But she fought against the swoon. The ironical laughter of the Augustas round her quickly brought her to herself.

"The heat is overpowering," she said calmly in reply to a coarse comment from the Cæsar.

CHAPTER XX

"His blood shall be on our head, if any hand be upon him."—
Joshua ii. 19.

The heat was intense! The glare from the tribunes opposite seemed to sear the eyes, and from below there rose to the nostrils that awful sickening stench of human blood.

The public, frantic with excitement, was clapping and cheering; thousands of necks were craned to get a better view into the floor of the arena, thousands of fans were fluttering, children were laughing and women chattered incessantly, like a pack of monkeys.

And down below the baffled panther sent roar upon roar of rage into the seething cauldron of a thousand sounds.

The creature had been cheated to the last; a score of victims had been pushed into his lair to tempt him. He had stalked them in play at first, then more earnestly, finally with a mad desire for blood. But always his prey escaped him, invisible hands showed the means of escape; the crimson ladders seemed to multiply their numbers until all round the walls they showed innumerable paths to safety.

The panther seemed to know that those streaks of crimson were his mute enemies. He made several ineffectual dashes for them, but always his claws slid against the marble, and he fell back into the sand, snarling with rage.

Once or twice his prey was more attainable. He caught a foot, a leg, a hand; thrice he brought a huge, panting body to the ground, but even then he was cheated of his victory. Long iron grapnels, wielded by unseen hands, dragged the mangled limbs and torn bodies roughly from his clutch, leaving behind them trails of torn flesh and streams of blood, which only helped to exasperate the beast by their insufficiency.

And now the panther was like a black, snake-like fury, blind with rage and unsatisfied lust, with tail lashing like a whipcord and yellow eyes that gleamed like tiny suns. His jaws were red and dripping, his claws had been torn by the same grapnels that had snatched his prey from him.

He had ceased to roar, but snarl upon snarl escaped his panting throat. The public delighted in him. They loved to see the ferocious brute maddened by these tortures, beside which the agony of Tantalus was but the misery of a child.

Then Caligula rose to his feet and his heralds blew loud blasts upon their trumpets. In a moment silence fell on the entire arena; the pandemonium of shouts and laughter and shrieks of agony was hushed as if by the magic of an almighty power.

The Emperor was standing and desired speech, and all at once silence descended upon this vast concourse of people. Everyone rose, since the Cæsar was standing; all heads were turned towards the tribune, all eyes fixed upon the misshapen figure with its halo of gold round the grotesque head, and the metal thunderbolts held aloft in the hand.

The only sound that was not stilled at the Cæsar's bidding was—down below—the snarl of the angry panther.

"Citizens of Rome," began Caligula, as soon as he could make himself heard, "patricians of Rome! soldiers! senators! all my people! I—even I—your Cæsar, your Emperor, your god, do give you greeting! I have sought to please you and to make you happy on this my first day amongst you all."

Here he was interrupted by vociferous cheering. Next to shows and spectacles, to games and theatres, there was nothing that the people of Rome loved better than to hear impassioned speeches thundered at them either from the rostra in the Forum, or from any convenient spot whence the voice of a good speaker would rouse a sense of excitement or elation in their hearts. Demagogues and agitators, rhetoricians and poets were all sure of a hearing, if only they were sufficiently inspired and sufficiently eloquent. But it was not often that the Cæsar himself would pour forth imperial oratory into the delighted ears of his people, and a fervent speech from the Emperor at this moment, when excitement and exhilaration were at fever-pitch, was a pleasure which no one had foreseen but which filled everyone with delight.

"Glad am I," continued Caligula, when the excitement had calmed down momentarily, "that my efforts to please you have met with success."

"They have! They have!" yelled the enthusiastic crowd.

"The gods have indeed rewarded me—not beyond my deserts, for that were impossible—but in a just measure, by giving me the love of my people."

"Hail Cæsar! Hail the greatest and best of Cæsars!" came in deafening echoes from every side of the immense Amphitheatre.

"I thank you all! Your loyalty to-day has greatly cheered me. I—as your supreme lord and god—will shower my blessings upon you. As a god I am immortal; always I will watch over you, sitting at the right hand of Jupiter Victor, my father, from all times. But in my earthly shape I may not be with you always. There may come a time when god-like duties call me to Olympus. Then must a wise and just ruler take my place at the head of this great Empire."

"No! no! Hail to thee Cæsar! Immortal Cæsar!" cried the people, and Caligula, stricken with vanity as if with plague, was deaf to the ironical cheers that accompanied these cries.

128

"Immortal am I," he said, whilst his bloodshot eyes travelled restlessly over the sea of faces spread out before him. "Immortal, yet destined to leave you one day. When that day comes, there will be weeping in the city and moanings throughout the Empire, but the wise and just ruler who will follow in my wake will—while not able to console you for my loss—continue the good works which I have commenced. Citizens of Rome, patricians, soldiers, all listen to what I say."

His face now looked purple with excitement, his hoarse voice shook as it escaped his throat, and his hair, thin and lanky, seemed to stand upon end all round his large, bulging forehead.

A gentle breeze had caught the folds of his purple tunic, and it fluttered all round him with a curious swishing noise, like the sighing of creatures in pain.

The hand that held Jove's thunderbolt trembled visibly, and the perspiration was streaming down his face. There was not a man or woman present there at this moment who did not look upon him as an abject and hideous monster, there was no one there who did not loathe and despise him! And yet everyone listened, and not one voice was raised in derision at his senseless oratory.

Only the panther snarled, and its tail beat against the ground with a dull, monotonous sound.

And Dea Flavia, standing beside the monster, white as the lilies which now lay withered at her feet, listened to every word that he said, whilst Taurus Antinor gazed on her and saw again in her eyes that look of anticipation and of understanding, as of one who knows what is to come.

"Citizens of Rome," resumed the imperial mountebank after an impressive pause, "I have spent days and nights in communion with the gods, thinking of your welfare—of your welfare when I no longer will be amongst you all. And this is what I and the gods have decided. Listen to me, for the gods speak to you through my mouth—I, even I, your Cæsar and your god, do speak.

"There dwells amongst us all one whose divinity is almost equal to mine own—one who by her beauty and her grace hath found favour with the gods and with me. She is of the House of Cæsar, and hath name Dea Flavia; and I, the Cæsar, have called her Augusta, and set her up above all other women in Rome. She comes from the House of great Augustus himself, and it is a descendant of the great Augustus who alone will be worthy to wield the sceptre of Cæsar when it hath fallen from my grasp. Therefore this have I decided. The son of Dea Flavia shall in time to come follow in my footsteps, and make you happy and prosperous even as I have done; and because of this my decision must I give Dea Flavia as wife unto a man who is worthy of her. Many there are who have aspired to her hand, but all of them have I hitherto

129

rejected, because not one of them had given proof of his courage or of his strength. Citizens of Rome, patricians, and soldiers all! What we must look for in your future ruler is valour in the face of death, coolness and intrepidity in the sight of danger. These qualities, which grace your present Cæsar, must be transmitted to his successor through Dea Flavia, the divine, and by a father who has given signal proof of his virtues. I have enjoined the Augusta Dea Flavia to bestow her hand on him who above all is worthy to be her lord. To this has she consented and to-day will she make her choice, and herewith do I call on you patricians who aspire to her hand to enter the lists in her honour. Give a proof of your valour, of your intrepidity, of your courage! Show that you are as valiant as the lion, as wary as the snake. Descend into the arena now, unarmed save for the hands which the gods have given you, and thus engage that unconquered monster in single combat! An even chance of life is given you! And I—even I your Cæsar—will give unto the victor the hand of the Augusta Dea Flavia in marriage!"

Even before his last words had echoed along the marble walls, deafening cries and cheers rent the air. Men shouted, women screamed and waved their fans, mantles were torn from every shoulder and swung overhead like flags.

"Hail to Cæsar! Hail to the best and greatest of Cæsars! Hail to the Augusta! Dea Flavia, hail!"

The shouts were incessant, even whilst Caligula, delighted with his oratory, exultant over the success of his plan, stood there trembling in every limb, with moist, purple face turned from right to left to receive the acclamations of his people. His tiny eyes blinked with the glare that struck fully at them from opposite, his throat was parched with screaming, his tongue seemed to cleave to the roof of his mouth.

Excitement was overmastering him; the effort to appear outwardly sane and calm was too severe a tax upon his raging temper. The heat, too, no doubt turned him giddy, for suddenly, even whilst the cries of "Hail!" buzzed in his ears, he threw up his arms and tottered backwards, rigid as a log, whilst drops of foam gathered at the corners of his mouth.

It was Taurus Antinor who received the swooning Cæsar in his strong arms. Everyone else around was too excited to move. The Augustas, inwardly consumed with jealousy, were striving to keep up an appearance of dignity in the face of the insult which they deemed had been put upon them by this semi-deification of their kinswoman.

Dea Flavia, pale and silent, stood facing the people, with eyes that seemed to look on something unearthly far away. Her white robes, shimmering with precious stones, fell round her like a shroud, her lips were parted as with a cry that had died even before it had found birth in her throat. The public thought that she looked proud, and acclaimed her because of this strange aloofness which seemed to envelop her whole person. She did not look of this world at all. Even the eyes appeared sightless and dead.

When the Cæsar fell back, half fainting, she seemed to wake from her dream, a shudder went right through her as her eyes slowly turned from their vacant gaze to the prostrate figure of this inhuman monster, lying stricken like a felled brute, in the arms of the praefect of Rome.

Once again, and for the third time to-day, her eyes met those of Taurus Antinor, but this time it seemed to him that within their still mysterious depths he read something akin to an appeal.

As on that day in the Forum, intense pity—which had given birth to love—filled his heart for this beautiful young girl who seemed so lonely in the midst of all this pomp.

The purity of her soul appeared to him undimmed, even though he knew now that she had expected this awful thing all along, and that she was no stranger to this monstrous barter of her person for the attainment of a crazy Emperor's whim, or to make holiday for the rabble of Rome. In his sight her pride remained unshaken; only her loyalty and allegiance had been given to the Cæsar in the same way as his own had been. She, in her simple, womanly way, was rendering unto Cæsar that which was Cæsar's, and Taurus Antinor, whilst tenderly pitying her, felt that he had never loved her as fondly as he did now.

The curse of the dying freedwoman was indeed bearing fruit. Dea's favours, her loyalty, were turning to bitter malediction for the recipients. More than one man to-day, mayhap, would die an horrible death in the hope of winning her grace. And Taurus Antinor, in the silent depths of his soul, prayed unto God that the woman he loved should never—as Menecreta had foretold—be driven to beg for mercy from a heart that knew it not and find a pitiless ear turned to her prayers.

Caligula had quickly shaken himself free from the arms that held him. The fainting fit which had threatened him passed away as swiftly as it had come. His lust of hate and revenge was so keen at this moment that it conquered all his physical weakness. When he realised that it was Taurus Antinor who was supporting him, he contrived to smile benignly and placidly upon him.

"I am well! I am well!" he reiterated cheerfully. "Did my voice carry all over the Amphitheatre? Did everyone hear what I said?"

"Everyone heard thy voice, O Cæsar!" said Taurus Antinor slowly, "and see the aspirant for the Augusta's hand has prepared to do battle for her sake!"

131

CHAPTER XXI

"But truly as the Lord liveth, and as thy soul liveth, there is but a step between me and death."—I Samuel xx. 3.

When the Cæsar had finished speaking, and he fell swooning back in the arms of the praefect of Rome, the conspirators remained quite still, staring at one another, dumbfounded.

Could any man at that moment have divined the secrets of the heart and looked into the thoughts of all these men, what a medley of terror and of lust, of rage and of jealousy, would have been unfolded before his eyes.

The plotters were like men who, falling to with axe and pick to demolish a building, had seen that same building collapse beneath their feet. They had sat quietly by all the day watching the events, content that these would shape themselves in accordance with their will. Young Escanes from time to time fingered the poniard which he had hidden under his tunic, Hortensius Martius gave free rein to his ardent admiration of Dea Flavia, Ancyrus, the elder, kept watch over every phase of the temper of the audience—its apathy, its excitement, its murmurs of dissatisfaction and cries of enthusiasm.

Only Caius Nepos, white to the lips, sat in terror lest the courage of the conspirators whom he had betrayed should fail them at the eleventh hour, and he—branded as a false informer—be left to encounter the fury of an almighty Cæsar, who had never been known to relent.

The speech of Caligula had of a truth struck strangely upon his hearers. The men who had been willing to wait upon chance for the success of their plot, now found that Chance had waited upon them. The thought of treachery did not at first enter their minds. The freaks of the crazy Emperor were as numerous and as varied as the grains of sand in the arena. That he should offer the hand of his kinswoman as a prize to a victor in the arena, was not inconsistent with his perpetual desire for new sensations, his lust of tyrannical power and his open contempt for all his fellow-men.

His allusions to his probable successor had seemed futile and of no account, and they all felt that they had wallowed so deeply in the mire of conspiracy together, that it could not have served the purpose of any one of them to betray the others.

The first moment of stupefaction had quickly passed away, and even before the Cæsar had recovered consciousness Hortensius Martius had risen to his feet. There had been no hesitation in him from the first. Whilst the others pondered—vaguely frightened at this turn given by Chance to her wheel—he was ready to stake his life for the possession of Dea Flavia and of the imperium. His passion for the beautiful woman would have led him into far wilder extravagances and into far graver dangers than an encounter in a public arena with a wild beast, and the momentary degradation of offering his patrician person as a spectacle for the plebs.

And because of this sudden decision, taken boldly whilst others wavered, he became tacitly the leader of the gang of plotters. When he jumped to his feet, ready to descend into the arena, he seemed to challenge them to keep their oath of allegiance to him, who would succeed in winning Dea Flavia for wife.

Hortensius Martius had proved himself to be a true opportunist, for he had seized his opportunity just at the right moment when the others hesitated. Thus are leaders made—one bold movement whilst others sit still, one step forward whilst the others wait.

"Thy chance, O Hortensius Martius," whispered Marcus Ancyrus, the elder, close to the young man's ear. "Escanes and the rest of us will be ready when the time comes, mayhap before thou dost return to us from below."

Escanes' hand beneath his tunic closed upon the dagger. Stronger and taller than Hortensius, he had not the sudden initiative of the brain. He was one of those men who would always be second to a bolder, a more resourceful leader.

Forty pairs of eyes encouraged Hortensius Martius as he rose. In their minds they had already crowned him with laurels. For the moment they had accepted him as their future Emperor and were prepared to acclaim him as Cæsar when Escanes had done his work.

It was at this moment that Caligula recovered from his swoon. His lust of revenge and of hate brought him back to reality. He had planned to make the arch-traitor betray himself, and now, when he caught sight of Hortensius Martius preparing to descend into the arena, a cry as of some prowling, savage beast rose and died in his throat.

He was sufficiently cunning to control himself, sufficiently of an actor to play his part without betraying his thoughts. Though he would gladly have strangled Hortensius then and there with his own hands, he called the young man to him with kindly benevolence and placed a fatherly hand upon his shoulder.

"Thou, O Hortensius Martius?" he said, in well-feigned astonishment.

"Even I, O Cæsar!" replied Hortensius calmly.

"For love of the Augusta thou wouldst risk thy life?"

"To prove my valour, gracious lord, since thou didst desire it."

"On thy knees then, O my son!" rejoined the mountebank solemnly, "and receive the blessing of the gods."

The public watched this little scene with palpitating interest. The Cæsar looked magnificent in his fantastic robes, and beside him Dea Flavia—like a goddess in her white tunic—was beautiful to behold.

The Cæsar laid three fingers on the young man's head, and turned his bloodshot eyes up to the vault of heaven. Then Hortensius Martius rose from his knees and went up to the Augusta Dea Flavia, and knelt down before her. She took no heed of him whatever. She did not look upon his bowed head as he stooped very low and kissed the hem of her gown; some who watched the scene very closely declared afterwards that she snatched her robe away from his hands.

And from the arena down below was heard again the snarl of the thwarted beast.

From the Emperor's tribune, to right and left, wide marble steps led down to the floor of the arena. At the bottom of these steps huge iron gates, wrought with gold and studded with nails, guarded them against access from below. Two legionaries were stationed at these gates.

When Hortensius Martius appeared at the top of the steps the audience screamed with delight and cheered him to the echoes.

He was indeed a figure like to please the most hardened spectator. Not over tall, and slight of build, he looked elegant and graceful in his short white tunic, with the deep purple bands that proclaimed his patrician rank.

A young exquisite, with well-groomed hands and hair delicately perfumed and curled, the tense expression of his face gave him nevertheless an air of determination and of strength. He had taken off his cloak and was winding it round his left arm, otherwise, of course, he was unarmed as the Emperor had directed.

The women blew him kisses across the width of the arena, and some of the more enthusiastic—or the younger—ones pelted him with roses as he came down the steps.

And down below the panther, as if scenting this new prey, sent a roar of expectation into the vibrating air.

Caligula smiled with hideous complacency as he looked down on the descending figure of the young man, and when the people cheered, and the shower of roses fell in a blood-red mass at Hortensius' feet, the Cæsar snarled even as the panther had done, showing a row of yellow teeth, like fangs.

At last Hortensius Martius had reached the foot of the steps. The massive iron gates stood alone between him and the black panther, which cowered some twenty feet away behind a low monticule covered with tufts of grass, its tiny eyes of topaz fixed upon the oncoming prey.

Hortensius gave the order for the opening of the gates. They swung upon their hinges and he passed out through them. And they fell to behind him with a mighty clang.

Thunderous applause greeted him when he set his foot upon the sands of the arena. The panther did not move. It had even ceased to snarl, but its sinewy tail beat a dull tattoo upon the ground.

Then over the whole arena there rose a curious sound, like the sighing of two hundred thousand souls, an indrawing of the breath in two hundred thousand throats. Hortensius Martius looked up, for the sigh had sounded very strangely in his ear, and it had been followed by a still stranger silence, as if two hundred thousand hearts had momentarily ceased to beat.

And as he looked he understood the sigh, and also the death-like silence that followed.

He saw that from the niches all round the arena the safety ladders of crimson silk had all been taken away.

And up in the imperial tribune the mighty Cæsar laughed loudly and long.

CHAPTER XXII

"Greater love hath no man than this, that a man lay down his life for his friends."—St. John xv. 13.

No doubt that for that first tense moment all thought of treachery, of the conspiracy, of the imperium and even of Dea Flavia, was absent from the young man's mind.

It must have come upon him suddenly then and there that his life was now in almost hopeless jeopardy. He was unarmed, and all around him the smooth marble walls of the arena rose, polished and straight, to a height of at least twelve feet, to the row of niches which alone might afford him shelter. From the bases of the fluted columns the iron rings to which the silken ladders had previously been attached, now hung at an unattainable height: the narrow ledge—four feet from the ground—had ceased to be a stepping-stone to safety.

All this, of course, came to him in a flash, as does to a dying man, they say, the varied pictures of his life. Hortensius Martius, in that one flash, realised that he was a doomed man, that he had been trapped into this death-trap, and that nothing now but a miracle stood between him and a hideous death.

Men up above in the tribunes held their breath; some women began to whimper with excitement. But the man and the panther stood for a moment eye to eye. No longer the hunted and the hunter, but the hungry beast of the desert and his certain prey. The baffled creature, tantalised with the blood of his other victims, was ready to satiate its lust at last.

There was a moment of absolute silence, while two tiny golden eyes, measured the distance for a leap.

135

The young man now, with the cunning born of a mad instinct for life, was waiting with bent knees, body slightly leaning forward and eyes fixed upon the brute. He had unwound the cloak from round his arm and held it in front of him like a shield. The man and the beast watched one another thus for a few seconds, and to many those few seconds seemed like an eternity.

Then with a snarl the panther bounded forward. The man held his ground for the space of one second, and as the brute landed within an arm's length of him, quick as lightning he threw his cloak right in its face. Then he began to run. The panther, entangled in the folds of the cloak, savage and snarling, was tearing it to pieces, but Hortensius ran and ran, driven by the blind sense of self-preservation. He ran and ran the whole length of the arena, skirted the oval at the eastern end, and still continued to run, with elbows firmly held to his hips and with swift winged steps that made no sound in the sand.

But already the creature, realising that again it was being cheated, started in pursuit. With leaps and bounds that seemed erratic and purposeless, it gradually diminished the distance between itself and the running man. Once it alighted on the outstanding branch of a gnarled tree, then from thence it took shelter in a clump of shrubs, then across the stream, swimming to the opposite shore; for the running man had rounded the oval and was now swiftly coming this way. Here in the tall grass it paused—cowering—once more on the watch.

And Hortensius, while he ran so blindly along, had failed to notice where his enemy lay hiding.

"In the grass!" shouted a dozen voices.

"There!"

"On ahead!"

"Further on!"

"No! no! Not there! Not there!"

There was little exquisiteness left in the young man now. It was but a few moments since he had stepped smiling into the arena, kicking aside the rose-leaves which enthusiastic hands had thrown in his path. It was but some minutes since he had begun to run, and now the perspiration was pouring from his body, his face was as grey as the sand of the arena, the fear of death had raised the death-sweat on his brow.

His breath came and went hot and panting through his nostrils, his eyes, dilated with terror, were vainly searching for the cowering enemy.

Once more he turned to run. The panther seemed to be playing with him. A dozen times it could have reached him, a dozen times it bounded to one side, giving his prey another chance to run, another short respite for the agony of despair.

Men, women and children screamed with excitement. No longer did they cheer the handsome young patrician, no longer did they throw roses at his feet. They shouted to him to run because they knew that running was no use. They urged the panther to leap because they fanned its rage with their screams.

"Habet! Habet!" they shouted with every bound of the ferocious creature.

"Habet! Habet!" now that Hortensius at last paused in his run.

He stood quite still for a veil had descended over his eyes. The whole arena began to spin and to dance before him, the marble columns were twisted awry, thousands upon thousands of distorted faces grinned hideously upon him. Over the trees and the grass and the stream there was a film of red, the colour of blood, and through this film—which grew thicker and thicker as he gazed—he saw nothing but just opposite to him, across the width of the arena, towering high above everything around, the tall figure of Dea Flavia with her white dress falling straight from the shoulders, her fair hair crowned with diamonds, her face white as her gown and her lips parted as if uttering a cry of horror.

The next moment that cry—it was a woman's cry—did rend the air from, end to end of the gigantic enclosure, and the cry was echoed and re-echoed by thousands and thousands of throats, as the panther, taking steady aim, leaped straight for the man.

The noise became deafening: men, women, children, everyone screamed, and right through this whirling orgy of sound a voice was shouting, strong and mighty as that of Jupiter when he sends his decrees thundering forth into the air.

"By his throat, Hortensius! By his throat, and I'll at him whilst he pants!"

Hortensius put out his hands with a last instinctive sense of self-preservation. The mighty voice rang in his ear, it reverberated through the hot noonday air, and clanged against the copper gates as if a powerful arm had smitten them with the axe of Jove.

The man saw the beast's leap, felt the hot breath in his face, felt the two yellow eyes gleaming on him like burning suns, and his ears buzzed with the din of thousands of shrieks; then he suddenly felt himself uplifted, whilst an agonised roar from the throat of a wounded beast overfilled the seething cauldron of sound.

The praefect of Rome was standing in the arena now, and in his strong arms lifted high above his head he held the swooning man, whilst some few paces away the panther was lying prone, with blood streaming from its quivering jaws.

It had all happened so suddenly that no one afterwards could say how it occurred. But there were those who retained a vision of the whole thing and afterwards shared their impressions with others.

Everyone recollected when my lord Hortensius first entered the arena and the iron gates closed in behind him, that a general feeling of horror fell upon the entire public when it realised that all means of safety, all chance of escape had been removed with those silken ladders, and that the young patrician had in truth been left at the mercy of a powerful brute, goaded to madness through baffled desire for blood.

At that same moment the praefect of Rome disappeared from the imperial tribune, and the terrible scene between the hunting beast and the hunted man had begun.

Time for the man to run round the arena! Time for the brute to stalk and play with its prey! Time, it seems, for the praefect of Rome to make his way from the imperial tribune to the east end of the arena, where was stationed the city guard of which he had full control!

A few precious seconds in making the soldiers understand what he wanted, a few more seconds to command them to obey for they stood as a phalanx against the gate, thinking the praefect mad in desiring to enter the arena—a few more seconds and Taurus Antinor was at last in the arena, shouting to the hunted man to have at the brute with his hands.

But Hortensius was weak from exhaustion brought on by a life of luxury and idleness and by the excitement of the last two days. He put out two feeble hands, and the panther was already on the leap.

And by that time Taurus Antinor was between him and the brute. With a blow of his hard fists—fashioned in far off Northern lands—and with the strength that is given to the barbarians of that sea-washed shore, he had drawn blood from the creature's jaw and sent it rolling back on its haunches, momentarily dazed.

Only momentarily, however, whilst two hundred thousand throats yelled in unison:

"Habet! Habet! Habet!"

A precious moment that! With a maddened beast, a swooning man and no arms save a pair of fists, hard as iron, made with a hand slender and supple like the finest tempered steel.

And while the panther fell back roaring, and before it could prepare for a new spring, Taurus Antinor had seized the swooning man. It was his turn to run now, for he had but a few seconds in which to save the life of his bitterest foe.

Straight to the walls of the arena did he run, and his voice was heard speaking loudly and commandingly:

"The arcade, man! Rouse thyself! The arcade! The rings in the columns! Quick!"

It needed the strength of a bullock to accomplish the deed: that, or the strength which comes from unbendable human will. The man, only half-conscious, returned to his senses by the force of that same will. The instinct of life was strongest in the end, and when Taurus Antinor leapt upon the ledge and hoisted Hortensius' body high up above his head, the young man, with the final effort borne of hope and built upon despair, reached up and caught one of the massive rings imbedded in the bases of the fluted columns.

For a few seconds he remained suspended, his body swinging against the marble wall, whilst the public cheered with an enthusiasm that knew no bounds. From below the praefect helped to push the feeble body up, then another jerk, a pull upwards, a push, and Hortensius Martius had found safety in one of the niches of the arcade.

"Hail to the praefect of Rome! Hail!" came in a continuous, thunderous roar from every corner of the arena, even as with a sudden bound the black panther had sprung upon Taurus Antinor, and, catching him unawares, had felled him to the ground.

CHAPTER XXIII

"Well done, thou good and faithful servant."—St. Matthew xxv. 21.

A tumult amongst the people?

Aye! it was here now fully aroused. The praefect of Rome was popular with the plebs. His action in the arena had called forth unbounded enthusiasm. When he fell rolling into the sand, with the black panther snarling above him, his steel-like grip warding for the moment the brute's jaws from off his throat, the people broke out into regular frenzy.

"The praefect! the praefect!" they shouted.

Men climbed down along the gradients leaping over other men, determined to jump down twelve feet into the arena in order to rescue the praefect from the jaws of the ferocious beast.

But above in the imperial tribune the Cæsar sat snarling like the panther and rubbing his hands with glee. His trap had been over-successful, one by one the arch-traitors fell headlong into it. First Hortensius Martius, that young fool! What mattered if he had escaped from a ravenous panther? The claws of a vengeful Cæsar were sharper far than those of any beast of the desert.

And now Taurus Antinor! the praefect of Rome! the man of silence and of integrity! the idol of the people, the scorner of Cæsar's godhead. Vague rumour had reached Caligula of the praefect's strange sayings, his refusal to enter the temples and to sacrifice to the gods. People said that the Anglicanus worshipped one who claimed to be greater than Cæsar and all the deities of Rome.

Well, so be it! There he lay now in the dust, a huddled mass of man and beast, the sand of the arena reddened with his blood. Caligula screamed like the rest of his people, but his cry was:

"Habet! Habet! Habet!" And in a frenzy of rage and hate his thumb pointed downwards, downwards, as if it were a dagger which he could plunge into the Anglicanus' throat.

But the city guard were the first to break their bounds. Even whilst the imperial madman exulted and shrieked forth his murderous "Habet!" they had rushed to the rescue of their praefect.

The powerful grasp on the panther's throat was on the point of relaxing; the brute was digging its claws in the shoulders of the fallen man, and he, feeling faint with loss of blood, looked upon death as it stared down at him from the beast's golden eyes, and all that he was conscious of was the feeling that death was good.

When the city guard rushed to his rescue, and by dint of numbers and strength of steel tore the ferocious creature from the body of its prey, Taurus Antinor lay a while half conscious. He heard the cry of the people round him, he felt a shower of sweet-scented petals fall upon him from above, he heard the last dying roar of the panther and a scream of rage from the imperial tribune.

Then the din became deafening: the trampling of feet, the rushing hither and thither, the cries, the imprecations, and from beneath the tribunes in their distant prisons, the roar of caged beasts like the far-off rumbling of thunder.

Taurus Antinor raised himself on his knees. Both his shoulders had been lacerated by the panther; he was bleeding from several wounds about the legs and arms, and his whole body felt bruised and stiff.

But he struggled to his feet, and now, leaning against a large tree trunk which had formed part of the setting of the scene, he tried to take in every detail of what was going on around him. There was, of course, a great deal of shouting and a general stampede in the tribunes of the plebs. In the midst of this shouting, which buzzed incessantly like the war of a great cataract, two cries resounded very distinctly above all the others.

Thousands of people were shouting:

"Hail to the praefect! Hail to the god of valour and of strength! Hail! Taurus Antinor, hail!"

Whilst others cried more dully, yet equally distinctly:

"Death to the tyrant! Death to the madman! Death to Cæsar! Death!"

That he himself was for the moment the object of enthusiasm of this irresponsible crowd, he could not doubt for an instant. That this same irresponsible enthusiasm was leading the crowd to treachery and rebellion was equally certain.

The city guard egged on by the people had forced open the heavy iron gates through which Hortensius Martius had passed a while ago, and which led up the marble steps straight to the imperial tribune.

Taurus Antinor looking up now saw the Cæsar standing pale and trembling, surrounded by his standard bearers, whose attitude seemed strangely irresolute. The Augustas were clinging together in obvious terror, their heads were pressed close to one another, and the jewels in their hair formed a curious shimmering mass of diamonds and rubies which caught the rays of the sun and threw back blinding sparks of prismatic colours. Dea Flavia was not near them. She was standing alone up against the dividing wall of the tribune, and leaning back against it, with eyes closed, and hand pressed against her heart.

All this did Taurus Antinor see, and also that Hortensius Martius, still deathly pale and trembling in every limb, had succeeded in making his way from the arcade where he had found safety, back to the patricians' tribune amongst his friends.

He was standing now in the midst of a compact group composed of those men who had been present two days ago at the banquet in Caius Nepos' house. They stood close to one another whispering eagerly amongst themselves. Hortensius Martius was obviously their chief centre of interest, and young Escanes held his hand concealed within the folds of his tunic.

And Taurus Antinor no longer paused to think. He had forgotten his lacerated shoulder and his bleeding limbs; even the horrors of the past quarter of an hour had faded from his mind. All that he saw was that murder and treachery were walking hand in hand, and that the murder of the insane Cæsar now would mean the death of thousands of innocent victims later on, that it would mean civil strife, and uncountable misery. And all that he heard was the voice of Him Who had bidden him to render unto Cæsar that which was Cæsar's, namely his allegiance, his fealty, his life.

The city guard loved him and knew his voice. He had no trouble in inducing the men to let him pass through their ranks and to mount the steps before them which led to the imperial tribune. They let him pass perhaps because they thought that their praefect would wish to take his revenge with his own hands. The gods themselves would have placed a poisoned dagger in the hand of him who had been so ruthlessly exposed to a most horrible death.

And as Taurus Antinor's massive figure was seen to mount the steps, the audience broke into cheers.

"Hail Taurus Antinor! the god of valour and of strength!"

Whilst more ominous than before came that other cry: "Death to the tyrant! Death to the Cæsar! Death!"

And whilst the city guard followed closely on the footsteps of their praefect, and men among the crowd prepared for the inevitable fight which they foresaw, the women and those who were feeble and pacific waved fans and cloaks about and threw dead roses across the arena, till the whole place seemed like a great pageant of many-coloured flags, over which the midday sun had thrown its veil of gold.

When Taurus Antinor reached the topmost step Caligula caught sight of him, and the intensity of his rage was such that his cheeks turned livid and blotchy and hoarse inarticulate sounds escaped his panting throat.

Even at this same moment the group composed of Escanes and the others seemed to sway in a mass toward the tribune of the Cæsar. They appeared to be consulting Hortensius Martius who had nodded encouragingly. Young Escanes was in the very centre of the group now, his hand was still hidden in the folds of his tunic and the look in his face told Taurus Antinor all that there was to fear.

At his feet as he stepped into the tribune lay his own cloak which he had discarded when first his instinct had prompted him to run to Hortensius' aid. Now he picked it up. It was of dark-coloured stuff, unadorned with the usual insignia of dignity and rank. With it in his hand he ran quickly toward the Cæsar.

Caligula saw him coming towards him, his yellow teeth were chattering in his mouth, he stood there palsied with fear, a prey to a deadly feeling of hate and to one of abject terror.

Even as Taurus Antinor, with a quick gesture, threw his own cloak round the shoulders of the Cæsar and whispered hurriedly:

"Let your praetorian guard escort you quickly to your palace, gracious lord—your life is in danger from the people, and...."

"In danger at thy hands, thou infamous traitor," broke in Caligula with a maniacal yell of rage; "take this then, in remembrance of the Cæsar whom thou hast betrayed!"

And quick as lightning the madman drew a short poniard from beneath his robe, and, uttering a final snarl of satisfied hate and revenge, he plunged the dagger in Taurus Antinor's breast.

Then he snatched the cloak from him, and, wrapping it quickly over his head and shoulders, he called wildly to his guard and fled incontinently from the spot.

CHAPTER XXIV

"The sorrows of death compassed me."—Psalm xviii. 4.

Dea Flavia lay upon her bed, with wide-open eyes fixed into vacancy above her.

Afternoon and evening had gone by since that awful moment

142

when the whole fell purpose of the Cæsar's plan was revealed to her, and she saw Hortensius Martius standing unarmed and doomed in the arena, face to face with a raging, wild beast. Afternoon and evening had vanished into the past since she saw Taurus Antinor, with Hortensius' body held high over his head, saving one life whilst offering up his own, since she heard that deafening cry of horror uttered by two hundred thousand throats when the panther sprung upon him unawares and felled him to the ground, whilst his blood reddened the sand of the arena.

Afternoon and evening had swooned in the arms of eternity since she saw the terror-stricken Cæsar treacherously stab the man who had rushed forward to save him.

After that last agonising moment she remembered nothing more until she found herself in her own house, lying on her bed, with Licinia's anxious, wrinkled face bending over her.

"What hath happened, Licinia?" she had asked feebly as soon as consciousness had returned.

"We brought thee home safely, my precious treasure," replied the old woman fervently, "all praise be unto the gods who watched over their beloved."

"But how did it happen?" queried Dea with some impatience. "Tell me all that happened, Licinia," she reiterated with earnest insistence, as she raised herself on her elbow and fixed her large blue eyes, in which burned a feverish light, upon the face of her slave.

"Yes! yes! I'll tell thee all I know," rejoined the woman soothingly. "Thy slaves were close at hand in the vestibule of the imperial tribune, and thy litter was down below with the bearers, in case thou shouldst require it. But I had stood on the threshold of the tribune for some time watching thee, for thy sweet face had been pale as death all the morning, and I feared that the heat would be too much for thee. Thus I saw much of what went on. I saw the traitor advance toward the Cæsar, trying to smother him with a cloak. I saw the Cæsar—whom may the gods protect—stab the traitor in the breast, and then leave the Amphitheatre hurriedly, followed by a few among his faithful guard. But my thoughts then were only of thee. I could see thy lovely face white as the maple leaf, and thou wast leaning against the wall as if ready to swoon. The traitor whom the Cæsar had justly punished lay bleeding from many wounds close to thy foot. The next moment I had thee in my arms, having caught thee when thy dear body swayed forward and would have fallen even upon the breast of the dead traitor."

"The traitor?" murmured Dea Flavia then.

"Aye! the praefect of Rome," said Licinia, with a vicious oath. "He had incited the rabble against the Cæsar, and—may his dead body be defiled for the sacrilege!—he was causing the populace to acclaim him

143

as their Emperor, even whilst he raised his murderous hand against him who is the equal of the gods!"

"He was striving to save Cæsar, Licinia, and not to murder him," said Dea Flavia earnestly.

"To save the Cæsar? Nay! nay! my precious, the praefect of Rome tried to murder Cæsar by smothering him with a cloak."

"It is false I tell thee!"

"False? Nay, dear heart, I saw it all, and thou wast beside thyself and knew not rightly what happened. Even a minute later thou laidst in my arms like a dead white swan, and I pushed my way through the soldiers, and past the other Augustas who cowered in the tribune, screaming and wringing their hands. Two of thy slaves were luckily close at hand. Together we carried thee down to thy litter and bore thee safely home for which to-morrow I will offer special sacrifice to Minerva who protected thee."

"And what happened after we were gone?"

"Alas! I know not. They say that the populace became more and more unruly: there were shouts for the praefect of Rome, who fortunately lay dead on the floor of the tribune, and there were even some sacrilegious miscreants who called for death upon the Cæsar."

"Do they say," queried Dea Flavia, speaking slowly and low, "that the praefect of Rome is dead?"

"If he be not dead now," retorted Licinia viciously, for her loyalty to the Cæsar was bound up with her love for Dea Flavia, and treachery to Cæsar meant treachery to her beloved, "If he be not dead now, he shall still suffer for his treason: and if he be dead his body shall be defiled."

"Oh!"

"Aye! a traitor must suffer even in death. His body shall be given to the dogs, his blood to the carrion...."

"Silence, Licinia!" broke in Dea Flavia sternly, "fill not mine ears with thy hideous talk. Every word thou dost utter is impiety and sacrilege, and I would smite thee for them had I but the strength.

"But I am so tired," she added after a slight pause, with a weary little sigh, even whilst Licinia, subdued and frightened, stood silently by: "I would like to sleep."

"Then sleep, my goddess," said the old woman, "I'll watch over thee."

"No! no! I could not sleep if I were watched," rejoined Dea Flavia with the fretfulness of a tired child. "I would rather be alone."

"But thou'lt have bad dreams."

"Order Blanca to lie across the threshold. I can then send her to fetch thee, if I have need of thee."

"I would rather lie across thy threshold myself," muttered the old woman.

"Good Licinia, do as I tell thee," said Dea, now with marked impatience. "And—stay—" she added as Licinia still grumbling prepared reluctantly to obey—"I pray thee find out for me all that is going on in the city. Mayhap Tertius will know what has happened—or Piso.... Go seek them, Licinia, and find out all that there is to know, so that thou canst tell me everything anon, when I wake."

She lay back on her bed with closed eyes whilst Licinia kissed her hands and feet, re-arranged the embroidered coverlet and the downy cushions, and after a while shuffled out of the room.

There was nothing that the old woman loved better than a gossip with Tertius, who was the comptroller of the Augusta's household, or with Piso, who was the overseer of her slaves: and even her fond desire to watch beside her mistress yielded to the delight of holding long and interesting parley with these worthies.

So it was with considerable alacrity that—having deputed the young girl, Blanca, to watch over her mistress—she made her way through the atrium, and thence across the vast peristyle to the quarters of the slaves.

Tertius—the comptroller—had, it appears, sallied forth into the streets, despite the lateness of the hour, in the hope of gleaning some information as to what was going on in the city. Even in this secluded portion of the Palatine, where stood the house of Dea Flavia under the shelter of the surrounding palaces, weird sounds of human cries and of the clashing of steel was penetrating with ominous persistency.

Piso—the overseer—who had remained at home, as he did not feel sufficiently valiant to face once again the disturbance outside, told Licinia all that he had witnessed before he finally found safe haven at home.

It seemed that the tumult in the Amphitheatre had not ceased with the flight of the Emperor, rather that it had grown in intensity when the populace saw the praefect of Rome fall backwards, stabbed by the Cæsar, and the latter disappear hurriedly, followed by a few from among the practorian guard.

There was no doubt that the temper of the populace had been over-excited by the cruel scenes of a while ago; lust of blood and of tyranny had been fanned to fever-pitch through those very spectacles which the Cæsar himself had provided for the people, with a view to satisfying his own ferocious desires of hate and of revenge.

Now that same fever-heated temper was turning against him, who had fanned it for his own ends.

Caligula had made good his escape, satisfied that his dagger had done its work upon the arch-traitor. He had fled through the private entrance of his tribune, and his guard had rallied round him. But a company of legionaries—some five or six hundred strong—was still in the place, as well as his knights and all his friends, and against these did the wrath of the rabble turn.

The lawless and the rough soon had it all their own way, and the peaceable citizen who would have liked to get wife and children safely out of the crowd found it well-nigh impossible to make his way through the throng.

After a few moments the disturbance became general; there was a great deal of shouting and presently missiles began to fly about. The rabble attacked the legionaries and a sanguinary conflict ensued. The former was in overwhelming number and succeeded in breaking the rank of the soldiers, and in putting them momentarily to rout.

After this there was a general stampede down and along the gradients of the Amphitheatre, during which hundreds of persons—including women and children—were crushed to death. The scene of confusion seems to have baffled description. Piso, who had succeeded in making his way home in the midst of it all, had even now to wipe his brow, which was streaming with perspiration at the recollection of the horrors which he had witnessed.

Whilst he proceeded with his narrative, Tertius had returned with further news. And these, of a truth, were very alarming. The lower slopes of the Palatine, as well as the Forum and the surrounding streets, were now in the hands of the mob. The few legions who were in the city had been cut off from the Palatine, and though they were making vigorous efforts to break through the close ranks of the crowd, they had, up to this hour, been wholly unsuccessful, owing no doubt to the paucity of their numbers, since the bulk of the army was not yet home from that insensate and mock expedition into Germany.

The whole of the troops in and around the city, including the town and praetorian guard, was on this day computed at less than one thousand, and the mob—so Tertius averred—was over one hundred thousand strong.

The law-abiding citizens had locked themselves up in the fastnesses of their homes, and the Cæsar—so it was believed—was inside his palace with a small detachment of his guard around him, one hundred strong, who already had had to repel numerous attacks delivered by the more forward amongst the rabble.

Tertius had not been able to get far beyond the precincts of the house, for fear had driven him back. The shouts which came from the streets below and from the Forum were ominous and threatening.

"Death to the Cæsar! Death to the tyrant!" could be distinctly heard above the din of stampeding feet, and a low and constant murmur that sounded like distant thunder.

There was no doubt that the Cæsar's life was in grave danger, seeing that only a handful of men stood between him and the fury of an excited populace; and these men were without a leader, for the praetorian praefect had been cut off from them, even as he tried to push his way through the crowd earlier in the day.

Thus, therefore, did this harbinger of evil news resume the situation. Caligula was in his palace, surrounded by the slaves of his household and guarded by a few soldiers against a raging mob—an hundred thousand or more strong—who had formed a ring around the Palatine, and was clamouring for the Cæsar's death. The legionaries, under the command of faithful Centurions, were cut off from the Palatine and from their Cæsar by the mob whose solid ranks they had hitherto been unable to break. The Augustas and their slaves were also safe within their palaces.

But what Tertius did not know, and was therefore unable to impart to his eager listeners was that the party of conspirators, with Hortensius Martius as their acknowledged leader, were taking advantage of the disturbance to place themselves at the head of the mob, hoping that the cry of "Death to Caligula!" would soon be followed by one of "Hail to the Cæsar! the new Cæsar, Hortensius Martius! Hail!"

CHAPTER XXV

"Watchman, what of the night?"—Isaiah xxi. 11.

And far away beyond the noise and tumult which ranged around the foot of the Palatine, the honey-coloured moon illumined with her weird and ghostly light the vast arena of the gigantic Amphitheatre, where a company of the town guard, under the command of an aedile, were busy collecting the dead.

A narrow streak of those same ghostly rays found its way through the folds of the curtains which spanned the window of Dea Flavia's room. It peeped in boldly, stirring up myriads of impalpable atoms and whipping them into a living line of silver. It wandered further, and finding a golden head that tossed restlessly upon a silk-covered pillow, it alighted on it, making the white face appear ghostlier still, and the wide eyes to shine like stars.

A timid step shuffled across the floor.

"Blanca, is it thou?" whispered Dea Flavia, as quickly she raised herself up, squatting now upon the bed, with one hand pressed against the pillow and the other to her breast.

"Aye, mistress, it is I!" came in whispered response.

"Well? Have they returned?"

"Aye! gracious lady. Half an hour ago."

"Did they find him?"

"Yes."

"Is he...?"

There was a pause, whilst from afar came that strange low sound of thousands of men murmuring, which is so akin to the booming of the waves upon a rocky shore.

"The praefect of Rome was in a swoon when they found him in the imperial tribune," said the young slave-girl, still speaking under her breath. "Nolus and Dion carried him to the litter, and once or twice he groaned whilst they carried him."

A gentle breeze wafted the curtains into the room; the rays of the waning moon fell full upon the huddled figure on the bed, with the stream of gold falling each side of the set, pale face, and the large blue eyes now strangely veiled with tears.

"Where is ... where is the praefect now?" asked Dea Flavia.

"In the room out of thy studio, gracious mistress, as thou didst direct. Dion did prepare a couch for him there, and hath laid him down."

"And the physician?"

"The physician hath seen him. He saith that the praefect is weak with loss of blood. His shoulders, arms and legs have been torn by the panther's claws, but these wounds are not deep."

"And ... and the dagger thrust?"

"The physician saith that the dagger must have glanced off the bone. I did not quite understand what he said, and Dion explained it badly."

"He did not say that there was poison in the dagger?"

"I think not, gracious lady; for the physician said that the praefect would soon be well if he were carefully tended. He is very weak with loss of blood."

"Did Nolus and Dion find it difficult to approach the praefect's body?"

"They had to parley with the aedile who was in command, and to give him all the money which my gracious mistress did entrust to them for that purpose."

"After which the aedile made no demur ... and asked no questions?"

"The aedile took the money, gracious lady, and Dion said that he asked no further questions, but allowed the praefect to be borne away."

"That is well," said Dea Flavia, after a brief moment of silence, whilst the girl stood awaiting her further pleasure. "Thou, Blanca, hath served me faithfully, so have Nolus and Dion, my slaves. Ye have earned your reward, and though I am grieved to part from good servants like you, yet will I fulfil my promise, even as I have given it to you. From this hour, thou, Blanca, art a freewoman, and Nolus thy brother, and Dion, thy future husband, are freemen, and the sum of six hundred aurei shall be given unto you to-morrow—two hundred unto each—and may you live long and prosper and be happy, for you have served me well."

Blanca fell upon her knees and kissed the coverlet on which reposed her mistress; but Dea Flavia did not seem to see her. She was squatting on her heels, with body and head erect, and slowly now, like the rosy kiss of dawn upon the snow-clad hills of Etruria, a faint crimson glow spread over her pale cheeks.

Blanca waited irresolute, not liking to leave her mistress before she could be assured that sleep had descended at last on those weary lids. The hour was very late, close upon midnight, and yet the city was not asleep. That constant murmur—like unto the breaking of angry waves—still sent its sinister echo through the still night air, and even in the house of Dea Flavia it seemed that hundreds of eyes were still open, fear having chased sleep away. There was a sound—like the buzzing of bees—that came from the slaves' quarters beyond the peristyle, and from the studio, which lay the other side of the atrium, came the sound of muffled footsteps gliding over the mosaic of the floor.

"Go to bed now, child," said Dea Flavia at last, "thou hast earned thy rest ... and ... stay! Tell Dion and Nolus to remain in the studio, and there to spend the night. They must be ready to go to the praefect if he calls.... Go!"

Then as the girl made ready to obey, the Augusta put out her hand to detain her.

"Wait! Hast seen Licinia?"

"No, gracious lady."

"She is not hovering somewhere near my room?... or in the atrium?"

"No, gracious lady."

"And the night-watchers?"

"They are in the vestibule, gracious lady."

"And all my women?"

"They are all in bed and asleep."

"That is well. Thou canst go."

Blanca's naked little feet made no sound as she crossed the room, and went out by the door which led to the sleeping-chamber of the Augusta's women.

Dea Flavia waited for a while, straining her ears to catch every sound which came from this portion of her palace.

Her sleeping-chamber, together with all those on this floor gave directly on the atrium, which formed a large irregular square in the centre of this portion of the house. The north side of it was taken up with the Augusta's apartments and those of her women, the south side with the reception rooms and with the studio and its attendant vestibules, whilst the main vestibule of the house and the first peristyle gave on either end.

From the main vestibule came the subdued hum of voices, and throughout the house there was that feeling of wakefulness so different to the usual placid hush of night.

Dea Flavia held her breath whilst she listened attentively. In the vestibule it was the night watchmen who were talking, discussing, no doubt, the many events of the day: and that sound—like the buzzing of bees—showed that the women were awake and gossiping, and that up in the slaves' quarters tongues were still wagging, despite Blanca's assurance and the overseer's sharp discipline. But on the other side of the atrium, where were the reception halls and the studio, everything was still.

The young girl threw herself back upon her bed. Sleep refused to visit her this night; the thin streak of silvery moon, which persistently peeped in through the curtain, flicked the tiny atoms in the air until they assumed quaint, minute shapes of their own, like unto crawling panthers and grotesque creatures crowned with a golden halo, and brandishing a mock thunderbolt in one hand and a dagger in the other. Then suddenly all these shapes would vanish, smothered beneath a cloak, and Dea Flavia, still wide awake, would feel drops of moisture at the roots of her hair, and her whole body, as if sinking into a black abyss, where monsters yelled and wild beasts roared and huge, black, snake-like creatures tore the flesh off human bones.

The hours of the night sped on, borne on the weighted feet of anguish and of horror. Gradually, one by one, the sounds in and about the house died away; the slaves in their quarters must have turned over on their rough pallets and gone to sleep, the women close by had done gossiping, only from the vestibule came the slow measured tread of the watchmen guarding the Augusta's house, and from far away that ceaseless, rumbling noise which meant that discontent was awake and astir.

Once more Dea Flavia sat up, unable to lie still. Her golden hair was matted against her temples and in her breast her heart was beating furiously. The waning moon had long since now sunk behind the western clouds, a gentle breeze stirred the curtains with a soft, sighing noise as of some human creature in pain. In the far corner of the room, in a tiny lamp of gold, a tiny wick threw a feeble light around.

Dea Flavia put her feet to the ground. The heat in the room was oppressive; no doubt it was that which had caused her restlessness, and the dampness of her brow. She shuddered now when her bare feet touched the smooth coldness of the mosaic floor, but she stood up resolutely, and anon crossed over to the door which gave on the atrium.

For a few seconds she listened. Everything was still. Then very gently she pushed open the door.

On the marble table, in the centre of the atrium, another light glimmered in a jewelled lamp; but the atrium was vast and the diminutive light did not reach its far corners. The gentle trickle of water along the gutters in the floor made queer, ghost-like sounds, and in the great pots of lilies all round currents of air sent weird moanings in the night.

Dea Flavia, like an ethereal figure clad all in white, and with waves of golden hair shimmering over the whiteness of her gown, glided softly across the atrium.

A tiny vestibule led into the studio, she crossed it, guided by her knowledge of the place, for the light in the atrium did not penetrate to this recess. Her bare feet made no noise as she glided along the floor, her hand pushed the door open without raising a sound.

Now she was in the studio. The place in which she did the work that she loved, the place in which day after day she loved to sit and to idle away the hours. In an angle of the room, stretched out upon the bare floor, Dion and Nolus were lying, their even breathing showing that they slept. On the right was another door, which led to an inner chamber, where she oft used to retire for rest from her work. It was a private sanctum which none dared enter save with special permission from herself. Blanca kept it swept and free from dust, and Licinia tidied it only when she was so allowed.

Dea Flavia went across the studio and pushed open the door. It was masked by a curtain, and this too she pulled aside, slowly and nervously like some small animal that is timid and yet venturesome. She knew every corner of the place of course, and the very creaking of the hinges and gentle swish of the curtain was a familiar sound to her ear.

Nevertheless she was almost frightened to advance, for the big dark shadow right across the stuccoed wall awed her by its mysterious blackness. It was caused by a large object in the centre of the room, a couch covered with coverlets of soft, white woollen stuffs, on which the night-light burning fitfully threw patches of ruddy lights.

Dea Flavia had paused on the threshold, with one hand behind her still clinging to the curtain, the other pressed hard on her bosom, trying to still the wild beatings which went on hammering inside her just below her breasts. She thought that she either must be dreaming now, or being awake, must have been dreaming before.

Once or twice she closed and then reopened her eyes, thinking that perhaps the flickering night-light was playing her drowsy senses some elusive trick. For surely Blanca had told her that Dion and Nolus had laid the praefect of Rome on an improvised couch in the chamber beside the studio, and that the praefect was helpless and weak with pain and loss of blood.

The improvised couch was certainly in its place, the light of the lamp danced upon pillow and coverlet, but no one was lying there, even though the pillow still bore the impress of the head which had rested on it.

The silence was oppressive, for through the thick walls and heavy curtains of the Augusta's favourite room there penetrated no sound from without, and she herself stood so still, so still by the door, that she

151

was sure the beatings of her heart must be heard through that awful stillness.

Suddenly she started, and her fingers closed more convulsively than before on the curtain behind her. Imperceptible as the sound of a swallow on the wing, there came a long-drawn sigh to her ear. Her brow contracted, her eyes narrowed in a great effort to peer past the light into the darkness.

On the further side of the couch now and masked by its shadow, she saw something that was immovable and yet seemed pulsating with life. Gradually as she peered, that something detached itself from the surrounding gloom. She saw a bowed head with wealth of tawny hair which gleamed like copper against the white coverlet, two hands white as the pillow beside which they rested, whiter still by contrast with the copper of the hair against them; she saw a pair of broad shoulders, and a powerful body and limbs that lost themselves in the darkness beyond the couch.

The face was hidden and the body was quite still. It would have seemed like that of the dead but for that long sigh, which, intangible though it was, had broken the silence of the night.

Dea Flavia could not now have moved, even if she would. Her small bare feet seemed glued to the cold mosaic of the floor, her hand seemed fastened with clamps of steel to the curtain which it clutched.

She had never seen a man thus kneeling alone in the stillness and in the gloom. Why should a man kneel thus? and to whom?

Yet she would not have disturbed him, not for all the world. She never dreamed that he would be awake; she had thought of him lying— as Blanca said—exhausted from loss of blood.

She had only meant to look on him for a moment, to look into his face as he slept, to try and read in its wonted harsh lines the secrets of his soul.

He had rushed to the Cæsar trying to protect him, when thousands on thousands of throats were acclaiming his name as future lord of Rome. Why?

He had rushed into the arena and risked his life to save a man who two days ago had insulted him, who—at best—was nothing to him. Why?

These questions she had meant to ask him when he was sleeping: now she could not ask them from that bowed head, nor yet from those clasped hands. And yet, somehow, it seemed that something of the man's soul was revealed to her at this moment, though she could not as yet fathom the meaning of this strange answer to her questions.

Her eyes had become quite accustomed to the darkness beyond the light. She could see clearly the powerful figure on bended knees, the wide shoulders with the bandages disposed over them by the physician for the healing of those horrible wounds, and the fingers linked together in a manner which she had never seen before. And now the

152

hands stirred ever so slightly, the light caught the fingers more directly, and Dea Flavia saw that—clasped between them—there was a small wooden cross.

And she knew now—all in a moment—that the answer to her questions lay there before her, not in the man's face, for that she could not see, but in his clasped hands and in the cross which they held. She knew that it was because of it—or rather because of that which had gone before, and of which that little cross was the tangible memory—that he had been ready to give his life for an enemy, and to give up all ambition and all pride for the sake of his allegiance to Cæsar!

A sigh must have escaped her lips, or merely just the indrawing of her breath; certain it is that something caused the kneeling man to stir. He raised his head very slowly, and then looked up straight across the light—to her.

For one second he remained quite still, on his knees and with that white vision before him, ghost-like and silent, against the crimson background of the curtain. Then softly, as a sigh, one word escaped his lips:

"Dea!"

He rose to his feet but already she had fled, noiselessly as she had come, but swiftly across the studio and the atrium and back to her room, but even while she fled it seemed to her that on the silent night air there still trembled the sound of a voice, vibrating with longing and with passion, mournful as a sigh, appealing as the call of a bird to its mate:

"Dea!"

CHAPTER XXVI

"There is no peace, saith the Lord, unto the wicked."—Isaiah xlviii. 22.

When after a few hours of light and troubled sleep Dea Flavia woke to partial consciousness, it seemed to her as if Phoebus Apollo had been driving his chariot through a sea of blood; for through the folds of the curtains over the windows she caught a glimpse of the sky, and it was of vivid crimson.

The heat was oppressive, and as the young girl tossed with ever increasing restlessness on the pillows, beads of moisture rose on her forehead and matted the fair curls against her temples.

She felt too tired to get up, even though she vaguely marvelled how wonderful must be the dawn, since its reflection was of such lurid colour. She lay back drowsy and with nerves tingling; she closed her eyes for they ached and burned intolerably.

Gradually to her half-aroused consciousness sounds too began to penetrate. It seemed to her that the usual stately quietude of her house was gravely disturbed this morning, shuffling footsteps could be heard moving across the atrium, voices—scarce subdued—were whispering audibly, and the shouts of the overseers echoed from across the peristyle, and through it all a dull, monotonous sound, distant as yet and faint, came at long intervals, the sound of Jove's thunder over the Campania far away.

Dea Flavia listened more intently, and one by one through the veil which kindly sleep had drawn over her memory, the events of the past day and night knocked at the portals of her brain.

She remembered everything now, and with this sudden onrush of memory of the past, came fuller consciousness of the present.

Through the hum of varied noises which filled her own house, she distinguished presently more strange, more ominous sounds that came from afar, like the thunders of Jove, and like them sounded weird and threatening in her ear; hoarse cries and shouts which seemed like peremptory commands, and groans that rose above the muffled din with calls of terror and of pain.

In a moment Dea Flavia had put her feet to the ground. She ran to the window, drew back the curtains and peered into the narrow street which, at this point, separated her house from the rear of the Palace of Tiberius.

A dull grey light enveloped the city in its mantle of gloom, and it was not the torch of Phoebus which had spread the rosy gleam of dawn over the sky! As Dea Flavia looked, she saw a canopy of dull crimson over her head, and from beyond the Palace of Tiberius there rose at intervals heavy banks of purple smoke.

Dea Flavia stood there for one moment at the window, paralysed with the dread of what she saw and of what she guessed, and even as a cry of horror died within her throat, Licinia, with grey hair flying loosely round her pale face, and hands held out before her with an agonised gesture of fear, came running into the room.

"The miscreants! the miscreants!" she shouted as she threw herself down on to the floor before her young mistress and squatted there on her heels, wringing her hands and uttering moans of terror. "They have set fire to the palace! They are on us, my beloved! Save thyself! Save thy house! Oh ye gods! protect us all!"

The awesome news which Licinia thus blurted out was but a confirmation of what Dea had already feared. Every drop of blood within her seemed to turn to ice, horror gripped her heart, the oncoming catastrophe appeared suddenly before her, vivid, swift and

154

inevitable. But she contrived to steady her voice and to appear outwardly calm as she said:

"I do not understand thee, Licinia, speak more clearly. What is it that hath happened?"

"The rabble are invading the Palatine," said Licinia, to the accompaniment of many groans. "They are on us I tell thee."

"On us!" retorted Dea Flavia scornfully. "Tush, woman! they'll not heed us.... But the Cæsar ... Hast news of the Cæsar?"

"No! no! my beloved, I have no news. I only know what the watchmen say."

"What do they say?"

"That the rabble is invading the hill. The miscreants have forced their way into the Forum. They have surrounded the palace of the Cæsar and set fire within its precincts."

"Ye gods!..." exclaimed Dea Flavia.

"Dost hear their shouts? the villains! the villains! Dost hear Jove's thunder, my beloved? His vengeance is nigh! May his curse descend on the villains and on their children."

"Silence, woman!" commanded the Augusta peremptorily. "Get me a robe—quickly—no, no! not that one," she added, as Licinia, with trembling hands had snatched up the gorgeous jewel-studded gown which Dea Flavia had worn the day before, "a dark robe—haste, I tell thee! go thou fetch it and send Blanca quickly to me."

Moaning and trembling, the woman endeavoured to obey and to make as much speed as her limbs, paralysed with terror, would allow her. She called to Blanca, who together with the Augusta's tire-women had her quarters close at hand, and the young girl hastened to her mistress's room whilst Licinia went in search of a dark-coloured robe.

"The praefect?" whispered Dea Flavia quickly, as soon as she felt assured that she was quite alone with her slave. "Hast seen Dion or Nolus?"

"My brother spoke to me in the atrium just now, gracious mistress," replied Blanca, who seemed scarce less excited than her mistress, "he and Dion heard a thud in the night, which roused them from a brief sleep which they had snatched, for they were very tired ... their long hunt in the Amphitheatre...."

"Yes! yes! go on! I know that they slept ... and they heard a thud ... what was it?"

"They ran to the resting-chamber, gracious lady, and found the praefect of Rome lying senseless on the floor."

"Great Mother!... and what did they do?"

"They lifted him as best they could; for the praefect is over tall and mightily powerful. But they succeeded in laying him back on to the couch, and Dion ran to rouse the physician."

"And now?"

"The physician hath given the praefect a drug to make him sleep, for it seems that fever was upon him with the pain of his wounds and he talked incoherently like one bereft of reason."

"Hush!..." interrupted Dea Flavia hurriedly, "not before Licinia."

Even as she spoke the old woman returned, carrying a robe of dove grey cloth, the darkest one that she could find. She had collected the tire-women round her, and they flocked in her wake like frightened sheep that have been driven into a pen. Licinia herself was evidently the prey of abject terror, for her teeth were chattering, and all the while that she helped her mistress to make a hasty toilet, she uttered low moans as if she were in pain.

"The traitors! the miscreants!" she murmured at intervals.

But Dea Flavia paid no heed to her. Her women had brought her fresh water, perfumes and fine cloths, and she was hastily bathing her face and hands. Then, she slipped on the dull-coloured robe and Licinia's trembling fingers fastened a girdle round her waist.

And all the while, from far away, came the dull sound of Jove's thunders hurled by his wrath, and above it as a constant din, like the roaring of a tempestuous sea, the hoarse cries which—borne upon the wings of the oncoming storm—seemed to gain distinctness as their echo reached this distant house.

"Dost hear the cries, Blanca?" asked Dea Flavia, as the young slave, leaning out of the narrow window tried to peer out into the street.

"I hear them, gracious lady," replied the girl in an awed whisper.

"And canst distinguish any words?"

"Aye, one word, gracious lady ... Hark!"

And that word sent its dismal echo even to Dea Flavia's ear.

"Death!"

Then Blanca uttered a terrified scream and quickly drew away from the window; from beyond the Palace of Tiberius, there where the new Palace of Caligula reared its gigantic marble pillars above the temples below, a huge column of flames had shot upwards to the sky. And a cry, louder than before and more distinct, came clearly from afar.

"Death to the Cæsar! Death!"

"Ye gods protect him," murmured Dea Flavia fervently.

"They'll murder him! they'll murder him!" shouted Licinia at the top of her trembling voice.

She had fallen on her knees and the other women squatted round her like a huddled-up mass of terror-stricken humanity, with hair undone and pale, quivering lips and staring eyes dilated with fear.

But Dea Flavia, now that she was dressed, took no further notice of them; she left them there on the floor, moaning and whimpering, and hurried out into the atrium. Here too the sense of terror filled the air. Beyond the colonnaded arcade in the corridors and the peristyle

156

could be seen groups of slaves—men and women—squatting together with head meeting head in eager gossip, or clinging to one another in a state of abject cowardice.

Here too, through the open vestibule, the sounds from the streets came louder and more clear. That awful cry of "Death" echoed with appalling distinctness, and to Dea Flavia's strained senses it seemed as if they were mingled with others, more awesome mayhap, but equally ominous of "The praefect of Rome! Where is the praefect of Rome! Hail! Taurus Antinor! Hail."

The noise grew louder and louder, and from where she stood now—it seemed to her that she could trace in her mind the progress of the rebels, as they spread themselves from the foot of the Palatine and from the Forum, upwards to the heights until they had the palace of the Cæsar completely surrounded.

It was from there that weird cries of terror came incessantly, and in imagination Dea saw an army of cowardly, panic-stricken slaves, huddled together as her own women had been, with palsied limbs and chattering teeth, whilst a handful of faithful men of the praetorian guard were alone left to protect the sacred person of the Cæsar.

Above her, through the apertures in the tiled roof, she could see the sky aglow with lurid crimson, and the smell of burning wood and of charred stuffs filled her nostrils with their pungent odour.

"Death to the Cæsar! Death!" The cry seemed almost at her door. Only the Palace of Tiberius, with its great empty halls and basilicas stood between her and the rallying-point of the rebels.

She called loudly for Tertius—her comptroller—and he came running along from the slaves' quarters with an army of howling men and women at his heels.

"What news, Tertius?" she demanded. "Hast heard?"

"They have surrounded the Cæsar's palace," said Tertius excitedly, "and demand his presence."

"Oh! the sacrilege!..." she exclaimed, "and what doth the Cæsar?"

"He will not appear, and his guards charge the mob as they advance upwards from the Forum. They have invaded the temple of Castor, and already some are swarming in the vestibules of the palace. The guard are behind the colonnades and were holding the crowd at bay with fair success until...."

"Until?" she asked.

"Until some of the rebels skirting the palace, set fire to the slaves' quarters in the rear. The flames are spreading. The Cæsar will be forced to face the people, an he doth not mean to be buried beneath the crumbling walls of his palace!"

"The miscreants have set fire to the palace of the Cæsars?" she exclaimed.

"Alas!" replied the man, "they will force the Cæsar to show himself to them. And they loudly demand the praefect of Rome."

"The praefect of Rome?"

"Aye, gracious lady. The people had thought that the Cæsar killed him; some strove, it seems, to recover his body in the imperial tribune, where he was seen to fall. But the body had disappeared, and the rumour hath gained ground that the Cæsar had it thrown to his dogs."

"It's not true," she cried out involuntarily.

"No, gracious lady. Men of sense do know that it is not true. But an infuriated mob hath no sense. It is like an overgrown child, with thousands of irresponsible limbs. It is tossed hither and thither, swayed by the wind of a chance word. But it were as well, mayhap, if it were true."

"Silence, Tertius, how canst say such a thing."

"I think of the Cæsar, gracious lady," rejoined the man simply, "and of thee. If the mob found the praefect of Rome now alive or dead, then surely would they murder the Cæsar and make of the praefect their Emperor if he lived, their god if he were dead."

And as if to confirm the man's words, the morning breeze wafted through the air the prolonged and insistent cry:

"Taurus Antinor! Hail!"

With a curt word, Dea dismissed her comptroller, and he went, followed by his train of shrieking men and women.

She remained a while silent and alone in the atrium, while the moanings of the slaves and Tertius' rough admonitions to them died away in the distance.

"If the mob found the praefect of Rome now alive or dead," she murmured, "then surely would they murder the Cæsar and make of the praefect their Emperor if he lived, their god if he were dead!"

Dea Flavia cast a quick glance all round her. The atrium itself was deserted, even though from every side beyond its colonnaded arcade came the sound of many voices and those persistent, cowardly groanings which set the young girl's nerves tingling and caused her heart to sink within her, with the presage of impending doom.

Only in the vestibule the watchmen sat alert and prepared to guard the Augusta's house; they were gossiping among themselves and seemed the only men in the place who were not wholly panic-stricken.

The hum of their voices sounded quite reassuring in the midst of the senseless groans of terror which came from the women's quarters near the Augusta's rooms, as well as from the men in the more remote parts of the house.

After that brief moment of hesitation Dea went resolutely toward the studio. She crossed its small vestibule and pushed open the door.

Dion was sitting there on guard as the Augusta had commanded. He rose when she entered.

"The praefect?" she asked hurriedly.

"He sleeps," replied the man.

"Art sure?"

"I peeped in but a few moments ago. His eyes are closed. I think that he sleeps."

"I would wish to make sure," she said curtly.

Too well-trained, or mayhap too indifferent to show surprise at so strange a desire on the part of the great and gracious Augusta, Dion stood aside respectfully to allow her to pass, then he followed her to the door of the inner room and held aside the heavy curtain, whilst she put her hand upon the latch.

"Dion," she said, turning back to him, "yesterday I gave thee thy freedom, since thou didst serve me well."

"Aye, gracious lady," replied the man as he bent the knee in submissive respect, "and I would kiss thy feet for this, thy graciousness."

"When the city is once more at peace, we'll before the quaestor, and thou and Nolus and Blanca shall all be declared free. But to-day thou art still my slave and must obey me in all things."

"As thou dost command, gracious lady."

"Then, 'tis silence that I do enjoin on thee, Dion," she said earnestly, "silence as to the praefect's presence in my house, until I bid thee speak: on pain of death, Dion, for thou art still my slave."

"I understand, gracious lady."

"Then wait for me now and on peril of thy life allow no one to enter."

But scarce had these words crossed her lips than there rose from the atrium behind her a series of weird sounds, cries, and imprecations, calls for the Augusta and curses on her slaves, as from one who is bereft of reason and screams in his madness.

"The Cæsar!" she murmured, as white to the lips now, she stood rigid by the door whilst her hand fell from the latch.

"Augusta! Augusta!" came the hoarse cries from the atrium, and the hideous, familiar sound of leather thongs whistling through the air reached her straining senses.

She put a finger to her lips, with a quick peremptory gesture to Dion, then she recrossed the studio with a firm step and the curtains of the inner door fell back behind her with a swish.

The next moment she was standing in the atrium facing Caligula, the Cæsar.

CHAPTER XXVII

"How art thou fallen from heaven, O Lucifer, son of the morning!"—Isaiah xiv. 12.

He had a score or so of his guard with him and they remained at some little distance, in a compact group, with their short, bronze-hilted swords naked in their hands.

Caligula was livid. He had donned a dark woollen robe and his head was uncovered. His knees, arms and hands were shaking and his mouth opened and closed as if he were gasping for breath. His eyes were bloodshot and staring out of his head like those of a man who is being strangled.

"Gracious Cæsar!" exclaimed Dea Flavia as soon as she was before him, and with the instinct born of long usage, she bent the knee before him.

"They have trapped me," he murmured inarticulately whilst weird choking sounds escaped his throat. "They have trapped me, hast heard?"

"Alas!"

"The miscreants! the sacrilegious miscreants! the hideous monsters! the villainous reptiles! Aye! punishment will overtake them; they shall rue this day! All Rome shall rue this day: her streets shall flow with blood and I'll invent such tortures for every man as will turn the firmament red with horror ... I'll...."

His mouth was twitching convulsively and his hands clutched spasmodically at his throat. Dea Flavia had risen to her feet, she stood before this raging madman erect and calm, with eyes downcast, for the sight of him filled her with loathing.

Suddenly he ceased in his ravings; a loud crash as of crumbling walls had rent the air, followed by shrieks and loud hissing sounds and that perpetual cry, awesome in its weird monotony:

"Death to the Cæsar! Death!"

Caligula's face was contorted with terror, his cheeks were grey like those of the dead. He made a quick movement forward and suddenly clutched Dea's wrist.

"Dost hear them?" he said in a hoarse whisper.

And she nodded in response.

"They want to kill me ... they have set fire to my house ... I escaped through the crypta.... But they were hard on my heels...."

And as if to confirm his words, the cries of "Death!" again rose in the air; the tramping of feet, the angry murmurs became more loud and appeared to be filling the street close by and tending toward the very door of Dea Flavia's house.

"Ah, monsters! miserable monsters!" shouted the Cæsar, crazy with fear, "to-morrow will come the awful reprisals ... to-morrow ..."

"To-day," broke in Dea Flavia coldly, "the Cæsar is in danger of his life."

"They'll kill me," he cried, whilst once more trembling—akin to palsy—seized his limbs. "They'll kill me, Augusta ... hide me, hide me ere they come."

And he fell on his knees, grovelling on the floor like a fawning beast, with quivering hands clutching the young girl's robe, his forehead beating the ground at her feet.

"Hide me, Augusta," he murmured through his groans, "hide me!... Do not let them kill me."

She drew back in horror and disgust, closing her eyes lest she should see this degradation of the Cæsarship, this breaking down of her highest ideals.

But two days ago this same abject creature had stood beside her, demanding from her obedience and loyalty which she was fully prepared to accord to him. He had called on her fealty in the very name of that Cæsarship which she worshipped and which he was now degrading and lowering to the dust.

Then as now Jove's thunders from afar had proclaimed the wrath of the gods. Then as now Jove thundered his warnings to that man not to defile the majesty of the Cæsars. But two days ago she had still believed in and acknowledged that majesty, she had bent her will, curbed her inclinations, smothered her every girlish inspiration, her every womanly instinct to the dictates of that power which came straight from the hands of the gods; now she felt actual physical nausea at the sight of this pitiable coward, who—wallowing in his own cruelty—had not even the unreasoning pluck of a brute defending its life.

Involuntarily her thoughts flew back to the man who was lying helpless in her house. She saw him in her mind as she had seen him yesterday, bounding into the arena to save another's life: strong and determined—measuring and accepting every risk, looking neither to right nor left whilst he carried his self-imposed burden to safety, and then falling without a groan, felled to the ground by the claws of the panther.

And outside the cries had become quite distinct.

"Death to the Cæsar! Hail Taurus Antinor! Hail!"

The people, in their fury and their exultation, had condemned one man and exalted another. Truly the gods themselves had guided them in their choice. And now it seemed as if the final choice rested with her: as if in some distant shrine, mysterious oracles had spoken and told her that the future of Rome lay in her hands.

161

And involuntarily she looked down on her hands and saw that they were tiny and weak, and yet one of them would within the next few seconds point the way to Destiny, show her whither she should go, carrying on her giant shoulders the whole empire of the world.

At her feet a cowardly and inhuman creature grovelled, abjectly praying for a life which by its continuance could only bring more sorrow, more horrors and more misery to thousands upon thousands of human beings dependent on this half-crazy monster.

Behind her, beyond two walls there lay a man amongst men, for whom the people clamoured, whose very presence betokened strength and whose every glance diffused peace. A man born to rule a people and to guide the destinies of an empire, and whose life of simple integrity had yesterday been crowned by an act of sublime sacrifice.

And the choice rested with her.

Her ears were buzzing with the hoarse cries from without: the cry of "Death!" mingling with that of "Hail!"—the name of Cæsar blended with that of the praefect of Rome; and through it all, drowning them by their hideous sound, the groans and shrieks of a bloodthirsty tyrant, brought down to the dust by his own cruelties, and even now thirsting for more.

The choice did rest with her.

She had but to run a few steps to the vestibule and there to call loudly to the populace that even now was invading the slope of the hill toward her house. She had but to rush to her door and to shout boldly:

"The Cæsar is here, and the praefect of Rome is nigh!"

And the twenty men who were waiting with naked swords would be as naught before the onslaught of the people.

She looked round her helpless and dazed whilst the fawning creature on the ground embraced her ankles and kissed her feet, and repeated with frantic persistence:

"Save me, Augusta ... save me ... do not let them kill me.... I have been good to thee.... I am thy guardian—thy Cæsar ... save me...."

"Save thee?" she repeated mechanically, "how can I?"

"Hide me somewhere—where they cannot find me"—he murmured, half raising himself from the ground. "Thou wouldst not give up thy Cæsar to the fury of the populace ... thou wouldst not soil thy hands with the blood of thy kinsman..."

Now he was embracing her knees and his hideous, distorted face was looking up appealingly at her.

"Thou wouldst not soil thy hands with the blood of thy kinsman...."

Even as these words escaped his flaccid lips a roll of thunder louder than any previous one came echoing from behind the Aventine Hill. Dea Flavia shuddered. Was it Jove's warning, or already Jove's curse, the curse of the gods on her for the treachery of her thoughts?

162

"Thou wouldst not soil thy hands with the blood of thy kinsman...." he repeated pitiably.

"No! no!" she said hurriedly. "Not that.... I'll help thee!... What can I do?"

"Let me hide in thy house...."

"Where?"

He pointed to the studio.

"There!" he said.

"No! no!" she exclaimed, and instinctively her arms were held out, as if she would protect a sacred shrine.

"Thy workroom is private," he urged in tones of abject entreaty; "no one would venture there ... only thy women slaves ever cross its threshold.... I should be quite safe in the inner room ... thy women would not betray me ... thou hast some that are mute ... they could attend on me there, and no one would know of my presence until this outrage hath subsided.... In a few hours mayhap the praetorian guard will succeed in forcing a passage through the raging mob ... my legions too are on their way from Germany ... they will be here soon ... they were only four days' march behind me and my convoy ... they are but a couple of days' march now from the city gates ... I could stay in there ... in thy private room ... with a few men to protect me ... and thy women to attend on me ... no one else would know...."

He talked volubly, at times incoherently, with hoarse voice and quaking lips. She tried with all her might to free herself from his convulsive clutch—but he clung to her like a dying man would cling to the last breath of life—like a drowning man would cling to the raft on which he might find safety.

"In there——" he entreated.

"No—no——"

"I should be safe and nobody would know."

And now he raised himself to his feet, and swaying like a drunken man he turned toward the studio, calling to his guard to follow him. But she was still between him and that door, between this raving, bloodthirsty maniac and a helpless man who was lying wounded and in a drugged sleep on a bed of sickness.

The oracle had not yet finished speaking. The last word still hung in the air. Her choice had not yet been made: but at this moment when Caligula and his guard turned toward the studio door, she knew that it would not be long in the making. Never should that demented tyrant cross the threshold of her studio and wreak his hatred and revenge upon the fallen hero. Rather than that should happen she would call to the people, and hand over the Cæsar—her kinsman—to an infuriated mob. Better that than to deliver a wounded man into the claws of a raging brute.

163

Then mayhap the blood of her kinsman would stain her hands for ever; then, too, no doubt would come horror, remorse and the malediction of the gods. Then so be it. That would she take upon herself. What must be suffered, that she would suffer: the torments of remorse would be infinitesimal compared with the awful sacrilege which the Cæsar's hand would perpetrate, were he allowed access to the praefect of Rome.

And even as the resolve became firmly implanted in her heart, she found herself murmuring softly words which she had heard in the Forum a very few days ago.

"I have but one soul and that is in the hand of God!"

Something of the serenity which had then shone from the man's face now entered into her heart. Horror and excitement fell away from her like a useless mantle. She felt herself absolutely calm and unswerving in her determination.

Therefore she did not make a rush for the studio door, she did not with dramatic gesture interpose her body between it and the Cæsar: she merely put her hand out and let it rest upon his arm.

"I should be safe in there—and nobody would know...." he murmured.

"My slaves would know," she said coldly, "and would betray thee."

"I only fear the men and they need not know," he said eagerly, even though at her words he had paused and turned back towards her.

"Many of them have seen and heard thee."

"Tell them I have escaped to the Palace of Augustus, through the crypta."

"They would not believe it—they would know it was not true."

"Canst thou not trust thy slaves?" he snarled.

"Couldst thou trust thine?" she retorted.

"I can change robes with one of my guard," he urged, "and he could then pretend to be the Cæsar escaping through the crypta to the House of Augustus."

"'Twere safest not to make pretence," she rejoined coolly; "rather let the Cæsar do what he suggests."

"What is that?"

"The Palace of Augustus would be the safest stronghold for the Cæsar until the arrival of the legions. It would be safer than the house of his servant, for prying eyes may have seen him enter it, and ears—sharpened by hate—may have heard his cries."

"Then am I lost!" he exclaimed.

"Not if my gracious lord will take counsel of his servant. The underground way is clear and safe. The Palace of Augustus would afford ample shelter. Twenty men well armed will watch over the Cæsar and the house of Dea Flavia will furnish the necessary food."

Caligula hesitated a moment, his shifty eyes wandered restlessly over the face of the young girl.

"Thou'lt not betray me?" he murmured.

"I could betray thee now an I would," she said simply. "The mob is at my gate. One call from me and the Cæsar is in the hands of those who desire his death."

"Hush! hush!" he said, once more clutching her wrist and gazing fearfully around him, "speak not of this, Dea! The very words might call down the decree of the gods.... I'll trust thee," he added, bringing his livid face close to her own and speaking with a fever of maddened fury, "but if thou shouldst fail me...."

"No need of threats, great Cæsar," she said, calmly disengaging her wrist from his grasp and stepping back from him, "if I failed thee to-day neither I nor thou would be alive on the morrow."

The truth of what she said must have struck his dulled mind, for the look of savage ferocity quickly died from his face, leaving it once more pale with abject fear. He must have realised that his own unreasoning cowardice had placed him entirely in this girl's hands, and that having feared to meet his people a few hours ago, he had cut off from beneath his own feet the bulwark of dignity and of unapproachable sanctity on which he should have stood.

"I'll to the House of Augustus," he said more quietly, "while the rabble vent their rage upon my palace and search for their Cæsar that they might murder him, I'll remain there in peace. Do thou send thy most trusted slave into the streets, and let him endeavour to reach the praetorian guard who are holding their ground behind the crowd of rebels. They might effect a flank movement, which, if unexpected, might put the miscreants to rout sooner than we anticipate. Hast a slave whom thou canst trust thus far?"

"I have two freedmen," she replied, "free since yesternight, who would give their life for me."

"Let them do it then," he retorted cynically. "And do thou lead the way to the triclinium. I am anhungered, and a halt at thy table will throw dust in the eyes of thy slaves. I can reach the crypta from there without being seen again."

"As the Cæsar commands," she said calmly, "but there is little time to be lost."

CHAPTER XXVIII

"Nothing is secret, which shall not be made manifest."—St. Luke viii. 17.

Caligula himself led the way to the triclinium and Dea Flavia followed him.

He threw himself upon a couch and she, with her own hands, served him with wine and fruit. He refused to eat but drank freely of the wine, whilst she stood beside him calmly waiting until he should be ready to go.

Seeing Blanca cross the atrium, she had called to her and ordered her to serve the soldiers. The men were grateful for they were exhausted. They had not tasted food since the day before, and had been on the watch round the Cæsar's person all night.

The underground passage which runs beneath the declivity between the two points of the Palatine, and by tortuous ways under the temple of Jupiter Victor on its highest summit, did connect the house which Dea Flavia now occupied with the Palace of Augusta. The latter, since the death of the great imperator, had been used entirely as a hall of justice: a few scribes alone inhabited the rearmost portion of the huge edifice.

The passage itself abutted in Dea Flavia's house on one of the small rooms that lay round the triclinium. There were several such passages connecting the various palaces on the Palatine, but their existence was not revealed to the army of slaves, only a few responsible ones knew that they were there. In this instance the Cæsar could, from the triclinium, reach this road to safety without again crossing the atrium and encountering the prying eyes of hundreds of cowardly slaves.

He had no thought of thanking Dea Flavia for what she did for him, but having drunk his fill, he rose from the couch and made ready to go.

She escorted him to the door of the passage and gave brief instructions to the men how to proceed. She had lighted a small lamp which would guide the Cæsar and his escort on their way. From the door, a flight of precipitous steps led down into the darkness. Caligula was the first to descend and his soldiers followed him; the one who held the lamp keeping close to the Cæsar's person.

Dea Flavia stood at the door until the footsteps of the men ceased to send their echo back to her along the vaulted passage. Then, with a sigh of relief, she closed the door on them and hastily fled from the room.

Her one desire now was to shut out, as completely as possible from her mental vision the picture of her shattered ideal, the degradation of that majesty which she had honoured all her life. So imbued was she with that sense of honour and of reverence for the Cæsarship, that she would not dwell in thought on that awful sight of the Cæsar grovelling in abject terror at her feet. She wished to forget it—to forget him—the man who, in her eyes, was already no longer the Cæsar, for the Cæsar was a god, and like unto a god in glory and in dignity—whilst Caligula, her kinsman, had sunk lower than the beasts.

Almost involuntarily she had turned back toward the studio. A while ago she had wished to look on the praefect of Rome as he lay in a drugged sleep, desiring to assure herself that all was well with him; then the advent of the Cæsar had interrupted her. Over an hour had gone by since then and the whole aspect of the world had changed.

The Cæsar was a fugitive and a coward, and the people who had the upper hand were prepared to acclaim the hero of their choice.

The atrium now was gloomy and deserted. The slaves—gathered together in their remote quarters—shunned the vastness and the enforced silence of the reception halls; they preferred to huddle together in close groups in corners, distant from the noise of the street.

Dea Flavia stood quietly listening. Still from afar came the insistent cries of "Death!" and of "Vengeance!" Still overhead that lurid light and smoke-laden atmosphere. But now those same cries seemed almost drowned by a sound more persistent if less ominous: the sound of heavy pattering rain on leaden roofs and into the marble basin of the impluvium, whilst the roll of Jove's thunders appeared to be more nigh.

It was obvious that the storm which had been threatening all the morning from over the Campania, had burst over the great city at last. It was Jove's turn now to make a noise with his thunder, to utter cries and howls of vengeance and of death through the medium of his storm, and to drown the fury of men in the whirl of his own.

Now a vivid flash of lightning rent the leaden sky overhead and searched the dark corners of the atrium. Dea Flavia uttered an involuntary little cry of terror, and hid her face in her hands.

A high wind howled among the trees outside the house; Dea could hear the tiny branches cracking under the whip-lash of the blast, breaking away from the parent stem and sending an eddy of dry dead leaves whirling wildly along the narrow streets and into the open portals of the vestibule. She could hear the fall of the torrential rain, and the flames, which sacrilegious hands had kindled, dying away with long-drawn-out hissing moans of pain. She could hear the wind in its rage lashing those flames back into life again, and could see through the opening overhead the huge volumes of black smoke chased across the sky.

Smoke and flames were fighting an uneven battle against the persistent, heavy rain. The wind was their ally, but he was gusty and fitful: now and then helping them with all his might, fanning their activity and renewing their strength, but after a violent outburst he

167

would lie down and rest, gathering strength mayhap, but giving the falling rain its opportunity.

The rain had no need of rest; it fell, and fell, and fell, steadily and torrentially, searching the weaker flames, killing them out one by one.

To Dea Flavia's straining senses it seemed clear that in this storm the number of rebels had greatly diminished; none, no doubt, but the most enthusiastic remained to face the discomforts of drenched skin and bone chilled to the marrow. No doubt too the gale blowing the flames and smoke hither and thither on the exposed slopes of the Palatine, had rendered a stand in the open unmaintainable.

All this of course was mere conjecture, but the young girl, worn out mentally and physically with the nerve strain of the past four-and-twenty hours was grateful for the momentary sense of peace. The steady fall of the rain acted soothingly upon her senses; her wearied thoughts flew aimlessly hither and thither on the wings of her imagination.

Only the storm frightened her because she was not sure if it were an expression of Jove's wrath, or whether his mighty hand had only scattered the infuriated populace so that she—Dea Flavia—could weigh the destinies of Rome in peace.

She thought of going quietly back to her room, to think a while in the solitude; the danger being less imminent gave her leisure to ponder and to weigh in the balance her allegiance to Cæsar, and that other nameless sense within her which she did not yet understand, but which invariably drew her wandering thoughts back, and then back again to the man who lay in a drugged sleep under her roof.

He slept, and throughout the great city the people called on him: "Hail Taurus Antinor! Hail!"

She sighed and involuntary tears gathered in her eyes: but the sigh was not one of sadness, rather was it one of longing for something intangible and exquisite, and this longing was so sweet and withal so mysterious, that instinctively she turned away from the magnificent reception hall toward her own room, with a wild desire to be alone and nurse that longing into an all-compelling desire.

It was at this moment that five or six men—all wrapped in dark woollen cloaks—entered the atrium from the vestibule, and catching sight of the Augusta, called to her loudly with greetings of respectful homage.

She paused, angered at the intrusion; peace and solitude seemed indeed denied to her to-day; but recognising the praetorian praefect as the foremost of her visitors, she could not—owing to his high rank—dismiss him from her presence.

Caius Nepos had already bent the knee before her. He looked flushed and agitated as did most of the others, only my lord Hortensius Martius who was in the background, looked pale and wan from the terrible exposure of yesterday.

She did not think to wonder how these men had entered her house, how they had found their way to her presence, past her janitors, and without the usual formalities and ceremonies of introduction which her high rank demanded. She knew that her slaves were demoralised, that men who had been friends of the Cæsar were now fugitives, and vaguely thought that the praetorian praefect and his friends had found their way into her house as into a likely haven of refuge, and would, the next moment, be kneeling at her feet begging for protection and shelter, just as their lord and Cæsar had done on this selfsame spot half an hour ago.

"Your pleasure, my lords?" she asked.

"To speak with thee privately, O Augusta!" said Caius Nepos, sinking his voice to a whisper. "My friends and I have tried all the morning to forge our way through the mob and to reach thine ear. But the praetorian guard, faithful to me, was unable to make headway. Then did we think of covering ourselves with dark cloaks and of following the crowd, as if we were one with it, until it led us to the precincts of thy house. The storm as it broke overhead was our faithful ally; the crowd has sought refuge against it under the arcades of the Forum, and the slopes of the Palatine are comparatively free."

"Yet, do ye want shelter and protection from me?" asked Dea Flavia.

She had no liking for these men, all of whom she knew. Caius Nepos, selfish and callous; Ancyrus, the elder, avaricious and self-seeking; young Escanes whom she knew to be unscrupulous; Philippus Decius whose ostentation and lavishness she despised. She vaguely wondered why my lord Hortensius Martius was among them.

"Nay, gracious lady!" said Caius Nepos suavely, "'tis not thy protection which we crave, save for a few moments whilst we lay at thy feet our desires for the welfare of Rome."

"The welfare of Rome?" she queried vaguely. "I do not understand ye! What hath your coming hither to do with the welfare of Rome?"

"Allow us to make the meaning clear to thee, O Augusta. But not here, where prying eyes might be on the watch or unwelcome ears be prepared to listen. Grant us but a brief audience in strict privacy ... the destinies of Rome are in thy hands."

She made no immediate reply, but, as was habitual with her, she tried to read with searching eyes all that went on behind the obsequious masks wherewith these men sought to hide their innermost thoughts from her.

And as she peered into their smooth, humble faces, all at once she knew why they had come. She knew it even before they put their proposals into words; she knew why the praetorian praefect was so servile, and why my lord Hortensius Martius, despite his obvious weakness, wore an air of triumph.

169

They had come to betray the Cæsar and to place the destinies of Rome in her hands. It was strange indeed that this mealy-mouthed sycophant should be using those very words which had stood before her eyes like letters of fire, searing her brain ever since she had stood here—half an hour ago—with the grovelling Cæsar at her feet.

The whirl of thoughts which rushed to her brain now made her giddy. Instinctively now, as she had done then, she looked down on her hands—those hands which were to guide the destinies of Rome—and her heart had a curious twinge of pain, almost of fear, for she realised more fully than before how small and delicate they were.

"Time walks closely on the heels of destiny, O Augusta!" urged Marcus Ancyrus, the elder, in his gently insinuating voice; "for the nonce Jove has damped the wrath of the people of Rome, but that wrath is only dormant, it will break out afresh. The storm in the heavens will pass by, but the tempest caused by a raging mob will reawaken with double fury. In thy hands, Augusta, in thy hands!..."

She knew that all these men wanted was to use her as a tool—a puppet to dance to their piping. She knew that anon they would be as ready to betray her as they were betraying their Cæsar now. Yesternight had they come to her with their proposals she would have rejected them with unqualified scorn; but since yesternight she had seen the Cæsar abject, cowardly, degraded, dragging his bespattered majesty across the floor of this house; she had measured him—not by what he represented, but by what he was, and she had taken his measure ... and that of another .... and the Cæsar was lower than the brutes—and that other was greater than men.

A silent voice, a whisper which mayhap was an inspiration, caused her to look toward the studio.

"In there, my lords," she said, pointing to the door, "we shall be safe from watchful eyes and ears, and I will listen to what you have to say."

She chose not to see the look of triumph which flashed from six pairs of eyes, but calmly led the way toward the studio.

Caius Nepos and the others followed her without a word. Dion and Nolus rose as she entered, and she dismissed them, whilst ordering them to wait her pleasure outside the door. The two men—brought up in the school of slavery, were too well drilled to marvel at the gracious lady's many moods; they did not even cast one look in the direction of the inner room where they knew that the praefect of Rome still lay in a drugged sleep.

As soon as they were gone Dea Flavia turned again to Caius Nepos and to his friends.

"I pray you sit," she said simply.

She herself sat on a high chair with circular back carved of citrus wood, but Caius Nepos and the others preferred to stand.

CHAPTER XXIX

"For the children of this world are in their generation wiser than the children of light."—St. Luke xvi. 8.

Caius Nepos was the spokesman of the party. His high rank and great influence with the guard under his command gave him certain privileges which his friends were always willing to give him. They did not know of his treachery to them; nothing, indeed, had occurred to make them guess that the man who, in a sense, had been the leader and organiser of their party, had betrayed them all to the Cæsar in the hopes of greater gains, once he knew that his adherents had no thought of offering him the imperium.

The events of yesterday had changed the whole trend of Caius Nepos' ambitions. The people in its present temper was not like to accept him as the Cæsar, even if he could persuade the praetorian guard to acclaim him as such.

His one desire being his own advancement and his own interests, he had already realised that these were best served by adherence to Dea Flavia's fortunes, since the Cæsar himself, whilst still in the fulness of his power had named her and her descendants as his successors for all times. Caius Nepos, quick to seize his chance, and seeing the party of patrician malcontents aimless without a leader, had grasped his opportunity and constituted himself once more their organiser.

Now whilst the others grouped themselves at a respectful distance round the Augusta, he stood quite close to her, with back bent and his face in shadow.

"Augusta," he began, "meseems that in thy heart thou hast already guessed the purpose of our coming. The hour is rife and we do but wait thy command. We are at one in this: the praetorian guard will follow my dictates, the patriciate of Rome will bow the knee to thee. Augusta, the hour is rife! a raging madman, a cruel mountebank and abject coward has this day forfeited all rights to sit on the throne of Augustus, thine immortal kinsman. Augusta, art prepared to deliver Rome finally from under the heel of a tyrant, and thyself to place the sceptre of Augustus in the hands of one who were worthy of the prize?"

"I, my lord?" she asked coldly, for Caius Nepos had paused in his oratory, "I? How can I—a woman—decide on this great point? 'Tis for the legions to proclaim their Cæsar...."

"The legions," he broke in quietly, "will follow in the wake of the praetorian guard, and the praetorian guard will listen to my voice. They believe that the Cæsar is dead; they will soon believe that the will of Rome lies in this, that the final choice of his successor shall rest with thee."

Then as she made no reply but sat quite still and thoughtful, her small hand shielding her face so that it was in shadow, her elbow resting on the delicately carved wood of the chair, Caius Nepos drew a step or two nearer: he bent his long back nearly double and sank his voice to an insinuating whisper.

"It was the Cæsar himself, O Augusta," he whispered, "who yesterday, before all the people, made an oath and declared that thy future lord and master should succeed to the imperium, so that the descendants of immortal Augustus should in time become the rulers of Rome."

"But the Cæsar is not dead," she said simply.

"He is dead to the people, dead to his guard, dead to Rome!" asserted the praefect solemnly. "Yesterday the dagger of Escanes was ready to do the supreme act of retributory justice, and to rid the world of a maniacal tyrant and Rome of a cruel oppressor; to-day the act was virtually done by the madman himself when he fled in abject terror from before the face of his people."

And—as if in direct confirmation of Caius Nepos' solemn words, there came from far away, rising momentarily above the roar of the tempest, that ever-persistent monotonous cry:

"Death to the Cæsar! Death!" even whilst Jove's thunder overhead gave forth its majestic echo.

Dea Flavia no longer hid her face in her hand. She sat serene and dignified, upright and pure as a lily, allowing her thoughts to be expressed in her blue eyes, letting these ambitious self-seekers see that she was not deceived by their pretence at loyalty and patriotism. They gathered closer round her, and she looked now truly a queen, dignified and serene, her head crowned by the glory of her golden hair—towering above their stooping forms.

There was a look of contempt in her eyes which they did not choose to see. They were having their will with her; they had fired her ambition and roused her enthusiasm, and that was all that these intriguers asked of this girl, of whom they but desired to make a tool for the carving of their own selfish ends.

Vaguely the older men wondered on whom the Augusta's choice had fallen, whilst my lord Hortensius Martius felt the hot blood rush to his cheeks at the hopes that had once more risen in his heart.

But now Ancyrus, the elder, began to speak and his voice was mellow and gentle.

"The people have spoken plainly, O Augusta," he said; "wilt set thy will against the might of the people of Rome? Hath not Jove spoken clearly too? Think on the events of the past two days! The Cæsar's pronouncement in the Circus, the tumult amongst the people when my lord Hortensius Martius courted certain death in order to win thy favours, the rage of the populace against the Cæsar!... think on it all! Did not Jove direct all this?"

"Aye! but meseems that he did!" she murmured, as her eyes

fastened themselves on the heavy door that led to the inner room, "but since then hath he not directed the people to acclaim the Cæsar of their choice?"

Caius Nepos shrugged his shoulders and Hortensius Martius broke in hotly.

"The rabble clamours for the praefect of Rome! but the praefect is dead...."

"Aye! I remember, my lord," she said quietly, "there is a rumour that he died soon after he had saved thy life."

Then as Hortensius Martius, feeling the sting of the rebuke, bit his under lip to check an angry retort, Ancyrus, the elder, rejoined suavely, trying to pour the oil of his honeyed words on the troubled water of the younger man's wrath.

"The praefect is dead, O Augusta, and the people will soon forget him. Rome deifies thee because of thy great kinsman. Having forgotten the hero of their choice they will readily turn to thee whom they love. They will accept from thy hands the Cæsar whom thou wilt choose."

My lord Hortensius after that first feeling of anger had soon recovered his serenity. He tried to put an expression of sad reproach into the glance which he fixed on the Augusta. Perhaps she had not meant to rebuke him and was already sorry that she had wounded him. He would have liked to put into his glance all that he felt in his heart for her; deep down within him, below the overlaying crust of his ambition, there was real love for the beautiful girl who had it in her power to bestow on him all the gifts for which he craved.

He firmly believed that the Augusta reciprocated his love. She had always received his admiration more patiently than that of others, she had more than once listened quietly to the protestations of his love. Yesterday he had risked his life to win her hand: she, a proud Roman lady, was not like to forget his valour. When from the arena he had caught sight of her face, it was terror-stricken and deathly pale; she had feared for him then, of that he was quite sure.

The horrible death which he had faced had given him the first claim to her favours in the sight of his friends. They had rallied willingly round him and had tacitly recognised him as their leader. Now it seemed as if Jove himself, with the help of his thunders, had ranged himself on his side.

He saw the glow of enthusiasm rise to Dea Flavia's face, suffusing her eyes, her lips, her throat. He believed that that glow had been partly kindled by his glance, and was too much blinded by his own ambition and his own desires to note that the young girl's averted gaze was persistently fixed upon the door of the inner room.

Dea Flavia, of a truth, had little thought of my lord Hortensius Martius, of his ambition or of his love; she could not tear her eyes away from the spot beyond the stuccoed walls where lay a man—helpless

173

now—but a man whose every deed proclaimed him the born ruler of men.

Then, as those around her were silent, hanging expectant upon her lips, she forced her thoughts back to them and to all that they had said.

"What would ye have me do, my lords?" she murmured.

"Make thy choice, O Augusta!" urged Caius Nepos eagerly. "Choose thy lord and master from among those who are ready to acclaim thy choice as final. The praetorian guard is prepared I tell thee. The mad Cæsar yesterday paved the way for our success. Choose thy husband, Augusta, and the praetorian guard will forthwith proclaim him as the greatest and best of Cæsars, princeps, imperator, the father of his armies. The people will go wild with joy and will deify thee and thy lord."

"But the Cæsar ... my kinsman...?"

"He will end his days in contentment and in peace," said Ancyrus, the elder, dryly, "in a villa on the island of Capræa. No harm shall come to him. We here present do pledge thee our oath."

"But I must have time to think," she said earnestly; "'tis no small matter ye ask of me, my lords. I am but a woman and still young in years, and ye ask me to weigh the destinies of this mighty Empire in the balance of mine own desires."

"We would not ask it of thee, O Augusta! were thou an ordinary mortal," said Hortensius Martius, speaking with passionate warmth, "but thou art a goddess; the blood of great Augustus doth deify thee."

"A goddess? I?" she retorted coldly; "nay! I am but a lonely woman who hath need of counsel to guide her in this supreme moment of her life."

"Are we not here to guide thee?" came in dulcet tones from Ancyrus, the elder; "we, thy faithful servants, thy obedient slaves? Have we not spoken and counselled thee?"

"Aye! you have spoken, my lords, and I have read the thoughts that lie behind your words. 'Tis not loyalty to dead Augustus that alone led your footsteps to my door."

"Our love for thee," interposed Hortensius Martius softly.

"And your own aims that you would follow, your own ambitions that you would feed."

Then as hot words of protest rose to the lips of most, she put up her hand and added with quiet dignity:

"Nay, my lords, 'tis but human to be ambitious, and Rome herself is great because she is ambitious. But I, for myself alone, have no ambition. The proud title which ye would offer me holds no allurement to my tastes. But if the gods will so guide my choice that a just and brave man shall bear the sceptre of imperial Augustus, then will I thank them on my knees that I was made a medium for their will."

Hortensius Martius, convinced that her eyes had rested on him

174

while she spoke, made an effort to disguise the look of triumph that shone from out his glance. But young Escanes, in whom all hope had not yet died, was under the same impression, as also was my lord Philippus Decius; for, in truth, Dea Flavia had looked round on them all marvelling how any of them could compare with the man who already, in her heart, was the chosen lord of Rome.

"And now, my lords," she said, paying no further heed to the sighs of restless desires that rose up round her as she spoke, "I pray you ask no more of me. I must think and I must pray. I entreat you not to urge a decision on me until I have thought and prayed."

"Time is precious, Augusta," urged Caius Nepos feebly, "and the people will not wait."

"The people have fled from before the storm," she rejoined, "and their will, remember, my lords, may not be in accordance with yours."

"They call for the praefect of Rome and the praefect is dead. We must be ready to acclaim a Cæsar who will be equally to their choice."

"Then," she said, "when to-morrow the third hour of the day is called, I pray you, my lords, come back to me for mine answer. But I must have until to-morrow to ponder and to pray. An you must press me now," she added decisively, seeing that protestations were again hanging on their lips, "then must my answer be 'No!' to all your demands."

Though in her heart she had already weighed all that she meant to do, yet she would not give her decision without speaking first to the man who already was the elect of her choice. He was sick now, lying in the arms of sleep. In a few hours probably he would be refreshed, and it would indeed be a mighty Cæsar whom she would proclaim on the morrow before the people of Rome.

"The people will not wait till to-morrow, Augusta," urged Ancyrus, the elder, "canst tell a raging tempest to pause or a thunderstorm to bide thy time? They are quiet for the nonce but in an hour they will again invade the imperial hill. Thy house will not be safe."

"Then must ye put a check upon the people as best ye can, my lords; I cannot make my choice at this hour," she said determinedly, "if ye cannot wait and if ye fear the people, then must you make your plans without my help."

They consulted with one another in whispers. The Augusta was obdurate and without her they did not care to act. Her personality was alone powerful enough at this crisis to satisfy the people, and she alone could stand for the success of their intrigues against the people's loud demands for the praefect of Rome.

Betwixt two dangers the plotters chose the lesser one. If the populace got once more out of hand they would, whilst invading the palaces, find the Cæsar and no doubt murder him. That act of vengeance once accomplished they would probably calm down for a while. They would expend their strength in clamouring for the praefect of Rome, but the praefect of Rome was certainly dead, else he would have appeared ere this. The darkness of the night would perforce put a stop to all street-rioting; under its cover the praetorian praefect could easily rejoin the guard, and by the third hour of to-morrow, everything would be prepared for the proclamation of the newly chosen Cæsar.

Not one of these conspirators had any doubt as to who that Cæsar would be. Chosen from among their ranks, he would be compelled to reward richly those who had placed him on the throne.

Dea Flavia waited quietly while these hurried consultations were going on. Now that she saw that her wishes had prevailed, she once more became gracious and kind.

With a sign of the head and a smile that contained a promise she intimated to them that they were dismissed.

"I beg of you, my lords," she said, "to look upon my house as your own until the morrow. My slaves will offer you food and drink, and prepare you baths to refresh you, and sleeping-chambers for the night. To-morrow you will have mine answer. May the gods protect ye until then, my lords."

She touched a small gong summoning Dion and Nolus back into her presence. To them she entrusted the task of seeing to the needs of these great lords and of watching over their comforts.

It would have been churlish and inexpedient after this to insist on further conversation. Moreover the presence of the slaves put a check on privacy. It was better on the whole to obey. These sybarites too were not averse to the thought of a rich table and of merry-making in the Augusta's house until the morrow. Her cooks were noted for their skill and hers were the richest cellars in Rome.

Caius Nepos, Ancyrus, the elder, and the others all walked out of Dea Flavia's presence backwards and with spine bent at an obsequious angle.

Hortensius Martius was the last to leave. He knelt on the floor, and taking the edge of her tunic between his fingers he touched it reverently with his lips. She looked down on him, not unkindly. Had he but known that his greatest claim on her graciousness was that his life had been saved by another, he would not have worn that look of triumph as he finally followed the others out of the room.

"She hath made her choice, my lord," said Caius Nepos amiably, taking the younger man by the arm, "a woman was not like to reject such brilliant proposals."

"I will ask for the praefecture of Rome," murmured Ancyrus, the elder, complacently.

My lord Hortensius Martius said nothing, but he disengaged his arm from his too familiar friend and walked ahead of all the others, squaring his shoulders and holding his head erect, as one already marked out to rule over the rest of mankind.

CHAPTER XXX

"Strait is the gate, and narrow is the way...."—*St. Matthew vii.*
14.

In the studio, upon the throne-like chair of carved citrus wood and heavy crimson silk, Dea Flavia sat silent and alone.

The footsteps of the men quickly died away on the marble floors of the atrium, their harsh voices and loud laughter only reached this secluded spot as a faint, intangible echo.

The patter of the rain from above into the impluvium was soothing in its insistent monotony, only from time to time Jove, still angered, sent his thunders rolling through the heavy clouds and his lightnings rending the lurid sky.

The people of Rome, wrathful against the Cæsar, vaguely demanding vengeance for wrongs unstated, had not gone to rest. Like the gale a while ago they had merely drawn back in their fury, quiescent for a while, but losing neither strength nor temerity. Dull cries still resounded from afar. "Death to the Cæsar!" was still the rallying cry, though it came now subdued by distance, and the majestic screens of stately temples interposed between it and the towering heights of imperial Palatine.

Dea Flavia at first—her musings one wild tangle of hopes, fears and joys—did only vaguely listen for each recurrent cry as it came; and thus, listening and watching, her ears became doubly sensitive and acute, and caught the words more distinctly as they rolled on the currents of the wind that blew them upwards from the arcades of the Forum.

"Death to the Cæsar!" That cry was always clear, and with it came, like a complement or a corollary, the name of the praefect of Rome.

"Hail Taurus Antinor Cæsar! Hail!"

The cry filled Dea Flavia's veins as with living fire. She longed to run out into the streets now, at this moment, with the rain beating about her and the storm raging overhead, and to call to the people to come into her house, in their thousands and tens of thousands, and here to fall down and worship the mighty hero who would rule over them all.

The people clamoured for him, and because of these clamours an almighty love for the people of Rome filled the heart of the Augusta. She saw now just what the imperium should be, just how supreme power should sit upon a man. And she loved the people because the people saw it too. They clamoured for the one man who would fulfil every ideal of Cæsarship and of might.

Valour yesterday, the sublimity of self-sacrifice, had appealed to

177

them with irresistible force, even though they did not understand the force that had set these great virtues in motion. The hero of yesterday should be the chosen of to-day, the god of to-morrow; let the brutish Cæsar be swept from before his path.

The people clamoured, and did they see the praefect of Rome standing virile and powerful before them, they would fall on their knees and acclaim him princeps, imperator, greater than great Augustus himself.

And in this very house, but a few steps from where Dea sat musing, were the men, the patricians who were ready to accept the decision of the people, who were all-powerful to make the legions acknowledge the new Cæsar, and ready to set the seal of official acceptance to the wild desires of the plebs.

The patriciate of Rome had combined with the people to place its destinies in Dea Flavia's hands. The Cæsar's insane pronouncement in the Circus yesterday had confirmed the wishes of the conspirators. All envies and jealousies would best be set at rest if the kinswoman of great Augustus chose the future Cæsar, and secured the inheritance of the great Emperor for his descendants later on.

And now there was but her choice to be made, and the imperium would descend on the noblest head that had ever worn a crown. Dea Flavia felt the hot blood rush to her cheeks at thought that the choice did rest with her, that the man who was so proud, so self-absorbed, so self-willed but a few days ago in the Forum, would receive supreme gifts through her; that he would be the recipient and she, like the goddess holding riches, power, honour in her hands; that she would shower them on him while he knelt—a suppliant first, then a grateful worshipper—at her feet.

Ambitious? He must be ambitious! Ambition was the supreme virtue of the Roman patrician! And she had it in her power to satisfy the wildest cravings of ambition in the one man above all men whom she felt was worthy of the gifts.

Those were the first thoughts that merged themselves into a coherent whole in Dea Flavia's head after Caius Nepos and the others had bowed themselves from out her presence, and there was her sense of the power of giving, that sense so dear to a woman's heart. As to the thought of love—of the marriage which this same choice of hers would entail—of that greatest gift of all—herself—which by her choice she would promise him—that thought did not even begin to enter her head. She was so much a girl still—hardly yet a woman—she had thought so little hitherto, felt so little, lived so little; a semi-deified Augusta, surrounded by obsequious slaves and sycophantic hangers-on, she had existed in her proud way, aloof from the bent backs that surrounded her—loyal to the Cæsar, loyal to herself and to her House—but she had not lived.

There had never been a desire within her that had not been

178

gratified or that had grown delicious and intense through being thwarted; she had never suffered, never hoped, never feared. The world was there as a plaything; she had seen masks but never faces, she had never looked into a human heart or witnessed human sorrow or joy.

Looking back upon her life, Dea Flavia saw how senseless, how soulless it had been. Her soul awakened that day in the Forum when first a real, living man was revealed to her; not a puppet, not a mealy-mouthed sycophant, not a tortuous self-seeker, just a man with a heart, a will, a temperament and strange memories of things seen of which he had told her, though he saw that he angered her.

Since then she had begun to live, to realise that men lived, thought and felt, that they had other desires but those of pleasing the Cæsar or winning his good graces. She had seen a man offering his life to save another's, she had seen him clinging to a strange symbol which seemed to bring peace to his heart.

That man she honoured and on him would rest her choice, and he would be exalted above everyone on earth because she believed him to be loyal and just, and knew him to be brave. Her own heart—still in its infancy—had not realised that her choice would rest on that man, not because of his virtues, not because of his courage and his power, but for the simple, sublime, womanly reason that he was the man whom she loved.

And as she sat there, musing and still, with her eyes almost involuntarily drawn toward the oaken door of the inner room, she saw it slowly swinging out upon its hinges, she heard the swishing of the heavy curtain behind it, and the next moment she saw the praefect of Rome standing on the threshold.

He looked sick and wan, but strangely tall and splendid in the barbaric pomp of the gorgeous robe which he had worn yesterday. Dion had cleaned it of blood and dust, and it still looked crumpled and stained, but as he came forward the purple and gold gleamed against the stuccoed walls of the studio, and his tawny hair and sun-tanned face looked dark in the subdued light.

She could see plainly through the robe the line of bandages which bound his lacerated shoulders, and her heart was filled with pity for all that he had suffered, and with pride at thought of all the joys that would come to him through her.

As he came nearer to her, he bent the knee.

"I crave leave to kiss thy feet," he said, "for thy graciousness to me."

"Thou art well, O Taurus Antinor?" she asked timidly; "thy wounds...."

"Are healed, O gracious lady," he broke in gently, whilst a smile lit up his dark face, "since thy lips did deign to ask after them."

"It was presumptuous of me to bring thee here," she said after a while. "I feared that thou wast dead, and the Cæsar...."

"Would have defiled my body. Then would I kiss the ground where the hem of thy gown did touch it, for thy graciousness hath made it sacred."

"I pray thee rise," she said, "thou art weak."

"May I not kneel?"

"Not to me."

"Not to thee, but before thee, Augusta; before thy beauty and thy purity, the exquisite creations of God."

"Of thy God, O Taurus Antinor," she said with a little sigh. "He hath naught to do with me."

"He made thee for man's delight, to gladden the heart of those on whom thy glance doth rest."

She had ordered him to sit on a pile of cushions which lay not far from her chair. Thus was he almost at her feet, and she could look down upon his massive shoulders and on his head bent slightly forward as he spoke.

She thought then how like unto a ruler of men he was, how much strength and power did his whole person express. She wondered, with a happy little feeling of anticipation, how he would take the news which she would impart to him, what he would say, how he would look when he knew that she was prepared to crown him with the diadem of Augustus, and to bestow on him the full gifts of her love.

Time was precious, and the next few moments would satisfy her wonderment. She longed to see the fire of ambition light up his earnest face: the glow of love smouldering in his eyes would render their glance exquisitely sweet.

But for the moment she would have liked to put the more serious issues off for a while, she would have liked to sit here for many hours to come, with him close by at her feet, her ears pleasantly tickled by his gentle words of bold admiration yet profound respect. Had he not said that she was made to gladden the heart of those on whom her glance did rest? And a sense of sadness had crept into her heart as he thus spoke, for memory had conjured up before her mind the miseries which had followed in her wake these few days past.

"I have brought naught but misery," she said with a sigh, "to those whom I would bless."

"Joy to me, Augusta," he rejoined earnestly, "since the day I first beheld thee."

"Menecreta is dead," she whispered; "dost remember?"

"I remember."

She paused a while, then said abruptly:

"And the Cæsar is a fugitive."

"Heavens above!" he exclaimed, and the whole expression of his face changed suddenly; "a fugitive?... when?... where...?"

"The people are wrathful against him," she said; "they surrounded his palace, and even...."

180

The words died on her lips. The shout of "Death to the Cæsar! Death!" had come distinctly from afar. He jumped to his feet, and she saw that his face now looked careworn and anxious.

"Where is the Cæsar?" he asked hurriedly.

"He is a fugitive, I tell thee. The rabble fired his palace to force him to come out of it and face them. But he ran away through the secret passage which leads through the house of Germanicus to mine."

"He is here then?"

"No! He grovelled at my feet and begged me to hide him ... here ... in my private chamber where he thought he would be safe ... but I would not let him come for I thought thee helpless in thy bed, and feared that he would kill thee."

"Great God!"

"Nay! why shouldst thou call to thy god on behalf of a tyrant and a coward," she said excitedly; "thou shouldst have seen that man cowering at my feet like a beaten dog. I could have spurned him with my foot, as I would a cur."

"The Cæsar, Augusta, the Cæsar!"

"Aye!" she rejoined firmly, "the Cæsar, my kinsman! Were he not that, I would have rushed to my door and called to the people, and would have handed over unto them that miserable bundle of rags which stood for the majesty of Cæsar!"

"And I lay a helpless log," he rejoined bitterly, "while the destinies of Rome lay in thy hands."

"Aye! The destinies of Rome," she said proudly, whilst a glow of intense excitement filled her whole personality, "but not in my hands, O praefect, but in thine!"

"In mine?"

She rose and went up to him and placed her white fingers upon his arm.

"Listen!" she said.

She held up her other hand and thus stood beside him with slender neck stretched slightly forward, her lips parted, a look of intentness expressed in the whole of her exquisite face.

"Dost hear?" she whispered.

Obedient to her will he listened too. The cry of "Death to the Cæsar!" monotonous and weird, seemed to strike him with horror, for his wan cheeks assumed a yet paler hue and his lips murmured words which, however, she could not understand. Then suddenly the cry was followed by another—indistinct at first, yet gaining in clearness as it rose on the waves of the storm from the Forum below.

"The praefect of Rome! Where is the praefect of Rome? Hail Taurus Antinor Cæsar! Hail!"

"Hark!" she said triumphantly, "dost hear? The people call to thee! They are ready to deify thee. They call for thee, dost hear them, O praefect?"

But though she turned her eager, questioning gaze on him, though excitement and enthusiasm seemed to emanate from her from every pore, the look of horror only deepened on his face and the whispered prayer did not cease to tremble on his lips.

"Dost hear them?" she reiterated once more.

He was looking on her now, and gradually horror faded from his eyes and pallor from his cheeks. A wave of tenderness seemed to pass right over his face, making the harsh lines seem marvellously soft.

"I hear thy voice," he murmured, "soft as the breath of spring among the leaves of roses."

"The people call for thee."

"And thy hand is on my arm and I feel the magic of thy touch."

She stood there quite close to him, tall and slender like those lilies which—ever since he first beheld her—had so sweetly reminded him of her. Her simple grey tunic fell in straight folds from her shoulders, not a single jewel adorned her hands or neck, only her hair, in heavy plaits, made a crown of gold above her brow.

Never had she seemed to him so beautiful as now, for never had she seemed so womanly and yet so young. Her soul—rising triumphant from its trammels of high rank and artificial living—emerged god-like, opening out to the advent of love, welcoming it as it came, enfolding it in its own ardour and in its purity. With this man's presence near her, with her hand upon his arm, she had suddenly understood. Ambition, power, dominion of the world had vanished from her thoughts.

She had found love, knew love, felt its empire and its yoke, and the vista which that knowledge opened up before her was more wonderful than she could ever have dreamed of before.

Her cheeks were glowing with enthusiasm, her lips were parted and her eyes were of a vivid, translucent blue, with the pupils like brilliant sardonyx, full of dark and mysterious lights. She was ready to meet love with a surfeit of the rich gifts which she had at her command.

"The people call to thee, Taurus Antinor," she reiterated eagerly; "they want a man to lead them. They are tired of tyranny, of bloodshed and of idleness. They want to live! Therefore they call to thee. Two hundred thousand hearts were opened to thee yesterday in the Amphitheatre! Two hundred thousand tongues acclaimed thee even as in thine arms thou didst hold my lord Hortensius Martius and didst bear him into safety. The people have need of thee, and are ready to follow thee whithersoever thou wouldst lead them. They are miserable and oppressed, they want justice! They are starving and want bread. Their fate is in thy keeping for thou wouldst give them justice, and thou wouldst feed the poor and clothe the needy. All this morning did I hear the moans of the down-trodden, the wretched and the weak, and felt that Rome could only find happiness now through thee."

"And the Cæsar?" he said. "Where is the Cæsar?"

"He hath fled like a coward. Let him be forgotten even whilst the people proclaim thee the Cæsar and a new era of happiness doth rise over Rome."

Then as he made no reply she continued more hurriedly, more insistently:

"There are those here in my house now who would be the first to acclaim thee as the Cæsar. The praetorian guard, fired by thy valour yesterday, sickened by the cowardice of Caligula, is ready to follow in their wake, whilst mine will be the joy of calling unto the whole city of Rome: 'Citizens, behold your Cæsar! He is here!'"

She would not tell him that the imperium should come to him only through her hands; a strange reticence seemed to choke these words in her throat. Anon he would know. Caius Nepos and the others would tell him, but it was so sweet to give so much and—as the giver—to remain unknown.

She made a quick movement now, half withdrawing her hand from his arm, but his firm grasp closed swiftly over it.

"No, no," he said, "take not thy touch from off my soul lest I sink into an abyss of degradation."

He kept her slender fingers rivetted against his arm, and she looked up at him a little frightened, for his words sounded strange and there was a wild look in his eyes. She remembered suddenly that he was sick and that a brief while ago fever had fired his brain. All her womanly tenderness surged up at sight of his drawn face.

"Thou art ill!" she said gently.

He fell on his knees, and still holding her hand he rested his forehead against the cool white fingers.

"I am dying," he said softly, "for love of thee."

There was silence in the room now whilst she stood quite still, like a grey bird in its nest. She was looking down on him and his head was bowed upon her hands.

A weird, ruddy light penetrated into the studio from above and the sound of the pattering rain awoke a soft, murmuring echo on the white walls. The noise of strife and rebellion, though distant, still filled the air around, but here, in this room, there was infinite quietude and peace.

Dea Flavia felt supremely happy. Love had come to her in its most exquisite plenitude; the man whom she honoured, loved her and she loved him. It seemed as if she had slept for thousands and thousands of years and had just woke up to see how beautiful was the world.

"Love is not death," she murmured gently. "It is life."

"Death to me," he whispered, "for I have seen thy beauty and felt thee near unto my soul. And when I no longer may look upon thee mine eyes will become blind with the infinity of their longing, and when I no longer can feel thy touch, my heart will become as a stone."

A quick blush rose to her cheeks.

"That time shall never come, Taurus Antinor," she said so softly that her words hardly reached his ears. "Have I not told thee that there are those in my house who are ready to acclaim thee as the Cæsar?... acting upon my kinsman's own pronouncement yesterday ... they have come to me ... to beg me to make the choice which will place the imperium in the hands of the man most worthy to wield it.... My choice is made, O praefect!... Look into mine eyes, my dear lord, and read what they express."

He looked up just as she bade him, and as he did so there fell on him from her blue eyes such a look of love, that with a wild cry of passionate joy he stretched out his arms and closed them around her.

"Love is not death, dear lord," she murmured, even as the tears gathered in her eyes and made them shine like stars.

The moment was too supreme for words. Even the whisper, "I love thee!" died upon their lips. He held her close to him, her dear head resting on his shoulder, his hand upon her cheek, the perfume of her loveliness mounting to his nostrils and making his senses reel with its exquisite fragrance.

This one great moment was love's, and it was love's alone. Each had forgotten strife, rebellion, ambition, the fugitive Cæsar and the murmuring people. Each only remembered the other and the perfect flavour of that first lingering kiss.

Whatever life held for them hereafter, glory or shame, joy or regret, this moment remained unspoiled, perfect in its esctasy, the world but a dream, love the only reality.

Overhead the thunder rolled at intervals, dull and distant now, with occasional flashes of vivid lightning which lit up Dea's golden hair and the round, bare shoulder which emerged above the tunic. Her face was in shadow; she lay against his heart like a young bird that has found its nest.

Then he awoke from this ecstasy.

"The Cæsar?" he said wildly, "where is the Cæsar?"

"Near me now, dear Lord," she murmured looking up at him with a smile; "my head is on his shoulder and I can hear the beating of his heart."

"The Cæsar, Augusta," he said more insistently, and now he held her away from him, her two hands still in his and held against his breast, but she at an arm's length from him.

"Augusta," he reiterated, "I implore thee! Where is the Cæsar?"

"Hid in the Palace of Augustus, whining like a coward for his vanished power.... Forget him, my dear lord ... he is not worthy of thy thoughts.... Whither art going?" she added suddenly, for with gentle force he had disengaged his hands from hers and had turned toward the door.

"To the Cæsar, dear heart," he said simply; "an he is a fugitive he hath need of friends: an he is afraid, he hath need of courage."

184

"Thou'lt not go to him, dear lord," she exclaimed indignantly, and her hands, strong and firm, fastened themselves on his arm. "A coward, I tell thee ... a madman ... a tyrant ..."

"The Cæsar, Augusta," he retorted; "deign to let me go to him."

"Thou'rt mad, Taurus Antinor! Fever is in thy veins and doth cloud the clearness of thy brain.... Hast not heard the people? They vow vengeance on him.... 'Tis on thee they call ... thou art their chosen, their anointed; the people call to thee. It is thou whom they acclaim."

"To-morrow," he said more gently, "they will have forgotten their disloyalty. To-morrow they will have forgotten me ... they will think me dead ... dead will I be to them to-morrow."

"Nay! but to-day," she urged, "to-day is thine and mine.... The praetorian praefect is here and the others ... the choice rests with me and my choice is made.... Rome even now rings from end to end with thy name: 'Hail Taurus Antinor Cæsar! Hail!' ... Hast no ambition?" she cried, for at her words he had remained cold and still.

"None," he replied gently, "but so to help the Cæsar, that he may gain the love of his people by acts of grace and mercy, and to see the wings of peace once more spread over the seven hills of Rome."

With a firm yet exquisitely tender touch he took her clinging hands in his, forcing her to release her grip on his arm. On her trembling fingers then he pressed a burning, lingering kiss.

"Thou art not going!" she cried.

"To the Cæsar, O my soul! He hath need of me! He has mine oath; my loyalty is his."

"A madman and a tyrant. If thou goest to him he will kill thee!... his guard is with him ... he will kill thee!"

"That is as God wills...!"

"Thy god!" she retorted vehemently, "thy god! Doth he wish to part us? Is my love naught that he should wish thee to spurn it...?"

"The value of thy love is infinite," he said earnestly and tenderly as, in perfect humility, he bent the knee for one moment before her and stooping to the very ground he kissed the tip of her sandal. "'Tis only on bended knees that such as I can render sufficient thanks to God and to thee for that holy, precious gift."

She bent down to him and said with earnest solemnity:

"Then I entreat thee, good my lord, in the name of that love go not to the Cæsar now.... An he doth not kill thee ... an thou dost help to bring him back to power, he will use that power to part thee from me.... Do not go from me now, dear lord—for if thou goest I know that it will be for ever.... The Cæsar hates thee now as much as he loved thee before ... his hatred is as insensate as his love.... He will kill thee or take thee from me.... In either case 'tis death, my good lord...."

"'Twere death to betray the Cæsar, O my soul!" he replied, still on his knees, his forehead bent low to the ground, "Death, a thousand

185

times worse than a dagger's thrust ... a thousand times worse than parting."

His voice was low and vibrant, and as his solemn words died away, they struck the murmuring echo that slumbered on the studio walls. And Dea Flavia was silent now: silent as he rose to his feet and stood before her with head slightly bent, silent, because borne on the subtle wing of that same dying echo there came to her the awful sense of unavoidable fate. She shuddered as if with cold, that sense of fatality seemed ready to spread over her soul like a pall.

It was only the Roman blood in her, the blood of victorious Augustus which would not allow her to yield to the spectre ... not just yet ... not until the last battle had been fought—the last unconquerable weapon drawn.

She waited in silence for a while, nor did she detain him by the slightest gesture although he once more made a movement as if to go, only her eyes rooted him to the spot even as she said very softly, her voice sounding full and mellow like the cooing of a dove.

"My lord, I entreat thee but to grant me one moment longer, for of a truth there is much that my mind cannot grasp. Of thy god we will not speak. Whoever he be, as thou dost worship him, I will be content to worship by thy side. But that will come in the fullness of time. Dost love me, my dear lord?"

"With every aspiration of my soul, with every beating of my heart, with every fibre of my body do I love thee," he said, and there was such intensity of passion in his voice, such a glowing ardour in the glance which seemed to envelop and embrace her whole person, that even she—the proud Augusta, the woman—exacting through the very magnitude of her love—was satisfied.

"Then, dear lord, I entreat thee," she said, "for one brief moment only think of naught but of our love. Let me rest in thine arms but that one moment longer, and remember the while that with my love, the world conquered will lie at thy feet."

She drew closer to him and once more lay against his breast. She was tender and clinging now, no longer the Augusta, the unapproachable princess but just a woman, loving and submissive, proud to give and proud to abdicate.

To him this was the torturing moment. He knew what she desired and what weapons she could wield wherewith to subdue his will. The battle he fought with himself just then was but a precursor of the fiercer one which anon he would have to fight against her. The rending of his soul was expressed in every line of his face, which once more now looked haggard and harsh; Dea Flavia saw it all. She saw how he suffered, whilst with every passing second the inward struggle became more difficult and fierce; his breath came and went with feverish rapidity, the frown across his brow deepened visibly, and for a

186

while his arms were rigid and his fists clenched, even though she clung to him, her frail body against his, her head upon his breast.

"Wouldst lose the world and lose me?" she murmured. "The world is at thy feet, and I love thee."

A moan escaped him as that of a wounded creature in pain; the rigidity of his arms relaxed and wildly now he was pressing her closer to him.

"I love thee," he murmured, "I love thee. The world is well lost to me now that I have held thee in mine arms."

"The world, dear lord," she whispered, "is not lost, rather is it won. My hand in thine, we'll make that world a happier and brighter one. Power is thine ... thou art the Cæsar...."

"Hush—sh—sh, idol of my soul! Do not speak of that ... not now ... when my arms are round thee and the whole world has vanished from my ken. Let me live in my dream just a brief moment longer; let me forget all save my love for thee. It hath burned my soul for an eternity meseems, for I have only lived since that hour when first I heard thy voice ... in the Forum ... dost remember?... when I knelt at thy feet and tied the strings of thy shoe."

"I remember!"

"And I loved thee from that hour. I loved thee for thy purity and because thou art exquisitely beautiful and I am a man thirsting for happiness. But God, who hath need of my soul, hath willed to break my heart so that I might remain pure and true to His service. It was so filled with thine image that even the glorious vision of His Passion became faint and dim. But with infinite pity He hath given thee to me just for this one brief, glorious hour that it might feed on the memory of thee, even whilst my feet trod the way that leads to the foot of His Cross."

"There is but one way, dear lord," she exclaimed, "for thy footsteps to tread! Tis the way that leads to mine arms first and thence upwards to the temple of Jupiter Victor where stands the throne and rests the sceptre of Augustus."

"The way of which I speak, dear heart," he rejoined earnestly, "also leads upwards, upwards to Calvary, on the uttermost summit of which stands a lonely, broken Cross. The wind and rains and snows of the past seven years have worked their will with it.... They tell me that one of its branches lies broken on the ground, that its stem is split from end to end. But it is there—there still, abandoned now and alone, but to eyes that can see, still bearing the imprint of the heavenly body that hung thereon for three hours in unspeakable agony so that men might know how to live—and might learn how to die."

She said nothing for the moment. Her excitement had not left her, but her lips were mute because that which was in her heart was too great, too strange for words. She did not understand what he meant; she still thought that fever had clouded his brain; anon, she felt sure, sane reason would return and with it ambition, which became every man. But she did not understand that his love for her transcended all human love she ever wot of; it was great and noble and sublime as all that emanated from him, and, womanlike, she was content to let other matters shape themselves in accordance with the will of the gods.

She looked into the face which in this brief period of time she had learnt to love, and tried to read that which to her was still hidden behind the earnest brow and the deep-set eyes. In them, indeed, did she read exultation, an ardour at least equal to her own, but an ardour for an object which she—the proud, exquisite pagan, the daughter of Augustus—wholly failed to comprehend. She had shown him the way to the imperium, to the diadem of Augustus, the sceptre of the Cæsars, yet in his eyes, which were unfathomable and blue as the ocean that girt his own ancestral home of far away, there glowed neither the fire of ambition, nor the desire for supreme power. Only the fire of love for her and the serenity of infinite peace.

"Dear lord," she said, "when the sceptre of Augustus is in thine hands thou canst wield it at thy pleasure. I know not the way of which thou speakest; the mountain of Calvary is unknown to me and thou speakest of things that are strange to mine ear.... But the gods have placed it within my power to make thee great above all men, the ruler of the mightiest Empire in the world, and on my knees do I thank them that they have shown me the way whereby I can guide thy footsteps even to the throne of Augustus."

"And on my knees do I thank God, O my soul, that thou didst show me the way to the foot of His Cross. God himself, dear heart!—oh! thou'lt understand some day for thy soul is beautiful and prepared to receive just that one breath from Heaven which will show it the way to eternal life—God Himself, dear heart, who lived amongst us all a lowly, humble life of patience and of toil! God—think on it!—who might have come down to us in the fullness of His Majesty, Who might, had He so chosen, have wielded the sceptre of the world and worn every crown of every empire throughout the ages, but Whom I saw—aye, I, dear heart—saw with mine own eyes as He toiled, weary, footsore, anhungered, and athirst, that He might comfort the poor and bring radiance into the dwellings of the humble. And I who saw Him thus, I who heard His voice of gentleness and of peace, I to desire a crown and sceptre, to betray the Cæsar and to mount a throne!!! Dear heart! dear heart! dost not understand that the sceptre would weigh like lead in my hands and the crown bow my head down with shame?"

"Then would my whispered words lift the weight from thy brow and my kiss dissipate the blush of shame from thy cheeks. Day and night would go by in infinite happiness, thy head upon my breast, mine arms encircling thy neck. I am ignorant still, yet would I teach thee what love means and the sweet lesson learnt from me thou wouldst teach me in return."

"And in mine ear the still, small voice would murmur: 'Thou hast seen the living face of thy God, didst break thine oath to Cæsar! thou didst betray him in his need, even as the Iscariot betrayed his Lord with a kiss.'"

"The voice of thy god," she retorted, "is no louder than that of the people of Rome, and the people proclaim thee the Cæsar and have released thee of thine oath."

"The voice of God," he said slowly, "spoke to me across the sandy wastes of Galilee and said unto me: 'Render unto Cæsar the things that are Cæsar's, and unto God the things that are God's.'"

His softly murmured words died away in the vastness around him. Dea Flavia made no response; a terrible ache was in her heart as if a cold, dead hand gripped its every string, whilst mocking laughter sounded in her ear.

That cruel monster Finality grinned at her from across the room. Love was lying bleeding and fettered at the feet of some intangible, superhuman spectre which Dea Flavia dreaded because it was the Unknown.

Taurus Antinor's eyes were fixed into vacancy, and she trembled because she could not see that which he saw. Was he looking on that very vision which he had conjured up, a cross, broken and tempest-tossed, a symbol of that power which to him was mightier than the Empire of Rome, mightier than the kingdom of her love?

She remembered how, a few days ago, in this self-same room she had in thought accosted and defied that Galilean rebel who had died the ignominious death; she had defied him, even she, Dea Flavia Augusta of the imperial House of Cæsar. She had offered him battle for this very man whose soul she now would fill with her own.

She had defied the Galilean, vowed that she would conquer this heart and filch it from the allegiance it had sworn, vowed that she would make it Cæsar's first and then her own, that she would break it and crush it first and then wrest it from its unknown God.

And now it seemed as if that obscure Galilean rebel had conquered in the end. She had brought forth the whole armoury of her love, her beauty, her nearness, the ardour of youth and passion which emanated from her entire being, and the intangible Unknown had remained the victor, and she was left with that awful ache in her heart which was more bitter than death.

"Have I thy leave to go, Augusta?" he asked gently at last, "the moments are precious. The Cæsar hath need of me...."

She woke as from a hideous dream. With a wild gesture of the arms she seemed to sweep away from before her those awful spectres that assailed her. Then she clung to him with the strength of oncoming despair.

"No—no," she cried, "do not go ... he will kill thee, I say ... do not go...."

189

"I must," he said firmly. "Dear heart, I entreat thee let me go."

"No—no ... think but a moment ... think!... My love?... is it naught to thee?... Has my kiss left thee cold?... Do not leave me, dear lord ... do not leave me yet ... not just yet ... now that I know what happiness can mean. I have been so lonely all my life.... Love hath come to me at last ... love and happiness.... I am young—I want both.... Dear lord, if thou lovest me canst leave me desolate?..."

"If I love thee!"

There was so much longing in the one brief phrase, such passion and such tenderness, that all her hopes revived. One more effort and she felt sure that she would conquer. Fever was in her veins now, the walls of the studio swam before her eyes; she fell on her knees for she could no longer stand, but her arms encircled him, clinging to him with all her might. Her face, lifted up to his, was swimming in tears, her golden hair escaping from its trammels fell in a glowing mass down her shoulders.

"I love thee," she murmured, "canst leave me now, dear lord.... If thou goest now 'tis for ever ... think, oh think! just for one moment ... the Cæsar restored to power will part me from thee ... even if anon in his madness he doth not kill thee. If thou goest 'tis for ever.... Think on it ... think on it ere thou goest.... My love ... my love, go not from me, and leave me desolate.... Dear lord, but think on it—of the kisses thou wilt taste from my lips—the ecstasies thou wilt find in my arms!... Thine am I—thine my heart that loves thee—my body that worships thee—my every thought is thine.... Go not from me ... not just now till thou hast felt once more the full savour of my love."

Her arms round his knees, and she was exquisitely beautiful, exquisite in her whole-hearted love, her whole-hearted abnegation— she, a proud Roman lady kneeling at his feet, her full red lips asking for a kiss.

He stood with his face buried in his hands.

"Oh God! my God!" he murmured, "do not forsake me now!"

The thunder crashed overhead while a human soul fought its desperate fight for truth and eternal life. A vivid flash of lightning lit up the white-washed walls of the studio, and to the poor fighting soul, tortured with temptation, with longing and with passion, there came in that swift bright flash a vision of long ago.

The sky lurid and dark, the soil trembling beneath the feet of thousands of men and women, and there, far away, outlined against that sky, a figure stretched out upon a Cross. The head was bent in agony, the eyes half-closed, the lips livid and parted, the body broken with torments had the rigidity of death. But the arms were stretched out, straight and wide, as if with one last gesture of appeal and of longing, and in this storm-laden air there floated tender words, intangible and soft as a memory.

190

"Come unto me, all ye that travail and are heavy laden, and I will refresh you."

It was but a vision, swift as the lightning flash that conjured it and the words had already died on the stillness of the air.

But the tortured soul had found its anchorage. Taurus Antinor's hands fell from before his face.

"In Thy service, O Jesus of Galilee!" he said, and the mighty effort of subjection brought the perspiration to his brow and caused his limbs to tremble. "I saw Thine agony, Thy sacrifice; it should be so easy to do this for Thy sake. Give me the strength to render unto Cæsar that which is Cæsar's, and do Thou take from me all that is Thine."

She heard his words, she saw the look and knew that she had failed.

Back on the cruel wings of remembrance came the words of Menecreta the slave.

"May thine every deed of mercy be turned to sorrow and to humiliation, thine every act of pity prove a curse to him who receives it, until thou on thy knees art left to sue for pity to a heart that knoweth it not, and findest a deaf ear turned unto thy cry!"

And the curse of the broken-hearted mother seemed like the tangible response to the defiance which she, in her arrogance and her pride, had hurled against him who was called Jesus of Nazareth. She would have blessed Menecreta and Menecreta was dead; she would have given her life for the Cæsar and the Cæsar was a cowardly fugitive, and now on her knees she had sued for pity, and the heart which she had fought for to possess had turned from her as if it knew neither mercy nor love, and whilst her very soul had cried with longing she had found a deaf ear turned to her cry.

That unknown Galilean who died upon the cross had been stronger than her love. It was he who was filching it from its allegiance, he who was brushing and crushing this heart ere he wrested it finally from her—Dea Flavia Augusta of the imperial House of Cæsar!

The Galilean had accepted her challenge and he had conquered, and she was naught in the heart of the one man she would have given her whole life to call her own.

She gave a cry like a wounded bird, she jumped to her feet, and for one moment stood up, splendid, wrathful, pagan to the heart.

"Curse thy god," she cried wildly, "curse him, I say, for a jealous, cruel god.... Go thy ways, O follower of the Galilean! go thy ways! and when lonely and wretched thy footsteps lead thee along that way which thou hast deified, then call on him, I say—thou'lt find him silent to thy prayer and deaf unto thy woe!"

Her body swayed, an ashen pallor spread over her cheeks, she would have fallen backwards like a log had he not caught her in his arms.

Reverently he carried her to the couch and there he laid her down, wrapping her grey shroud-like tunic closely round her feet.

He bent over her and kissed her golden hair, each blue-veined lid closed in unconsciousness, the perfect lips pallid now and still.

"In the name of Him Who died before mine eyes, take her in Thy keeping, O God!" he murmured fervently.

Then without another glance on her, he fled precipitately from the room.

CHAPTER XXXI

"Wherefore take unto you the whole armour of God, that ye may be able to withstand in the evil day, and having done all, to stand."—Ephesians vi. 13.

Without looking to right or left he strode across the atrium.

"A cloak quickly," he commanded as Dion and Nolus, obedient and expectant of orders, rushed forward at his approach.

From the triclinium on the right came the sound of loud laughter and the strains of a bibulous song, voices raised in gaiety and pleasure: Taurus Antinor recognised that of Caius Nepos, fluent and mellow, and that of my lord Hortensius Martius resonant and clear.

To what their revelries meant he did not give a thought. Dea had told him why these men had come to her house. The intrigues hatched two days ago over a supper-table were finding their culmination now. The Cæsar was a fugitive and the people rebellious: the golden opportunity lay ready to the hand of these treacherous self-seekers: and Dea Flavia was to be their tool, their puppet, until such time as they betrayed her in her turn into other hands that paid them higher wage.

Taurus Antinor wrapped the dark cloak which Dion had brought him closely around his person. He gave the slaves a mute, peremptory sign of silence and then quickly walked past the janitors, through the vestibule and out into the open street.

The midday light had yielded to early afternoon. It still was grey and lurid, with a leaden mist hanging over the distance and moisture rising up from the rain-sodden ground. The worst of the storm had passed from over the city, but the thunder still rolled dully at intervals above the Campania and great gusts of wind drove the heavy rain into Taurus Antinor's face.

It seemed to him, as he walked rapidly down the narrow street in front of the Augusta's palace, that the noise from the Forum below had gained in volume and in strength. When the raging tempest of rebellion was at its height earlier in the day, he had lain in a drugged sleep, unconscious of the shouts, the threats, the groans which had resounded from palace to palace on the very summit of the Palatine. When he awoke these terrifying sounds were already more subdued. The people had been driven by the storm-fanned conflagration which they themselves had kindled, to seek shelter under the arcades of the tabernae in the Forum below. But now, after a couple of hours of enforced inactivity, they were ready once more for mischief: in compact groups of a dozen or so they were slowly emerging from beneath the shelters, and it only needed the amalgamation of these isolated groups for the fire of open insurrection to be ablaze again.

Time, therefore, was obviously precious. At any moment now, if the rain ceased altogether, the populace—in no way cooled by the drenching—would once more storm the hill and would discover the fugitive Cæsar in his retreat. Already from afar there came to the lonely pedestrian's ear the roar of a mighty wave composed of many sounds, which, gathering force and fury, was ready to dash itself anew upon the imperial hill.

But up here on the summit there still reigned comparative quietude. True that as he walked rapidly along Taurus Antinor spied from time to time groups of excited, chattering men congregated at street corners or under the shelter of a jutting portico; whilst now and then from behind the huge piles of builders' materials, which littered this portion of the Palatine, darkly swathed figures would emerge at sound of the praefect's footsteps on the flagstones, and as quickly vanish again. But to these Taurus Antinor paid no heed; they were but the remote echoes of the angry storm below.

Soon the majestic pile of Augustus' palace loomed before him on the left, with its unending vistas of marble and porphyry colonnades. On the right was the temple of Jupiter Victor on the very summit of the hill.

An undefinable instinct led the man's footsteps to that lonely height. He skirted the temple and anon stood looking down on the panorama of Rome stretched out at his feet: the Palatine sloping downwards in a gentle gradient—covered with the dwellings of the rich patricians which formed here a network of intricate and narrow streets; below these the great Circus redolent of the memories of the past four-and-twenty hours; beyond it the Aventine and the winding ribbon of the Tiber now lost in a leaden-coloured haze.

The streets from the valley upwards all round the hill were swarming with men, who from this distance looked like pygmies, fussy and irresponsible, spectral too in the rain-laden mist as they appeared to be running hither and thither in compact groups, but with seeming aimlessness, whilst shouting, always shouting, that perpetual call for vengeance and for death.

The watcher looked down in silence, for that crowd of Pygmies was the people of Rome, who at a word from him would proclaim him Cæsar and master of the world. The immensity of the sky was above him, the far horizon partly hidden in gloom, but down there were the people whose voice was raised to deify their chosen hero in the intervals of demanding the death of a tyrant.

And the people were the lords of Rome just now. Entrenched in the narrow streets a crowd—one hundred thousand or more strong—held the imperial hill in a solid blockade. Down below, in and around the Circus, steel and bronze glittered in the distant vapours. One thousand men of the praetorian guard, cut off from the Cæsar, had been unable to forge a way through the serried ranks of the populace.

Dark masses—that lay immovable and stark in the open space around the Circus—spoke mutely of combats that had been fierce and bloody: but the people had remained victorious; the people held their ground. One hundred thousand fists and staves, a few agricultural and building implements had asserted their mastery over one thousand swords and shields.

The people were the masters of Rome, and they had chosen their Cæsar in the hero whom they had already deified.

Taurus Antinor's gaze swept over the vista that lay stretched out before him: it pictured the entire political situation of the world-city. With treachery lurking on the hill and a determined mob in the valley, the murder of the Cæsar was but a question of hours.

And after that?

After that the Empire of Rome and the dominion of the world for this man who stood here on the watch. He had but to say the word and that Empire would be his. He had but to go back now, to find his way with softly treading footsteps to the couch where Dea Flavia's exquisite body lay stretched out in semi-unconsciousness. He had but to take her once more in his arms, to murmur the words of love that—unspoken—seared his lips even now; he had but to close his ears to the still small voice that was God's, and Rome, the mistress of the world, and Dea Flavia, the peerless woman, would be his at the word.

Rome and Dea Flavia! the two priceless guerdons of the earth! They called to him now on the wings of the distant storm, from over the hills and from across the grey, dull mist that obscured the sky.

The man stretched out his arms with a gesture of passionate longing. How easy it were to take all! How impossible it seemed to give up everything that made life glorious and sweet.

A voice low and insinuating trembled in the air.

"Take all!" it said, "it is thine for the taking. Thine by the will of thousands, thine by the call of one pair of perfect lips ... Rome, the unconquered queen ... Dea Flavia holding in her white hands a cup brimming over with happiness ... all are thine at the word."

The silent watcher cried out in his loneliness and his agony; he

194

held his hands to his ears, for the voice grew more insidious and more real:

"The Empire of the world and Dea Flavia ... and in the balance what?... an oath rendered to a tyrannical madman, the scourge and terror of mankind ... an oath which reason itself doth repudiate with scorn ... even thy God would not exact obedience from thee at such a price...."

His head fell upon his breast and his knees bent to the earth. It was all so difficult ... it seemed well-nigh impossible now....

No words escaped his lips; he knelt here silent and alone before the face of Rome that but waited to be conquered—before the face of God veiled to his gaze, and around him the distant roll of thunder and the confused shouts of the people from below.

Christian! this is thine hour! In silence and in tears thou must make thy last stand against temptation greater mayhap than suffering manhood hath ever had to withstand alone.

Everything in the man cried out to him to yield; his love for Dea and his love for Rome, and that pride of manhood in him that calls for power over other men. Born and bred in luxury-loving paganism, in the worship of might and the deification of the imperium, the Christian had to choose between the world and the Master. The battle was fierce and cruel. Gone now was the consciousness of strength, the dignity of the patrician! Here was but a lonely wretched human creature fighting the tempter for his own soul.

He cowered on the ground, the while driving rain beat against the tawny masses of his hair, and lashed the proud stiff neck that found it so difficult to bend. The tearing wind searched the loosened folds of his mantle and the purple silk of his tunic, the emblem of patrician rank. His face was buried in his hands, heavy sobs shook his broad shoulders. The face of Dea Flavia, exquisitely fair, smiled at him through his closed lids, the warm, mellow masses of her hair entwined themselves around his tear-stained fingers, her cooing voice called to him with the ineffable sweetness of love.

Christian, it is thine hour! and the battle must be fought out in anguish and in loneliness, with no one nigh thee to comfort and to succour, with no one to see the rending of thy soul or the slow breaking of thy love-filled heart.

"When thou art lonely and wretched," Dea Flavia had cried in the agony of her wounded love, "call on thy god then and thou wilt find him silent unto thy prayer and deaf unto thy woe."

And the cry was wrung out from the depths of the tortured heart: "Oh, God, my God, if Thou be willing take this cup from me!" whilst the man prayed to his God to take his soul into His keeping ere it became perjured and accursed.

But God was silent, because the soul, though racked and tempted, was too great for the tasting of an easy victory. God was silent, but He saw the tears that fell heavy and hot upon the ground. He was silent, but He heard the cries of anguish, the bitter moans of pain.

Christian, this is thine hour! for when thy soul and heart have suffered enough, when they have been weighed in the crucible of divine love and not been found wanting, then will the peace of God which passeth all understanding descend in exquisite comfort upon thee.

Gradually the tears ceased to fall, the sobs to shake the massive frame of the kneeling man. His hands dropped from his face and his gaze went up to the storm-tossed firmament, there where land and sky merged in the grey mists of approaching evening.

And on the horizon, as he gazed, beyond the valley, beyond the Aventine and the murmuring Tiber, already wrapped in gloom, a ray of golden light had rent the lowering clouds.

It shone serene and bright, illumined from behind limitless depths by the slanting rays of a slowly sinking sun. Taurus Antinor rose to his feet; he looked and looked upon that light until it tore a wider and ever wider gap in the angry clouds, and its golden radiance spread right across the horizon far away.

The very mist now seemed aglow; the waters of the Tiber, tossed by the gale, throw back brilliant sparks of reflected lights.

From the low-lying marshes among the reeds two birds rose in rapid flight and disappeared in that golden haze.

"My God, not mine but Thy will be done!" murmured the lonely man; and anguish folded its sable wings and the tortured heart was at peace.

CHAPTER XXXII

"For whom the Lord loveth He chasteneth, and scourgeth every son whom He receiveth."—Hebrews xii. 6.

The gorgeous palace of Augustus appeared quite deserted when the praefect of Rome finally made his way to the vestibule. He crossed the magnificent inner peristylium, the tall, uncut pillars of which, sharply defined against the sky, enhanced its majestic grandeur and its air of mysterious solemnity.

As a rule these vast halls were peopled with scribes, and though shorn of its original imperial splendours the palace of the great Emperor presented at times a certain air of animation and of official bustle. But now these scribes, no doubt awed by the sound of terror and of strife which must have reached even this hallowed spot, had fled into the more remote portions of the palace, or mayhap had even joined the throngs in the Forum, on the principle that 'tis better to form an unit in an angry crowd, rather than to be its butt.

The peristylium itself, despite its mute and lonely magnificence, bore traces of the turmoil that reigned throughout the city; there were obvious signs that men had lived and worked here but a very little while ago, that they had been afraid and then had run away.

The marble floors were stained with mud. The sedate chairs that usually lined the walls were pushed aside and left to stand crooked and awry, the very mockery of their former dignity. Here and there a roll of parchment, an ink-stained pen, a cast-off cloak littered the hall and looked curiously provocative and out of place—an insult to the majesty of the dead and mighty Cæsar, who had caused the stately columns to be reared, and the massive walls to raise their pure lines upwards to the sky.

But on all this Taurus Antinor did not pause to think. On his right he heard sounds which proclaimed the presence of men, and thither did he immediately turn his footsteps.

Peering through the long vista of numberless columns, the further ones of which were merged together in the dim light, he saw that the score or so of the praetorian guard who had escorted the Cæsar in his flight were assembled at the end of the gigantic hall, some lolling against the marble pillars, others lying or squatting on the hard floor, as much at their ease as circumstances would allow.

They had not discarded their accoutrements and each man had his sword by his side. Not realising that the fury of the mob had been momentarily damped by the storm, they remained prepared to defend the Cæsar's life at any moment with their own.

More than one of them had apparently been wounded in one or other of the hand-to-hand combats which they had sustained against the mob earlier in the day, for more than one head was wrapped in a rough piece of bandage and more than one tunic was stained with blood. All the men looked fagged and dirty and for the most part worn out with sleeplessness and want of food.

As the praefect's firm tread resounded from end to end of the colonnaded hall and woke the slumbering echoes of the deserted palace, weary, lack-lustre eyes were turned in his direction, and now when his tall figure appeared between two pillars the men recognised him, for his head was uncovered.

One or two of them gave a cry of terror since all of them had thought that the praefect was dead, and this tall, dark presence, wrapped in a long cloak and with tawny hair still dripping from the rain, looked very like an apparition from another world.

"The Cæsar?" queried the praefect curtly.

Some of the men struggled to their feet. The voice they knew well; it was as of old, loud and peremptory and not like to be coming from a grave. All did their best to assume a respectful bearing, and one who was in command made ready to show the praefect into the Cæsar's presence.

"I want no escort," said Taurus Antinor in that same commanding voice which no one in Rome had ever tried to resist. "Tell me only where I can find the Cæsar."

"In the lararium, O praefect," replied the soldier without hesitation. "He ordered us to remain here."

Without looking to right or left Taurus Antinor walked past the soldiers into the gorgeous tablinium beyond, where great Augustus had been wont to administer justice. This vast hall was deserted, but from an inner room on the left there came to the praefect's ear a curious sound like the snarl of an angry feline creature, a sound which he knew could only come from one human throat. Without hesitation he turned to whence that sound had come. On the right of the huge semi-circular apse, which contained the now vacant throne of Augustus, a narrow door led to the small temple-like room which had once contained the great Emperor's household gods.

A heavy curtain of embroidered silk masked this entrance. Taurus Antinor pushed it back and walked in.

The temple derived its light solely from a small opening in the vaulted ceiling; that light which came down in a narrow shaft was grey and dull and failed to penetrate the dark and mysterious corners of the room.

Taurus Antinor's eyes were narrowed beneath his frowning brows as he tried to pierce the gloom that lay beyond that shaft of light. He could hear heavy breathing proceeding from there and the muttering of curses, and anon he was able to spy a bundle of stained silken clothes that lay in a heap and which seemed to shrink and to shrivel, to tremble and to cower on the altar steps: a bundle of rags and a gleam of flaccid flesh which stood for the majesty of Cæsar.

All at once there was a raucous cry and a growl as of an animal enraged, and the next second something hot and heavy threw itself with violent force against the praefect, even whilst the sharp blade of a dagger caught a gleam of reflected light.

But Taurus Antinor—well knowing the man whom he had come to help—was fully prepared for the treacherous attack. With a rapid movement he had made a shield of his mantle by winding it closely round his arm, and holding it before his face. The dagger glanced against the woollen material, rendered heavy and sodden with the rain, and Caligula, unnerved by the futile effort, staggered back against the altar steps while the dagger fell with a sharp sound upon the marble floor.

"Traitor!" came in hoarse gasps from the Cæsar's throat. "Hast come to murder me!"

"Ho! there! My guard! My guard!"

He was trying to shout, but terror was evidently choking him. He struggled to his feet, and still trembling from head to foot, made pitiable attempts to work his way round to a place of safety behind the altar, whilst keeping his bloodshot eyes fixed upon the praefect.

"Hast come to murder me?" he gasped.

"I came to place my body at thy service, O Cæsar," replied Taurus Antinor quietly. "I have been sick for nigh on twenty-four hours, else I had come to thee before. They told me that thou wast cut off from those whose duty it is to guard thy person. An thou wilt grant me leave I'll conduct thee to them."

"Aye! thou'rt ready enough to conduct me to my death, thou treacherous son of slaves," snarled the Cæsar from behind the safe bastion of the stone altar. "I have learnt thy treachery, I, even I, who trusted thee. Thou didst lie to me and plan my death even whilst I heaped uncounted favours upon thee."

"On my soul, O Cæsar, thou dost me infinite wrong," rejoined the praefect calmly. "But, an it please thee, I am not here to justify myself before thee, though God knows I would wish thee to believe me true; rather am I here to serve thee, an thou wilt deign to accept my help in thy need."

"To accept thy help. Nay! By Jupiter, I would as soon trust myself to the snakes that creep under the grasses of the Campania, as I would place my life in the keeping of a traitor."

"Had I thought to betray thee, O Cæsar," said Taurus Antinor simply, "I had not come unarmed and alone. Even the dagger wherewith thou didst threaten my life lies at my foot now, ready to my hand for the mere picking up of it."

As he spoke he gave the dagger a slight kick with his foot, so that it slid clinking and rattling along the smooth floor, until its progress was stopped by the corner of the altar steps against which the Cæsar cowered in abject fear. "My guard is in the next room," said Caligula with an evil sneer, "an I call but once and they will kill thee at my word."

"That is as thou commandest and as God wills," said Taurus Antinor, "but remember ere thou strikest, O Cæsar, that with my death thou wilt lose the one man who can save thee now."

He spoke quite calmly nor did the tone of deference ever depart from his speech. He stood in the dim light which came in a straight shaft down through the opening above, his splendid person in full view of the Cæsar who still crouched in the shadow. The power of his individuality imposed itself upon the miserable coward who threatened him. Caligula—tyrant and half crazy though he was—had sufficient shrewdness in his tortuous brain to recognise the truth of what the praefect had told him. Had this man come with evil intent he would not have come alone and unarmed: had he wished to gain his own ends, he would have had but to say a word and the mob had been ready to wreak its desired vengeance upon the Cæsar.

"The people of Rome," resumed Taurus Antinor after a while, seeing that Caligula was silent and more inclined to listen to him, "are angered against thee. Thou knowest, O Cæsar! what the anger of the people portends. For the moment a violent storm has driven the malcontents away from the vicinity of thy palace. They are congregated under the arcades of the Forum and nurse there their thoughts of rancour and of revenge."

"Until such time as my wrath overtakes them," broke in Caligula with one of his most evil oaths. "I am not dead yet, and whilst I live I'll not forget. Rome shall rue this day in blood and in tears. Vengeance and rancour, sayest thou?" and he drew in his breath with a moist, hissing sound like the snakes of the Campania of which he spoke just now. "Vengeance and rancour will overtake the rebels! My vengeance and my rancour, beside which all others shall pale! Rome can wait, I say: the Cæsar is not yet dead."

The words fell choked and thick from his quivering lips, nor did Taurus Antinor attempt to interrupt him; but as the Cæsar finished speaking, exhausted and breathing heavily, there was a moment's silence in the room, and through that silence could be heard quite distinctly the call of the people from the distance below.

"Death to the Cæsar! Death!"

Caligula uttered a loud cry of rage and of fear and struggled to his feet. He staggered forward out of the darkness and into the light, his trembling arms outstretched, his sparse hair plastered against his moist forehead, his eyes, protruding and bloodshot, fixed upon the praefect.

"They'll murder me," he cried, as he almost fell on his knees and only saved himself by clinging desperately with both hands to Taurus Antinor's outstretched arm. "They'll murder me! Save me, O praefect; save me! and I'll heap wealth upon thee—money, honours, power, all that thou dost desire! Save me! Do not let them murder me! I will not die.... I will not! I will not!... Cowards! cowards! I am a defenceless man!... I will not die ... I cannot die.... Cowards!"

Taurus Antinor had to brace himself up against the sickening sense of almost physical nausea that came over him at sight of this pitiful creature, more abject than any cur.

Among the many moments of terrible doubt and still more terrible temptation through which he had fought to-day, this was perhaps the most intolerable because the worldly man in him cried out against the futility of his own sacrifice.

To give up every hope of happiness, every aspiration for the welfare of an entire nation for the sake of this miserable coward, whose thoughts of self-preservation only alternated with those of maniacal tyranny, seemed indeed insensate mockery. Duty could not possibly lie in this. This base creature's worthless life surely could not be weighed in the balance against the countless others which—despite any promises that might be wrung from him now—he would inevitably sacrifice to his own lust for blood and for revenge.

The worldly man, the thinking philosopher, the pagan in fact, faced these propositions and placed them before the Christian. But the time had gone by for mental conflict. The Christian had fought until his numbed soul had almost lost the power of suffering; all he knew now was that he must not reason, he must neither think nor philosophise. The Master whom he had seen with limbs stretched upon a Cross in unspeakable agony and humiliation, might also have overturned a Cæsar and ruled the world from the heights of a throne. He chose to rule it from a place of infamy, and when His dying lips proclaimed to that same world the supreme finality of its salvation: "It is accomplished!" it was not to the sound of triumphal music, with banners flying and the spoils of conquest around, it was to the accompaniment of taunts and of derision and with body stripped naked before a jeering world.

"I have offered thee my service, O Cæsar," said Taurus Antinor with a mighty effort at deference and calm. "An thou wilt follow mine advice I can shield thee from the wrath of the people until such time as that which has occurred to-day, lies buried in the bosom of the past."

"What must I do?... What must I do?" muttered Caligula between his chattering teeth. He was clinging to the praefect with both hands, for his knees were shaking under him and he would have fallen had he attempted to stand up alone. "Save me, praefect.... Save me.... Do not let them kill me.... I cannot die.... I will not ... and those cowards would murder me...."

"Wilt trust thyself to me, O Cæsar?"

"Yes, yes, what must I do?"

"Come forth with me into the streets. Wrapped in dark cloaks the people will not recognise us. They would never expect the Cæsar to leave his palace while his life is in danger, and well disguised thou couldst come with me through devious ways to a house I know of on the Aventine where thou wouldst be safe."

But at this suggestion that he should leave the security of this lonely palace for the open dangers of the streets, Caligula's terrors increased tenfold. His teeth chattered more loudly in his head, and his hands on the praefect's arm became convulsive in their grasp.

"I dare not go, praefect," he stammered, and it had been pitiable were it not abject to see the look of insane terror which he cast around him. "I dare not go.... They would kill me if they saw me ... and I don't want to die...."

"No one would recognise thee," said Taurus Antinor with ill-restrained patience, "dressed as scribes we can mingle with the fringe of the crowd. The shades of evening will be on us in an hour and our dark mantles will excite no attention. Have no fear, Cæsar! no one would suspect thee of running in the teeth of danger."

The tone of bitter irony was lost on the dulled perceptions of this miserable coward.

"I would not dare," he murmured intermittently, "I would not dare."

"Then do I take my leave of thee, O Cæsar," retorted Taurus Antinor coldly. "For here alone, with but twenty men to guard thee, I can do naught to save thy person from outrage."

"If I were quite sure that I could trust thee...."

"That is for thee to decide. I have offered thee my services ... an thou'lt not accept them I crave thy leave to go."

"No, no, do not leave me, praefect," cried Caligula with despair, clinging now with all his might to this arm, which every instinct in him told him was staunch in his defence. "Do not leave me ... I'll do as thou dost advise.... I'll don a slave's garb ... and slip out into the street in thy wake ... and ... after that...?"

"Thou'lt find temporary shelter in an humble house on the Aventine. There thou canst rest for a few days even while thy legions, distant from here but three days' march, I believe, do approach the city."

"Yes, yes! my legions," cried the Cæsar in a hoarse whisper. "I had nigh forgotten them. They are not far ... if I could but reach them...."

A sudden fire of malicious hatred once more lit up the dull misery of his face.

"At the head of my legions I can soon show this miserable rabble who is the master of Rome."

"At the head of thy legions, O Cæsar," retorted Taurus Antinor firmly, "and preceded by a proclamation of universal pardon for all the events of the past few days, thou wilt make thine entry into Rome amidst the rejoicings of thy people."

"Pardon!" hissed Caligula through set teeth. "Never!"

"Yet is a proclamation of universal pardon necessary for thy safety," said Taurus Antinor with solemn earnestness. "As soon as I have placed thee under the protection of that sheltering roof on the Aventine, I would return to Rome with thy proclamation, and with the news that in three days' time thou wouldst enter the city at the head of thy people. The people, frightened at first, would imagine that divine interference had led thee triumphantly out of danger, thy clemency would allay their fears and fire their enthusiasm; they would soon make ready to welcome thee with rejoicings. But without thy promise of pardon fear would gain the mastery over those who led this rebellion, and fear quickly would beget despair. In their terror of thy coming vengeance they might oppose thy coming, and such is the temper of the people just now that all the strength of thy legions—half-spent in this last expedition—might be powerless against it; thy chosen soldiers even might turn against thee."

The Cæsar was silent, and even in this dim light it was easy to read on his ghastly face the inner workings of his tortuous mind—rage, malice, a raging thirst for revenge fought against his own cowardice and the steady influence which the praefect's calm and firm attitude was exercising over him, much against his will.

"Time is precious, O Cæsar," continued Taurus Antinor earnestly; "the people will not wait. The shadows of evening will soon be drawing in and the storm has not yet wholly passed away. The hour is propitious now, an thou wilt accept my service, we can slip away and mingle with the few straggling groups of malcontents before the crowd has again rushed the hill. An thou wilt not tarry and canst brace thyself up to indifferent demeanour in the streets, I swear to thee that thou wilt be under safe shelter in an hour."

"If I but dared to trust myself so entirely in thy keeping...."

Taurus Antinor shrugged his broad shoulders with marked contempt for his forbearance was threatening to give way.

"Is there anyone else," he asked, "whom thou wouldst rather trust? Name him then, O Cæsar, and, alive or dead, I'll bring him to thy presence within the hour."

But to this the Cæsar made no reply. He knew better than anyone could tell him that the man whom he had called a traitor, whom he had twice tried basely to kill, was the one man in the entire patriciate of Rome who would be true to him. Even madmen have such instincts at times. Caligula knew that he was doomed, the cries from below could leave no doubt in his mind that, isolated as he was, cut off not only from his legions but even from his guard, nothing could save him from the fury of vengeance which threatened him from his entire people.

A wave of fatality swept over his maniacal sense of terror. He knew and felt that if this man was a traitor then indeed could nothing save him; and he knew and felt at the same time that while he was under this man's protection no great harm could come to him.

Gradually this sense of fatality got the mastery over his cowardice, and as Taurus Antinor watched the twitchings of that distorted face, he could note that insensibly a resolution to follow his advice had found its way in this madman's brain.

"I'll come with thee," said Caligula at last, and now his voice sounded more firm, even whilst his hands released their grip on the praefect's arm and his short body straightened itself out upon his trembling limbs. "I'll come with thee, but may thy flesh wither on thy bones, thy hands be palsied and thine eyes become sightless if thou hast a thought of betraying thy Cæsar."

To this senseless speech Taurus Antinor vouchsafed no reply.

"Then I pray thee," he said quietly, "wait here a while till I find

203

the necessary garments for thy disguise and mine, and also pen, ink and parchment."

"Pen and ink? For what?"

"Thy proclamation of pardon, Cæsar, signed by thy hand...."

"When I am in safety I will see to it," said Caligula with sudden blandness, "thou saidst it thyself there is no time to lose."

"There is time to fulfil a promise and time to take what is the most important measure for thy safety," rejoined Taurus Antinor.

"Thou dost not trust thy Cæsar," said Caligula with a vicious snarl.

"No," was the praefect's curt reply.

It was characteristic of this tyrannical despot that at the praefect's rough answer he laughed with obvious satisfaction. At the back of his shrewd sense of self-preservation there had come the thought that the man who had spoken that unequivocal "No!" had learnt to its fullest the lesson of truth. He said nothing for a while, and when his laughter died away in a kind of hysterical gasp, he made a gesture expressive of indifference and also of submission to the other's wish.

Taurus Antinor turned away from the loathsome presence without another word and with a firm step. And Caligula, standing motionless in the middle of the room waited quietly for his return.

CHAPTER XXXIII

"Come, take up the cross, and follow me."—St. Mark x. 21.

Taurus Antinor had some difficulty in finding the clothes that he wanted, which would serve as a disguise for the Cæsar and himself, and he had to explore the huge deserted palace from end to end before he came on the block of the slaves' quarters; here in one of the cubicles he ultimately discovered a few bundles of garments, which had apparently been hastily collected and then forgotten by one of the runaway scribes.

These he found on inspection would suit his purpose admirably. Writing tools and desk he had already collected; there were plenty of these littering the building in every corner.

Armed with all these necessaries, he made his way back to the lararium without again crossing the peristylium where the soldiers were assembled.

Sitting on the altar steps, with the desk between his knees and the light from the narrow shaft above falling full upon the parchment, he wrote out carefully and laboriously the proclamation of pardon which was destined on the morrow to assure the people of Rome that all their delinquencies against the majesty and the person of their Cæsar would by him be forgotten.

It was necessary so to word it that not a single loophole should remain through which Caligula could ultimately slip and break his word. More than one beginning was made and whole lines erased and rewritten before the praefect of Rome was satisfied with his work.

The Cæsar in the meanwhile was tramping up and down the tiny room like his own favourite black panther when it was in a rage. Throwing his thick, short body about in a kind of rolling gait, he only paused at times for a moment or two in order to hurl a vicious snarl at the praefect.

His fingers were twitching convulsively the whole time, with longing no doubt to grasp the leather-thonged whip which they were so fond of wielding. At intervals he would gnaw his nails down to the quick while snorts of bridled fury escaped through his pallid lips.

But Taurus Antinor went on with his work, absolutely heedless of the Cæsar's rage. When the wording of the proclamation satisfied him, he held out the pen for Caligula to sign. He knelt on the floor with one knee, holding up against his forehead, as custom demanded on a solemn occasion, the desk on which rested the imperial decree. He rendered this act of homage simply and loyally, as the outward sign of that sacrifice which the Divine Master had demanded of him.

Faithful to his instincts of petty tyranny, the Cæsar kept the praefect of Rome kneeling before him for close on half an hour; all this while volleys of vituperations poured from his mouth against all traitors in general, and more especially against the praefect whom he accused of selling his services only in order to gain his own ends.

It was only when Taurus Antinor had reminded him for the third time that he was placing his life in grave jeopardy with all this delay that he ultimately snatched up the pen and put his name to the decree.

After that both the men donned the dark garments of the fugitive scribe. With the proclamation of pardon rolled up tightly and hidden within the folds of his tunic, Taurus Antinor led the way out of the lararium.

The afternoon light was slowly sinking into the embrace of evening. The vast deserted palace, with its rows of monumental columns and statues of stone gods looked spectral and mysterious in the fast gathering gloom.

When exploring the building in search of disguises Taurus Antinor had taken note of the minor exits which gave on the more isolated portions of the imperial gardens; to one of these did he now conduct the Cæsar and suddenly the outer air struck on the faces of the

205

two men and they found themselves in the open, in the waning light of day.

Unbroken now by the solid marble walls which had shut out most of the noise from the streets, the shouts that came from the slopes of the hill struck more clearly upon the ear. The sound travelling through the mist-laden air seemed to come more especially from the northwestern front of the palace of Augustus, which here faces that of the late Emperor Tiberius, with the new gigantic wing built recently thereunto by Caligula.

Here a vast multitude appeared to have congregated. The cries of "Death!" seemed ominously loud and near, and through them there was a dull murmur as of an angry mob foiled in its lust.

The Cæsar uttered a cry of terror and his knees gave under him. He cowered on the ground, clutching at the praefect's robe and hiding his face in the folds of his mantle.

"They will kill me!" he stammered thickly. "I dare not go, praefect!... take me back ... I dare not go!"

Taurus Antinor, none too patient a man at any time, had to clench his fists and drive his finger-nails into the palms of his hands, else he could have struck this abject, miserable coward. He wrenched his cloak out of the Cæsar's grasp and with a firm grip pulled him roughly up from the ground.

"An thou canst not control thy cowardly fears," he said harshly, "I'll leave thee to perish at their hands."

And holding the wretched man tightly by the wrist, he quickly sought shelter behind a pile of building material which lay some distance away. He hoped that this cringing dastard would not hear that other clamour of the people which invariably followed the call for vengeance: "Hail Taurus Antinor! Hail!"

Did these words perchance reach Caligula's ears he would no doubt even at this eleventh hour have refused to trust himself to the praefect; he would rush back into the palace, like a tracked beast that seeks its burrow, and all the sorrow and the renunciation of the past twenty-four hours would turn to the bitter fruit of uselessness.

Fortunately Caligula's senses were dulled by his own terrors. He heard the shouts and the ceaseless din of rebellious strife but the only word that he could distinguish was the ominous one of "Death," and whenever this word struck upon his confused mind a violent fit of trembling would seize him and he would stumble and stagger along like a drunken man.

Taurus Antinor, however, held him tightly by the wrist and thus he half led, half dragged him in his wake. The towering masses of building materials, huge blocks of stone and of marble, scaffoldings and ladders piled up on the open ground which encircled the rear of Caligula's palace, afforded him the protection which he had counted on and foreseen.

Keeping well within the shadows, he thus gradually worked his way on from pile to pile until he reached the brow of the hill. The crowd which was swarming up the slopes was just beginning to appear in isolated detachments in the roads and streets that led upwards from the Forum. Apparently the mob had not forgotten its former purpose to entrap the fugitive Cæsar and to force him to come out and to face his people.

The dull evening light creeping up from below, the thin drizzle which had succeeded the heavy rain and which mingled with the rising vapours from the sodden ground, the aimlessness of the onrushing crowd as it spread itself in confused masses all round the foremost palaces on the hill, all favoured Taurus Antinor's plans. Emerging from behind a monumental block of granite, looking in their dark clothes for all the world like the scribes who had been seen running about here all the day, the two men attracted little or no attention.

Their faces in the gloom could not easily be distinguished, nor did anyone in that excited throng imagine for a moment that the Cæsar would leave the safe shelter of his palace and, dressed in slave's garb, affront the multitude who clamoured for his death.

The audacity of this flight carried success along with it. Dragging the quaking Cæsar after him, Taurus Antinor soon plunged into the very thick of the crowd.

The tumult here and the confusion were intense. Men running and shouting, women shrieking and children crying, all in a tangled mass of noisy humanity. Some of the men brandished sticks, shovels or rakes, any instrument they had happened to possess; they shouted loudly for the Cæsar, demanding his death, urging the more pusillanimous to rush the palace and drag the hiding princeps out into the open. Others carried tall poles on which they had improvised rude banners made of bits of purple-coloured rags: they were proclaiming the new Cæsar of their choice in voices rendered hoarse with lustiness.

The women clung to their men-folk, their shrill accents mingling with the rougher ones. Some of them clutched small children to their breasts, others dragged older ones at their skirts, and it was terrible to hear the cries of frightened children through the shouts of vengeance and of death.

Now as the gloom gathered in a few lighted torches appeared here and there, held high above the sea of surrounding heads; they flickered feebly in the damp air, throwing fitful lurid lights on the faces close by: dark faces, flushed and excited, with sullen eyes and dishevelled hair, above which the black smoke from the sizzling resin formed weird and shifting haloes.

The crowd carried the fugitives along with it, pressed shoulder to shoulder in a living, breathing, panting vice. Damp rising from thousands of rain-sodden garments mingled with the mist and with the rain and formed a grey, wet, clinging veil over this restless mass, kneading it all together into a dark, swaying entity from which rose the cries of the children and the hoarse shouts of the men.

Drifting with the throng, Taurus Antinor, still holding his trembling companion by the wrist, soon found himself being carried down the long flight of steps which leads from the heights crowned by Caligula's palace to the Forum below. Without attempting to work against the crowd, he presently crossed the Nova Via, and turning sharply on his left he found himself behind the basilica whose every arcade and precinct was densely packed with men and women and whose marble walls echoed and re-echoed with a multitude of sounds.

The crowd!—always the crowd! Always these shouting men, these screaming women, these puny crying children! It seemed as if their numbers were being fed by invisible masses that came from out the darkness which was closing in around. On ahead the height of the Aventine hid the horizon line from view, and on its slopes tiny lights began to appear that seemed to mock the weary fugitives by their distance and their elusiveness.

Taurus Antinor had all along intended to reach the Aventine by a devious way. Now the crowd had brought him and his companion to the river bank, there where the Tiber winds its sudden curve at the foot of the three hills. That curve of the river would have to be followed its whole way along the bank, and the slope of the Aventine looked so immeasurably far.

But progress had become more easy at last. Taurus Antinor pushed his way along now as quickly as he dared. More than one angry glance followed the tall, powerful figure as it forged a path for its burden, regardless of obstruction; more than one oath was uttered in the wake of those broad shoulders that towered above the rest of the crowd.

With a man who was shivering as with ague dragging upon his arm, with his body racked with fever and his temples throbbing with pain, the man set out with renewed energy upon this final stage of his journey.

In the constant pushing through the crowd the bandages on his shoulder had shifted, and he could again feel the claws of the panther tearing at his flesh, and the hot breath of the beast scorching his face. The sodden garments clung cold and dank to his skin, he felt chilled down to the marrow, and yet he felt as if the fire of his body would burn his skin on to his bones.

Perhaps the physical misery which he endured numbed the more unendurable agony of the soul; certain it is that a kind of torpor gradually invaded his brain, leaving within it only the sensation of a terrible longing to drop down on the wet ground and to yield to the unconquerable desire to stretch out his aching limbs and to lay down his head in the last long sleep which would bring eternal rest.

But now the ground had begun to rise, the Aventine stretched out its slopes into the arms of darkness and its summit was lost in the gloom above. The weary ascent had begun.

Then it was that through the torpor of the man's brain a vision had suddenly found its way, searching those memory cells of the mind that contained the sacred picture of long ago. A mountain rugged and steep, a surging crowd, a Man, weary and with body tormented by ceaseless pain, toiling upwards with a heavy burden.

His naked feet made no noise upon the earth, the burden which He bore was a heavy Cross.

Above on the summit death awaited Him, ignominy and shame, but He walked up in silence and in patience, so that men in long after years, who had burdens of sorrow or of misery, should know how to bear them till they too reached the summit of their Golgotha, there to find ... not death, not humiliation or pain, but eternal life and the serenity of exquisite peace.

The Cæsar hung like a dead weight on Antinor's left arm, and the right one, lacerated by the panther's claws, burned and ached well-nigh intolerably. But the glorious memory of long ago now preceded him, the Divine Martyr walking on ahead with sacred shoulders bent to the sacrifice, and he seemed to hear again the swishing of the tunic, stained with blood and the mud of the road; he seemed to hear the shouts of the jeering crowd, the rough words of the soldiery, the sobs of faithful disciples and women.

And he too plodded on with his burden. The crowd, now far away, seemed to mock him for the uselessness of his sacrifice; Dea Flavia's sobs of sorely wounded love called to him to turn back.

But memory now would be held back no longer. The picture which it conjured up became more distinct and more real, and its gold-lined wings, as they fluttered around his head, made a murmur gentle and intangible as the flitting of the clouds across the skies of Italia.

The murmur was soft and low, and it reached the aching senses of the weary pilgrim like the cooling breath of multitudes of angels in the parched wilderness of his sorrow:

"If any man will come after me, let him deny himself and take up his cross and follow me. For whosoever will save his life shall lose it, and whosoever will lose his life for my sake shall find it."

"For Thy sake, oh Jesus of Galilee!" said the man as he toiled up his endless Calvary and left behind him with every step, far away in the valley below, all that had made the world fair to him and all the promises of happiness.

On ahead the Divine Leader had fallen on his knees: the burden of His Cross seemed greater than He could bear. Rough hands helped to drag him up from the ground and set Him once more on His tedious way. His cheeks were wan and pale, blood trickled from the thorn-crowned brow, but there was no wavering in the lines of the face though they were distorted with pain, no giving in, no drawing back, not though one word from those livid lips could have called even now unto God, and ten thousand legions of angels would have come down at that word to avenge the outrage and to proclaim His godhead.

And in the wake of his Master the Christian plodded on, dragging his burden on his arm, the cross which he had to bear. Gradually behind him the noise became more and more subdued, then it died down altogether—all but a confused and far-away murmur which mingled with the sighing of the Tiber.

And the Christian was alone once more—alone with memory.

Taurus Antinor's breath came in short, stertorous gasps, his throat was parched and his tongue clove to the roof of his mouth. The slope of the hill is precipitous here, and the house—nigh to the summit—seemed to recede farther and farther with devilish malignity.

And the sense of silence and of solitude became more absolute, a fitting attendant on memory. On and on the two men walked, the Christian and his burden; their sandalled feet felt like lead as they sank ankle-deep in the mud of the unpaved road.

"Come, take up thy cross and follow me!" and the Christian plodded on in the wake of the Divine Presence that beckoned to him upwards from above.

From time to time Caligula's hoarse and querulous voice would break the death-like silence.

"Are we not there yet?"

"Not yet. Very soon," the praefect would reply.

"I am a fool to have trusted myself to thee, for of a truth thou leadest me to my death."

"Patience, Cæsar, yet a little while longer."

"May the gods fell thee to the earth. I would I had a poisoned dagger by me to kill thee ere thou dost work thy treacherous will with me. Thou son of slaves, may death overtake thee now ..."

"God in heaven grant that it may, O Cæsar," said the praefect fervently.

Now at last the houses became more sparse. Only here and there up the side of the hill a tiny light glittered feebly. Taurus Antinor's senses were only just sufficiently alert to keep in the right direction. The house which he wished to reach was not more now than six hundred steps away.

The darkness had become almost thick in its intensity, even the houses were undistinguishable in the gloom. The two men stumbled as they walked, loose stones detached themselves under their feet and their heelless sandals slid in the mud. Once the Cæsar lost his foothold altogether; but for his convulsive hold on the praefect's arm he would have measured his length in the mud.

Taurus Antinor felt after the wrench as if this must be the end, as if body and brain and soul could not endure a moment longer and live.

A mist akin to the one that enveloped the hill seemed to fall over his brain. He no longer walked now, he just tumbled along, blindly stumbling at almost every step with that dead, dead weight upon his arm which an invisible force compelled him to carry up the precipitous height to the place of safety which was so far away.

"What shall a man give in exchange for his soul?" asked that heavenly murmur on the wings of memory. "For the Son of Man shall come in the glory of the Father with His angels; and then He shall reward every man according to his work."

With his burden lying like an insentient log on his arm, Taurus Antinor fell up at last against the door of the house; his foot had stumbled against its corner-stone.

A moment or two later the door was opened from within and the feeble light of a tiny lamp was held above him whilst a kindly voice murmured:

"Who goes there?"

"The Cæsar is in danger, and a fugitive. He asks shelter and protection from thee," murmured Taurus Antinor feebly, "and I would lay down my burden in thy house for I am weary and I would find rest."

"Enter friend," said the man simply.

The Cæsar, trembling and nerveless, fell forward into the room.

The praefect of Rome lay unconscious upon its threshold but the Christian had laid down his cross at the foot of the throne of God.

CHAPTER XXXIV

"Finally my brethren be strong."—Ephesians vi. 10.

The younger men were still inclined to rebel. They felt that they were in great numbers and that they were strong: they believed—with that optimism of excited youth—that their will must prevail in the end. In their opinion the Cæsar had done nothing to atone for his crime against the praefect of Rome, or for his dastardly cringing before the power of his people.

But the older men, those who had mayhap more than once witnessed street rioting and the bloody reprisals that invariably followed open rebellion—they counselled prudence, an acceptance of what had come about, since the imperial decree had been fixed to the rostrum of the great Augustus, promising pardon for all delinquencies.

And—what would you?—but was not the praefect of Rome dead? The consul-major had stated it positively to all those who asked the question of him, and he had it on the positive authority of Folces, the praefect's most trusted slave. It was the consul-major who, preceded by his lictors, had caused the imperial decree to be read out aloud to the people of Rome from the topmost steps of the Temple of Mars, and it was he who had then ordered the decree to be affixed to the wall of the rostrum. The consul-major had received the precious parchment at the hands of the special messenger sent by the Cæsar himself: that messenger was none other than Folces, and he had stated positively that the praefect of Rome was dead.

It was useless to demand that a man be proclaimed to the principate if that man be dead. True that some of the malcontents—those young men who were hot-headed and whose raging tempers were not easily curbed—refused to accept the news and loudly demanded the body of the hero so that divine honours might be accorded to it, to the lifelong shame of the Cæsar who had so basely murdered him.

But the praetor urbanus had declared that the body of the praefect could not be found, and the rumour had gained ground that it had been defiled and thrown to the dogs. A sullen discontent reigned amongst the people for this, and it could not be allayed by all the promises of pardon and of rejoicings which the imperial proclamation decreed.

There had been some calls too for Dea Flavia. The Cæsar had nominated his successor to the imperium in the Circus the other day. If the Augusta would but make her choice, the people would perhaps be ready to accept her lord now as Consort Imperii, with the ultimate hope that a just and brave man would succeed to the principate in due course.

But no sound had as yet come from the house of Dea Flavia, and the people hung about the Forum in desultory groups, discussing the situation. That the gods had intervened in the Cæsar's favour no one could reasonably doubt. Even whilst the anger of the populace was at its height and dense masses had surrounded his palace to which he had been known to flee, he had been spirited away out of the city. His proclamation had come from Etruria, showing that he was already far from his city and on his way to join his legions.

How did he succeed in making a way for himself through the dense masses that had thronged the streets for nigh on forty-eight hours, since first the tumult broke out in the Circus when the praefect of Rome was stabbed?

Had Jupiter sent down his thunders yesterday, his lowering clouds and heavy showers of rain, only in order to aid the Cæsar in his progress? What hand had guided him down the declivities of the Palatine? What arm shielded him from the anger of the people?

Dea Flavia had heard the news even as soon as the first hour of the day had been called. Yesterday, bruised in mind and heart and body, she had lain for close on an hour in a dreamless, semi-conscious state. It was only when she awoke from that that the knowledge of her misery returned to her in full.

She had found love, happiness, pride, all that makes life exquisite and fair, only to lose all these treasures even before she had had time to grasp them.

Love had been called to life by the look, the touch of one man, happiness had come when she saw the love-light in his eyes, born in response to hers: pride came with all the rich gifts which she could lavish upon him. Now everything was gone, he had taken everything from her, even as he gave it; and he took everything in order to offer it as a sacrifice to his God.

Now her heart was numbed and her brain tried in vain to conjure up the images of yesterday: the happy moments when she had lain against the noblest heart in Rome. But the only vision that her dulled senses could perceive was that of dying Menecreta speaking that awful curse, or of herself—Dea Flavia—gazing with eyes of anger and of pride into vacancy wherein her imagination had traced a glowing cross, and uttering words of defiance that seemed so futile, so sacrilegious now.

The storm then had obscured the sky, drove the rain in heavy patter overhead, the air was dismal and dark: now a brilliant sunshine flooded the imperial city with its radiance, the wet marble glistened in the dawn and a roseate hue tipped the seven hills of Rome with glory. But in Dea Flavia's heart there was sorrow darker than the blackest night, sleep forsook her eyelids, and all night long she tossed about restlessly on her couch listening to the sounds that came from the city in rebellion, counting them out as they died away one by one.

She had gone to her room quite early in the day; her guests she knew were being well looked after, and she could not bear to remain in the studio whose every corner reminded her of that powerful personality which had lately filled it, and whose very walls still echoed with the sound of that rough voice, rendered at times so exquisitely tender.

Blanca attended on her and put her to bed for she could not bear to have Licinia near her. The old woman's gossip jarred upon her nerves and she was physically afraid to hear indifferent lips utter the name of the praefect of Rome.

Only the call, "Hail Taurus Antinor Cæsar! Hail!" which still came half the night through from afar dulled her agony of mind for a few seconds when it struck upon her ear. It set her wondering, thus allowing her momentarily to forget her misery. Then she would lie, wide-eyed, looking upwards and pondering.

Who was this god whom Taurus Antinor worshipped?

Who was he and what had he done? All she knew was that he had died upon a cross, the most ignominious death mortal man could suffer, and the praefect of Rome, the proud Roman patrician, had been content to obey him as a slave.

213

Who was he and what had he done? On this she pondered half the night through, while fever coursed through her veins and her brows were moist and aching, her heart palpitating with pain.

The dawn found her wearied and sick. But she rose when Blanca came to her in the first hour. She summoned Licinia and all her women and ordered them to dress her in one of her richest robes. She looked very girlish and very pale when she stood decked out in the embroidered tunic which she had chosen; it was of a soft material, clinging to her graceful figure in long straight folds, there was some elaborate embroidery round the hem, below which her feet peeped out clothed in sandals of gilt leather.

When she was dressed she went out into the atrium and then sent word to the praetorian praefect and his friends that she was ready to receive them.

Some of the news from the busy world outside had already reached her ears. Licinia was not like to be chary in imparting to her mistress the scraps of gossip which she had collected.

The Cæsar was outside the city, he would in due time return to Rome at the head of his legions, and in the meanwhile he had by a comprehensive and gracious act of clemency pardoned all those who had offended against his majesty.

The noble patricians who yesterday had already deposed him, and had called on her to name his successor, had been foiled in their ambitious schemes by the very man whom she—Dea Flavia—would have set upon the throne.

And once more that one all-absorbing puzzle confronted her: who and what was this god who had exacted this all-embracing sacrifice?

She wandered somewhat aimlessly through the halls, for the great lords were not yet ready to appear before her, and as she crossed the atrium and went into the peristylium, looking with somewhat wistful longing toward the open portals of the vestibule and the vista of open air and sky from whence a breath of pure fresh air struck pleasingly on her nostrils, she saw that in spite of the early hour a large number of the poorer clients, suppliants at the door of the great Augusta, had already assembled there.

Foremost amongst them was an elderly man dressed in the plain garb of a slave, and wearing, embroidered on his tunic, the badge that proclaimed him in the service of the praefect of Rome.

The man appeared to be very insistent, and to be receiving in consequence, somewhat rough treatment from the janitors. Dea Flavia turned to one of her own slaves and ordered the man to be brought to her presence in her studio where she would receive him.

The man told the janitors that his name was Folces, that he belonged to the praefect of Rome and desired speech with the Augusta. He walked in very humbly, with back bent nearly double, and when he was shown into the studio where the Augusta sat alone he fell on both knees before her.

"Thy name is Folces, I am told," she began graciously, "and thou art of the household of the praefect of Rome?"

"I attend upon his person, gracious lady," replied the man.

"And thou hast brought me a message from him?" she asked, even as with this hope her heart began to beat violently in her breast.

"Not from him, gracious lady," said Folces humbly, "for the praefect of Rome is dead."

"Who told thee that he was dead?" she asked.

"Taurus Antinor named Anglicanus," replied the man simply; "he sent me my freedom this night and a message to lay at the feet of Dea Flavia Augusta."

"Give me the message," she said.

Still on his knees, Folces fumbled in the folds of his mantle and from his breast he drew a roll of parchment which he offered to the Augusta.

"Rise, Folces, and go while I read," she said; "wait outside the door till I do summon thee."

She waited until the man had closed the heavy door behind him: she wanted to be alone with these last words which he had penned for her. Now she untied the string that held the roll together, then she unfolded the parchment and read:

"Idol of my soul, beloved of my heart. Aroused from dreams of thee, my wakening soul takes its last flight to thy feet. This is farewell, my dear, dear heart, even as my hand pens the word the dawn around me turns to the likeness of the night, and it is peopled with all the sorrows that wear out the heartstrings slowly, one by one. The Cæsar is safe. Even as I write he starts forth on his way to join his legions. Having left him in charge of those who do not know how to betray, I succeeded in the night in reaching the detachment of the praetorian guard encamped around the Circus: a small company of them returned with me to the lonely house on the Aventine, and from thence at break of day they started with the Cæsar toward Etruria, where the legions home from the expedition against the Allemanni were still known to abide. In three or four days, or mayhap five, the Cæsar will re-enter his city. His proclamation of pardon is so worded that his keeping of his word is closely bound up both with his honour and with his personal safety. The people therefore have naught to fear from his vengeance: those who have more actively conspired against him, and who would have drawn thee in their selfish schemes, have time before them to put themselves and their belongings out of the immediate reach of the Cæsar. Tell them to live in retirement as far from Rome as they can until such time as the events of the past few days have been erased from the tablets of memory.

"The Cæsar is safe, and I, dear heart, do bid thee a last farewell.

When I parted from thee yesterday we both knew then that the parting would be for ever; even though thine exquisite hands clung to me and twined themselves round the very fibres of my soul, and thy voice called me back with the ineffable sweetness of thy love, I knew that it would be for ever. The Cæsar will never forgive me that I witnessed his abject humiliation. Even at dawn, when he stood surrounded by his praetorian guard, as secure from danger as human agency could make him, a gleam of hatred shone in his eyes whenever he looked on me. He never would give thee to me, dear heart, and would vent his wrath also upon thy dear head. 'Tis better that he too should think me dead, for dead will I be to Rome and to the people among whom my name might yet give cause for strife and for discontent.

"The Cæsar is safe, and I can go my ways in peace. He hath no longer need of me but my Lord hath called and I His servant must take up my cross and follow Him. The priceless gifts which thy pure hands did hold out to me are registered in His book of Heaven, and He never forgets. As for me I were less or more than a man were I to ask thee to forget. I would have thee remember, yet would I think of thee as happy and radiant as the stars wherewith He hath gladdened the darkness of our nights. But think not of me as unhappy. My Lord has called, and I the servant am bound to follow. He laid a burden on me and this burden must I bear even though I may bear with it all the pain that is greater than the pain of the earth, greater than the ceaseless travail of the sea, even though I may bear with it that bitterest of all bitter fruits the labour that is nothing worth. That I know not! Who knoweth, oh God? Truly not I. There was grief in the world, dear heart, even before the stars were made or the sky stretched its blue dome above; and as hour follows hour, day succeeds day and the cycles of years come and go, even so do fresh griefs and greener sorrows spring around us; like each recurrent season they too come and go. Only one thing abideth, dear heart, and that is the will of God, who made happiness and woe, love and pain, sleep and death. And 'tis the will of God that I should lose thee and yet continue to live, even though life to me henceforth will be one long dream of death.

"Idol of my soul, beloved of my heart, farewell. I go to find comfort from that bitter word on the summit of Golgotha, at the foot of an abandoned, broken Cross. When my soul hath found peace then will it be ready for the service of God.

"Farewell, my beloved! May God have thee in His keeping, even as thy soul hath already been touched with His grace. Farewell! Mine eyes are dim, my hand trembles, hot tears blur the writing on this parchment. And as I look up through the open doorway to where the limitless horizon lies beyond Rome's seven hills, I see stretched out before me the long vista of years throughout which my heart will be for ever weaving with threads of longing and of sorrow the tether which binds undying memory to thee."

Her hands, which held the roll of parchment, dropped down upon her lap. Her eyes too were dim and the hot tears fell from them one by one. A sadness that was in no way bitter and yet was immeasurable as death had filled her entire being as she read.

Slowly she laid the parchment in the bosom of her tunic, then, like one who walks in sleep, she rose and crossed the studio, her hand—white and slightly quivering—pushed back the heavy door that masked the inner room. Silently it swung upon its hinges, disclosing the sanctum where yesterday the stricken hero had lain helpless and sick.

The couch had not been touched since he had lain on it. It still bore the imprint of the massive figure as it lay inert in the embrace of drugged sleep. The pillow only had been smoothed out as if by a loving hand, and as Dea Flavia came nearer to it she saw that a small object had been laid there, as if reverently, right in the centre.

The tears in her eyes obscured her vision momentarily, but when they fell one by one down her cheeks, she saw a little more clearly, and having approached the couch she took up the small object that lay there upon the pillow.

It was the wooden cross which she had last seen held between the clasped hands of the man whom she loved.

She gazed on the small symbol, and gazed, even though the tears gathered thick and fast in her eyes and the image that she saw was scarce discernible as it rested in her hand.

How puzzled she had been two nights ago when she stole softly into this room and saw him kneeling here beside the couch, clasping this wooden symbol between his fingers—intertwined in a gesture of passionate prayer. She had been puzzled because his actions of the day before had seemed incomprehensible to her: his attitude to my lord Hortensius Martius, an enemy whose life he saved at risk of his own, his loyalty to the Cæsar whom everyone abhorred!

All this had puzzled her then, but how infinitely more profound was that puzzle now. A riddle more mysterious than any sage could propound lay hidden in the words of the letter which she had just read. The man who had penned that letter had poured out his heart in it, and it was not a heart that was void of pity or of love. It brimmed over with pity, it was bruised with the intensity of love: but, crushed and broken though it was, it did not murmur, it only endured.

Dea Flavia looked down upon the small object which to Taurus Antinor had been an emblem of that god whom he worshipped and who had been man and had died a shameful death.

Who was this god whom Taurus Antinor worshipped? for whose sake and at whose bidding he was content to give up all the superheights of ambition to which a Roman patrician could aspire? Who was this god? and what had he done that a man like Taurus Antinor—a man filled with all a man's strength and all a man's heroism, a man worshipped of the people and glorified by an entire nation—

should thus give up the lordship of Rome in order to do him service? that he should give it up, too, without a murmur, content to offer this final and absolute sacrifice.

"Think not of me as unhappy. My Lord has called me and I, His servant am bound to follow."

Thus had the man written in loneliness and in peace after the sacrifice had been accomplished, even after she—the Augusta—had, with love-filled heart and generous hands, offered him everything that man could desire on this earth. He had written it in loneliness and in peace, having given up the world to follow his God.

Who was this god? and what had he done that his power over Taurus Antinor's heart was greater than her own?

Yesterday she had cursed him loudly and called him cruel and unjust, four days ago she had defied him and now he had conquered. Taurus Antinor had obeyed him and she who loved him and whom he loved was left desolate.

For this she never doubted: he loved her, that she knew. She was no child now! The last four days had made a woman of her: in the past four days she had tasted of and witnessed every passion that rends a human heart, love, ambition, cruelty, hatred! She had seen them all! seen through passion men brought down to a level lower than the beasts, and through passion a man become equal to a god. No! she was no longer a child, she was a woman now, and there was much that if she did not understand she at least could not doubt. The man whom she loved, loved her with an intensity at least equal to that which even now made her heart throb at the memory of his kiss. He loved her, longed for her, would have laid down his life for her even at the moment when he tore himself away from her arms. He loved her and longed for her even whilst his trembling fingers penned this last impassioned farewell.

He loved her and he loved Rome! But his god called to him and he, the proud Roman patrician, the accepted lord of the Augusta and of Rome, followed as would a slave.

Slowly she dropped down on her knees just where he too had knelt two nights ago, and like unto him she clasped her hands together, scarce conscious that the tiny wooden cross still lay between her fingers.

"Thou hast conquered, oh Galilean!" she murmured, whilst great sobs that would not be suppressed rose to her throat. "At thy call he left everything that makes life beautiful and happy: at thy call he left me to mourn, he left the people of Rome who acclaimed him, he left the throne of Augustus and the Empire of the world! Everything he left at thy call! What hast thou in thy nail-pierced hands to give him in return?"

For a while now she was able to give way to her immeasurable sorrow. Her head buried in the pillow whereon his head had rested, she sobbed out her loving, aching heart in a passionate fit of weeping.

Just like the Christian yesterday up on the heights, so was she—the pagan—alone now with her grief. More lonely than he—she had no anchorage, and in her ear had never sounded those all-compelling words, sublime in their perfect gentleness:

"Come unto Me!"

But who shall tell what divine hand soothed her burning forehead? what divine words of comfort were whispered in her ear?

Gradually her tears ceased to flow, the heavy sobs were stilled, her aching and bruised body felt numb with the pain in her heart. But outwardly she was more calm. She rose from her knees, and hiding the small cross in the bosom of her gown, she drew forth the letter and read it through once more.

"If only I knew!" she murmured. "If only I could understand!"

After a while she bethought her of the slave Folces, the one human link left now between herself and the man whom she loved and who was gone from her.

With reverent hands she smoothed out the couch, the pillow which had supported his head, the coverlet which had lain over him. She was loth to go from this room whose every corner seemed still to hold something of his personality and whose every wall seemed to hold an echo of his voice.

She would have stayed here for hours longer, talking to that absent personality, powerful and mysterious more than ever now, listening to the rugged voice which she would never hear again. But there was something that she must do ere she gave herself over finally to her dreams; there was a duty to accomplish which she knew he would ask of her.

Therefore—after a last, long, all-embracing look on the place which would for ever be as a sanctuary in her sight—she went back to the studio at last, and herself going to the door she called Folces back to her.

"The praefect of Rome, good Folces?" she asked as soon as the man had entered, "wilt see him again?"

"Taurus Antinor named Anglicanus hath left Rome to-day on his way to Syria, O Augusta!" said the man, humbly insisting on the name of his master.

"Dost not go with him?"

"He hath commanded me to stay here and to look after his household until such time as he doth direct."

"His household?" she said. "I had not thought of that. What is to become of his house in Rome, his villa at Ostia and his slaves?"

"The praefect of Rome," said Folces, "made ere he died a testament wherein he did command the freedom of all his slaves, and ordered a certain sum of money to be set aside which will enable even the humblest amongst us all to live decently like freedmen. The house in Rome and the villa at Ostia are to be sold, whilst the remainder of Taurus Antinor's private fortune is to be administered by his general agents. He said that he would see to it later on. I am still his slave; he did not confide in me."

"Yet he asked thee to look after his household."

"It will take a little time until the manumissio testamento can take effect. In the meanwhile we all are Taurus Antinor's slaves and must look after his houses until they have been sold."

"Wilt be happy as a freedman, Folces?"

"Yes, Augusta," replied the man simply, "for then I shall be at liberty to follow Taurus Antinor as his servant."

She sat quite silently after this, her tear-stained eyes fixed into vacancy. Folces was on his knees waiting to be dismissed. It was some little while before she remembered his presence, then in a gentle voice she bade him go.

"Shall I take a message back to my master?" he asked humbly. "I could find him, I think, if I had a message."

"I have no message," she said; "go, good Folces."

CHAPTER XXXV

"We are unprofitable servants: we have done that which was our duty to do."—St. Luke xvii. 10.

Half an hour later Dea Flavia Augusta was in the tablinium. She had received Caius Nepos, the praetorian praefect, Marcus Ancyrus, the elder, my lords Hortensius Martius, Philippus Decius and the others, and they, who had heard so many conflicting rumours throughout the morning and were beginning to quake with fear, for none of the rumours were reassuring, were grouped trembling and expectant around her.

"My lords," she began as soon as she had received their obsequious greetings, "I know not if you have heard the news. The Cæsar hath succeeded in quitting Rome; he is on his way to rejoin his legions and nothing can stand in the way of his progress. In a few days from now he will make his State re-entry into the city, and the city will resound from end to end with rejoicings in his honour."

"We had all heard the news, Augusta," said Caius Nepos who was vainly trying to steady his voice and to appear calm and dignified, "and also that a proclamation of pardon hath preceded the entry of the Cæsar into Rome and hath been affixed to the rostrum of the great Augustus by the consul-major himself this morning."

"And what do you make of all this, my lords?" she asked.

"That some gods of evil have been at work," muttered young Escanes between set teeth, "and spirited the tyrannical madman out of the way for the further scourging of his people."

"The spirit, my lords," she interposed quietly, "that led my kinsman to safety last night was one which actuated the noblest patrician in Rome to do his duty loyally by the Cæsar."

"Then curse him for a traitor," muttered Caius Nepos, whose cheeks had become white with terror.

"He was no traitor to you, my lords," she retorted hotly, "for he was not one of you. He was true to the oath which he had rendered to the Cæsar; aye, even to the Cæsar whom we, my lords, all of us here present had been ready to betray."

Then as she saw nothing but sullen faces around her and not a word broke the silence that ensued, she continued more calmly:

"Yesterday you came to me, my lords, with proposals of treachery to which I, alas, did listen because in my heart I had already chosen one man who I felt was worthy to rule over this great Empire. I had made my choice and myself offered him the imperium, the throne of Augustus and the sceptre of the Cæsars.... But he refused it all, my lords, and went forth in the night to place himself body and heart at the Cæsar's service."

"And his name, O Augusta?" queried Ancyrus, the elder.

"He hath name Taurus Antinor and was once praefect of Rome."

"He is dead!" broke in Hortensius Martius hotly.

"He lived long enough, my lord," she retorted, "to show us all our duty."

There was silence after that, for many a heart was beating spasmodically with fear or with hope. My lord Hortensius Martius sat on a low stool, with his elbow on his knee, his chin buried in his hand. His eyes, glowing with dull and sullen hatred, searched the face of Dea Flavia, trying to read what went on behind the pure, straight brow and those liquid blue eyes, deep as the fathomless sea.

"What is to be done?" said Ancyrus, the elder, with a pitiable look of perplexity directed at the Augusta.

"To make our submission to the Cæsar," she said simply, "those of us at least who are not afraid of his wrath. For the others there is still time to seek a safe retreat far away from Rome."

"But this is monstrous!" cried Hortensius Martius, suddenly jumping to his feet and beginning to pace up and down the room in an outburst of impotent wrath. "This is miserable, cowardly, abject! What? Would ye allow that stranger, that son of slaves, to thwart your plans by his treachery? Are we naughty children that can thus be sent, well-whipped and whining to bed? Up, my lords, this is not the end! Cæsar is not yet in Rome! The people are still dissatisfied. Hark to the noise in the Forum below! Does it sound as if the populace was accepting the news with rejoicing? Up now, my lords! It is not too late! Acclaim your new Cæsar; it is not too late, I say. When the legions return with that mountebank at their head let them find Dea Flavia Augusta and her lord the acknowledged masters of Rome."

He looked flushed, excited and proud, feeling that even at this eleventh hour he could carry these men along with him if Dea Flavia put the weight of her power on his side. Now he paused in his peroration, standing above his fellow-conspirators as if already he were their ruler, and looking from one face to the other with eager restless eyes that expressed all his enthusiasm and all his hopes.

But the two older men had evidently no stomach for the situation as it now was. It had been easy matter enough to murder the Cæsar treacherously and while his legions were three days' march away. But now everything was very different, the issues very doubtful; no doubt that a safe retreat away from the city would be by far the wiser course.

Caius Nepos, with vivid recollections of his last interview with the Cæsar, shook his head with slow determination. Ancyrus, the elder, was silent and only the three younger men had followed Hortensius Martius in his heated argument.

"What sayest thou, Augusta?" asked Philippus Decius at last, looking doubtfully upon the young girl.

"That ye must make your plans without me, my lords," she said coldly. "Since, as you say, the praefect of Rome is dead, I can make no choice worthy of him who is gone. I choose to return to mine allegiance, my loyalty to the Cæsar and to my House."

"If the Cæsar returns," urged Hortensius Martius, "he will vent some of his wrath on thee."

"Then will I suffer for my treachery, my lords," she rejoined proudly, "in accordance with my deserts."

"But Augusta ..."

"I pray you, my lord," she interposed haughtily, "do not prolong your arguments. My mind is made up. An you value your own safety in the future, 'twere wiser to make preparations for a lengthy stay away from Rome."

"Hadst thou listened to us yesterday ..." sighed Ancyrus, the elder.

"A heavy crime had lain against us all," she said. "Be thankful, my lords, that in the history of Rome when it comes to be written, your deed will not have sullied the page that marks to-day. And now, my lords, I bid you farewell! You are in no danger if you leave the city forthwith. The rejoicings at the entry of the Cæsar and the homecoming of his legions will last many days, during that time your names will be erased from the tablets of my kinsman's memory."

"The gods grant it!" murmured Caius Nepos. "But thou, Augusta, what of thee?"

"I, my lords," she said with a gentle smile, the irony of which was lost on their self-centred intellects, "I pray you have no thoughts of me. I have been placed in the keeping of one who, I am told, is mightier than Cæsar. There must I be safe; so farewell, my lords; we meet again, I hope, in happier and more peaceful times."

She stood up and one by one—for was she not still the Augusta and the favourite kinswoman of the Cæsar?—they bent the knee before her and kissed the hem of her gown. After which act of homage they retired with backs bent and walking backwards out of the room.

My lord Hortensius Martius was the last to take his leave. He went down on both knees and would have encircled the Augusta with his arms, only she drew back quickly a step or two.

"Dea ... in the name of my love for thee ..." he began.

But she interrupted him gently, yet firmly.

"Speak not to me of love, my lord," she said. "'Tis but love's ghost that moves to and fro when you speak."

Then as he would have protested, she put up her hand with a gesture of finality.

"It is no use, my lord. What love there is in me, that you could never have aroused—not even in the past. I entreat you not to insist. Love cannot be compelled. It is or is not. Whence it comes we know not; mayhap the gods do know ... mayhap there is only one who knows ... and he seems to give much, but also to take all.... Therefore mayhap love comes from him, and when we are not prepared to give up all for love's sake, then doth he withhold the supreme gift and leave our hearts barren.... Mayhap! mayhap!" she sighed, "alas! I know not! and you, good my lord, do not look so puzzled and so scared. I bid you farewell now. I'll not forget you; to remember is so much easier than to love."

He had perforce to accept his dismissal. He felt rebellious against fate and would have liked to have forced her will. But as she stood there before him, clad all in white, so young and so chaste and yet a woman who knew what love was, an awed reverence for her crept into his heart and he felt that indeed he would never dare to speak again to her of love.

He too kissed the hem of her tunic now, just as the others had done, and just as they had done he walked out of her presence backwards with back bent and an overwhelming disappointment in his heart.

CHAPTER XXXVI

"The peace of God, which passeth all understanding."—
Philippians iv. 7.

Three months had gone by since then. Rome had acclaimed the
Cæsar and rejoiced over his homecoming. There were holidays and
spectacles, chariot races and gladiatorial combats, and the people of
Rome forgot that it had ever shouted: "Hail Taurus Antinor Cæsar!
Hail!"

Now the calls were for Caius Julius Cæsar Caligula, and those
who had most loudly shouted for his death, cringed most obsequiously
at his feet. The very name of the ex-praefect of Rome was already
forgotten.

His testament, made, it appears, just before his death, had been
copiously commented on at first. All his slaves had received their
freedom together with a sufficient sum to enable one and all to live in
comfort in the new state of freedom. The rest of the vast property
owned by the late praefect was being somewhat mysteriously
administered, and up to this hour no one had been able to gain any
definite information with regard to its ultimate destination. There were
those who averred that a great deal of ready money—including the
proceeds of the sale of the late praefect's house in Rome and of his villa
at Ostia—had found its way to a section of very poor freedmen who
lived on the Aventine and who formed a somewhat isolated little colony
not viewed altogether kindly by the official magistracy of the city.

But all that was mere gossip and did not withstand the test of
time. After three months people had plenty of other matters to think of
and to talk about.

There were the festivals and games which had accompanied the
re-entry of the Cæsar into Rome. The city had been beflagged and
adorned with banners and with garlands. For thirty days did the
rejoicings last, and brilliant sunshine shone over the golden glories of
autumn and kissed the foliage of oleanders until they blushed a
brilliant crimson, and tinged the marble of palaces and temples every
morning with rose.

The games in the great Circus went on without intermission for
thirty days; there were military and naval pageants, combats between
the lions from Numidia and the new hyenas and crocodiles; there were
gladiatorial contests and chariot races. Much human blood was shed
for the delectation of the masters of the world, much skill displayed,
much prowess vanquished by prowess greater, much valour laid to
dust.

But the Cæsar's pet black panther did not appear again in the
Circus. The mighty fist of the dead praefect had mayhap laid the

224

creature low; in any case it were not safe to re-awaken dormant memories.

And Caius Julius Cæsar Caligula, the father of his armies, the best and greatest of Cæsars, showed himself at all these pageants more crazed than ever; he hardly ever spoke now to the people. 'Twas averred that Cæsonia, his wife, had given him a potion to cure him of his infatuation for Dea Flavia, his kinswoman, whom he had exalted above all the other Augustas, and whose absence from Rome and from all festivities had rendered him half distracted with wrath.

He would have liked to vent that wrath on Dea, but he could not lay hands on her. She had left her palace even before his re-entry into Rome, taking none but two of her most trusted slaves with her; the others did not know whither she had gone. Some thought that she had gone on a journey to a villa which she possessed in Sicilia, others thought that she was living a life of retirement in a lonely dwelling on the Sabine Hills, preparatory to devoting her virginity to the glory of Vesta.

Caius Julius Cæsar Caligula prepared to have her sought for throughout the length and breadth of his Empire, and would no doubt have succeeded in time in this search had not a few months later Chaerea, the praetorian tribune, done the work with his hands which the dagger of young Escanes had failed to do.

The winter had been slow in coming, but it had come at last. An icy wind blew from across the sea. Overhead the sky was the colour of lead and great banks of clouds chased one another wantonly above the hills that tower over Jerusalem.

There was hardly a path up the rugged incline, the rains and winds and snows of the past seven years had obliterated the marks which a surging crowd had once made in the wake of the sacred feet.

It was close on the ninth hour and the shadows of evening were already drawing in very fast. A tall figure dressed in sombre garments walked slowly up the hill which is called Calvary.

His head was uncovered and he had no wand wherewith to ease his footsteps; the blustering gusts of wind blew the tawny hair over his brow.

He held his head erect and his eyes did not watch the places where trod his feet. They were fixed on ahead, up toward the summit of the hill, there where a Cross stood broken and lonely with wooden arms outstretched and the birds of heaven circling all round it.

Every day for seven days now had the pilgrim wandered up the steep desolate hill. Every day for seven days he had reached the summit ere the ninth hour was called from the city walls. He lived at a small inn just inside the third wall, and every day at noon he set out upon his pilgrimage and only came home when the darkness of the night lay dense upon the valley.

To-day he was more weary than he had ever been before. His feet

225

felt like leaden weights that seemed to be dragging him down and ever downwards, and the loneliness of the place had its image within his heart.

On the summit he fell on his knees and knelt at the foot of the Cross, leaning his aching forehead against the cold, dank wood.

"How long, oh my God, how long?" he murmured. "The misery is more than I can bear. I am ready to do Thy work, oh God, to speak Thy Word where Thou dost bid me go, but take her image, dear Lord, from before mine eyes, it stands for ever 'twixt Thy Cross and me. Break my heart, oh God, since her image fills it and its every beat is not in Thy name. Take the cup from me, dear Lord! It is too bitter and I cannot drink!"

The night drew in around him; the lights in the city below were extinguished one by one. The croaking birds on the lonely Cross had found a home far away in the gloom.

The pilgrim knelt against the Cross, he could hardly see the objects nearest to him, the small prickly shrubs, the rough grass, the loose stones that looked so white and spectral in the waning light. He could hardly see, for his eyes ached with the dull misery of tears that would not fall; but suddenly a sound softer than that made by a night-bird in its flight struck upon his ear.

It was like the drawing of a garment upon the rugged ground. One or two small stones detached themselves from their bed of wet earth and rolled away from under the tread of feet that walked upwards toward the summit.

The pilgrim did not move, and yet he heard the sound. It came nearer to him, and nearer, and suddenly he was not alone; something living and warm knelt on the stony ground beside him, and gentle fingers that had the softness and the coolness of snow were laid upon his burning hands.

"I came as quickly as I could," said a tender voice close to his ear. "But it has taken me some time to find thee. Had it not been for Folces and his devotion I might mayhap never have found thee. We came to Jerusalem yesterday. To-day at noon I saw thee starting forth from out the city. I followed thee, but the way was rough.... I feared I should never reach the summit ... and yet 'twas here I wished to speak to thee."

All this while he had remained numb and silent. He knew even when first her hand touched his that God had ended his sorrow and taken his aching soul into His keeping at last. But for the moment he thought that sweet death had kissed his eyelids and that this was the first taste of paradise. Darkness was closing in around them both; he could scarcely distinguish her features, but it seemed to him as if glory shone out of her eyes, glory so radiant that it illumined the darkness and pierced the walls of the night.

"Is it thou?" he murmured. "Oh God! have pity on me! Her

image, her sweet image, allow it to fade from my mind ere my brain becomes a traitor to Thee!"

"'Tis not a vision, dear heart," she whispered softly, "'tis not a dream. It is I, Dea Flavia, whom thou didst call the beloved of thy heart. I came because I loved thee and because here on this spot I would learn from thee the mysteries of thy God."

"Is it thou? And hast thou come to me from heaven?"

"No, dear heart, only from far-off Rome. And I have come to thee, to be with thee and to follow thee wherever thou wilt lead me."

"Yet will my wanderings lead me far," he said, "my Lord has called and I must go."

"Then will I go with thee," she said.

"To far-off lands, dear heart, to speak the Word of God to those who heard it not."

"I will go with thee," she reiterated simply.

"To far-off lands whence I came, a sea-girt land which once was mine own. My fathers lived there. I would go back and tell my people of all that I saw here on Calvary seven years ago."

"Then thither will I go with thee," she replied, "thy home will be my home, thy people my people and thy God shall be my God, for thine am I now and always. I am ignorant yet but this I do know, that thy God must be the great, the true and only God. None other God but He could have put in thy heart the strength of sacrifice which hath brought thee—who had Rome at thy feet—a lonely wanderer to the foot of this Cross."

She knelt beside him and he no longer cowered, limitless joy was in his heart and immeasurable gratitude.

"For the Son of Man shall come in the glory of the Father with His angels, and then He shall reward every man according to his works."

The wings of the wind brought the sacred words to his ears. He kissed the rough wooden Cross there where the Divine feet had rested, and Dea Flavia pressed her lips on it too, and the peace that passeth all understanding descended upon them both.

Overhead the clouds had parted, their silver lining showed clearly against the dull blue sky, and in the midst of that rent in the firmament, far away in the limitless beyond, a star shone out bright and clear.

Then they both rose, and hand in hand they walked slowly down the hill.

THE END